What readers are
The Batch Magr

Have you read them all?

Treat yourself to the whole Batch Magna Chronicles series:

Turn to the end of this book for more information about Peter Maughan, plus – on the last page – **bonus access to a short story by the author.**

THE BATCH MAGNA CAPER

THE BATCH MAGNA CHRONICLES, VOLUME THREE

Peter Maughan

This edition published in 2019 by Farrago,
an imprint of Prelude Books Ltd
13 Carrington Road, Richmond, TW10 5AA, United Kingdom

www.farragobooks.com

ISBN: 978-1-78842-129-4

To the memory of Neil Marr

Chapter One

In the office of Sneed's Pawn Shop in a Birmingham city backstreet, Major Smythe, late of the Royal Dragoons, who, as prison librarian, had spent his time improvingly when last inside, was expanding on the origins of the three brass balls suspended above the shop's entrance.

He was standing with his back to a steel cabinet, his attention largely on what his hand was up to behind him. He was working that part of a penknife intended to extract stones from the hooves of horses in the lock of one of the drawers of the cabinet, its contents filed under the initial J, which he was hoping meant jewellery, a store perhaps of the better, fenced pieces.

"They were part of the Medici family's coat of arms, you know. The three balls," he said, and was put off his stroke by a loud snigger from the youth called Brrm-Brrm, for whom the Major's accent was an entertainment on its own, and who'd been following the lecture as if watching some bloke on the telly.

"The – er – the three brass balls," the Major pressed gallantly forward, "go back to fifteenth-century Italy. To Florence actually. They, the Medicis, were held in such esteem, that – er – that other moneylenders of that time adapted the symbol which stands, or rather hangs, up, over – er – above the door of Sneed's establishment today. Their considerable fortune, the Medici's considerable fortune, was built, it is true, on commerce, but they were persons of culture and refinement."

The Major looked for a moment as if he could have wept at those words, said here, in this place, among the company he was obliged to keep these days, his face a brief mask of fastidious suffering.

He gave another sharp twist in vain with the penknife, and fumbling in a pocket of his British Warm with the other hand, pressed a crisp linen handkerchief to his brow.

"People of culture and refinement. They—"

"You've already said that," Tony Seperelli, sitting over the racing pages of his newspaper, his feet up on the desk, said without looking up. "People of culture and refinement, you've already said it."

"Ah, yes, thank you, Tony. They made the – er – they made Florence the cultural centre of Europe—"

"Like the Common Market," Brrm-Brrm put in brightly.

The Major gave a short abstracted laugh. "Well, yes, yes, something like that, Brrm-Brrm. Anyway, as I say, they – er – they started as traders, businessmen. In fact, interestingly enough, they developed the double-entry method of bookkeeping, you know," he said, going nostalgically off on a tangent, having used his own version of the double-entry method of bookkeeping during a business venture which ended with the Fraud Squad on the doorstep.

"But – er – but anyway, under their patronage, under the Medici's patronage, the Renaissance flourished. They were responsible for the – er – for the majority of Florentine art, you know, sponsoring—"

"Oh, dear, Major," Harold Sneed said, conversationally, coming in from the shop. "You'll have your work cut on that lock. You'll need at least a drill for it."

The pawnbroker, in tartan carpet slippers and pinstriped trousers, and with a waistcoat like a railway porter's over a sweater and shirt, had shuffled in unnoticed, as he went largely unnoticed in life, until his services were needed, until life found itself in a Birmingham backstreet.

"My dear Sneed!" the Major blustered, hurriedly shoving the penknife back into his overcoat pocket. "I really must protest!"

The Major's expression was a brief, shifting mixture of embarrassment, furtiveness and indignation, through which he appeared to peep, giving his middle-aged, patrician features in that instant a curiously boyish look, a look stuck in time, the look of a schoolboy caught with a hand in his mother's purse.

The pawnbroker ignored him. He knew what he'd seen and he knew the Major, his association with him going back to a time when he first came through his door as a customer, with a raincoat over his uniform, furtively lugging in two plastic bags of mess silver.

"Sorry about that. I forgot to turn the Open sign over," he said to the others, closing the door on the used clothes smell of the shop. "Honestly, it's pathetic, some of the things people bring you. Bit of gilt on a cheap chain. Like something a kid would wear." He sniffed and then smiled through his distaste. "Still, that's what I'm here for, I always say. And I like to help, if I can," he added confidingly, and made a face as if confessing a weakness.

"I thought he was scratching his bum," the man called Clothesline said with ponderous humour, grinning at the Major, enjoying his discomfort.

"We're not all quite as uncouth as you, Clothesline," the Major bristled.

"Hey, you wanna watch it," Clothesline said slowly, deciding that whatever uncouth meant he didn't like it. He lumbered to his feet, an ex-professional heavyweight wrestler whose trademark had been a 'clothesline', a blow delivered with the arm straight out, sweeping his opponent off his feet as if he'd run into one.

"Sit down please, Clothesline," the pawnbroker said, as the Major nippily put the cabinet between him and the wrestler. "*Sit down*," he had to tell him again, voice rising in a near shriek, and grinned suddenly at the bigger man, his eyes shrill with it, a flash of the real Harold Sneed.

"This is a business meeting, Clothesline," he explained primly when Clothesline was sitting again.

"Yeah, well…" Clothesline grumbled.

"Yes, and can we get on with it? This place gives me the creeps," Tony said, glancing round at the bars on the window behind him.

"If I might have my chair back, Tony, then yes we can," Sneed said in the same prim tone.

Tony got up and squatted on a corner of the desk.

"So, what's it about then?"

The pawnbroker, settling himself back behind his desk and running a suspicious eye over the invoices and other paperwork on it, took his time answering.

"Money, Tony," he said then, as if it should be obvious, and regretting that it was so, looking up at Tony with a small doleful smile. "Isn't it always? It makes the world go round, they say."

The Major made a sound like a laugh. "I think you'll find, Sneed, that it's love that makes the world go round," he said, getting some of his own back. He struck his breast with a hand. "With the earth and the sky and the water, remade like a casket of gold. For my dreams of—"

"How much?" Tony cut in abruptly. "How much money?"

Sneed leant towards him. "A hundred grand's worth of money, Tony. One hundred thousand pounds," he said softly, spelling it out.

Even Tony, who made a point of never being impressed, was impressed.

He gave a low whistle.

"Crikey!" the Major said, immediately forgetting about love and drawing nearer to the desk, to the potential source of all that wealth.

"One hundred thousand pounds," Clothesline told himself wonderingly. "I wonder how much that is?"

Brrm-Brrm laughed. "A bleeding lot, Clothesline, my son, that's how much. And I know what I'm going to get with my cut! *Brrm-brrm.*"

"Twenty apiece. That's how much. Nice wage, Harold," Tony congratulated him.

"That's what I meant," Clothesline said defensively. "How much apiece."

"I can't wait!" Brrm-Brrm said.

"Well, not quite the full twenty, Tony," Sneed said. "There's an informant to pay on this one."

"And what's that going to cost us?" Tony asked suspiciously.

"That's our Tony, always doing the figures," Sneed said, smiling his pawnbroker's smile at him, while mentally going through a few figures of his own. "Fifteen percent," he decided. "He wants fifteen of it." Sneed spread his hands. "Which is fair enough, considering."

"Fifteen? A bit steep," Tony said. "What is it?"

The pawnbroker's smile came and went. "A bit steep? A bit steep, he says. It's three each, that's all. And cheap at the price. It's quality information, Tony. From the horse's mouth. He could sell it for double that."

"Is it a bank job, Mr Sneed?" Brrm-Brrm asked, shifting eagerly in his seat. He hadn't done a bank job yet, hadn't sat at the wheel outside one in the high street in a souped-up motor, ready to take off with the doors still open and legs sticking out, like on the telly.

"You and your bank jobs," Sneed said indulgently.

"Keen type," the Major approved.

"All in good time, Brrm-Brrm," Sneed said. "All in good time. But we'll need the same hurry-up skills on this one."

He glanced around, as if he could be overheard. "It's wages, mates. A wages snatch. An engineering company in Shrewsbury. My informant used to work there. In accounts," he added for Tony's benefit.

"Where's that then, Mr Sneed, Shrewsbury? Where's that?" Brrm-Brrm asked, and grinned at the others, sharing the prospect of a day out.

"Shropshire," the Major said briskly, and brushed at his moustache. "Adjacent to the Welsh Borders. Damn fine hunting country around there. Plenty of stiff hedges to put at, you know."

"Get away!" Brrm-Brrm said, happy to be impressed whatever the old bloke was on about.

"We'll be going down together later, Brrm-Brrm," the pawnbroker said. "In the Wolseley. You can drive," he added, making him a present of it. "I don't think I've had it full out yet. You'll like that. And there'll be a three-ton lorry to nick on this one, as well as another car, a getaway, to tickle up for us. How about that then, Brrm-Brrm?"

"Brrm-Brrm," Brrm-Brrm said.

"Just make sure it's not a Mini this time," Tony muttered broodingly.

But Brrm-Brrm was not to be deflated. "And what about guns, Mr Sneed?" he asked, moving again in his chair. "We gonna have guns? We gonna be carrying?"

"We've got a hocked Luger. Only came in yesterday. There's no ammo for it, but they won't know that. And the sawn-off, loaded with birdseed in case you don't get their attention the first time. And there's Clothesline."

"Yeah," Clothesline grinned, and shot an arm straight out. "Do as you're told or you're washing!"

Tony, reaching into the inside pocket of his well-cut silk suit, pulled out a flick-knife. He held it up, and looking steadily at Sneed, released the blade with a well-oiled click.

"Tony's pig-sticker." The Major said, and chuckled uneasily. He prided himself on being a sound judge of both horseflesh and men, and he was of the opinion that the Italian, like most Mediterranean sorts, was not only erratic, but was also becoming increasingly unstable.

"Plus Tony's contribution, of course," Sneed said, smiling at him as Tony dipped the blade and began cleaning his perfectly manicured nails with it.

"Now," the pawnbroker went on, "when Brrm-Brrm collars the transport, the lorry and car we'll need, he'll get them to your yard, Clothesline, for a change of plates and a paint job for the lorry. So let him have the spare key for the gates."

"Right, boss," Clothesline said.

The pawnbroker ripped off the used top sheet of a notepad, and making sure they could all see, drew a blob on the new page.

"Just to give you—" he started, when Clothesline, who'd been thinking about it, interrupted.

"What colour, boss?" he wanted to know.

Sneed frowned. "Eh?"

"What colour do you want me to respray the lorry?" Clothesline said patiently.

"Whatever colour you've got handy. Long as it's not shocking pink, or anything like that. Nothing that will stand out. All right? Got that?"

"Yeah, course I've got it."

Sneed went back to his drawing, adding another smaller blob to the bigger one. And then a thought struck him.

"And make sure you don't respray it the same colour as when it come in. OK?" He waited, making sure Clothesline had got that as well.

Clothesline looked offended. "Well, I know that!"

"Yeah, well, just make sure, Clothesline, that's all. We don't want any cock-ups on this one."

Sneed went back to his blobs. "I'll fill in the details in a minute, but to give you a rough idea this," he said, tapping the bigger blob with his pen, "is the factory, Wrekin Engineering Limited. And this is their back yard and loading bay. The bay's here, and the yard gates are there," he went on, sketching them in with his pen. "The armoured carrier comes into the yard and backs up to the bay to offload the money. And that's when we take it."

"When we gonna do it?" Tony asked. "This pay day? This Friday?"

"No, no. A week from then. I want this one gone over until we could do it blindfold. Right? This is the big one, so it's got to go like clockwork. And not that in some cheap Mickey Mouse job you're looking for a couple quid on, either. This has got to be top quality, Swiss precision work."

"The big one," Clothesline said, smiling at the description. "Hey! It'll be in all the papers."

"And on the telly!" Brrm-Brrm added.

"Ah, and when it is," the pawnbroker said less enthusiastically, "we don't want our faces on with it. So let's try and get this one right for a change, shall we? Eh?" he added almost pleadingly.

Chapter Two

Not more than seventy miles from Sneed's Pawn Shop, and not more than thirty from where the gang's big one waited for them, in a place where England shared the border with Wales, and Wales with England, plans were also being made in Batch Hall, an Elizabethan manor house sitting with its village in a valley with a river running through it.

Or rather, Lady Clementine Strange and Annie Owen were making plans, going over the events diary together at the long pine kitchen table. Clem's husband, Sir Humphrey Strange, the unlikely-looking 9th baronet and squire of Batch Magna and this March, was on his hands and knees, playing horse with his two-year-old daughter, Hawis, on his broad back squealing delightedly, hands gripping his shirt collar, and squealing even louder then, when her father's Yankees baseball cap she was wearing slid over her eyes again.

"Oh, and they've confirmed the wedding party on Saturday," Clem said, adding it to the diary.

"Oh, good! That'll be fun," Annie said.

"Yes, as long as we don't get the arguments we had last time. Talk about happy families!"

"Well, they were from Sedbury," Annie said, naming a village firmly on the English side of the border. "Funny lot there, they are."

"And we've another at the end of the month. Word's getting round."

"And the Kingham Music Festive thing, at the castle," Annie said. "I'll get Sion to have a bit of a tidy up there, and get the grass down." Annie had been housekeeper at the Hall to the 8th baronet, the late General Sir Humphrey Myles Pinkerton Strange, and was now back, as a friend and factotum, working with Shelly and Clem on whatever needed to be done.

"Well, we've got a few weeks yet for that. They've hired it for two days," Clem said, looking at the diary. "Lovely."

"What if it rains?" Shelly, Humphrey's mother, asked. Since moving there with her son from their native New York she'd come to know about rain.

"Well, they're aware of the risk, Shelly," Clem said.

"They can bring brollies," Annie said.

"Yes, it's all part of the fun," Clem said, "drinking fizz in wellies and your best frock."

"Specially if you've got a bloke to cuddle up to," Annie added.

"Oh, sure," Shelly agreed, looking wistful, a widow whose last date with a man had been on the other side of the Atlantic.

"We're hiring the Hall out to a film company later on that month as well," Clem said. "That's another new one."

"Ohh!" Annie said. "Any film stars? Anybody we know?"

Clem laughed. "I don't know, Annie. But if it's Rick Todd, I saw him first."

"Maybe it's for *Upstairs, Downstairs*," Shelly, who never missed an episode, said. "The Bellamys on a visit. And I serve Conies and coffee to Sir Richard," she added dreamily over the rolls she was buttering.

"Well, whatever it's for we should get a bit of local publicity from it. And lots of lovely money, I hope," Clem said on a practical note. "Sarah dealt with it. I must give her a ring, see what sort of fee she agreed. Do have a care, darling," she added then to Humphrey, mindful of the flagged floor, and speaking above the yapping of the Jack Russell, one of their three dogs keeping the pair company on their canter, the large kitchen echoing with it.

"Yeah, be careful, honey. If she falls on that stone…" Shelly, who'd been keeping a dubious eye on them, said.

"She won't fall off, she's got her mother's seat," Humphrey said, which, as Clem had taken a tumble while point-to-pointing last week, and still had the stiff back to prove it, didn't help make his case.

Shelly was sitting at the other end of the table preparing the rolls for that morning's batch of Coney Island Specials, ordinary hotdogs dressed with diced onions and then turned into something quite extraordinary by the addition of a secret recipe, a pickled relish, a family heirloom she'd brought over with her. Shelly's Conies were famous as far afield as the police station in Kingham, officers from there regularly turning up at the back door for them.

She also did a sandwich run in the shooting brake to businesses in nearby towns both sides of the border, and took her Conies to all the local outdoor events during the summer, borrowing from Annie something called a De Luxe Cook Centre from the Patio Living department in one of Bryony Owen's mail order catalogues. Bryony, the Owens' eldest daughter, had introduced the village to life on the never-never, and had at least a dozen catalogues on the go at any one time.

Shelly's contribution went with whatever other income could be wrung from the Hall and what was left of the estate to help towards keeping the whole thing afloat. Which, apart from the staples of shooting and fishing, could mean anything from business conferences in the servants' hall – when, that is, it wasn't being used on Tuesday and Thursday nights for bingo, with further enticements in the one-armed bandits in the entrance hall and kitchen, bought second hand from an amusement arcade in Rhyll – to cream teas, bed and breakfast, and Open Days with tours of the Hall and its history conducted by the 9th baronet himself, in a shirt.

"Yeah, OK. Come on, honey, off you come," Humphrey said, swinging his daughter round and lifting her with him as he stood.

He retrieved his baseball cap and Hawis toddled off to help her grandmother with the buttering.

"Hey, and don't forget the historical acting thing, honey," he said then to his wife, adding his bit. It was another first for the estate and one he was really looking forward to, even more so than the film company thing.

"Historical re-enactment, darling," Clem corrected him. "Yes, that's in the book. A few weeks before the festival," she said, finding it in the diary. "They're based in Birmingham. They're doing a show, or whatever they call it, in the morning at the castle, and one here in the afternoon. On the lawns, I suppose, although I'd better check. If it's inside as well we'll have to move vases and things out of the way. Oh, hello, Georgie," she said then, looking up.

The age of the pale young lad who had wandered into the kitchen might have been anywhere between perhaps twelve and seventeen. He had that sort of face, the smaller size, as it were, of more or less the face he'd have at forty, or even older, under a shock of thick, dark adult-looking hair which seemed to have got there before him.

George, who had just turned ten, was on his holidays from school, and helped out around the place.

"Historical actment?" he said warily, thinking that, whatever it was, it sounded like school.

"Historical *re-enactment*, George," Clem said absently over the diary.

"Hitting people with swords," Humphrey told him cheerfully.

"Oh, knights and wenches, is it?" Annie asked with relish. "Ohh, I'll have a go at that. Some knight slinging me across his saddle and galloping off with me. You can put me down for that, Clem."

"As long as he brings you back again," Clem said. "You're needed here."

"No, it's Cavaliers and Roundheads," Humphrey said. He'd read up on it, that part of history from which his title had evolved, for the Open Days, the first baronet, Sir Richard Strange, awarded the baronetcy for his allegiance to the crown. "The Civil War, and all that, Annie."

"The *Rebellion*," his wife, daughter of a Shropshire baron, corrected him, deftly rolling a cigarette. Clem's family, which went back even further than her husband's, had a long memory.

"They're re-fighting the Battle of Batch Magna. And we get half the entrance money, so let's hope the weather's on our side as well," she added, flicking a Zippo lighter at her roll-up, and going back to the diary. Today the sun was shining, but so far most of the summer had been a washout.

"Yeah, we won that one, Georgie," Humphrey said. "The Cavaliers. In between drinking and swashbuckling, and all that. We kicked the butts of the Roundheads for the King of England."

George was unimpressed. "I don't know what you want with *swords*, Humph," he said scornfully, "when you've got a Chicago piano under the bed." Clem to George was Lady C, but Sir Humphrey was Humph, on Humphrey's insistence. Humphrey was a man who liked to be called Humph.

That got Clem's attention.

"A *what* under his bed?"

Shelly laughed. "A Chicago piano, honey," she told her, looking at her son and shaking her head.

"What on *earth* is a Chicago piano?"

George couldn't believe it.

"What, you don't know what a Chicago piano is, Lady C! It's a Tommy-gun," he told her, and fired off a few rounds, chips of wood in his imagination flying from the dresser and the crockery exploding.

"Humph, now what have you been telling him!" Clem said. "Don't take any notice of him, George. It's just one of his daft stories."

"I know what I know," George muttered darkly.

George said that his mum had made him toast before he came out, when Clem asked him if he'd had breakfast. Clem had befriended George's mother, a widow, when she'd arrived in Batch Magna a while ago. She had taken a job in a chemist's in Church Myddle, and George, while she was working, was now a fixture at the Hall, and about the yards of the Batch Valley Chase, the local hunt, of which Clem was the joint master.

Humphrey finished off the coffee in his Yankees souvenir mug.

"Come on, Georgie, you can give me a hand again in the lodge now it's dry."

"OK, Humph," George said, one chap to another.

"Not in the house, Humphie," his mom, who didn't watch *Upstairs, Downstairs* for nothing, instructed him, when her son donned his baseball cap.

"Dames! Eh, Humph?" George said, as they left together.

The Elizabethan confection that was Batch Hall formed three sides of a south-facing square, its white, lime-washed walls striped ornately with black timbers under red sandstone flagged roofs, the tall, herring-bone red-brick chimneys glowing in the sunlight, mellow with an ancient warmth, holding the suns of four hundred summers as if baking gently on in them.

And peacocks trailed their bright feathers in its gardens, and under horse chestnuts heavy with summer, what was left of its park ran down to a boathouse and the river.

Humphrey, as Humphrey frequently and wonderingly reflected, had come a long way from a second-floor walk-up in the Bronx.

He'd been working in a downtown diner when a great uncle he never knew existed died in a place he'd never heard of, and his life turned into a movie, starring Sir Humphrey Strange, a baronet with an estate, or what was left of it, in England, or Wales, depending on what bend in the road you took.

He had even got the girl, the right girl, in the end.

He had the feudal law of entailment to thank for it, a law enacted on the death of General Sir Humphrey Myles Pinkerton Strange, which moved down through the empty ranks where once potential male heirs had been, to his next lineal descendent, a large, overweight short-order cook from the South Bronx, flipping burgers for a living.

They walked down the long twisting drive, with its screens of rhododendrons and the stands of ancient beeches, to the lodge. The lion and otter rampant surmounting the gate pillars were patched with lichen, the red sandstone boundary walls, cut from the same quarry that had first been mined to build the castle, crumbling under blankets of ivy, and the filigreed, wrought-iron gates which had once been run back to welcome carriages and the first motorcar of the valley, had long stayed open, rusted on their hinges.

The walls would for now have to wait. Bit by bit, over the past three years, Humphrey had rebuilt those in the gardens, and used the demolished stone from one of them to repair the terraces. And now it was the turn of the lodge.

Like Sir Winston Churchill, another overweight guy who smoked cigars, it had pleased him to learn, Humphrey had discovered bricklaying. He'd even done a night school course in Kingham, an exotic figure, this Sir Humphrey, this large baronet in a baseball cap and with a Bronx accent, among the other trainee bricklayers, slapping them on their backs and calling them buddy.

Like the garden walls much of the stone used to build the lodge had come away, and had been buried by time under bramble and nettles. Humphrey had cleared the undergrowth and the salvaged stone sat in piles on the small front lawn, with the roof tiles he'd also rescued, all waiting to go up again.

There was much to do. New floors to be laid and new roof timbers hammered into place, but for now they were cleaning the old stone among the piles of sand and gravel and bags of lime and cement, a small building site for them to get dirty in, the man and the small boy together – or, as even Humphrey's family and friends might have had it, two small boys together.

George listening fascinated to more of Humphrey's tales of New York, the blood-stained sidewalks echoing to the sound of Tommy-guns, and somebody called Jimmy Legs getting his in a barber's chair, and Fat Tony, face down in his last plate of spaghetti.

A New York he'd been astonished to learn existed outside of the Saturday morning black and white gangster films at the Kingham Odeon – a New York that many of its good citizens would be astonished to learn existed still outside of the Kingham, or any other, Odeon.

Chapter Three

The folds of small hillocky fields, when seen from the encircling hills of Batch Valley, appear to be held untidily together, as if rough stitched, by high-banked lanes twisting and turning this way and that between them.

And there are woods on the slopes of the hills, birdsong echoing from their ancient gloom, and farms among orchards. And snug in the palm of the valley, the pinnacled tower of its church St Swithin's and the chimneys of its manor house standing over it, the border village of Batch Magna, the red dragon above the door of the post office and shop claiming it for Wales, the flag of St George flown from the Steamer Inn for England. A story first told in the ruined stone of a castle above a river called the Cluny.

And strung out along a meander, with the island called Snails Eye at its heart, more history in the four Victorian paddle steamers which were once part of the Cluny Steamboat Company. They'd been converted to houseboats after the venture went bankrupt with duck-shooting parties in mind, and later for holidaymakers, who came in even fewer numbers, and had then served at various times as storage sheds and as accommodation for estate workers, until gathering their present tenants.

And those present tenants, as it was a Saturday, and raining, were all in the saloon bar of the Steamer Inn, the bigger of the pub's two bars, a dim room of worn Welsh slate flags, high-backed settles and beams of estate oak seasoned with centuries of smoke, and a fireplace like a cave. And on one of its walls mementoes of the old CSC, tickets and sailing bills and advertisements, and among the photographs Humphrey's forebear, Sir Cosmo, the man who shipped the side-wheelers from the River Thames, making a speech in a silk topper, addressing the pens and cameras of the local press from the deck of the PS *Felicity H*, a portentous figure of empire, one hand on the lapel of his frock coat, a finger pointing as if to horizons far more distant and exotic than Shrewsbury, twenty odd miles upstream.

The *Felicity H* had been the flagship of that tiny fleet and was now the home of Annie Owen and her family. Annie had stopped off at the pub with Shelly, after helping her with that morning's sandwich run. Clem had taken Hawis with her to the discount shop across the border in Penycwn, but Humphrey was there, in the public bar in his builder's clothes, rained off, as he'd put it, playing bar billiards with John Beecher the village coal merchant and joint master, with Clem, of the Batch Valley Chase.

Jasmine Roberts, off the *Cluny Queen*, was also in working clothes, a voluminous purple silk printed with stars and moons, rainbows and comets. No one ever seemed quite sure just how many children, mostly with different fathers, Jasmine had – even Jasmine at times seemed unsure of it. But whatever their number her eldest daughter was babysitting them, a sensible and capable fourteen-year-old who, in reaction to the family's crowded and shambolic life, threatened to train as a social worker when she left school.

Jasmine, a psychic, a world famous one, according to her ads in the local newspapers, with a special rate for pets, was on her way to do a private reading in Nether Myddle, but couldn't resist dropping in first with a titbit of local gossip she'd heard in the village shop, picked up with her change from Mrs Pugh in the post office.

"How *frightful!*" Priny Cunningham said in a satisfied sort of way when Jasmine had finished. "And that wretched wife of his. Poor *woman.*"

"Jeez!" Shelly said, "I thought the guy I knew back in the States, the husband of a pal of mine, I thought he was bad enough…"

"Go on, Shelly." Annie urged. "What did he get up to…?"

"Yes, do tell, darling," Priny said, settling herself expectantly in her seat.

Priny and her husband, the Commander, lived on the *Batch Castle*, tied up at what used to be the CSC's landing stage and offices. Priny seemed to carry a party around with her, one she was always at the centre of, a cocktail party on this occasion, in a sequin and chiffon apricot dress, hair fresh from the hairdresser's, waving a cigarette in an amber holder about in one hand, a large Plymouth gin in the other.

They were sitting where they usually sat when inside, at a table in the bow window overlooking the river and the small terrace with its summer chairs and tables, and the upended mahogany sculling boats on the bank below, waiting in the rain for someone to hire them.

The Commander at the other end of the table was having a discussion with Annie's husband, Owain, on the subject of rainbow trout. Owain, who worked for the estate as a ghillie and water bailiff, was so involved he'd let his pipe go out.

"Man! I'm bloody telling you," he said, slapping the table, "there's only one bloody way to catch your rainbow, and that's bloody worms!"

The Commander regarded his friend placidly with his good eye, while in his other an engagement raged under sail in a miniaturised detail from Pocock's painting of the *Battle of St Vincent*.

"Leeches," he said calmly.

Lieutenant-Commander James Cunningham, DSO and bar, RN (rtd), late of the Fleet Air Arm, had suffered a wartime wound to his leg which also caused him to have an eye removed. He had then turned the vacant space into a miniaturist gallery by commissioning an artist to paint a set of plain glass ones, depicting scenes from British naval victories and landscapes that speak of England, and one flying the Union Jack when a bit of swank, a bit of defiance, in the face of whatever, was called for. And a bit of swank had been called for on more than one occasion in his and Priny's years together.

"*Lee-ches*," Owain said, drawing the word out with Welsh scorn. "You're talking through your – it's worms, man, *worms*. That's the only bait for 'em. *Worms*. On eight or ten gang hooks. Ain't a rainbow breathing that'll swim past that." He shook his head in disgust. "All I can say, is that it's a good job we had a bloody army." During the same war Owain had worn the uniform of the Welsh Borderers, among the first to volunteer to fight for his country, even, generously, the half of it that was in England.

"Leeches. *Leeches*, he says." Owain turned to one side of him, as if for someone to share the Commander's idiocy with. And finding women there turned the other way, and found Phineas Cook.

"Duw!" he growled, giving up, and took his matches out again.

The Commander laughed. "Never mind, Owain, old man, have another pint. It's my shout."

Owain blew out smoke from a stubby briar.

"Now you're talking some bloody sense for a change."

"Number One?" the Commander enquired, taking orders for drinks, and addressing his wife, the First Lieutenant, as he called her. And then he looked at the pint of Sheepsnout cider on the table in front of Phineas and saw that it had barely been touched.

Phineas just sitting there, staring fixedly off into the middle distance.

"Are you ailing, Phineas?" he asked.

Phineas blinked and came back among them.

"My trouble," he said slowly, narrowing his eyes at the revelation, "is women."

"No!" Owain said in mock astonishment. "You don't say! Well, I never. Fancy that now."

"Keep it in your pants, my boy," the Commander briskly advised him. "Best place for it. I've told you often enough. Now stop wasting the pub's time and see that off, I'm in the chair. Then you can tell us *all* about it."

"Ah, and don't spare us the juicy bits, either," Owain said, and waggled his bushy eyebrows suggestively. As far as he was concerned, Phineas's love life was as good as a read of the *News of the World*.

But Phineas couldn't bear to think about it longer than a few painful seconds, never mind talk about it. It was horrible. *Horrible.*

He had only the foggiest notion how he had got into this extraordinarily undesirable situation, and no idea at *all* how he might get out of it, apart that is from chucking himself in the river.

And things had started so *well*. His girlfriend Sally, a district nurse, had signed on for a ten-day package holiday, and was sunning herself in Jersey – a much *needed* and much *deserved* holiday, he always reminded himself at this point, rubbing it in. She had wanted him to go with her, but he'd just smiled and patted her hand, and told her to go ahead and enjoy herself, he had a book to finish.

She'd gone with a friend in the end, and had told him not to work too hard while she was gone, her way of showing approval of him doing just that, starting to put more into things, as she had long hinted he should. Meaning of course demonstrating that he was serious about the relationship, serious enough to pop the question.

Which as far as he was concerned, with three marriages behind him, was reason enough *not* to start putting more into things. And he'd been proved right not to do so, as it turned out. Because when he *did* start putting more into things, stopping only for a much needed supermarket shop, that's *precisely* where it had led him.

The problem was that it hadn't been Sally he had ended up popping the question to.

He *had* gone straight back to his paddler, the *Cluny Belle,* and he *had* started immediately getting on with things, if only because he had a deadline to meet and he badly needed the cash, the sure thing in the 4.20 at Chepstow having turned out to be nothing of the sort, pounding away on his typewriter as his alter ego, Warren Chase, crime writer, all morning until noon.

And then he'd broken off for a shopping trip, leaving his dog, Bill Sikes, on watch in case one or two of the more importunate of his creditors had done what they'd been quite unnecessarily threatening to do, and set the bailiffs on him.

Sikes, a hulking white boxer with the face of the spike-collared dog in a cartoon backyard, was as likely to bite a bailiff, or indeed anyone else, as he was his master. But it would be a brave or foolish man who would call his bluff, with Bill's fearsome-looking bulk snarling down at him from the top of the gangway, dripping spittle as if drooling over the prospect of a human limb to chew on.

Leaving him with a few of his favourite dried pigs' ears as a sop for not taking him, he had climbed into Ginny, his old canary-yellow Frogeye Sprite, and driven straight to the Imperial Stores in Kingham.

And it was there, while browsing the cheaper shelves of the wine section, that he had walked into calamity in the shape of a friend. A friend who was having a party tomorrow evening and would Phineas like to come? And Phineas, never one to turn down a jolly, said my dear chap, yes, of *course*.

Words which would return to haunt him.

He had met her in the kitchen at the party where he was busy with the corkscrew, a tall, jolly hockey sticks, toothy sort of girl, miserably sipping wine. She was upset because she'd given back her engagement ring to her fiancé that morning, after he'd come up with yet another excuse not to set a date.

Serve the bounder right, he'd said, and patted her back when she'd sobbed briefly on his shoulder. And then, after having a good blow on a piece of kitchen roll, told him through the last of her tears that her name was Petunia.

And for Phineas, at that stage of the evening, the sound of it was like the beginning of a song, a song he could have *sworn* he'd heard before somewhere.

The words to which came to him later, under the stars in the back garden of a semi in Kingham, a song which ended with him quoting Shakespeare at her with one knee in a flowerbed. *Romeo, poor Romeo, stabbed with a white girl's black eye, cut through the ear with a love song.* And that's when he had asked her for her hand, for no reason he could remember except that he thought he might as well while he was down there.

He'd called her Petal, his Petal, and said, "Would you, Petal? Could you? I've no fortune to offer and nothing grand by way of a name, I'm afraid – just good plain Cook, with no E and only one of the Os working. But could you – would you? *Will* you, Petal?" he'd asked of the tall, gauche, toothy girl standing coyly above him on the back lawn.

A tall, gauche, toothy girl who, only that morning, had broken off one engagement and who now lost no time snapping up another offer.

And after three years of doggedly avoiding asking the same question of Sally, Phineas woke the next day to find he'd asked it of someone else. And not only that, that someone else had said yes.

He couldn't remember any mention of a ring, but he was now, if unofficially, affianced. To a woman called Petunia Cholmondeley-Jones.

Otherwise known in the personnel files at Kingham police station as WPS 76.

He had, as he'd told himself wonderingly over and over the next day, somehow managed to get himself engaged to a woman police sergeant.

And he still hadn't met his deadline.

Chapter Four

It was also raining when Sneed and his gang met early on the morning of the big one, the potholes in Clothesline's scrapyard steadily filling with it.

They were crowded into the dilapidated caravan he used as an office, having a last run-through. The pawnbroker had moved a half-bottle of congealing milk and a couple of mugs out of the way on a table, with its cloth of a few pages of an old *Daily Mirror*, and was taking them through the blobs again.

When he'd finished he said, "Right, the Major carries the Luger—"

"Yeah," Tony said, "we know that. We know that."

"I'd have preferred a British make of weapon, of course," the Major said stiffly.

"The Major carries the Luger," Sneed went on patiently, "and Tony the sawn-off. The Major and Clothesline travel in the back of the lorry, Tony driving. The Major leaves his railway station gear, his overcoat and that, in the Wolseley."

Tony flicked an impatient hand. "We've gone through all this. Over and over."

"One last time won't hurt, Tony. We're leaving nothing to chance on this one."

"We're leaving nothing to chance on this one," Clothesline echoed, having heard his boss say it enough times, and looking vaguely threatening at Tony.

"Brrm-Brrm follows the lorry on to the job after I turn off for the switch-over place. The lorry pulls up there, not too near the gates, and Brrm-Brrm stops behind it. Tony sits at the wheel, pretending to be checking delivery notes, while waiting for the wages to arrive."

"At oh-nine-thirty," the Major said crisply, pulling a cuff back on his watch.

"Every Friday, on the button, my informant tells me. Without fail. They never learn, do they. Lucky for us."

"And what if we can't park when we get there? What happens then?" Tony said, finding something to fret about.

"Well, you've seen that stretch yourself," the pawnbroker said. "It's mostly used as a service road. I've visited it what – at least five times now, including a Friday, and I don't remember seeing anything parked there. Just have to hope it's the same today, that's all."

Tony jumped on it. "But what if it's not? What if—"

"Statistically, Tony," the Major cut in, "it is highly unlikely to be any different from the five other occasions. So can we please get on?"

"Thank you, Major" Sneed said, leaving Tony staring at both men, as if making a note of who said what when they got there and found a traffic jam.

"Right," Sneed went on, "so the lorry waits for the carrier to back into the yard and offload the money. Then it pulls up past the gates, reverses in, and stops between them, blocking the entrance. You two jump out of the back, joined by Tony, and make the snatch. The lorry stays – 'ere, Brrm-Brrm, you didn't forget to bring the stocking masks, did you, son?"

"Got 'em in me bag with me sandwiches, Mr Sneed. Mum sorted out three pairs of her tights. Two legs each, she said, in case of accidents."

"Ah, that was thoughtful of her. Tell her thanks. You can give 'em out when I've finished. And you've all got your gloves, I hope? Good. Right, so the lorry stays there, blocking the way, in case some hero in the yard gets it into his head to drive after us. A nice touch, that, I thought. And don't forget to take the keys with you, Tony, when you get out."

Tony waved it away. "Yeah, yeah."

"Yeah, well, don't forget, that's all I'm saying. Easy to overlook a detail like that when the job's on. Right, so, you grab the money – paper only – and leg it out of the yard to where Brrm-Brrm, who's pulled up in front of the gates, is waiting with the Triumph on ready."

"Goes like a bleeding bomb now." Brrm-Brrm shared that gleefully with them, leaving passing expressions of unease on the faces of the Major and Tony, both with experience of Brrm-Brrm at the wheel of a car that went like a bomb.

"Then he drives to where I'll be waiting. You've got the route down all right, Brrm-Brrm, have you?"

"I should have, Mr Sneed. I've been over it enough times."

"'Cause we don't want you getting lost. On the way there the money goes into the holdall with the guns. That's Plan A. If it's not in canvas bags, as we've been told, but in something we can't open there, then it comes back with us, and we'll have to risk a pull. That's Plan B. In Plan A we drive to the railway station in Shrewsbury and drop the Major and Tony off. They go in separately, the Major carrying the holdall. He takes—"

"Why him? Why does he have to carry it?" Tony demanded.

Sneed sighed. "I've told you, Tony. Because he's the best one of us to do it. He's the least likely of us to get stopped. Just look at him. With his brolly and bowler, and that accent of his. Do *you* want to risk it? Eh…?"

Tony said nothing, just moved his mouth as if chewing, and stared at the Major, his eyes sullen.

"Right, then" Sneed went on. "So the Major takes the Bristol train—"

"With Tony following," Tony added. "In case the Major forgets to get off."

The Major closed his eyes briefly at the remark, its implication beneath him.

"Followed separately," Sneed went on with heavy patience, "by Tony. They get off at this Church Myddle place, the first stop down the line, for their Birmingham connection – the train they could have caught thirty minutes later at Shrewsbury, but we want you and the money out of there soonest. That will take them straight through to New Street, where I'll be waiting with the Wolseley, after dropping Clothesline and Brrm-Brrm off at the shop first. As I've said, no need for us all to be at the station, hanging about. The less we advertise ourselves the better. Then back to the shop for the share-out. Now, are there any questions?"

Brrm-Brrm said no, he hadn't, and Clothesline frowned and started thinking about it.

Sneed left him to it. "Major? Tony? 'Cause now's the time to ask."

The Major shook his head, and looked out of the window at the rain.

And Tony had only one question from the beginning. And it didn't take him long to come up with the answer to that. The Major wouldn't be a problem, not with a blade at his throat.

And then on to Charing Cross from platform four and the night train for the Continent. Sneed wasn't the only one who could read a timetable.

And then Monte Carlo, Monte, as he thought of it in his imaginings. A playboy then, a big spender known at all the fashionable nightspots and at the tables, in a white tuxedo and gardenia buttonhole, with beautiful women in evening dress crowded admiringly at his shoulder as the chips piled up, like on the films. And people bowing and scraping, and vintage champagne for two in his suite at a grand hotel.

He'd known something of that life, from the outside looking in, as a waiter in top hotels and restaurants, doing his share of bowing and scraping for tips, for the crumbs from rich people's tables. Now he wanted his share, his place at the feast.

And as far as he was concerned he was due the means to get it.

It still rankled with him, still ate into him, the way they'd copped for that last lot of nick. They'd broken into an office in the city to crack a safe. They had all the tools, electric drill, lump hammer, cold chisel and jemmy, drilling and banging industriously away most of the night like a small machine shop, but the lock wouldn't budge.

They were on their way out of the building at first light, going home like a night shift, having decided to cut their losses, and ready for bed, when Clothesline came to a halt.

"'ere," he'd said, looking surprised. "'ere, I've had an idea."

That should have warned them, Clothesline having an idea. That should have told them something.

Instead they followed him like idiots as he lumbered back up the stairs to the office.

Bending to the safe, which came to above his waist, he hugged it in a wrestling hold, and grunting as if for a ringside audience, slowly lifted it.

He turned and took a couple of grinning, triumphant steps towards them, and started slowly sinking into the carpet, the combined weight of a half-ton Chubb and his 20 stone disappearing with a splintering crack of floorboards.

They shone their torch down through the hole and picked out his unconscious form and the safe on the floor below, its door sprung and rolls of banknotes spewed out of it, with more visible inside.

They made a dash for the stairs, scrambling to get down them at the same time, and were stuffing the plastic bags they'd brought with them, when the police, finally driven to responding to the numerous complaints of the row they'd been making, walked in on them.

Tony dated his habit of biting his nails from that time, and his twitch, his eye twitch, he'd developed that then as well.

Because the thing that had *really* got at him over the long years inside, the thing that could bring him snarling out of his sleep, was that even if Clothesline *had* managed to walk out with the safe, it wouldn't have come anywhere near fitting into the getaway car. *They* barely fitted into it.

Because the idiot Brrm-Brrm, simply because he'd never driven one before, had nicked a Mini.

"Foul weather," the Major remarked glumly, gazing out at it, in his bowler hat and with that hallmark of an English officer and gentlemen, a tightly furled umbrella.

"Ah, and let's hope it keeps up, Major. Best weather for us, this is. People are either under a brolly or have their heads down. So cheer up, you'll be one of the idle rich in a few hours."

But the Major wasn't at that moment in the mood to cheer up.

He was having one of his periodic bouts of asking himself where it all had gone wrong, while knowing perfectly well where it had all gone wrong.

You were born with a silver spoon in your mouth and you ended up pawning it, was his judgement on himself, standing hangdog in a dock of his own making. Along with the regimental silver, he always threw in then, as if asking for it to be taken into consideration.

Where are they now, he asked himself, the snows of yesteryear? The days of his gilded youth, a leisurely social stroll through his education, summer afternoons on the Cherwell and sherry mornings with his tutor at New College. And the pomp and swagger of the Royal Dragoons, croquet in Cairo, polo in the brilliant white dust of India and sundowners at the

Bengal Club, and ceremonial parades under a London sky. And the last war, when the horse was turned into a tank, the medals awarded him then, despite a determination to keep his head down, long since sold.

And the dear old school, the boyish trebles in his memory lifted again in song – *Games to play out, whether earnest or fun, fights for the fearless and goals for the eager. Twenty, and thirty, and forty years on...*

The Major, more than forty years on, staring out at the rain falling on a scrapyard in Birmingham, sniffed, and wiped at his moustache, as if at tears.

And then he straightened, steadying the ranks.

"Time to go, Sneed, what?" he said, turning smartly back into the room.

"Mount and form line, Sar'major!" he barked, and drew an imaginary sword.

"Cor! Hark at 'im," Brrm-Brrm said delightedly, as if it were all part of the day out his mum had got up early to make sandwiches for. His dad was out of the business for a while, banged up in Winston Green nick with three years on his card still to do. But he'll be that proud of you when I tell him, his old mum had said, getting all soppy about it as she saw him off on his first big one.

Sneed led the convoy out of the yard in his Wolseley, followed by the re-sprayed three-ton lorry Brrm-Brrm had lifted a couple of nights back from outside the city's fruit and vegetable market, and then the getaway car.

They paused while Clothesline snapped the padlock to on the gates, and then the pawnbroker pointed his bonnet eastwards.

The pawnbroker's black Wolseley was immaculate inside and out. He was wearing the jacket to his pinstriped trousers, a combination he now thought of as his going-away suit, and a tie he'd sponged down that morning. He was also wearing yellow leather driving gloves with string backs and a Homburg hat. He was rehearsing saying goodbye to his old life.

There *was* another world, one of pawnshops full of other people's scrapings, and junkyards, and bent majors and psychopathic waiters called Tony, and other riff-raff. But this was where he really belonged, in a Homburg hat and pinstriped suit, and yellow driving gloves at the wheel of a Wolseley.

And if Plan A didn't turn into Plan B, if they didn't have to take the money back with them in the car, he had his own version of Plan B. And if all went well with it he'd be in a position to make that way of life permanent.

Chapter Five

Phineas was not the only one who had enjoyed the intimacy of calling Sergeant Cholmondeley-Jones Petal. She had been known by that name to her immediate superior and erstwhile fiancé, Inspector Edward Worth.

And Inspector Worth was at that moment calling it her again, tenderly, while she sat on his lap at his desk, fiddling with a button on his uniform shirt.

"So who's your little prisoner now, then? Anyone I know?" she asked coyly.

"It's you – you goose!" he said, and chucked her under the chin.

"Oh, Tedders!" she cried, throwing herself about petulantly, still not satisfied. "Then why, oh way, did you let your little prisoner *escape?*"

"It was you, my dear, who said you *wanted* to escape," he pointed out gently.

"Well, I simply couldn't take any more. You kept putting it off. And putting it off. And putting it off…"

He shifted her weight on his lap.

"I told you, Petal, I wanted to come to you with an extra pip. As a chief inspector."

"As if that matters," she said sulkily.

"It does to a man, my dear. But, anyway, as it turned out the powers that be didn't see fit to offer me the promotion. So, once again, I stand before you as a mere double pipper."

The Inspector chuckled. "Or should I say *sit* before you, hmm? Or even *under* you, hmm? An inspector under a sergeant for a change, eh…? Don't I even get a smile? Not even just a little one?" he coaxed. "*That's* better."

"I think they're absolute *rotters* not to have offered you that promotion. Honestly I do."

"Well," he said, chuckling again, "they, they obviously didn't consider Inspector Worth was worth it. Hmm…?"

But a smile was all he was getting for now.

"And only a couple of nights before that you cancelled our date to see *South Pacific*. And you *knew* how much I wanted to see it. It was all too much, really it was."

"I told you, Petal. I was called in at the last moment. And I still had a chance at that stage of promotion. But Petal, that was before I realised what really mattered. What was of far more importance than a mere extra pip. What I'm trying to say, my dear, in my rather clumsy way, is that I still have your ring at home. I shut it away that day with a heavy heart. I had sacrificed love and happiness for promotion and ended up with neither."

"Oh! Tedders!" she said, the cry wrung from her despite herself. This was passion as if it were written on the cover of one of her Mills & Boon romances.

"It's still waiting for you, you know. If you can forgive a foolish male his pride, and do him the honour of once more saying yes."

"Oh, yes, yes – *yes*!" she cried, and clasped him to her.

"And now I've got you in custody again, my dear," he said, emerging from her bosom and smoothing down his hair, "you're staying there. Under lock and key. What have you to say to that? Mmm?"

"I say throw away the key," she said simply, and put her face to his to be kissed.

"Now, as we're both off this afternoon," he said after obliging, "I suggest a jolly good run. I've neglected to exercise since we broke up. Just didn't feel like it somehow. And then this evening, I will return that ring to its rightful finger. A nice meal, with a bottle of something special, and – what*ever* is the matter, my dear?"

The Sergeant was staring into space with a stricken expression.

It was saying yes twice in one week and the mention of a bottle that did it.

"Phineas...!" she gasped.

"Phineas?"

"Phineas Cook."

"And who or what is Phineas Cook, may one ask? Mmm?" he said, and chuckled.

"He's a – he's a man."

"A man, eh?" he said, indulging her with another chuckle. "Well, and what about him, this man?"

"He's a man I met when we – when I..."

"A man you met, eh?" he said.

And then he frowned.

"A man you met? Do you mean you met a man? Met someone else? Is that what you mean?"

"No. Well, Yes... But—"

"I think you had better explain yourself, my girl," he said, leaning back to get a better look at her.

She concentrated on his shirt button. "I thought you didn't love me..."

"*And...?*"

"Oh, Tedders, I've been such a fool!"

"Well...? I'm waiting..."

"I was vulnerable. My heart was bruised. I felt cast aside and unloved, unwanted. And you know I shouldn't drink more than a glass of red wine. It goes straight to my head."

"Well – go on..."

41

"And well, he – er – he asked me to marry him…"

"He… He asked you to *marry* him!"

"Yes."

"*Yes.* Is that all you have to say?"

"I said yes."

"You said—?"

"I thought, well, Tedders doesn't want me, so I said yes."

"I see. So, you thought, oh, well, I'll get married to someone else then." He snorted. "I suppose I must be thankful you remembered it in time."

"It's not like that. It wasn't—"

"Well, what was it like? I think I have a right to know."

"It was just…"

"When did you meet him? This – this other man."

"Saturday. In the evening. The same day I – we—"

"The same day? Well, it certainly didn't take you long!"

"It wasn't like that. It was because—"

"Do you love him?" the Inspector broke in, and stared stiffly ahead, a man prepared to do the decent thing.

"No, of *course* I don't. It wasn't – it was because I was upset, and the wine and everything. It's you I love. You *know* that."

"Not so sure I do now. And did he – have you—?"

"Tedders! Is that what you think of me!"

"I don't know what to think of you, my dear. You give me my ring back in the morning and pick up another one in the evening. What am I to think?"

She glumly held her bare left hand up in evidence.

"Perhaps you'd rather I went."

"I didn't say that," he said, as if he hadn't reached a decision either way. "Where did you meet this – this *other* man?"

"Here. In town. At a party."

"At a party, eh?"

"Tina Norman, a WPC, she invited me to one she and her husband were giving. She found me weeping in the Ladies'.

Tedders, I don't even *like* him particularly," she burst out. "And he's an awful slacker. When I asked him did he like exercising, trying to find *some* common ground, something to talk about, he made a joke about his right arm getting a lot of it. He meant drinking. And he smokes."

"And how many times did you and this – this *Phineas Cook*," he said, as if suggesting an obvious and rather absurd alias, "go out together, may one ask?"

"Just the once. We met again the next evening."

"To see *South Pacific*, I suppose. Back row of the Odeon."

"No. No, of course not. If I couldn't see *South Pacific* with you, then I didn't want to see it at all. We were supposed to be going for a meal."

"A meal, eh?"

"I could see then, when he turned up, what sort he was. In fact I thought there was something suspicious about him. He had dark glasses on and his collar turned up, and kept looking around. He looked thoroughly shifty."

"Mmm. And did you enjoy your meal together, hmm? You and this – Phineas Cook?"

"What meal?" The Sergeant rolled her eyes. "He took me straight to the nearest pub. Said he had to see a man about a dog. And then we had to sit facing the door. I wouldn't be surprised if he's on the wanted list."

"He certainly bears checking out by the sound of it."

"I wanted to tell him then that it was a dreadful mistake, but every time I brought it up he changed the subject. Perhaps he somehow knew what I was trying to say and couldn't bear me to say it. Love leaves us defenceless," she added, speaking both for herself and Phineas Cook.

The Inspector was unmoved. "Couldn't you have phoned him?"

"I don't have his number. He's not in the book, and directory enquires couldn't help. I don't even know if he has a phone. He lives on a boat on the river at Batch Magna. The *Cluny Belle,* it's called. It's the gipsy in his soul, he told me in the back garden."

"In the back garden…?"

"At the party. It's where he proposed. In the back garden."

"In the back garden, eh?"

"Kneeling in a flowerbed. He said we were going to sail away together so he could show his prize off to the world."

"Did he indeed!"

"I went over there, to Batch Magna, and found out where his boat was moored – went quite a few times in fact, to break it to him face to face. To tell him that it could never be. That two broken hearts can never a whole make. But he never seems to *be* there, Tedders. Just his dog, a large white brute, snarling and barking at me from the deck. And you know I don't like dogs."

"And what does this Phineas Cook do for a living, may one ask? When, that is, he's not sailing the seven seas."

"He couldn't sail anywhere on that old thing. It's not a proper boat, just some old tub he lives on. He wouldn't say what he did. He said it was best I didn't know. As if he were a secret agent or something. Oh, Tedders, I've been such a fool!"

"You've certainly been that, my girl," he agreed.

He gazed judiciously off into the middle distance.

The Sergeant cast down her eyes and waited.

And then he appeared to arrive at a judgement.

"Well, it seems to me that no great harm has been done, and that I am at least partly to blame for this unfortunate occurrence. So I suggest we put the whole thing behind us. Forget it ever happened."

"Oh, Tedders, you're so…"

"You'll have to break it to this Phineas Cook person, of course. Tell him the best man won, and all that."

"The best man never lost in the first place. The heart you won was and is still yours. But yes, you're right, of course. He must be told. I at least owe him that. Not to allow him to go on hoping. To be cruel only to be kind. When, that is, I can find him."

The Inspector looked amused.

"My dear girl, there's no need to actually *see* the man. Just write him a letter. That's all you have to do."

"Oh," she said immediately, "I feel I really ought to—"

"And address it to this tub of his at Batch Magna," the Inspector went on patiently. "The postman will do the rest. It's quite simple."

She hesitated. "Well, yes, I – yes, I suppose I could do that."

"Well, of course you could. And I suggest you do so. Now, this morning."

"Yes, all right, Tedders," she said meekly. "I'll get it off by the lunchtime post."

"That's the idea. And now we've got that out of the way, I can go ahead and book that table for two. Hmm?"

"Oh, yes…"

"And if something turns up again this evening they can jolly well get someone else to deal with it. Oh, yes, my dear, I too have learnt a lesson. Tonight, my girl, belongs to us."

"The night they invented champagne!" she cried gaily, tossing her head back, and then the phone rang.

"Oh, let it ring!" she said wantonly.

"No. No, I'd better answer it. I've never been less than conscientious, even if that's something that's obviously been overlooked by others. Worth here," he said curtly into it, and winked at her.

And then he sat up abruptly, almost dislodging her.

"Where… ?… *How* much!… Yes, yes, I'll let CID know – if, that is, any of them are in yet. How about the press…? Well, if and when they do give me as the officer in charge," he said, knowing that they would get on to it, he'd make sure of that, just as soon as he put the phone down. "I'm on my way."

He stared at her.

"It's a big one, Petal. A wages snatch. In Shrewsbury, but just within our patch. Something like a hundred thousand pounds was taken. The biggest robbery on this manor for... Well, the biggest robbery here ever, surely! You do realise what this means?"

"Yes," she said, sighing and taking herself off his lap. "It means I won't get my ring tonight."

"It means, my girl," he said, lifting the phone again, "that if I can bring this one to book they can hardly refuse me promotion."

After alerting his local press contact, the Inspector picked up his uniform hat and swagger stick and regarded himself in the mirror above the fireplace.

"They'll come to see then that the pip went to the wrong man," he murmured to himself, presenting first one profile and then the other, while the Sergeant stood glumly by his desk.

He had, he decided, the jaw for leadership.

"With our shiny new Chief Inspector away on his introductory course, the baton falls to me. And I shall not fumble," he told his reflection. "Shall not drop it."

The Sergeant sighed. "I'm fed up," she said to herself. "Honestly I am."

Chapter Six

They didn't need to fire off the birdseed, just the sight of the sawn-off, along with the Major's soldierly way with the Luger, and the terrifying, lumbering hulk of Clothesline, their features squashed into a leg apiece from Brrm-Brrm's mum's tights, was enough.

The armoured van driver and his mate, losing no time in complying with company policy, immediately handed the bags over, while the two warehousemen there to collect the money just as immediately shot their hands up.

The robbers then dashed with their loot past the three-ton lorry blocking the entrance and out to the Triumph, waiting with the engine revving.

There was a brief hiatus when Clothesline and the Major tried to get into the front passenger seat at the same time. But apart from that it went as sweet as a nut, as Tony put it, slicing open the six locked canvas bags in the back with his flick-knife, and kissing the first, thick bundle of notes, before starting to empty them into the big holdall, helped eagerly by the Major, the Triumph juddering and rocking as Brrm-Brrm picked up speed, going through the gears like a rally driver.

The rain had followed them from Birmingham, stopping shortly before they arrived at the factory, the road slick with it, which didn't slow down the Triumph.

Brrm-Brrm would never be more Brrm-Brrm than at the wheel of a souped-up getaway car with his foot down, his face lit with it. Brrm-brrming away to himself as if playing at it, a ten-year-old racing driver on the dodgems, throwing the car in and out of the morning traffic on the outskirts of the town, using both sides of the road, horn blaring, leaving a few oncoming vehicles, with nowhere else to go, climbing on to the pavement, scattering pedestrians.

The Triumph was swaying with speed as it hit the roundabout, Brrm-Brrm yelling with laughter as he glimpsed the frozen white faces of drivers who thought they had the Highway Code on their side, Clothesline with his eyes shut tight in the front seat, meaty hands rigid on the dashboard, the Major almost on Tony's lap as they screamed round the roundabout, the rear slewing in the wet, throwing up spray, the car turning to face the opposite direction before straightening.

They tore up the road leading into the town, and the Major was flung against Tony again as Brrm-Brrm then threw a left, down a rough track running between some of the back yards of an industrial estate and the arches of a railway viaduct, the car bouncing along it.

This was the switch-over place that the pawnbroker had found after a couple of days trawling the area, the polished nose of the Wolseley poking out from under one of the arches a marker.

The Triumph swung into the arch next to it and they piled out.

Sneed watched in his rear-view mirror as the holdall was dumped in the boot.

"All right? No problems...?" he asked then.

"Nah. Sweet as a nut," Tony said, getting into the back first.

"Good, good. Well done, mates. Well done," Sneed said, smiling the smile of the newly rich.

"Do mind my bowler," the Major said testily, hurriedly following Brrm-Brrm into the back and rescuing the hat before he could sit on it. "It's a Lock's Town Coke."

"Get away!" Brrm-Brrm said. "How did I do, Mr Sneed? Was it all right?" he asked excitedly.

"Stirling Moss couldn't have done better, son. I clocked it at a tight ten minutes on the practice runs. You did it in just over four."

"Did I, Mr Sneed? Did I?"

"You did, son, ah," Sneed said.

He switched on, and then glanced at Clothesline sitting next to him and chortled. "'Ere, Clothesline, have you got your stocking mask on or off?" he said, referring to the ex-wrestler's cauliflower ears and squashed nose, making a rare joke, but in the mood for a bit of levity. Clothesline checked his head with a hand, and then looked blankly at him.

"Got it all, did you?" Sneed asked then, glancing in the rear-view mirror as the Wolseley bumped its way carefully along the track.

"All except the coin," the Major said, his mind on the other sort in the boot.

He was wondering how he might lose the Italian when they got to the station.

The Major also had his dreams, the more modest, English ones, of Bournemouth and early retirement. A villa perhaps, with housekeeper and someone to do the garden, or a service apartment with a balcony and sea view. Morning promenades along the front, and the mannered click of bowls on a club green, concerts and the refinements of sherry and bridge, and who knows, now the evenings of his life were drawing in, some suitable lady perhaps to come home to.

"Right, now get your heads down," Sneed said, when they reached the road Brrm-Brrm had just left, and which would take them the short distance up into the town and the railway station. "They're bound to be busy. Although," he added, "the time Brrm-Brrm got it down to, I wouldn't be surprised if they haven't even got their helmets on yet. It means you'll have about a twenty-five minute wait for the train. But by the time you've got your tickets and found the right platform, and maybe had a cuppa…

"Major," he said then. "Major, are you listening?"

The Major grunted, his head down in a scrum with Tony and Brrm-Brrm.

"Just to recap, Major. The Bristol train leaves from platform seven—"

"The train now standing at platform four is the gravy train," Tony said in a mock station announcer's voice, and stifled a giggle.

Sneed went on patiently, "At five past ten. When you get to this Church Myddle, the first stop down the line, you want number one platform for the ten fifty-five Birmingham. The journey time to there is twenty minutes, which means another wait, thirty minutes if the Bristol's in on time, but at least you'll be clear of Shrewsbury. That will take you direct to New Street. Where I'll be waiting. OK…? Major? Tony?"

"We'll be there," Tony muttered.

"I do hope so, Tony," Sneed said, pulling up at the station entrance.

"It says I'm discreet and confidential on my shop window, but I won't be at all discreet and confidential if you don't turn up. Be on the blower to the Lane in no time, I will. And they've got both your details and mug shots on file, ready for the six o'clock news. You wouldn't get very far. Best to leave it at your share, eh mates, than have nothing and a large helping of porridge to go with it. Have a good journey…"

Chapter Seven

The Major donned his British Warm and bowler hat, restoring some of his dignity as the Wolseley pulled away from the station front. The impertinences and incivilities that are one's lot these days, he thought, gazing after it with distaste.

He picked up the holdall, the one hundred thousand in banknotes, and marched briskly with his umbrella towards the station. Tony, who had gone ahead, was loitering by the entrance, pretending to study a wall poster extolling the summer joys of Prestatyn.

What, the Major wondered, had happened to trust?

He glanced casually back on his way into the station. The Italian was following on, keeping close to the wall, skulking behind him like some damn native wallah.

The Major paused on the concourse, seeking the booking office.

There had been a flurry of activity from a few taxis pulling up behind Sneed, the passengers from them hurrying into the station, and people on their way out.

But now there was a lull, and Tony saw his chance.

He slipped a hand into the inside breast pocket of his suit and crept towards the Major with elaborate intent, a cartoon cat closing in on the mouse, the blade of the flick-knife springing into oiled, bright deadly life with the quietest of clicks.

The point of it was touching the cloth of the Major's British Warm, and Tony was about to give him a warning prod with it, his other hand stretching for the holdall, when the Major spotted the sign he wanted and abruptly moved off.

Caught off balance, Tony stumbled forward a few paces, the knife jabbing at the air, leaving him standing there with it held out at arm's length, just as the concourse suddenly sprung more passengers.

He shoved it hastily away in a side pocket.

And then he realised what he'd done and his eye started twitching.

He hadn't retracted the blade he'd honed earlier that day to a razor sharpness, and not only had it gone straight through the pocket of a 100 guinea silk suit without stopping, it had also neatly opened up a rent in the side of the coat on its way there.

He shoved the knife back into his breast pocket and stalked on after the Major, one arm covering the gaping slit in his coat.

The Major bought his ticket, leaving Tony smouldering a couple of places behind him in the queue.

Following the signs for platform seven, he stopped for a train of caged flat-bed wagons, pulled by an electric tug and piled with luggage and goods, that was about to cross his path.

He glanced casually back. Tony was occupied buying his ticket.

The Major, taking the initiative, nipped smartly in front of the wagons, and looked back again. The Italian was lost to view behind them.

Facing him was a newsagent's kiosk, a buffet, and two public lavatories either side of offices of some sort.

The Major made a dash for them.

Confounding the anticipated expectations of the enemy, as they'd taught him at Sandhurst, and trusting to his luck, he tripped straight down the stairs to the Ladies'.

His luck was out.

He thought at first the place was empty. His idea was to lock himself in a cubicle, and bunker down there until it was safe to assume Tony had given up. But his luck was out.

He heard her before he saw her, and when she emerged from the end cubicle with a mop and bucket he recognised her immediately. He'd seen that face before, or something very much like it, under the peak of one sort of uniform hat or the other. It had bawled at him on the parade ground at Sandhurst, and could be found on the landings of the various HM prisons he'd been a guest of, and in a different uniform, implacably writing out parking tickets.

He opened and closed his mouth a couple of times, attempting an explanation, even an amused chuckle at the situation, while she, without a word, walked stolidly towards him with her mop.

The Major, deciding on a strategic withdrawal, turned and scrambled back up the stairs.

He saw Tony when he came out again, standing in the middle of the concourse, peering about, looking for him.

He tried the door of the first office he came to. It was locked. He had his hand on the doorknob of the second office, had half-turned it, when his eyes met with the sign on the dark blue door. British Transport Police, it said.

He snatched his hand away as if burnt, and considering the buffet too obvious, made a dash for the Gents'.

The Gents', like the Ladies', had steep flights of stairs down to it from two different parts of the concourse. Unlike his visit to the Ladies', the Major didn't intend staying, but to go down one flight and then straight up the other, hoping to put enough station between him and the Italian, maybe even allowing him to sneak out of another entrance and grab a taxi.

But, again, the Major's luck was out.

He'd reached the bottom of the stairs when there was a rush of footsteps on them and Tony appeared, looking heated.

The Major chuckled briefly. "Frightfully amusing, Tony. You'll never guess what happened. I was caught short, and—"

"Give me the bag," Tony said in a low fierce voice, one eye on the other occupant there, standing with his back to them at the urinals. "Give it to me."

"My dear fellow—!" the Major blustered.

"You heard me." Tony's hand slid towards his inside coat pocket. "Hand it over... Yes, I – er—" he said then in a louder voice, innocently brushing at the front of his jacket. "I – er—" he said again, stalling as the other occupant went past them and up the stairs.

"Right. Give it to me," he went on, just as the clatter of more footsteps sounded on the stone stairs, a man coming down them in a hurry.

Tony stalled again. "Got a light, mate?" he said to the Major.

"Terrible sorry, old chap, afraid not," the Major said, seeing his chance and starting to edge round him. "I don't smoke."

Neither did Tony, but he bit his nails. And his eye had started twitching again.

He grabbed the Major's sleeve. "Give me the bag. Give it to me or I'll cut you! Open you up!"

"You won't get far with it. You heard what Sneed said he'd do," the Major said, both men speaking in near whispers.

"I'm not going far," Tony lied. "I don't trust you with it, that's all. Now hand it over."

"The reason I'm carrying it, Tony," the Major said primly, "as well you know, is because I'm the one least likely to be stopped. You heard—"

"I haven't seen any coppers about to do any stopping – have you? Eh?" Tony demanded, blinking rapidly at him, and looking, the Major considered, even for a Mediterranean type, quite demented. And then he noticed the state of his coat. The Italian was coming apart in more ways than one.

"Now, why don't we talk about it, hmm, Tony?" he said soothingly. "Perhaps over a cup of tea. We've got time." The Major thought again. "Or a coffee. An espresso," he said brightly, thinking that that sounded Italian. "You'll like that."

"Give it me!" Tony hissed, and made another move towards his knife pocket.

The Major put a hand on Tony's to hold it there. Tony's eye twitched, winking at him. The man who'd been in a hurry was now less so, and took in the scene on his way out.

"Disgusting!" he snapped. "I've a good mind to report you."

"This is becoming all rather unsavoury," the Major said stiffly. "And may I remind you, Tony, that we have a train to catch."

"No more talking, Major," Tony said, pulling the flick-knife out and releasing the blade.

He jabbed it towards the Major's throat, dimpling the skin with it, and as the Major's head went up removed the holdall from his limp grip.

And then more footsteps sounded on the stairs.

They both looked up and saw two pairs of uniform trousers descending.

"That chap reported us," the Major said, and found himself holding the bag again as Tony thrust it at him and bolted up the other flight of stairs, with the Major close behind, both of them missing the rest of the uniforms, the appearance of the two railway porters taking advantage of the facilities after a prolonged tea break.

Chapter Eight

Tony, with no more opportunities presenting themselves, had to walk, tantalisingly, past platform four for Charing Cross, and the Continent and Monte, following the Major to platform 7, for Church Myddle and Birmingham.

They sat at opposite ends of the same coach for the twenty-minute journey, the Major, holdall on his lap, gazing out of the window, watching the hunting fields of Shropshire go by, Tony watching the Major, one arm covering the tear in his jacket, his eye beating steadily, like a pulse.

They didn't have to look far for platform one at Church Myddle. Church Myddle only had two platforms, and they got off at one of them, platform two.

A few other passengers alighted with them and walked down towards the station entrance at the end of it. The Major, followed by Tony, had simply to walk the few yards across to platform one running parallel to it.

And it was then that fate, as Tony saw it, beckoned again. With nothing but the shine of railway tracks curving into the distance on their left, and the blank whitewashed wall of a waiting room on their right, he saw that they were, for that brief space, completely cut off from view.

He moved quickly, the blade flicking out, closing on the Major as he was about to step clear of the shelter of the building's wall, out on to platform one. Just as the Major had one foot on the platform, turned and saw a couple of uniformed police officers talking to a railway official halfway along it.

He jerked back and spinning round collided with Tony, almost knocking him down, the knife clattering to the floor.

"Whaddya doing – whaddya doing!" he hissed.

The Major couldn't tell him for a moment.

Then he waved a hand feebly in the direction of what he'd just seen.

"The police. The police are there," he got out then, and clutched at his heart. "Two of them."

Tony looked at him suspiciously. He picked up the knife and pointed it at him. "Stay there!" he warned.

He peered round the corner of the building, and then jerked his head back as if singed, and after remembering in time to retract the blade first, hastily pocketed the knife.

"I told you, Tony, didn't I. The police. But why here? Why *here*?" the Major implored plaintively. "That's what I don't understand. We didn't see them at Shrewsbury, so why *here*?"

"There wasn't time, maybe," Tony said, eye jumping. "Maybe that was it, like Sneed said. With that madman driving we were in and out before they could toss the net. They didn't have time to do it. And now they've got time. And they're just making themselves busy, that's all. Just routine enquiries," he said, a phrase he was familiar with.

"That's all," he said again, and nibbled furiously on a fingernail.

"But on the platform the Birmingham train leaves from, Tony. That's what I don't like about it."

The Major removed his bowler, mopped at his forehead and wiped the inside of the hat with a handkerchief. He really was getting too old for these sort of games.

It was obvious Tony didn't like that about it either.

He sidled along the wall and took another peek.

"One of them, a sergeant, he's writing something down in a notebook," he reported.

"You know what I'm thinking, Tony. I'm thinking that maybe they caught the others and they peached on us."

Tony frowned. "Peached?"

"Peached. Sneaked. Told on us, Tony, told on us."

Tony went back to his nails.

"That don't make sense," he decided then. "They'd have pulled us when we got off from Shrewsbury. They'd have been waiting for us. That don't make sense."

The Major clutched at it. "Then perhaps it's not us they're after," he said, and smiled hopefully at him.

Tony thought about that as well.

"And perhaps it is," he decided.

The Major's smile wobbled. "But, as you say, it doesn't—"

"You wanna risk it?" Tony jerked his head at the holdall the Major had put down. "Eh? You wanna walk out there with that?"

"Well, I – er…"

"No. No, I thought not."

"Well, we can't just *stand* here," the Major said, just standing there.

Tony was struck by an idea. "Left luggage," he said, and scuttling the few steps back to platform one peered round the corner of the building that end. Then beckoned the Major over.

"Thought I'd seen it when we got off. A left luggage place. We drop it in there, get it off our hands. Pick it up later."

"What, with a hundred thousand quid in it? It's not even locked."

The Major found that, like the Italian, he was whispering.

"Then whaddya suggest? Whaddya suggest, huh?" Tony flung his hands up, the fingers spread and rigid, and shook them, his face fierce with the effort of keeping his voice down. "If we're copped for this we're gonna do double, you know that don't you? Don't you? It'll be a ten stretch and more this time, straight off. With an extra helping for the guns. You wanna do that? Go down for all that? You'll be old when you come out."

The Major's sigh was heartfelt.

"Well, I suppose we've no choice."

He looked dolefully at the holdall sitting on the ground, saying goodbye to it, saying goodbye to Bournemouth.

"That's right, you got it. We got no choice. Well, go on, what you waiting for? You carry it. As you all say, who's gonna suspect you, nice English gent like you?"

The Major reluctantly picked up the bag, and, for a change, started following Tony.

Platform two was bare of police officers or anyone else.

Tony tried the door of the left luggage office. And then tried it again, turning the worn brass doorknob first one way and then the other, pushing and then pulling it. Then he shook it. The door stayed locked.

"Tony. Tony, it's closed," the Major noticed then despairingly. "Look, the shutter's down."

"There might be somebody in there. Having *tea...*" Tony sneered

"Try knocking, then," the Major suggested, and fretfully checked out the platform.

Tony winked at him.

"Knocking. Try knocking," the Major said, miming the action.

Tony knocked, rapping sharply on the door. Then he knocked again, and when there was still no answer, banged on it.

The Major winced, his head sinking into his British Warm as if braced for a hand on his collar.

And then Tony in a sudden fury grabbed the doorknob and started shaking it violently, the door rattling in its frame.

"My dear fellow!" the Major protested, his imagination seeing the two officers on their way round to investigate a sudden outbreak of vandalism on platform two.

But Tony wasn't listening. As far as he was concerned there was only him and the door there.

He stared at it, eye jumping and breathing as if from exertion – or as if getting ready to hurl himself at it.

The Major looked wildly around for escape.

The station entrance was at one end of the platform, and nothing but railway tracks at the other. Across from platform two, over the rails, a steep embankment rose to a perimeter fence of railway sleepers.

At his age it had to be the entrance.

The Major dithered in an agony of indecision, held by the sight of all that money, just sitting there.

And then his heart lurched as someone shouted from the direction of the entrance.

Chapter Nine

It was a porter, hurrying towards them and holding something up and waving it at them, which turned out as he drew near to be a bunch of keys.

"I saw you trying to get in. Sorry to keep you, gents," he said, blowing and looking harassed. "We're one short today. Which means I had to do the announcement for the inbound Shrewsbury, and then rush round and take the tickets off it. Then I was supposed to do the booking office, for when they start turning up for the outbound Birmingham. Well that will have to wait now. If I'm not there they'll just have to pay on board or at the other end. I can't be in two places at once."

"Indeed not!" the Major agreed, hearty with relief.

"Not that they don't expect it sometimes, I can tell you. And of course our blessed station master's busy, isn't he," he said, going through the keys. "Having a chin-wag on one. You must be off the Shrewsbury," he added.

The Major hesitated. "Yes," he admitted, realising that they had to be off the Shrewsbury. "Yes, we're off the Shrewsbury."

"Yes, we're off the Shrewsbury," Tony echoed, one arm covering the tear in his jacket, his head to one side as if comforting his twitching eye.

"There we are," the porter said, inserting one of the keys.

"Splendid!" the Major beamed.

"No we're not," the porter said, taking it out again.

"More like the parcel office, come to think of it. Not that there's a lot of parcels in it these days. Mostly stuff people have dumped there. Old destination boards, a broken weighing machine, a couple of luggage trolleys with their axles gone, that sort of thing... No, it's not that one either," he said, discarding another key, while the Major whistled through his teeth and glanced casually around.

"Well, at least the rain's stopped," the porter said. "Although it saved the station master having to water his blessed roses, so that's all right. Between you and me I sometimes think that's all he turns up for... No, nor that one. We don't get much call to use this office, see, little local station like this, not these days. But don't get me started on that... It's not that one, either. Still, I suppose we have to consider ourselves lucky we've still got a station, that we haven't gone under the Beeching axe... And it's not *that* one. And I know this one, with the dab of whitewash on it, that's the booking office.

"Time was, you see, when the keys were all kept separate, hung on a board in the station master's office, each with a wooden tag with the name of what it opened on it."

He looked at them.

"Well, I ask you, what could be clearer than that?"

"What indeed," the Major muttered.

"What could be more simple than that?"

"Quite," the Major said tightly.

"Then somebody went and lost a key. And the station master had one of his brain waves, didn't he. Decided in his infinite wisdom to put them all on one ring. Got the lot on it, this has. Office keys, sheds, staff room, locker keys, cupboards, signal box, toilets, every blooming thing. His thinking was – no, that's the waiting room key, I think... Now let me see... Don't worry, gents, it's on here somewhere. Though to tell the truth, I'm not sure anyone knows what all these are for now, me included...

No, it's not that one, either. And that's the grit box. I can tell you that straight off, by the shape. We have to keep grit on the platform, see, for when it's icy. Because if somebody slips and breaks a leg, we're for it. But we have to keep the box locked, otherwise the blooming school kids chuck the stuff about all over the place. Yes, his thinking was, that by putting them on one ring – ah, there we are," he said, turning it in the lock. "I knew we'd get there in the end. Hang on, and I'll open up…"

"Come on, come *on*!" Tony growled when he'd disappeared into the office.

"Yes, his thinking was," the porter resumed, reappearing behind a counter after the shutter had rattled up, "that it's harder to lose a bunch of keys than a single one. Well, that's all very well, as far as it goes. But you saw where that left us…"

"Quite," the Major said.

"You saw the result of that yourselves."

"Indeed," the Major grunted, hurriedly heaving the holdall up onto the counter, the sound of the sawn-off and pistol clunking together, adding to his nerves. The Luger was empty but, sawn-off or otherwise, shotguns have gone off accidentally.

He chuckled briefly, and then said, "Camera equipment. Yes, we – er – we're both rather keen on the photographic art, you know. Aren't we – er – Mr Smith."

"Yes, we're rather keen on that," Tony mumbled.

"Ah, I see," the porter said, smiling politely.

"We're waiting for the Birmingham train, actually. Is it – er – is it on time, do you know?" the Major said, pushing the bag towards him, and doing a quick sweep of the platform.

"Yes. Yes, it is." The porter was frowning. "But you could have boarded it at Shrewsbury, sir, the ten thirty-five, and gone straight through with it."

The Major, never short for long of an answer to an awkward question, drew himself up. "That's precisely what my colleague and I intended doing," he said huffily. "But we were misinformed by a member of staff there, told that what turned out to be the Bristol train was the Birmingham. Fortunately for us a fellow passenger put us right, and suggested we pick it up here."

"I see…" the porter said, one hand on the holdall, and not sounding as if he did entirely.

The Major came up with the rest of the story.

"But as it turns out we didn't mind terribly, because we – er – we intended anyway to – er – to return and tour the area. A short holiday, as it were, after concluding our business. A chance to indulge our joint interest in photography, and, given this part of the world, in – er – in archaeology. Without the digging, of course. The remains of castles, that sort of thing. The Saxon and Norman ruins which are known to abound here. The past through which the wind blows, carrying its voices, and all that, you know."

"I get you," the porter said.

"Not to mention of course the stone footprint of the Roman. One thinks in particular of the glory that was once Uriconium, the Romanised capital of Cornavii, to be found in modern day Wroxeter. Or, to give it its Latin form, Viroconium Cornoviorum," the Major went on, warming to it, while Tony shifted and muttered. "Or simply Viroconium. Or, no doubt to its plebeian order of citizens, the demotic Viro. A city established as a legionary fortress around AD fifty eight. Academics dispute among themselves, as academics will, as to the precise date."

"Oh, ah," the porter agreed, and smiled vaguely.

"By hire car," the Major added, stitching up that detail. "We intend visiting the various sites of interest by hire car. Far more convenient. But we had to make a business trip to Birmingham first, do you see."

"Ah, I *see*… I was wondering about that. So your thinking was—"

"Our thinking was that we'd leave our holdall here, attend the business meeting as scheduled, and return on a later train?" The Major turned it into a question.

The porter sucked in a breath.

"Not today, sir, I'm afraid," he said, shaking his head. "Not today. The last inbound Birmingham today is due in just over an hour. Outbound Birmingham, yes. There's two more today. But no inbound, I'm afraid."

"Oh, dear," the Major said. He hadn't expected that.

"Do you hear that, Mr Smith?"

Tony, his back to the wall, where he could keep an eye on both sides of the platform, grunted.

"Tomorrow, yes. There's an afternoon one tomorrow. Gets in at four thirty-seven, that does. And the same service runs on Tuesdays and Thursdays. But not today. Sorry…"

The porter waited.

"Oh, dear," the Major said again. "That does rather put a different complexion on things. Still, can't be helped, can't be helped. It will just have to be tomorrow then. Our main luggage, do you see, is in our hotel in Birmingham. Which served as our base, as it were."

"I see…"

"It's – er – as I say, our main luggage is in Birmingham." The Major indicated the holdall with his umbrella. "That contains our cameras, and overnight kit for our various business excursions. So the question now—"

"So the question now," the porter said, leaning on the counter, "is whether you take it with you on the Birmingham. Or leave it here and come back for it tomorrow."

"In a nut shell."

"And if I've got it right – and correct me if I haven't – you'll be leaving Birmingham with your main luggage to come back this way again for your little holiday."

"Precisely."

"Right. Well, sir, as I see it, it seems to me that there's not much sense in you taking it with you if you've got to come back again tomorrow, is there. That's the way I see it, anyhow."

"Yes. Yes, you have a point there. He has a point there, Mr Smith."

"That would be my thinking…"

"Yes, quite. Well, that settles it," the Major said with a little laugh.

The porter shot up a finger in a sudden afterthought.

"Ah. Unless of course, as it probably does do, it contains your overnight stuff, your shaving things and pyjamas, and so on."

"Yeeees" the Major said slowly, realising that he could hardly say otherwise. "Yes, it does, as you say, contain our toilet kit and pyjamas, and so on."

"*Just put the bloody thing in,*" Tony snarled out of the corner of his mouth.

"Ah, well then."

And then the porter had another thought. "Course, you could always take your pyjamas, and so on, out."

"Yeeees. Yes, we could do that," the Major had to agree.

The porter, having solved the problem, smiled and obligingly returned the holdall.

"There you are, sir. And I dare say I could even find you a couple of carrier bags for them."

The Major stared at it, his mind blank. Tony detached himself carefully from the wall.

And then the Major brightened.

"Ah. Ah, yes, thank you. Most considerate of you. But come to think of it, the hotel provides a complimentary shaving set. And towels and so forth, you know? And we have a change of pyjamas, and what have you, there, with our main luggage," he said, pushing the bag back again.

"Oh, well, in that case…"

"Quite," the Major said.

"You might as well leave it here then."

"Yes, I rather think that's the answer"

"That's what I'd do, anyhow."

"Yes, I suggest we do that, Mr Smith. Leave it here and retrieve it tomorrow."

"Be one less bag to carry coming back."

"As you so rightly say."

"And it'll be safe enough here, gents," the porter said, scribbling on a label and tying it to the handle of the holdall. "As you know, when there's no one in here the office is kept locked."

He handed the Major a ticket torn from a book of them.

"There you are, sir. You pay when you pick up your luggage. That number on your ticket," the porter went on, "matches the number here on your luggage label. It's a good system, couldn't be simpler. And we've never had a problem with it. Which means of course that any day now it'll be changed. Have a good journey."

Chapter Ten

Tony relieved the Major of half of the ticket, tearing it neatly between the four numbers on it, on their way down platform two to get to platform one that way, as if they had just arrived at the station.

There, Tony sat down on the first bench he came to, while the Major, distancing himself from him, strolled to the other end of the platform and leant nonchalantly on his umbrella, both men affecting indifference to the uniformed figures standing in the middle of it.

It was the older of the two police officers, a sergeant, and the station master who appeared to be doing all the talking. The other officer, a tall, lanky young constable, looked alertly restless, lifting himself up and down on his heels, stretching his neck as if his collar or chin strap were too tight, his eyes busy now and then under the peak of his helmet, moving among the waiting passengers.

The Major peered into the distance where the tracks led, and then glanced at his watch, a man waiting for a train.

He was hot under his Lock's Town Coke and trying not to show it. He didn't at all like the look of the constable. He was obviously a keen type, and a keen type who now seemed to be showing an extra interest in him.

He couldn't help thinking that this latest caper, the wheels on it already starting to wobble, was about to come horribly off the road.

Tony, watching the constable out of a corner of his eye, was also of the same opinion. But considered he would be the one the young rozzer would decide to take a closer look at.

He was aware that out here in the sticks he looked like a foreign import in more ways than one, with his dark looks and silk, city slicker suit. If he had to turn his pockets out he'd be done for, and so would the Major, if they put one and one together and came up with a left luggage ticket.

He sat with an arm over the tear in his jacket, his knife hand still on his lap, eye opening and closing slowly as if, as it were, idling.

Because inside Tony was ready to go, ready to put his foot down and to explode into action as soon as the rozzer came within striking distance, strolling casually his way, like they do, saying good morning, and then casually asking first one question, and then another and another, all casually leading back to Shrewsbury.

Well this time there would be no conversation. No questions to get him confused. This time he was getting in first.

And then the platform suddenly became busy, with the sound of a train rushing it, and people getting to their feet and picking up their luggage, and the Tannoy crackling into life as the porter, wearing his announcer's hat again, broadcast the arrival of the Birmingham service.

Tony walked slowly towards whatever fate had waiting for him. Towards a carriage door a departing passenger had left open, his knife hand resting lightly near his inside breast pocket, tensed and ready for whatever came next.

But nothing came next. He had a hand on the door, and one foot on the step, and nothing happened.

He glanced down the train.

The constable was standing by a carriage door which he appeared to be holding open for the Major.

Tony boarded the train, closed the door and running the window down, waited for developments.

The constable may have been new to the job and Church Myddle, on his first posting after his probationary period at Kingham, but he knew a toff when he saw one, and a local one obviously, seeing that he had no luggage.

A local toff who might be anyone – big landowner, chairman of the bench, on all the important committees, including the police one, and a golfing partner of the Chief Constable.

The Major hesitated, suspecting some sort of trap. The last time a police constable had opened a door for him it had been on a cell in Birmingham's Steelhouse Lane, with five years waiting for him at the other end of it.

And then looked at the constable's expression and put it together, and like an old trouper came in on cue.

He inclined his head, and with a smile of acknowledgement showing just the right amount of reserved warmth, accepted his proper due.

"Thank you so much, Constable. Most kind of you," he said, with a suggestion of agreeable surprise at finding at least one young man today who knew the meaning of manners.

The constable brought a finger up to the peak of his helmet. "You're welcome, sir. Have a good journey."

The Major paused before boarding and peered at the silver on the shoulder of his uniform, as if making a note of his number.

The constable shut the door smartly after him and smiled to himself. If you couldn't go collaring armed robbers in Shrewsbury then you had to find other ways to start climbing the ladder.

After the train had borne the Major and Tony away, leaving the proceeds of the Wrekin Engineering robbery and the entire complement of Church Myddle's police force behind on the platform, the two officers walked back towards the station entrance. They'd got what they had come for. Or rather the sergeant had.

He stopped just before the entrance at a raised flower bed straddling the space between the two platforms, the air after the rain sweetened with the ripe scent of roses, bushes of them blooming on both banks in soil turned with cow manure and composted tree bark, and all gleaming with freshened, unblemished health.

The sergeant drank the sight in. A prettier picture he could not imagine, the clusters of dewy pinks, reds and yellows framed with immaculate whitewashed stones

"And not a green or black fly in sight," he murmured. Which was more than he could say at present for his own ruddy beds.

But that was about to change. In the notebook pocket of his tunic he carried the recipe for the station master's home-made spray against aphids, used for the first time a few weeks back. A weapon which had not only vanquished their enemies but which had now been proved to keep them vanquished. The station master had put much work, and trial and error, into his concoction, and his flowers triumphantly paraded his success.

The sergeant wasn't a vindictive man, but he had seen the ruined beauty of the blooms he had so lovingly tended in his own garden, and he was resolute.

While his sergeant was gazing on what his roses would once again look like, the constable, waiting impatiently, rocked on his heels, and hands behind his back, surveyed the rest of the station, as if hoping it might yield at least a vandal or two, or the idiot who had drawn dirty bits on the holiday posters on platform one. He had joined the police to catch villains, as he thought of them, and had ended up under the wing of a middle-aged plodder in a sub-station in Church Myddle, a place where nothing ever happened – or if it did nobody bothered them with it.

While just that morning, not more than ten minutes away by car, one of those new high-speed jobs, say, with a two-tone air horn they've got at Kingham, a big armed blagging had gone down, as he'd learned to call it from television, shooters, stocking masks, the lot, and a hundred grand's worth of notes nicked, cool as you like. A pro job, if ever he'd heard of one. The lads would have been issued guns, and maybe there'd be a car chase, with the two-tone and lights going and the radio chattering away, ending in a road block, and both sides banging away at each other from behind their cars, until the villains threw down their weapons and came out with their hands up.

And then a press conference and the Chief Constable handing out commendations.

While he stood there, on a deserted railway platform in Church Myddle, waiting for his sergeant to finish smelling the blasted roses.

Chapter Eleven

Plan B, the one Sneed was keeping to himself, also involved a left luggage office, this one at Birmingham's New Street Station.

With Brrm-Brrm and Clothesline safely tucked away in the pawn shop office, he was lurking in the littered gloom of an alcove between two telephone boxes at that station on platform six, waiting for the incoming Shrewsbury train, waiting for his future to arrive.

His lease was almost up on the shop and flat above, as it was on his life here. He was on his way with a change of identity, turning himself into the person he'd always wanted to be, the person he felt that if it wasn't for others he would have been. A new life, with a new lease on a nice little shop in one of the better London suburbs, a quality jeweller's, starting it off with the fenced stock from the steel cabinet the Major had attempted to open with his boy scout's penknife.

He'd cleaned out his safe and bank account, and had sneaked the collection of fenced jewellery and two suitcases, one containing his own clothes and the other pawned old clothes, along with everything else he wanted to take with him, out of the shop while Brrm-Brrm and Clothesline were waiting in the office, and locked it all in the boot of the Wolseley. They, or whoever, were welcome to have a sale with what was left.

He'd even tidied the informant neatly away. He'd told the others that the man had asked for fifteen per cent simply out of habit. The real figure was the more normal ten per cent which he, Sneed, seeing as he wouldn't be paying that, or any other amount, had offered straight off, not starting with five per cent, as he normally would have. The informant, a delivery driver, an amateur, as nervous as he was greedy, had then easily been persuaded to wait for payment until the heat was off – by which time it would be he, Sneed, who would be off, he'd thought then, indulging himself in a small witticism.

His Plan B meant urgently calling Tony and the Major into the alcove and telling them that a watch had been put on the station. That in the car park, he'd happened by sheer chance to spot a detective from Steelhouse Lane CID, someone he'd had dealings with in the past, climbing into the back of a plain white van tucked away there. It was obviously a surveillance job, and he'd probably nipped out to spend a penny or to buy cigarettes.

Of course it may not be for them. But there again, maybe it was.

Maybe a connection had somehow been made with the Wolseley and Shrewsbury, or perhaps with the pair of them, both known, travelling from the station there. Whatever it was about, the fact was that they were staking out the car park. And, if it *was* down to them, then his bet was that they were waiting for them to leave, instead of risking collaring them in a crowded station, seeing that firearms had been involved.

Of course, he'd add, as he'd said, it may have nothing at all to do with them. But there again, did either of them want to risk it? He knew he didn't. Not when getting it wrong this time meant a sentence that would put them into double figures.

And then, while they were thinking about it, the Major having gone pale and Tony twitching away, he'd have an idea.

To be on the safe side, mates, he'd say, they *had* to lose the evidence, the holdall. So how about left luggage? And in case it was just the two of them in the frame, that they'd been placed at Shrewsbury, and, as there were sure to be, there were plain clothes dicks in the station and watching the other entrances, he'd better do it, while they left separately, their hands clean.

And if Tony, who wouldn't trust his own mother, insisted on waiting and taking half of the ticket, he could oblige him there as well, having deposited in left luggage when he arrived the suitcase of pawned clothes. Using a bit of sleight-of-hand he could have half of that ticket, and welcome to it.

Sneed heard the announcement for the incoming Shrewsbury and minutes later, peering round one of the phone boxes, spotted the Major's bowler hat bobbing along among the other passengers leaving the train.

He hissed at him as he walked past, and the Major jumped.

Sneed urgently beckoned him over, and had opened his mouth to give him the bad news, when he saw that the Major wasn't carrying the holdall.

"Sneed..." the Major started.

The pawnbroker ignored him. He poked his head round the telephone box again, and then stepped out on to the platform, the need for the alcove and story redundant now, as Tony wasn't carrying the holdall either.

Tony spread his hands, as if to show them empty.

"Sneed," the Major said, following on behind. "We—"

"We had to get rid of it," Tony said.

"We really had no choice," the Major added.

The pawnbroker showed his teeth in a grin, looking from one man to the other as if waiting to be let in on the joke.

"It's perfectly safe," the Major quickly assured him. "It's in left luggage at the station where we changed for the Birmingham train, Church Myddle," he said, and the pawnbroker wondered if he was listening to their version of Plan B.

The Major told him how it had got there, the three of them standing in the middle of the platform, people moving round them.

"I came to suspect afterwards," the Major went on, "that the two officers were there merely on a spot of local business of some sort, but at the time we didn't care to risk it. Anyway, nothing lost, but a couple of hours. We can head straight back there in the car and tell the left luggage chappie there's been a change of plan."

"No," Sneed said, and flashed a grin at them, his mind darting about behind it.

"No, I – er – we can't do that, mates, unfortunately. Not at the moment. No, the – er – the car's got engine trouble. Electrics, I think. It started playing up on the way here. I wouldn't risk it, to be honest, not on a long journey. And especially coming back. My garage is chock-a-block with work – I rang 'em soon as I got here, before I knew about all this. Still, I'm a good customer. They might be able to squeeze me in, if I tell 'em an emergency's come up. But not in time, I shouldn't think. I'll try, course I will. But I think we'll probably end up having to scrub that one. They couldn't even offer me a courtesy car. Both of 'em are out apparently."

Sneed tutted and shook his head. "I don't know, what a time for it to happen, eh?" he said, his mind still frantically busy, anticipating the next move and lost for an answer to it.

The Major provided it. "Well, there isn't a train, not today. We know that much. It would not only have been quicker but perhaps safer that way, rather than showing up in the area again with the Wolseley."

Sneed managed to look disappointed. "Well, I was about to suggest that, that we take the train back and get it. You sure of that, Major?"

"They told us that at the left luggage place," Tony said, and took a bite at a fingernail.

"Tomorrow afternoon, yes," the Major elaborated. "That gets into Church Myddle at four thirty-seven. And there's a regular service at that hour on Tuesdays and Thursdays. But not on Fridays."

"That's torn it," Sneed said.

The Major thought about it. "Perhaps not. Don't go away," he told them.

He marched off, and returning a short while later explained tersely, "Booking office. There's a train to London Euston departing platform seven at one-ten, arriving at two thirty-five. And a regular service from Euston departing for Shrewsbury thirty-five minutes later."

"Right – right!" Tony said, nodding eagerly, seeing what that meant.

"Ah," Sneed said, less enthusiastically.

"Changing at Wolverhampton," the Major added.

"Wolverhampton?" Tony said. "That's even better. That's just up the road. We could get a train there from here, easy. That's even better."

But the Major hadn't finished. "Or rather *would* be departing thirty-five minutes later for Shrewsbury, via Wolverhampton, were this a Saturday. Or, indeed, a Monday or a Wednesday. The service operates on all those days but not today."

"Right, well—" Sneed started.

"Shrewsbury is also served," the Major went on, "by a service from Waterloo Station."

"When does that leave?" Tony asked hopefully.

The Major looked at his watch. "If on time, the last train today departs in exactly twenty-three minutes from now."

Tony went back to his fingernail.

"And – er – and that's it, is it, Major? As far as the trains go today, like?" Sneed asked cautiously.

"I'm afraid, so, Sneed, yes."

"Right, well—"

"How about a bus, then?" it occurred to Tony.

The Major's eyebrows went up. "A bus?"

"The Midland Red. From Digbeth. They might have something. They go everywhere. They might have something."

"Worth a try, I suppose," the Major said.

"Yeah, yeah, it is," Sneed said, forcing a smile. "Good idea, Tony. Hadn't thought of that one. Right, well, I'll tell you what, mates, let me give my garage a ring first, see what I can swing there. Be easier if we can do it by car. I shouldn't think there's much risk. It's not as if the Wolseley was stopped earlier," he added, already on his way back to the alcove and one of the telephone boxes.

He shut himself in and had an animated conversation with the Speaking Clock, and then, after making a show of looking up a number, picked up the phone again, while the other two tried to look inconspicuous on the platform.

He came out shaking his head.

"Would you believe it? The last Midland Red to Shrewsbury left just over an hour ago. Not our day, is it. Anyway, it's not all bad news. My garage, just as a favour to me, like, says they'll fit me in at the end of today's list. But that's going to be sometime late this evening. It's the best they can do, they say."

The Major took the initiative.

"Well, in that case, as public transport appears to be out of the question, I suggest a hire car. I happen to have a company cheque book on me. You produce the licence, Sneed, and I'll pay as someone employing you on a courier assignment."

"That's a good idea, Major," Tony said. "That's a good idea," he told Sneed.

The pawnbroker was shaking his head. "Mates, mates, call me over-cautious if you like, but you won't get me using a hire car. Not for business." He put up a hand. "Now, I know there's no reason for the busies to be sniffing around in that direction. It's just that I don't like the idea of leaving my name and details on paper. And another thing, what happens, Major, what happens when your kite bounces and they lay a complaint? Eh? Have you thought of that?"

He snorted a laugh. "All it needs then is for your bogus company, or a description of you, to ring a bell at the Lane. You see what I'm getting at?"

"What if we pay in cash?" Tony suggested. "The Major can do a kite at a bank on the way there and we can pay in cash."

"Tony, son, you're still leaving a name behind. I mean, if you and the Major want to do it, fine, all right. Go ahead. You've both got licences. Just leave mine out of it, that's all I'm saying. You might think I'm being an old woman about it, but people have found themselves going up the stairs before, making that sort of slip up. It's sometimes small things like that. I mean, you know yourself what coppers are like, once they find something to start picking at there's no knowing what they might end up unravelling. I wouldn't even do it in a cab, frankly, mates, not that sort of journey. Giving the driver something to talk about afterwards, and putting my description on offer. No thanks."

Tony thought about it, staring down sullenly at the platform.

"I mean," Sneed added, "as I say, if you two want to risk it, well…"

The Major had also been thinking about it.

"No. No, you have a point, Sneed," he decided briskly. "Well, I don't like the idea, of course, not one bit, but in that case, it seems to me we've no alternative but to leave it until tomorrow morning."

"I don't like the idea either, Major," Sneed said, "but I don't see what else we can do. I mean, Clothesline doesn't drive and Brrm-Brrm doesn't have a car. And it'd be mad of us to take the risk of him nicking one."

"Quite, quite," the Major agreed. "And at least we know it's safe enough there. As we were told, Tony – indeed, as we found for ourselves – the office is locked when there's no one in attendance."

"Right, well, that's it then," the pawnbroker put in quickly, when Tony didn't object. "I'll pick the Wolseley up tonight and we'll get off nice and early. And – er – and until then," he added, thinking it worth a try, "I suggest we stick the ticket, the left luggage ticket for it, in the safe at the shop. Just in case. Then we'll all know where it is. How about that, mates, eh?"

"It's in two halves, actually," the Major said. "We—"

"And I'm hanging on to my half," Tony added.

Sneed grinned at him. "Eh, Tony," he said with a surprised little laugh, "that sounds like you don't trust me!"

Tony nodded. "That's right, Harold. I don't trust you."

If the way Sneed was staring and grinning at him didn't unnerve Tony, it did the Major.

"I say you fellows…" he said shakily.

"Your coat's torn, Tony," Sneed said then. "And you're usually so dapper. What happened, son?"

Tony's eye twitched. "I caught it on a nail."

"You ought to be more careful," Sneed advised him softly.

"I will, don't worry, Harold," Tony said, placing a hand near his inside pocket.

"Now, now, come along, you chaps," the Major said, nervously jovial. This one had handle with care written all over it. If it went off here it could take them all up with it.

"No need for this. And certainly not here, in a public place. Look – look, Sneed, how about taking *my* half of the ticket, as a guarantee. And then Tony can keep his. Hmm?"

Sneed came slowly back from wherever he'd been.

"Eh…? Yes. Yes, all right, Major. I'm open to any reasonable suggestion, as you know. Thank you," he said with dignity, taking the half ticket the Major had dug out of his wallet.

The Major beamed fraternally on them. "Well, there we are then. That's cleared that up."

"Little business misunderstanding, that's all," Sneed said, smiling in the same spirit on Tony. "And tomorrow morning,

Tony, my son, you bring your half of the ticket to the shop at, say, eight, and we'll conclude the business to our mutual satisfaction."

He couldn't see Plan C yet but there was always tomorrow. And tomorrow, as they say, is another day.

Chapter Twelve

The police had also returned empty-handed.

After cars of the sort the Church Myddle constable had thought wistfully about had screamed here and there, the uniform branch's contribution to the investigation, and the usual suspects rounded up and questioned, the CID's contribution, their two senior representatives at Kingham had been summoned to the top floor to bring Superintendent Jenkins up to date.

"No problems with cooperation from our colleagues in Shrewsbury, I trust?" the Superintendent wanted to know first.

Both men said there hadn't been. "Offered whatever resources we needed," the CID inspector, Berry, said. "Including all local intelligence, names, addresses, form and so forth."

"Not that they turned out to be all that intelligent," Inspector Worth said, and chuckled. "Gas meter bandits, mostly."

The Superintendent got down to it. "So, gentlemen, what's the state of play?"

Inspector Worth opened first.

"Well, sir, not to put too fine a point on it, the runs so far have all been made by the robbers," he said, continuing with the cricketing metaphor. The Superintendent was a fanatical fan.

The Inspector spoke frankly, but with steely-eyed determination, a man who, for his part, had done all that could be expected of him at this stage, but who hadn't finished yet by a long chalk.

"We were on to it soon enough. The chain of communication went like clockwork, I'm pleased to be able to report. And immediately I got a description of the getaway vehicle, I had the cars out covering the field – the new high-speed ones," he added with some satisfaction.

"Yes, we heard them," DI Berry said. "The sound of a stable door being hurriedly bolted."

"It's PR, as much as anything. Public perception, and all that. You should try and keep up with the latest thinking, Roger," the Inspector said jovially, but his eyes were saying something else, glancing at the middle-aged figure next to him, the greying hair, beer belly and heavily nicotine-stained fingers, yesterday's man, the past, that's what his look said.

"Latest thinking, my eye," the DI said. "Your lads couldn't wait to start playing with them."

Superintendent Jenkins looked pained. "Can we get on, gentlemen, do you think…?"

"Quite right, sir," the Inspector said briskly. "Yes, as I say, I had cars quartering the area, and road blocks on all roads out of the town, in case it was a bluff, their heading up that way. But no sign of them. We know they took the A458 down to the Bicwood roundabout, there were enough reports of that, all right, and then back up Moreton Hill in the direction of the town. And that so far is all we do know. But I'll have the cars out again tomorrow morning, parked up at the same time and on the same route, seeking witnesses."

Inspector Worth cleared his throat. "And I – er – I deployed men at Shrewsbury railway station, as well, sir, and had all recent deposits in left luggage opened up, just in case. Don't want to hand the local press another present."

He didn't look at Inspector Berry sitting next to him when he said it. He didn't need to. The Superintendent was doing that. While the DI seethed inwardly and stared at a point just below the top of the Superintendent's desk.

It was the DI who had been in sole charge of the investigation last year into the robbery by a gang of local thieves of a guard's van at Kingham railway station, when the contents of a couple of sacks of registered mail had been stuffed into a suitcase and deposited in left luggage, sitting under the noses of the police as they swarmed all over the station. It only came to light when the robbers involved were arrested, and then the front pages of the local papers made hay with the story.

"Well done, Mr Worth," the Superintendent said. "That's what lessons are for. To be learnt."

"Well, thank you, sir," the Inspector said, and hid a smile.

The Superintendent looked at the DI. "Mr Berry...?"

"Well, sir, I'm afraid we haven't got anywhere locally, so far. But then, that doesn't surprise me, because Shrewsbury doesn't believe they have anyone capable of fielding that sort of team. And we certainly don't. No, it says big city to me. Birmingham, London, or Cardiff maybe. I've telexed forces both sides of the border, and we're still putting feelers out of course locally. The lorry used had false number plates, and had been resprayed. But we're working on it. It might help if we had the getaway car. Either they didn't transfer from it, and the uniform lads let the ball go past them—"

"Not likely," Inspector Worth put in.

"Or they did transfer, and it's sitting there, waiting for them to find it in the long grass."

The Inspector smiled. "In which case, Roger, we can be assured that it's one ball that *will* be found. I think I can safely say—" he started to add, when the Superintendent's phone went.

While on the ground floor of the building, at her desk in the Sergeants' Room, Petunia Cholmondeley-Jones was tapping away quite happily, typing up in triplicate a pile of statements from shop owners after an outbreak of shoplifting in the high street by a marauding gang of sticky-fingered school children.

She didn't mind the paperwork, not now her world had two in it again – well, three if you count Phineas Cook, but she intended doing something about that, once and for all. And Ted had dropped in just before attending the briefing with the Superintendent upstairs, to tell her that, as absolutely nothing was moving on the wages robbery front, tonight was on again. Tonight, the ring would be back where it belonged.

"Honestly! They really are the giddy limit, these children!" she said with an indulgent chuckle, glancing over a new list of property stolen from a large newsagent's.

"Bloody little thieves!" a colleague at another desk snarled, stabbing out with two blunt fingers stained with fluid eraser his own burden of paperwork, and without a candle-lit meal for two and an engagement ring to look forward to.

"Good heavens, Barry – these are *children*," she said, with another little laugh. "I mean, I grant you they're a nuisance, and technically of course, yes, it is theft. But to brand them as thieves at such a young age is a little harsh, surely?"

"Well, what else then," Barry wanted to know, "do you call people who thieve?"

"Well, yes, as I say, technically it is theft. But these are impressionable young people, their concept of morality not yet fully formed, coming together in a group and subjected to peer pressure – it's all there, Barry, in all the latest thinking."

She was about to further educate her colleague in the latest thinking, when the door opened and Inspector Worth poked his head round.

She smiled up at him.

The door opened, she thought, and love walked in.

"I'm not stopping," he said cheerily. "Just popped in to tell you that we've located the getaway car."

"Oh, well *done*, Te – Inspector!" she said.

"Back of some industrial estate in Shrewsbury. I know it wouldn't be long, the way I'd mapped out the search. I'll have to get over there, of course. Make sure the finger-printing's being done thoroughly. You'd be surprised where people put their hands sometimes," he said, sharing that with both sergeants. "And also that nothing is overlooked. Sometimes a crime, even as well executed as this one, can be solved by the finding of what, to an inexperienced or negligent eye, would be considered insignificant."

The Sergeant, if not her colleague, gazed at him adoringly, and wondered again at the sheer *blindness* of their superiors when it came to promotion.

"Well, duty calls, and all that." The Inspector lifted his swagger stick in salute, closed the door, and immediately opened it again.

"Oh, Pe – Sergeant, incidentally, in view of this development we'll have to re-schedule this evening of course. No telling where a lead like this might take us."

The door closed and opened again. "Oh, and don't worry about the table reservation. I've already cancelled it," he assured her, and winked, a man on top of the smallest detail.

The Sergeant stared at the closed door, listening to him whistling his way down the corridor.

She returned to her paperwork, staring blindly at the new list, noticing then that among the other stolen items was a large quantity of cigars.

She glared at the entry as if personally affronted by it, and then burst out, "Well I hope it makes them jolly well sick! Rotten little thieves!"

Chapter Thirteen

The Pughs' post office and shop in Batch Magna's High Street had seethed all morning with talk of yesterday's robbery. And now, having exhausted what *was* known, they had moved on to what *wasn't* – not for sure, that is.

But Wilf Stoner said that, although he couldn't swear to it, he thought there'd been a mention somewhere by somebody of blood having been found at the scene, as they had learned to call it. And Mrs Beddoes, dropping in nearly an hour ago to buy stamps, and still there, jumped in and said that she thought she'd heard something about that, too, on the radio, she thought it was. A pool of blood, she was sure they'd said. While the normally socially aloof Mrs Templeton forgot she was above this sort of thing long enough to eagerly go one further, and declare that she'd heard blood had been found at the scene *and* in the getaway car.

And then Mrs Pugh, perched behind her post office counter, where she'd been passing on the latest news of the robbery in an official sort of way, and when running out of it had simply made up more of her own, asserted her position and said she *knew* blood had been found, and then shook her head firmly when asked for details, as if not at liberty to say any more.

Colonel Ash, who had come in for his football pools postal order, was puffing with barely concealed impatience on his pipe while waiting for Mr Morgan, ahead of him at the counter, to take his change. Mr Morgan, it seemed, was sure that he, too, had heard blood mentioned somewhere. That might have been on the radio, now he came to think of it, he said to Mrs Beddoes. Or perhaps he'd read it in a newspaper. Or maybe it was on the telly. He couldn't be sure, not absolutely, like, but there had *definitely* been a reference to blood somewhere. Blo-od, he said again, nodding emphatically, and investing the word with two syllables of Welsh doom.

The Colonel had had enough. He removed his pipe and enquired trenchantly why there should have been blood, of any quantity, found at all, anywhere, given that there had been no reports of shots having been fired, or indeed any other weapons used. Not in his late edition of the *Shrewsbury Chronicle*, there hadn't. Nor, he emphasised, had there been a mention made of such on the wireless *or* television reports.

No one had an answer to that, except Miss Wyndham, who had forgotten what she came in for, and no longer cared.

Miss Wyndham was an expert, in company with Phineas Cook, of all things murderous, their conversations littered with stranglers, poisoners, mass murderers, fatal wielders of blunt instruments, and homicidal amorists.

To Miss Wyndham this business was small fry, but, considering the amount involved, and in the current absence of anything gorier in the news, it was not without its interest.

"No reports of shots fired *during* the job, Colonel," she pointed out astutely. "But shots could have been fired *after* it. The classic falling out of thieves. An argument perhaps breaking out for some reason and one robber shooting another. Not unknown," she pronounced crisply.

The Colonel took his pipe from his mouth again. "In which case, my dear Miss Wyndham, they obviously didn't wait long before falling out. And where did the body of the wounded or deceased robber go, may one ask? I rather think we can assume the boot would have been searched."

"He's got a point there," Mr Morgan agreed, looking at Miss Wyndham.

Miss Wyndham trained her bloodhound gaze on the Colonel. "You are forgetting, Colonel, that they transferred from the getaway car to another vehicle, which no doubt also had a boot. Or, if a van, room in it for a body. Either way, dead or wounded, it was imperative for obvious reasons that they take him with them. Imperative!" she insisted vigorously, jowls shaking.

"She's right there," Mr Morgan said, and waited for the Colonel's response.

The Colonel struggled manfully with it for a few moments, looking for flaws, and then said obstinately that he still considered it unlikely they've have fallen out in such a remarkably short space of time, and put his pipe back. Then immediately took it out again and enquired of Mr Morgan if he had finished his business, because, the Colonel added pointedly, *he* had things to do.

While young George, sucking on one of the gobstoppers he'd just bought out of the wages Humphrey paid him, had drifted in from the shop and was all ears.

Blood or no blood, it was the nearest in his life he'd been to a big one, as Humph had called it, with guns and stocking masks, and that, and it might pay him from now on, he told himself darkly, to keep his eyes skinned.

In the female officers' locker room at Kingham police station Sergeant Cholmondeley-Jones, at the end of her shift, was sharing a wall mirror with WPC Tina Norman, standing behind her and running a comb through her hair.

She made a face at the result, and prompted perhaps by that blurted out to Tina as she put away the comb that she had misled Ted.

In fact, she confessed miserably, snapping her handbag shut, the shame of it in her cheeks, to be absolutely truthful, she had jolly well lied to him.

Tina paused, her eyes moving in the mirror from the hair she'd been brushing to her friend. This, from Petunia, the most truthful and least complicated person she knew, promised to be an interesting complication.

She gave the Sergeant her full attention.

"What about, Pet…?"

The Sergeant sighed. "Phineas Cook."

Tina knew of course about Phineas Cook. It was in Tina's back garden that he had popped the question, and she had been the first to hear about it. She didn't know Phineas well, he was a friend of her husband's, but quite frankly, as far as she was concerned, almost anyone was better than that pompous, conceited creep, Inspector Worth.

"Have you changed your mind about him, then? About Phineas?" she asked avidly.

The Sergeant shook her head. "No – no, of course not. He's *hopeless*."

"Oh, I dunno," Tina said vaguely, seeing it was her husband's friend. "Well, what is it then? What did you lie about…?"

"Well, you know I said I wanted to tell Phineas to his face? Well, I haven't been able to find him. He's not in the phone book—"

"No, he's ex-directory. Ray doesn't have his number, either," Tina said, referring to her husband. "He said that Phineas has a thing about phones." Tina thought it more likely that he had a thing about creditors. "But I know where he lives, Pet."

"I *know* where he lives. I've gone over there several times, but he never seems to *be* there. And this morning Ted suggested I write him a letter. But – but, well, I don't think it's right, doing it that way. I think he deserves to be told to his face, so… so I told Ted that I would, that I'd write to him this morning. And then just before going upstairs later for his briefing with the Superintendent, he asked had I done it. And I said I had, and that I'd posted it. But I hadn't. I haven't even written it."

"Well…? Is that all?" Tina said, after waiting for the rest of it.

"Isn't that enough? I *lied* to him, Tina."

Tina laughed. "Well, of course you did, love. You have to sometimes, with men. The truth's too complicated for them, so you tell them something else instead. It makes it easier for them. And they like it really, men do, bless 'em. They like things being made simple for them."

She smiled at her friend's expression. "You'll see what I mean, Pet, after you've been married for a bit," she said, and went on to tell her friend about a few of things she had simplified for her husband.

While the Sergeant, fascinated and feeling married already, in conspiracy with another married woman, told herself firmly that tomorrow, when she'd have more chance to get away, she must finish this business with Phineas once and for all. Before the simple became, for her, far too complicated.

Chapter Fourteen

When they met again in the pawnbroker's shop the following morning, pay day as Sneed put it, rubbing his hands together, Sneed, before anything else was done – before what he had in mind *could* be done – had to persuade Tony and the Major that Brrm-Brrm and Clothesline should collect the money from Church Myddle. Plan C depended on it.

"Right, well," Sneed started, "the first thing is to decide who picks the wages up. We can't all go. It's not a coach outing."

"Well, me and the Major, of course, we'll go – we're the ones what put it in there," Tony said immediately, not having given up on his own plans for the money. "We'll go."

Before the pawnbroker could come back with his answer to that, the Major stepped in and did half his work for him.

"I'm afraid I have to report, Sneed, that I'm somewhat *hors de combat* at present," he said, remembering what happened when he and Tony last travelled together. "A touch of the old trouble, a recurrence of the beriberi I picked up in Risalpur, on the north-west frontier. India, you know. Symptoms include fatigue, weakness, sometimes numbness, of the limbs, with complications affecting the muscular, nervous, cardiovascular, and gastrointestinal systems."

Sneed made a sympathetic face. "Oh, dear. Sorry to hear that, Major."

"So, I'm sure you'll appreciate…"

"Yeah, course, of course. And I think I should stop here as well. Don't want it noticed that the shop's been closed two days running. Just to be on the safe side."

"Well, we'll go then, the three of us," Brrm-Brrm said.

Sneed looked doubtful. "Three men in a car, the day after a major robbery in the area? Be as bad as five – worse, in fact, considering the actual robbery was carried out by a three-man team. Unnecessary risk, Brrm-Brrm, that comes under. Especially on the return journey." He shook his head. "No, that would be begging for a pull, that would."

"But the job was yesterday, Mr Sneed," Brrm-Brrm pointed out.

"Yes, and did they get a sniff of it then? No, they did not. Oh, they'll be out in force today, you can bet on it. Stopping people along the route we took and on the main drags, looking for witnesses. They'll have cars out all over the shop, on the alert for anything that looks the least bit suspicious, then doing a stop. Making themselves busy to keep the brass and the taxpayers happy. I've seen it all before, son."

Tony, a bit suspicious himself, if not sure why, pounced on it. "What about yesterday? You were happy to use the motor yesterday with the three of us in it then. What about that then?"

"Yes, you're right, Tony," Sneed promptly agreed. "I would have done. I admit it. I was too eager. And I'm just glad now, thinking about it afterwards, that the car did throw up that bit of trouble. That's what happens when you don't think things through, mates. There's a lesson there for all of us."

"Well, in that case," the Major said, "I suggest that they take the train, the afternoon service."

Sneed was ready for that one. "And what if there's not a train back today?"

"Well, we can soon establish—"

"And even if there is, there's bound to be a wait. And what if whoever picks it up is standing there with the holdall when your two local law, who have also been told to get busy, decide for some reason to pay another visit? Eh...?" he said, and the Major harrumphed and brushed at his moustache with a finger.

"Yes, that's what I mean about thinking things through, Major. Anyway, there's no need. I've been thinking about that. We'll use the Wolseley, and for a start I suggest that just two go. So, you're keen, Tony, you can go, with Clothesline. He'll make sure you come back, won't you, Clothesline?"

"Yes, boss," Clothesline said, nodding solemnly. "I'll make sure he comes back."

"We're not all called Harold," Tony said, staring at him.

"Just a joke, Tony," Sneed said. "Just a joke."

"Anyway, send Brrm-Brrm. He's the best driver," Tony said, having had second thoughts, prompted by the sort of activity Sneed had described.

"Yeah... *Yeah*," Sneed said, as if he'd just realised it, and looking at Brrm-Brrm. "Of course..."

"Hey, hang on a minute What about the fuzz being all over the place, and that!" Brrm-Brrm wanted to know.

Sneed held up a placatory hand. "I was about to come to that, Brrm-Brrm, when we've sorted out who's doing the driving. I've had a look at the road atlas and there's a route through the back doubles which will keep you well clear. Takes a bit longer of course, but it's worth it. And I have to say, son, Tony's right. I should have thought of it myself," he went on, shaking his head over his short-sightedness. "Must be slipping. You're by *miles* the best driver here, course you are. The one far less likely to get involved in an accident, with the police being called, and all that. Especially coming back. In fact, son, the more I think about it, you're the only one here *for* the bloody job," he added with a little laugh, sharing it with the others.

"Oh, quite, quite," the Major agreed

"I told you, didn't I," Tony said. "There's no one here to touch him."

Brrm-Brrm hesitated, pulled between the flattery and his own misgivings.

"Yeah, all right," he said then. "I'll do it."

"Good boy. So that's settled then. You and Clothesline. Right," Sneed said, moving quickly on. "And we'll wait here and keep ourselves company till you get back."

"And after all," the Major said, "they also serve who only stand and wait, as Milton observed, what?" He lifted his head, and hand on breast, quoted, "When I consider how my light is spent, ere half my days in this dark world and wide, and that one talent—"

"Well, they'd better get on with it, hadn't they," Tony cut in, surlily abrupt, saying goodbye again to a white tuxedo and gardenia buttonhole. "The sooner they go the sooner we get paid."

He produced his half of the left luggage ticket and Sneed added his and put both pieces in an envelope. He handed it to Brrm-Brrm with the road atlas.

"I've turned down the page you want, and marked the route. Now, when you get to the station, Brrm-Brrm, you go in, leave Clothesline in the car. You're a minicab driver, right, picking up luggage for a couple of clients, OK? You tell the bloke there that these clients have had a change of plan. That they were going to tour the area but had to stay in Birmingham on business. Say—"

"No, no, no, Sneed. You're over-egging it," the Major broke in, professionally affronted. "He's merely an envoy, sent to pick something up. He should also of course have a letter of release, which I'll supply in a moment. The most he should say is that his clients apologise for the condition of the ticket. It was inadvertently torn. No more than that."

"There you are, son. Never try to con a conner, eh?" Sneed said to Brrm-Brrm, and winked at him.

"It should ideally be on hotel writing paper," the Major grumbled then, scribbling the letter with a fountain pen and a flourish on a blank sheet of Sneed's. "But needs must, I suppose."

"Now, guard it with your life, son," Sneed said, handing Brrm-Brrm back the envelope. "And straight there and back. There's no need for you to stop. I filled the tank up last night at the garage, when I picked it up," he added for Tony's and the Major's benefit. "And remember, Brrm-Brrm, remember, son – and this is the most important bit – drive like an old lady. *Especially* on the way back. Keep to the speed limits, stop at red for a change like everybody else, and wear your seatbelts," he added, opening a desk drawer and handing him the car keys, minus the one for the boot, just in case Brrm-Brrm got nosy.

He saw them out of the shop, the Wolseley, sitting half on the pavement, gleaming from yesterday afternoon's valeting at a local garage, for the journey it had yet to make, sunlight adding an extra shine to its paintwork.

It was wasted here, Sneed thought, looking dismissively at the street. He blew on the Wolseley badge on the radiator and gave it a polish with his sleeve.

"Oh, almost forgot," he said, as Brrm-Brrm was about to get in. "The boot key snapped off when I was locking it up after we got back yesterday. My garage can fix it of course, and sort me out another one, but for now you'll have to keep the holdall with you in the car."

"All right, Mr Sneed," Brrm-Brrm said. "Well, we'll be off then."

"OK, son. Have a safe journey. Hey, and don't forget to come back, will you, Brrm-Brrm. Remember you've got a mother waiting for you at home, won't you, son," he added on a sentimental note.

"Well, if you don't trust me, Mr Sneed," Brrm-Brrm said indignantly.

"It's not that I don't trust you, Brrm-Brrm. It's just that we all do silly things at times. Things we regret then – when it's too late. Know what I mean? And I feel responsible for you, especially now your own dad can't be here. You're like a son to me, Brrm-Brrm, you know that, don't you… Eh?"

"Yeah, right, Mr Sneed," Brrm-Brrm said.

"So, just take care. That's all I'm saying. OK?"

"OK, Mr Sneed."

The pawnbroker watched the Wolseley drive off, its polish carrying the sun with it up the backstreet, before turning off for the main road out as if taking it with it.

Back in the office they settled down to wait, Tony sitting at the desk, shuffling a pack of cards, the Major sucking the end of his fountain pen over *The Times* crossword. While Sneed, telling them he'd be in the shop if he was needed, doing a bit of stocktaking, used the time to check again that he'd be leaving nothing behind he wanted.

Chapter Fifteen

Brrm-Brrm felt he was driving with the handbrake on, strapped in and keeping to the speed limit as instructed, waiting just like any other motorist for the lights to change, and even parking legally when they arrived at the railway station.

"Nothing to it. Sweet as a nut," he told Clothesline, dumping the holdall in the back of the car. He said he'd had to listen to some old bloke rabbiting on about keys, and how he was expected to do everything, but there had been no problem with the torn ticket or anything else.

"Oh, and there was a message left us by old Sneed. We've got to ring in. I tried the phone there," he said, indicating the box outside the station, "but it's out of order. We'll have to find another one on the way out."

"What for?" Clothesline asked. "What have we got to ring for, Brrm-Brrm?"

"I dunno. Scared we'll do a runner, I s'pose."

"Don't he trust us then?"

"He don't trust nobody, Clothesline. If he had a mother he probably wouldn't trust her neither."

He was about to switch on when he grinned.

"Hey, we could do that. We could just keep on driving. We could go anywhere. Hey – we could go to America!" it occurred to him. "We could drive to Southampton and get on the *Queen*

Mary, or whatever it is. They've got them big jobs over there – Caddies and Buicks, and all that. And hot rods, and road rigs…"

His grin spread. "*Hey*… I could buy a road rig. Like on the pictures! A massive Freightliner, with a cab up in the air, and big exhaust stacks, and loads of chrome…"

Brrm-Brrm gripped the wheel, the distances of America in Technicolor in his eyes, driving through them on an endless highway with his foot down.

"Brrm-brrm," he said softly. "Brrm-brrm…"

Clothesline was frowning with thought.

"No. No, we can't, Brrm-Brrm. We've gotta go back."

"Eh…?" Brrm-Brrm said, returning to Sneed's Wolseley and Church Myddle.

"We've gotta go back. The boss said. He said—"

"Yeah. Yeah, I know, mate," Brrm-Brrm said wistfully "'Sides, I told me mum I'd buy her a colour telly. And I'm buying an Aston Martin," he said, his face alight with it, "like James Bond drives. A DBS-Six with ZF five-speed gearbox, retractable blades in the hub caps, an ejector seat and revolving number plates. In red. What are you gonna buy, Clothesline?"

"A fish and chip shop," Clothesline said happily.

"Eh?" Brrm-Brrm said.

"I'm gonna buy a fish and chip shop. I like fish and chips."

Brrm-Brrm laughed delightedly at it all, at a fish and chip shop, and an Aston Martin with an ejector seat and retractable blades, and a colour telly, and all the other extravagant possibilities that were now theirs.

"Innit great to be rich!"

There was a phone box just down from the station, but it was occupied, the woman in it talking away with the air of someone with a lot more yet to say. Brrm-Brrm couldn't see another one on their way out of town, and as they weren't going to do a runner, didn't see why he should go to the trouble of searching for one.

They took the same route they'd followed coming there, down through the town, and out through the back lanes to the main road and the A458 and home.

They had almost reached the main road, when Brrm-Brrm glanced casually in the rear view mirror and found a car sitting in it, with a police sign on the roof topped with a blue light like a little helmet.

His first, unthinking, instinct leapt gleefully in him, the thought of a burn-up with a law car.

And then he remembered what was in the back and eased his foot off the accelerator, giving it a chance to pass.

It stayed there, and was still there, sitting on their tail, after the Wolseley had gone past a couple of roads turning off.

Clothesline noticed him checking the rear view mirror then, and took a look himself.

"Strewth!" he said.

"It's right, Clothesline, it's just a Noddy car, a Panda. A local job. They're just going the same way we are, that's all."

But when they reached the main road and the roundabout where he should have gone right for the A458, he took the road off to the left. And then a right, blindly, and then another left, and then right again, in the direction, a signpost told him, of somewhere called Batch Magna.

"It's still there, Brrm-Brrm…" Clothesline said out of the corner of his mouth.

Sitting in the passenger seat of the Panda, helmet on lap, the constable was holding forth eagerly about the criminal mind, while his sergeant at the wheel made the odd interested noise and thought about his roses.

He'd sprayed them as soon as he'd got home yesterday, and although the station master had warned him it would be at least a week before he started to see results, he was convinced that, when inspecting them immediately on getting up that morning, he had noticed the very first stirring of renewal, that there had been the faintest rallying of colour and bloom, a suggestion of freshness, like the intimations of a summer dawn.

"… Oh, yes, it's the future of police work, all this sort of stuff, Sarge," the constable was saying. "Make no mistake about it. *The Application of Psychology in the Modern Police Force.* That's what I'm studying at the moment. They've already started teaching courses on it at Hendon. Ah, but where, I hear you ask, is its practical application to everyday coppering?"

The constable's expression suggested that he was more than ready with the answer to that one. "Right, well, you take that car in front, the Wolseley. Now, I can tell you that it would be a waste of time doing a stop and search on that. Complete waste of time. Why? Two things," he went on, without waiting, and ticked them off on his fingers. "First, we came up on it from round a bend, so the driver couldn't have seen us approach, but there he was, obeying the speed limit all nice and legal. You see, Sarge, your villain, be he armed robber or gangster, drives like he lives – ignoring society's rules and doing what he wants, usually with his foot down. And second, apart from the fact that the Met uses them, the Wolseley is a nice, respectable sort of motor, the transport of your professional class, doctors and solicitors, and such like. Not like some local tealeaf's old banger, or the flash Jags or Rollers your London gangsters favour. Easy to imagine that, all nicely washed and polished as it is – which is another indicator, incidentally – parked up where the neighbours can see it on the driveway of a nice semi somewhere. All of which gives us, you see, Sarge, what is called a psychological composite. In this case, one of a respectable, law-abiding, middle-class citizen…

"Hello, he's going the same way we are," he said then, when the sergeant took the same turning off for Batch Valley, following the Wolseley.

"Hmm…?" the sergeant said, coming back from his blooms. He was a widower and he'd been thinking how nice it would be to have someone to share his triumph with when dawn finally broke on his rose garden.

"I said that Wolseley, in front there, it seems to be going wherever we're going."

"We're going, my lad, to Batch Magna. To Batch Hall, to be precise. I thought it was time to broaden your education – and I'm not talking about this psychological business of yours, neither. It's time, Constable, that you were introduced to Shelly's Conies. That's Mrs Strange to you, by the way," he added, touching at his tie. "The mother of Sir Humphrey, the squire of Batch Magna. So watch your manners. Shelly's Coney Island Specials…" he said fondly. "They're just ordinary hotdogs with fried onions – but then, ah, but then, my lad, she adds this special relish of hers, from a secret recipe that's been in her family for generations. And…"

The sergeant was lost for words. "And, well, if I've tasted anything better, then I don't remember it, that's all I can say."

Chapter Sixteen

"What are they following us for?" Clothesline demanded indignantly. "We ain't done nothing. We're keeping to the speed limit, and all that, ain't we. Ain't they got nothing better to do."

"They're just going the same way we are, that's all, Clothesline," Brrm-Brrm said again, and started whistling tunelessly.

"*Ooh*, birds! Big coloured birds…" Clothesline said then wonderingly, as the Wolseley, travelling deeper into the valley, hugged the edge of a wood, scattering a few pheasants wandering about the lane.

Brrm-Brrm wasn't interested in birds, coloured or otherwise. All Brrm-Brrm was interested in was shaking off that image that was starting to look like a permanent fixture in the rear view mirror.

He came to a junction of three lanes and immediately went left. And then left again, and then took a sharp right, straight into a farmyard, scattering geese and chickens.

He reversed out at speed. He couldn't see the Panda but he had the feeling that it was there somewhere, waiting for him to make the next move.

He followed the lane and took a left at the end of it, hoping that it would take him out of the valley, but it then turned right, feeding him downhill again, and then up, and then down again, twisting and turning along lanes hillocky with sudden dips and rises, putting his foot down and hoping nothing was coming round the bends on the flat stretches, while Clothesline held on with his eyes closed.

He hadn't spotted them once in the mirror, and he pulled up on the edge of another stretch of wood, cut the engine, wound the window down and sat with an ear cocked.

And then he grinned.

All he could hear was the engine cooling and birds singing.

He looked at Clothesline and grinned. "We can go home now, Clothesline."

He pulled the atlas out from under his seat and found Batch Magna and the two roads leading in and out, either side of the valley. He'd come down one of them and calculated that if he kept going right he must sooner or later hit the other.

"Right. Nothing to it when you know how, Clothesline," he said cheerfully, and switched on again.

"Where we going, Brrm-Brrm?" Clothesline asked plaintively, nearly an hour later.

"I don't know, do I!" Brrm-Brrm snapped. "We came down *into* the valley, so I've been trying to get *up* again. But I can't find neither of the roads out. It's these bleeding lanes, they drive you mad! They don't go nowhere except to another bleeding lane! It's like they want to keep us here."

"P'raps we ought to ask somebody."

Brrm-Brrm looked at him. "Who, Clothesline? One of them sheep there?" he said, pointing them out as they passed a field gate. "Or that bleeding bird up there sitting on a bleeding twig, singing its little bleeding heart out?"

"Don't be funny," Clothesline warned him heavily a couple of minutes later, having thought about it.

But Brrm-Brrm wasn't listening.

Brrm-Brrm's habitat was the city. It was bred into his bones and he was never at home anywhere but on its streets. And he now had the curious feeling that the place they were in knew it, and was not only playing with him, but out to get him. He'd seen the film, the one which opens just like this, with the sun shining and the birds singing, and all that – and something watching from a wood.

He wound up the window and wetting at his mouth started whistling, not looking anywhere but straight ahead.

And then, coming downhill again, and sweeping round yet another bend, wondering what was waiting for them round the other side, he saw ahead of him a bridge.

He put his foot down and went straight over it, escaped over it, as he saw it, with the feeling of leaving whatever it was behind.

"Cor – ducks," Clothesline said. "And *ships*, look!"

Brrm-Brrm glanced left in time to catch a glimpse of the blue and gold funnel rings of the Owens' paddler, the *Felicity H.*

He drove past a sign telling him that Batch Magna Welcomes Careful Drivers, and then another sign which told him he was in the High Street, a proper road, even though there only seemed to be one of them, with pavements and a few people on them.

"That's it, Clothesline, we've cracked it. We'll stop and ask how we get out to a main drag and we're on our way again."

It was Clothesline who spotted the car this time, just as Brrm-Brrm was about to pull up and ask directions.

"Brrm-Brrm..." he said.

Brrm-Brrm looked where Clothesline was looking, in the rear view mirror.

It wasn't a Panda this time but a serious-looking white job with orange markings.

Brrm-Brrm kept going, past a shop, and a church and pub, followed by the police car.

"What's going on, Brrm-Brrm?" Clothesline wanted to know. "Why are they following us again?"

"It's just a coincidence," Brrm-Brrm said. "That's all," he added a few moments later, glancing again in the mirror as they left the village, the orange and white car tucked in behind. What was worrying him was what it was doing there, in the middle of nowhere.

When they reached a crossroads just outside the village he went straight across, taking the police car with them, and saw another sign on the other side of it, a notice board on the grass verge, with a cut-out pair of cowboy boots on top.

The sign read:

> BATCH HALL – 100 YDS ON LEFT.
> BED & BREAKFAST MERRIE BATCH HALL STYLE – SUNNYSIDE UP!!!
> TREAT YOURSELF TO A FAMOUS SUNNYSIDE-UP BED & BREAKFAST AT OLDE WORLDE BATCH HALL, WHERE THE BEDS ARE BIG & SOFT, THE FOOD FRESH & DELICIOUS – AND THERE'S A MIGHTY, HEAPING HELPING OF GOOD OLE HOSPITALITY!
> REASONABLE RATES – PETS INCLUDED IN THE WELCOME.

When they reached the entrance to the Hall, Brrm-Brrm indicated a left and turned in through the open gates.

"Where we going, Brrm-Brrm?" Clothesline asked.

"Nowhere. It's called using your loaf, Clothesline, my son. The old grey matter. We're just pretending to, that's all, to let the rozzer motor go past. We'll go up this drive here, see, like a couple of normal punters, then turn round and out again. And then back to the village to get directions. Like I said, it was—"

A coincidence, just a coincidence, that's what he'd been about to say, when he glanced in the mirror and saw the police car behind them on the drive, emerging from around a screen of rhododendrons.

"Brrm-Brrm…" Clothesline said.

"I know, I know. I see it," he said fretfully. "I ain't bleeding blind. Well, we'll just have to call their bluff, that's all."

"What's that mean?" Clothesline wanted to know.

Brrm-Brrm didn't look entirely sure. "Well, we'll just have to park up and go into this Batch Hall bed and breakfast gaff, as if we're checking in, like, that's all. See what they do then. I mean, if they're going to pull us they'll do it then. Won't they," he added, not expecting an answer, and not getting one. He suddenly felt very alone.

Clothesline was smiling to himself. "I like having bed and breakfast. I hope it's a full English one."

"Yeah, well, let's just hope it's not a mug of cold bleeding tea and a couple of slices of bread and marg," Brrm-Brrm said, remembering the sort on the menu at Steelhouse Lane. "And anyway, we're not going to actually *check in*, just pretend to, that's all," he said, pulling up in the forecourt.

"I'll bring the bag in," Clothesline said helpfully, freeing his seatbelt.

"*No!*" Brrm-Brrm almost screamed. "Just – just get out, casual, like. And don't look back at them. Just walk straight in with me, nice and normal."

Chapter Seventeen

The wooden cut-out of cowboy boots on top of the Hall's recently erected bed & breakfast sign were Humphrey's idea, and so were some of the words, taken from *The Beverly Hillbillies*, a favourite TV show. The rest were from the pen of Phineas Cook.

And Phineas, determined to get something right before his girlfriend, Sally, came back, and doing so out of guilt as well as the need for money, had met his publisher's deadline and was working for the Hall again. He was busy writing a brochure for another of Clem's ideas, country house weekend breaks, his fee the two months' rent he owed the estate.

A gregarious man, he was scribbling away in the kitchen where a steady supply of coffee and gossip was at hand, sitting at the table facing the open back door, alert for the sound of a vehicle pulling up, a white one with orange markings and the word 'Police' on it. And he was working at the Hall instead of on his boat, because, he'd said, he wanted to draw inspiration from his surrounding – a process, he was able to tell them, he expected to take about a week.

By which time his advance cheque should have arrived, allowing him to throw his creditors something to keep them quiet.

That would then only leave him with the small problem of a fiancée.

And next week, Monday, to be precise, Sally returned from her holiday. Sally, who, if she expected him to be engaged at all, perfectly reasonably expected it to be to her. How *had* he got himself into this! He knew of course what he had to do, he'd told himself it enough times. And he told himself it again now, and a little more pressingly, seeing that Monday was the day after tomorrow.

There was nothing for it but to confess to the Sergeant. He considered writing to her, getting it down like a statement, before telling himself that she deserved better, and suddenly resolute, decided he would phone her. Doing so as if that were the decision he'd been putting off making, instead of the one he'd actually been putting off making, and was still putting off making. The one which meant speaking to her, face to face.

He'd tell her he'd been drunk, or drugged, or he'd had a touch of his old mental troubles, or something. She's a police officer, she'll understand, he assured himself, and bit at his lip.

But for the moment he'd put all that stuff, real life, aside, and had returned to the brochure.

If the games children play are a preparation for the adult world, then Phineas wasn't ready yet. Fiction to Phineas was what the toy soldiers, cowboy sets and death-dealing ray guns of his childhood had been. The world he played with now, peopled with Inspector MacNail and all the other characters he moved around in it, also did what he wanted it to do. And the last word, or rather words – 'The End'– were *always* his.

And he was contentedly working on a bit of fiction now, a story entirely of his own invention featuring a lone Cavalier holding off with cool, contemptuous swordplay a bumbling troop of Roundheads on the main staircase, which he considered called for that sort of thing, when the hand bell on the hall table sounded.

"I'll get it. The onions are about done," Shelly said, a frying pan of them diced and turning golden on the stove in front of her, ready to go with the jumbo hotdogs Annie was keeping hot in a preserve pan on another ring.

Shelly covered the pan, turned down the heat, and gave her hands a quick wipe on a cloth.

"Just in time for more customers, by the sound of it," Annie said, peering out through the open back door.

Phineas leapt to his feet and watched by the two women flattened himself to the wall one side of the door.

He sneaked a look round it and then pulled back as if shot at. It was an orange and white job from Kingham.

He chanced another cautious glance and saw with relief that both officers were male.

"You won't take me alive, cops!" he snarled, and then laughed, inviting the two women to share in the joke.

They looked at each other. He had gone through exactly the same business a short while back when the Panda car from Church Myddle had turned up.

Shelly shook her head and went to see who was waiting in the hall.

Phineas started getting his work together on the table, muttering something about doing a bit of research in the library.

Coming as the two officers did from Kingham, he couldn't run the risk of having them congratulating him on his engagement to one of their sergeants. He had no doubt, knowing women, that the happy news would be all over the station by now, and possibly a good deal of Kingham. But as far as he was concerned here, in Batch Magna, he was the only one who knew about it. Something that would change immediately, if not sooner, once Annie got to hear of it.

Annie watched him leave, her eyes narrowed suspiciously.

"Hi, boys!" Shelly said, coming out into the hall. "What can I do for you?"

Brrm-Brrm, who, as no cops had followed them in, simply wanted to get out of there, had opened his mouth to ask for directions to somewhere, anywhere, when Clothesline, who had rung the bell, simply because it was a bell, got there before him.

"Bed and breakfast, please," he said happily.

"Bed and breakfast. Right, well, you're in luck there, because we happen to have two singles free at the moment."

They had more than two singles free at the moment. In fact there was only one other guest staying, a commercial traveller who was using it as his base of operations, as he put it, and who sat morosely over his breakfast each morning staring at his order book.

"I'm moving into the library, Shelly," Phineas said, following on out of the kitchen and crossing the hall.

"OK, Phin," Shelly said.

"Some research needed. And to get a bit of peace and quiet."

"OK, Phin. Right, boys," Shelly said, opening the register on the hall table, "if you'd sign the book."

"The place is stiff with ruddy cops," Phineas muttered, before disappearing.

The words galvanized Brrm-Brrm. "No! No, actually, lady, we—" he started when he heard a heavy tread behind him.

He froze, and waited for it to end there, with a hand falling on his shoulder. And then his gaze met the wide, brilliant expanse of one of Humphrey's shirts and he blinked.

"Hi, fellows!" Humphrey said, beaming at them.

"Cap, Humphie," his mother reminded him.

"Sorry, Ma," Humphrey said, removing his baseball cap.

"These two gentlemen want bed and breakfast. I think we can just about squeeze 'em in."

"Softest beds and best breakfast in town, boys!" Humphrey boomed at them.

"Actually, we—" Brrm-Brrm started again.

"A full English breakfast?" Clothesline asked hopefully.

Humphrey looked taken aback. "You're darn right it's a full English breakfast. We don't serve none of them foreign bits and pieces here. And you look like a man who leaves a clean plate."

"Well," Clothesline admitted, "I do like a good fry-up, I must say."

"Then you've come to the right place!" Humphrey assured him.

"And all our eggs are fresh every morning," Shelly told him. "From our own chickens."

"Ahh," Clothesline said.

"And there's bangers, and back bacon, black pudding, baked beans, fried tomatoes," Humphrey told him, ticking them off on his meaty fingers.

"And as much toast as you want," Shelly added.

"Oh, lovely!" Clothesline said.

"I like mine with fried bread," Humphrey said. "Doorsteps, cut from the loaf."

Brrm-Brrm tried again. "Actually, mate, we—"

"Where's your baggage, guys?" Humphrey asked.

"Well, as I say, actually, we—" Brrm-Brrm started.

"We ain't got none," Clothesline said, looking worried. Then he brightened. "But we've got a holdall. It's in the back of the car."

"I'll get it in," Humphrey said.

"No!" Brrm-Brrm said.

"All part of the service," Shelly told him.

"No," Brrm-Brrm said on a lower note. "No, that's all right, mate. I'll get it. Only it's – er – it's locked, see, and the key sticks a bit, know what I mean. Won't be a sec."

Humphrey was telling an appreciative Clothesline about the sort of bangers, as he'd long learned to call them, he could expect on his plate in the morning, plump succulent goods made in the back room of Stretch's, a butcher in Church Myddle, when Brrm-Brrm, after standing for a few moments by the Wolseley, seeing eyes watching him everywhere, and dithering over whether or not to make a bolt for it, came reluctantly back in carrying the holdall.

Afterwards, while Clothesline lumbered excitedly from one bedroom to the other, as if on holiday, clutching a few tourist brochures from the hall table, babbling about the local attractions and comparing the views from his bedroom window with those from Brrm-Brrm's, and how from his he could see the river with the ships on it, Brrm-Brrm sat on his bed, going over it again, explaining to himself how they had ended up there.

Because, whether the place was stiff with cops or not, he'd then have to go downstairs to the phone and explain it to Mr Sneed.

Chapter Eighteen

Not long after the Wolseley had once again turned eastwards, the pawnbroker, offering to make tea, said that he'd run out of milk, and left to get a bottle from the corner shop.

The opening moves of Plan C.

The early morning sunlight falling on the backstreet looked tired already, as if discouraged, as if not seeing much point bothering to shine there at all, a brightness spent elsewhere wasted here, on drab, grey brick and a city's grime, its sparkle half-hearted on the plate glass of the shops, the junk shop that called itself an antique shop, the second-hand furniture shop, betting shop, and the undertaker's – the linchpin of Sneed's plan.

When he came back a few minutes later, he turned that part of Plan B which had involved spotting a detective getting into a surveillance van at New Street Station into Plan C, which involved him spotting a few minutes ago a detective constable he knew letting himself into the undertaker's.

The pawnbroker stood framed in the doorway of the office, clutching the milk.

"We're being watched," he said tightly.

The Major shot to his feet and grabbed his bowler and umbrella from the desk.

Tony, who'd been busy cheating himself at solitaire, froze with a palmed card in his hand.

His eye twitched. "Who? Who's watching us?"

"The Old Bill – who d'you think? Where are you off to, Major?" The Major was on his way to the door, a man who'd suddenly remembered a pressing appointment elsewhere. "No use panicking."

"Doing nothing of the sort!" the Major bridled. "To quote Wellington, I am daring to retreat. When——"

"How do you know? How do you know we're being watched?" Tony cut in, and Sneed told his story about spotting a detective he'd had dealings with in the past letting himself in through the side door of the undertaker's.

"There used to be a flat up there but old Payne the undertaker had trouble with the drains. A lot of the buildings that side do, something to do with the canal at the back. He uses it now as a storeroom for his coffins."

"Well, perhaps he's let it again. Perhaps the detective chappie's moved in there?" the Major suggested, a small hopeful smile coming and going.

"And perhaps he's a bleeding vampire. And even with the coffins out it's a dump. I've been up there. It stinks," Sneed said, putting the milk on the desk. He didn't think he'd be called on now to make tea. "No, it's a surveillance job, that much is obvious. The question is – who?"

"What's he doing, just walking in like that, when anybody could see him?" Tony said, sounding indignant.

"There's no other way for him to get in. Maybe he'd just arrived to take over a shift, or had nipped out for fags or something. I don't know. But I know they'd have no trouble getting a key off old Payne. We had a big barney over parking not long ago. He'd jump at a chance to help get me nicked."

"Did this chap spot you, d'you think?" the Major asked.

"No. No, I'm sure he didn't He had his back to me, on that side of the road."

"Then how'd you know who it was? How'd you know that?" Tony said, quick with suspicion.

Sneed had an answer for that as well.

"Well, I didn't like the look of him when I first noticed him. I've got a nose for the law. And when he walked past here he turned his face away, so I nipped into the shoe shop doorway and watched from there. Before letting himself in he had a quick dekko up and down the road. And that's when I clocked him. It's him, all right. I'd know him anywhere. I've sat across an interview room table from him a couple of times. He's one of that lot from the Lane, from the CID office."

The Major had sidled up to the window and was peering cautiously out between the bars on it.

"Careful, Major," Sneed warned him. "They're not directly opposite us but they'll have a view of that window."

Tony, sitting with his back to it, moved carefully away from the desk.

"Perhaps it's not us they're watching." The Major shared another little hopeful smile with them.

Sneed shook his head, and as if he'd been considering that himself, said, "Yes, well, if it isn't, I can't think who else it might be... There's Jane's, the hairdressers next door here, almost directly across from them, and Bright's Launderette next to her. But I can't see her or the old couple who run the wash place being of any interest. Still, you never know, I suppose," he added, looking dubiously at them.

Tony took a quick nibble of a fingernail.

"What do they want then? Why are they watching us?"

"We don't know it is us they're watching," the pawnbroker said, without much conviction.

"Well, if it is, what do they want? Why are they here?" Tony insisted, winking furiously at him.

"I don't know," Sneed said, his tone and expression suggesting otherwise.

The Major said it for him, despairingly. "It's the robbery. They're on to us."

Tony rounded on him. "How do they know? How do they know it's us, Major?"

"My dear fellow! Don't look at me," the Major protested, and sneaked a look at Sneed. Tony also looked at him.

"So it was me, was it?" the pawnbroker said, sounding angry. "What, so I go to all the bleeding trouble of setting the job up, and then go and tell them about it, do I? Maybe it was you, Tony, eh, son? Maybe you lost your nerve, and did it to cut a deal with them."

"Your mouth will get you into trouble one of these days, Harold."

"Now – now, look here, you chaps," the Major said nervously. "That's not going to help. We should be addressing the matter in hand, not rowing among ourselves."

The pawnbroker looked at him as if surprised to find him there. Then he smiled at Tony.

"He's right, Tony, son. This is no time for friends to fall out."

"Because may I point out," the Major went on querulously, pulling a cuff back and tapping his watch, "that in approximately one hour's time the money will be turning up here – under their very noses."

Sneed looked at him. "Eh – eh, that might be it. They might have been there when the Wolseley left and are waiting for it to come back. With the money and guns in it, all nicely bang to rights."

"Yeah, but how did they get on to us, that's what I'd like to know?" Tony muttered obstinately, looking from one to the other, eyes sullen.

"Here we go again," Sneed said. "Who knows, Tony? Maybe just on the off-chance, seeing as I'm known. Maybe they're under pressure to put themselves about, a job that size. One chief constable having a word with another. And the lorry and getaway were both nicked from Brum. But the main thing now, as the Major rightly says, is to stop the car turning up. Just be thankful I spotted him in time," he added, picking up the phone on his desk. "Even Brrm-Brrm couldn't have got there yet."

He got the number of Church Myddle railway station from directory enquires and asked to leave a message for the minicab driver collecting luggage for a Mr Smith and business associate, telling him to ring this number and emphasising that it was of the utmost importance.

He put the receiver down and stood there, one hand resting on it, a man deep in thought.

"The Old Bull in Deritend, that's got a car park," he said then, as if to himself.

He looked at them. "You know it, don't you, the Bull? In Deritend? On the corner there? Well, that's got a car park at the back, down the side street. We could get Brrm-Brrm to drive straight there."

"Better than drive straight here," the Major said heartily.

"And then what?" Tony wanted to know.

"Well, he leaves the Wolseley there, in the car park. Then… I don't know, we pick it up later. When we think it's safe. They have residents there, so it won't stick out. Well, it's better than having Brrm-Brrm and Clothesline wandering around with it," he said, when the other two didn't seem too impressed with the idea.

"I don't know, Sneed. I don't at all like the thought of leaving the car there," the Major said. "Not when one considers the crime rate in the city."

"Well – well, in that case we'll have to meet them there, and… I dunno, drive somewhere else for the share-out. Unless one of you can think of something better."

Tony left off chewing on a fingernail. "And how are we supposed to do that, Harold? How are we supposed to leave here and meet them, when we're being watched? How we gonna do that?" He flung up his hands. "Tell me that, tell me that!" he cried, slipping back into an accent he had long got rid of.

"Calm down, Tony, calm down," Sneed said. "Take a few deep breaths, and let me have a think."

While the pawnbroker was thinking Tony went back to his nails. And then Sneed said, "Right, well, there's not a lot of choice. There's no back way out of here, so it will have to be the front. But it's unlikely there'll be more than two of them up there, so if you two leave separately, in different directions—"

"They can't follow both of us," the Major finished for him. "One of them will have to stay on post to watch the shop."

"And for the Wolseley to turn up," Sneed reminded him.

"As you say, as you say," the Major agreed, moving hurriedly on from that prospect. "Sound thinking, Sneed. Strategy – the art of the general." He drew himself up. "I shall go first. I shall go left."

"OK, Major. Then Tony goes right. And I suggest you both pick up a—"

"Eh! What do you mean, what do mean, Tony goes right!" Tony said, having worked it out. "Let *him* go right. Let *him* walk under their noses, so they can take a nice photo of him. Tony will go left. He can go right."

"The choice of direction, Tony, was purely arbitrary," the Major said haughtily.

"Well, whatever it was Tony still goes left."

"You can both go left," Sneed said soothingly. "There's no difference. One leaves, then a few minutes later the other does. Simple. And when you get to the main road I suggest you pick up a black cab. He can't follow if you do get a tail, he'll be on foot."

"And what if he's got a car?" Tony said, holding out his hands as if making him a present of the problem.

Sneed sighed. "Have I got to do all the thinking? For one thing, it's quicker with the town traffic to walk from the Lane to here. And for another thing, even if they did have a car, and even if they did find somewhere to park round here, your tail would have to go back to wherever and get the bloody thing, wouldn't he!"

Tony hadn't finished. "All right, all right. Well, what if he gets another cab and follows? Or what if he commands a car? They can do that, command a—"

"Commandeer," the Major couldn't resist correcting him "Commandeer, Tony,"

"Yeah, commandeer. What if he does that? Commandeer. Huh?"

Sneed smiled to himself. He knew he could rely on Tony and his paranoia.

"Yeah..." Sneed said. "Yeah, I hadn't thought of that. Or even the cab bit, to be honest..."

"Huh?" Tony said again, looking at him, rubbing it in, and then looking at the Major, sharing being one move ahead of the pawnbroker.

Sneed shook his head. "Must be slipping. Have to have another think about that."

A few moments later he pointed a sudden finger at the Major. "Major – Major, didn't you say something about having moved digs?"

"Yes, that's so, Sneed. I managed to secure more congenial quarters. In a better class of establishment."

"Done a runner, more like," Tony muttered.

"Really, Tony – I do wish you wouldn't judge others by your own standards!"

"What I meant was, Major," Sneed said, before Tony could come back, "was that the Lane wouldn't have the new address on file."

"Certainly not," the Major said indignantly.

"Then that's it. If you're followed, I'll phone the Bull, asking to speak to – er..."

"Como," Tony put in. "Ask to speak to Mr Como. Like Perry," he added, and looked challengingly at them.

"All right, son. Mr Como. Go into the lounge bar. I'll—"

"I wouldn't dream of doing otherwise," the Major said stiffly.

"I'll ask to speak to a Mr Como. And then, if you have picked up a tail, you can nip out through the back way, through the car park, while he's out front waiting for you to make the next move. And then get over to the Major's drum. You'd better write the address down, Major. You got a phone there?"

"There's one in the hall."

"Better stick that down, while you're at it," Sneed said, a man clearly intending to keep in touch. "If it does come to it, I'll tell Brrm-Brrm to wait in the car if you're not there. And then I'll follow on. Either to the Bull, if there's no tail, or the Major's."

"And what if you're followed? What if it's you they're waiting for?" Tony said. "What if you pick up—"

"If I've got a tail, Tony my son, I'll know about it – I'll make sure of that. Remember, they don't know that we know. So don't worry, I won't lead him to you. I'll lose him, even if I have to go round the town a few times to do it. So bear that in mind, won't you, if I'm late for the share-out. Anyway, cheer up – who knows, eh, mates? Perhaps it's not us they're watching after all. Or maybe the dick really is a vampire and he's up there with his arms crossed waiting for the night shift."

Thirty minutes later the pawnbroker rang the Bull, and telling Mr Como that he had to be quick because Brrm-Brrm was due to call in, gave him the news that they had picked up a single tail.

"Did you get a cab? . . . Right, well, either you lost him then, or, as you suggested he might, he did the same. Or commandeered a car. So to be on the safe side, you'd both better do what we said and scarper out the back. Go separate ways again, take a bus to somewhere, anywhere, do that a few times to be on the safe side, and then take another cab. I'll get there when I'm sure it's safe. But I will be there, Tony, my son, so don't get any ideas about my share, will you…?" he finished, and allowed himself a small smile.

Chapter Nineteen

Now he had the milk to go with it, and plenty of time, with the other two still travelling round the city, Sneed made tea and waited for Brrm-Brrm to call.

The pawnbroker didn't intend provoking fate by counting his chickens quite yet, but nevertheless, when he reflected on how Plan C was shaping up, he whistled quietly and tunelessly to himself, and his movements as he bustled about with the tea things and biscuits, the tray laid with a lace cloth, an unredeemed silver plated teapot, milk jug and sugar tongs, had an air of fussy, self-satisfaction about them.

Forty-five minutes or so later his mood was turning into something else. Even allowing extra time for the back roads they should have been there, at Church Myddle station, well before now.

He rang the station again, to check that Brrm-Brrm had actually got the message, that he'd actually arrived there, wasn't in hospital, or a local nick, or waiting for a tow truck somewhere.

After some delay, while the station master found the porter who'd been in left luggage, Sneed was told that the person in question had indeed been given the message, nearly an hour ago.

He put the phone down.

Anger didn't warm Sneed, didn't heat his blood or pound in a hot flood in his ears. Rather he felt it like a sudden body chill, as if he were coming down with something. A symptom, for whoever, of something much worse to come.

It was true, as he'd said, that he had no bullets for the Luger. But he had for the other gun, a wartime Enfield 38 service revolver put across his counter sometime back with a full box of them. And if they had scarpered with his money, he promised them there and then that it would go to war again.

He would find them, no matter where or how far they ran. He would find them.

And then the phone rang. Sneed snatched at it.

It wasn't Brrm-Brrm but a local burglar, a regular customer, asking if could bring a bag of tom, meaning jewellery, round for him to take a look at.

"No!" he almost screamed, before remembering that there was no one actually watching the shop.

"No, not today, son. I'm – er – I'm busy. Hang on to it, will you, and give us a tinkle tomorrow," he said, hedging his bets, thinking that his tomorrow might well end up looking very different from the one he had planned.

He was sitting at his desk a short while later, staring fixedly into space, lost to his thoughts, when the phone went again.

He reached for it as if in a trance, and came back from dreams of revenge to find Brrm-Brrm alive and well and on the other end.

"You're late, Brrm-Brrm," he said quietly, softly, as if not wanting to scare him off.

Brrm-Brrm rushed in and told him about trying to phone him, but couldn't find a phone box, and then being followed by a cop car, and getting lost in the sticks, and then getting followed by another cop car, right up the door of this big posh gaff, where they were now.

Sneed thought he must have misheard the next bit, and asked Brrm-Brrm what he actually had said. And Brrm-Brrm said what he actually had said again, he said that they had just booked in there for bed and breakfast.

There was a silence at the other end and Brrm-Brrm hurried to fill it, saying that they'd had to do it, because Clothesline had opened his big gob first, and that he, Brrm-Brrm, was just going to ask directions, but, well, he didn't want to draw attention to themselves then. But they seemed to have gone now, the cops, so perhaps they should leave, come straight back, and what did Sneed think?

And then had to ask if the Sneed was still there.

The pawnbroker had his head to one side over the receiver, eyes narrowed in concentration, trying to work out Brrm-Brrm's Plan B. Before reminding himself that this was Brrm-Brrm, Brrm-Brrm and Clothesline. Their plan if they wanted to steal something would be to steal it, grab it and run, in this case in the Wolseley.

"Tell me again, son, what happened," he said, sounding tired.

Brrm-Brrm went through it again, and said that as the coast seems to be clear perhaps they should check out, say they'd had an emergency or something, and come straight back. What did Sneed think?

"No. No, son, don't do that," he said after a few moments' temptation. "As you say, you'll draw attention to yourself. And that's something we don't want. If they were there because of the snatch they're probably just having a trawl round the area, asking about any suspicious characters, and all that. Eh – you didn't use your real names there, did you...? Yeah, well, that's something. Anyway, you'd better stay there today, come back tomorrow morning. That's the best thing."

Brrm-Brrm lowered his voice then and said then that the place was run by Americans and wondered if that had something to do with the cops being there.

Sneed, about to tell him about the change of plan, a plan now moved on a day, said, "How d'you mean?"

"I don't know – the FBI, or something."

"You watch too much telly, son. Now listen, Brrm-Brrm – never mind the FBI, this is important. When you do leave tomorrow, don't come here, to the shop. Right? We've got a problem – that's why I wanted you to ring in," he said, and told him the same story he'd told the other two, but with a different finish, the closing moves of Plan C.

"I'll give you the Major's new address, and you drive straight there tomorrow, OK? Be better than risk any local law noticing out-of-hours activity at Clothesline's yard."

He didn't need to consult the address the Major had scribbled down, and which was now in the waste-paper bin. The pawnbroker had his own address for him.

"Have you got a pen on you...? Well, it's easy enough to remember. It's Fieldhouse Avenue. Got that? Fieldhouse Avenue. Number ten," he decided. "Like where the prime minster lives. Take the turnoff for the Mosley Road on your way in, and it's the first junction you come to on your left. On the corner of it you'll see a bingo hall, what used to be a cinema. It's got a large car park in front. Leave the Wolseley there and walk down. Whatever you do – and listen now, Brrm-Brrm – whatever you do, don't try and park in the road itself. Got it...? Right. Because it's important, that. It's residents' permits only there and by all accounts they are very, very hot on it, even on a Sunday. There's been a lot of trouble over it, apparently. We don't want the coppers called, which happened only last week, so the Major said. Get there between ten and ten thirty. Try not to be later than that, but don't speed. Leave the holdall in the car... Well, use your loaf, son," he said then, when Brrm-Brrm wanted to know why.

"Suppose some uniform who knows you happens to be driving past when you're on the street with it, eh? Nice big bag like that, could have anything in it... No, of course you hadn't thought of it. That's why I'm the boss. Right, so you leave it in the motor – and make sure you bloody well lock it. And whatever you do, don't lose the keys, I don't have a spare set," he added, a nice reassuring touch that, he thought.

"We'll be waiting for you there, at the Major's. Then we'll all drive out somewhere for the share-out. We've got a load of carrier bags with us all ready. You'll be going home to your mum with a nice bit of shopping, Brrm-Brrm. So, have you got all that…? Good. All right, son, well, I'll see you tomorrow then. Drive carefully, won't you."

And so he would see him tomorrow. He'd be the one standing in a bus shelter on the other side of the junction, keeping an eye on the car park from behind a newspaper, and with the spare set of keys to the Wolseley in his pocket.

He retrieved the Major's telephone number from the waste-paper bin, and then made himself another pot of tea. He had plenty of time. They were probably still changing buses. Then he'd have to listen to him and then Tony going on about it. If it wasn't for the fact he was taking the lot he'd have been justified in asking for a bit more on top, the work he was having to put into it.

Chapter Twenty

The sun climbed up into the morning, the River Cluny smoking under its gathering heat as it burned off the last of a river mist, leaving behind, like steam on a glass fading, a perfect summer's day.

Swallows swooped, twittering, over it and ducks paddled in and out of the islands of water lilies, and a kingfisher dropped from the sky as if too hot to hold, a bolt of orange and blue fire striking the water, and coming up with a fish in its beak.

And on board the Owens' paddler, the *Felicity H,* Humphrey, wearing a pair of Bermuda shorts bought in another life, for vacations among the rich at Malibu and Palm Beach, closed his eyes and jumped from the top of the riverside paddle box in an explosion of spray.

He came back up, shedding water like a hippopotamus surfacing, and rolling over on his back grinned up at his wife who was about to dive.

"Careful!" he called, vaguely and needlessly, Clem, who was pregnant again, breaking the water a few yards from him with scarcely a ripple.

On the deck of the boat their young daughter Hawis, with one of Bryony Owen's children of the same age, splashed happily in a patched rubber dingy that had once kept Bryony herself quiet, supervised by the Owens' second oldest daughter Ffion.

And more children ran in small riots about the deck, or jumped from the starboard rail as if the ship was going down, and there was more yelling, and shouting of orders, from the river where a wooden raft, flying the Jolly Roger, floated on empty oil drums, Bryn the Owens' collie riding on it like a mascot.

While ashore, among ducks, geese and scratching chickens, on one of the long trestle tables the WI regularly borrowed for their sales in the village hall, sat bottles of wine and beer and plastic gallons of Sheepsnout cider, and salad bowls and plates and cutlery and glasses, and watched with a sort of know-all amusement by Megan, a tethered Anglo Nubian milking goat, chewing the cud in the long grass, Owain, blatted away smoke, wrestling with the De Luxe Cook Centre, meant for patio living. And Jasmine, perched with her guitar on a kitchen step-stool, had her eyes closed on 'Rocky Mountain High', a John Denver number carrying freedom on its wings, her voice effortlessly taking off with it.

On days such as this, life on the river was moved outdoors, or in this case one particular set of outdoors, the Owens' large patch of land in front of their paddler. On it, an old gamekeeper's field hut, with rusty iron wheels and a stovepipe, and what was left of a Fordson tractor, half buried in the grass. And there were a few old wooden railway containers, used as sheds and a house for the deep-freeze, and stove logs weathering under wraps, and coils of old mooring cable, the bones of a beached sculling boat with grass growing through it.

The river had gathered there for a lunchtime jolly, along with a few landlubbers from the village, Miss Wyndham among them, in a straw hat dressed with a silk rose, sitting in a deckchair in the shade of an alder tree, with a glass of Annie's home-made cherry port.

She was airing her views on the wages snatch, contending that the money was still in Shrewsbury, or somewhere in the neighbourhood.

"No, you may take my word on it, it didn't go back with them to London, or anywhere else."

Priny, who'd been watching with mild interest a Muscovy drake trying to mount a chicken, put in, "The police apparently checked the left luggage office at Shrewsbury."

"I bet they did!" her husband said on a laugh. "After the shambles of the Kingham mail robbery last year. Probably went straight there. Don't worry, we know where the money will be – in left luggage at the railway station."

That had got Phineas's attention, the mention of the police. He was sitting at an angle from them, to give himself a better view of the Owens' gate, slumped in his deckchair behind dark glasses, the brim of his Gent's Superior Panama pulled down, and nursing a pint of cider.

"Too obvious, James," Miss Wyndham said, and laughed briefly. "*Far* too obvious. This is a pro mob they're dealing with. No, the loot was dropped off somewhere. Handed over to a sleeper, I shouldn't be surprised. A member of the gang, planted in a hotel or guest house in the area beforehand. And who is now waiting to slip quietly away with it once the heat is off."

She glanced at her fellow authority on crime, Phineas.

But Phineas wasn't listening. He'd spotted movement at the gate and had carefully eased himself down as far as he could go in the chair without sliding off it.

But when he sneaked another look from under his hat he saw that it was only Sion, the Owens' oldest son, and old Tom Parr, bearing bottles and shopping bags of salad vegetables from Tom's garden in one of the Masters' Cottages. Tom was wearing at a jaunty angle his aged company cap with its gold CSC ribbon, and a flannel vest, his scrawny arms browned and knotted like willow roots. He was one of the few villagers still alive who had worked on the paddler steamers when they were the Cluny Steamboat Company, an ancient, time-locked Lord Jim, a castaway from the Cluny's past.

"What *are* you doing, Phineas?" Priny asked, frowning over at him.

Phineas looked startled. "Who...? Me? Nothing... Just relaxing, that's all. Why? Aren't I allowed to relax? Is there a law against it now, or something?"

Priny, who hadn't brought up three children for nothing, ignored it.

She fitted a cigarette into her amber holder and lit it with a slim gold Dunhill lighter which, along with her pearls, had been put across a few pawn shop counters in its time, and asked Miss Wyndham what the latest was on the blood found in the getaway car. Or was it at the scene?

Priny too was wearing sunglasses, large film star bowls of glass in thick white frames, a red beret with a pompom, a poppy print shirt, cream Capri pants and red deck shoes, and crimson lipstick to match her nail extensions.

Miss Wyndham, changing her position somewhat from yesterday, was now scornful at the suggestion of blood. "A figment of people's rather silly imaginings. There was no such thing. Either in the getaway car *or* at the scene," she said dismissively.

"Mrs Pugh said—" Priny started.

"Mrs Pugh *would*," Miss Wyndham said tartly.

Priny looked disappointed. "Well, anyway, it was still an awful lot of money," she said, reluctant to relinquish quite all sensationalism.

Her husband regarded Miss Wyndham with his good eye, in the other Turner's sky was on fire, burning with light as *The Fighting Temeraire* was tugged to her last berth.

"Well, whether they did or whether they didn't end up shooting each other, I have to say, Hattie, that I'm not altogether sure I can agree with you that the money's still around. I should think it's long gone."

Miss Wyndham smiled tolerantly. "I doubt, James, considering how professional they so obviously are, that they'd have risked a roadblock, not with that amount at stake."

The Commander snorted. "I don't think there would have been much chance of that, Hattie. They'd have been in and out before our local guardians of the peace could get their boots on. And anyway, they've more important things to do." Like charging him with doing ninety on the dual carriageway the other week, and making after-hours raids on the Steamer Inn. "No, I've no doubt the miscreants are now back whence they came, busily spending their ill-gotten gains."

"One hundred thousand pounds of it," Priny said. "One could do an awful lot with a hundred grand," she almost purred, sensuously moving her shoulders as if snuggling into a mink coat.

The Commander glanced at his Number One, the First Lieutenant. Buy a house on land for a start, he thought, and immediately felt disloyal even thinking about that which he would never voice to her. It would feel like letting down the side. It would feel like surrender.

It would be to admit that they were both now old and that her arthritis was getting worse and that sitting on water in the winter wasn't helping. That their indomitable younger selves, who had come through a war and who had met life on their terms since, had at long last been vanquished.

So the Commander, who had never let any side he had fought or played on down, busied himself filling his briar and stayed silent.

Phineas, dragging his gaze away from the gate, couldn't resist telling them what he'd do with the money.

"I'd buy a pier, a seaside pier, that's what I'd do. I've always wanted a pier. With an amusement arcade, and a ghost train, and summer shows on the end of it, '"Happy Days are Here Again"', and all that," he said gloomily.

"Make a note of that, James," Priny said to her husband. "He's got a birthday coming up."

"I'd get my roof done. And buy a new refrigerator and new curtains, and have the house repainted," Miss Wyndham said. "And I'd go on a cruise. A luxury world cruise," she added, grand with wealth.

"It must be nice to be rich," Phineas said wistfully, thinking of another advantage of it. Thinking of the ease which members of that class, surrounded by lawyers, all experts in breach of promise, must be able to extricate themselves from such fantastically undesirable situations.

The miscreants, or at any rate two of them, hadn't yet gone back to whence they came, as the Commander had supposed, but they *were* busy spending their ill-gotten gains, and doing so at a place not all that far from where the Commander and company were sitting. Brrm-Brrm and Clothesline were at the seaside, eating ice-cream in Aberystwyth.

It was a good one hour and a half's drive from Batch Magna, but with no incriminating holdall in the back to worry about, Brrm-Brrm had done it in just over half the time.

Removing a wad of money for what he called expenses, and leaving the rest locked in his bedroom, they'd headed for the attractions of that town as advertised in one of the tourist brochures on the hall table.

They had paddled in the sea, gone up and down twice on the Electric Cliff Railway, changed notes for coins in the amusement arcade on a pier Phineas would happily have bought, had he been in charge of the holdall, played crazy golf and wacky football, went go-carting, listened with a sort of dutiful air to a brass band on the green, signed on for a boat trip around the bay, had hotdogs and candy floss and a sit-down meal of fish and chips, and were now tucking into another ice-cream each, reclining on deckchairs on the promenade in novelty hats, and wondering what to have a go at next.

Sergeant Cholmondeley-Jones wasn't having nearly as much fun. She was in Kingham, knocking on doors in the Claypit Lane area, calling on suspects in the shoplifting case.

The mother of one of the girls involved had come home unexpectedly to find her daughter lavishly experimenting with a range of make-up, part of the haul from Boots in the High Street. She had marched her to the police station where the girl had tearfully given up the names of the others.

Which was all very well for the clear-up rate, but it left the Sergeant with no time today to finish what she had been determined to finish – this wretched business with Phineas Cook. That would now have to wait till tomorrow because tonight was spoken for. Now it was clear that the armed robbers had almost certainly left the area, the pressure was off, which meant Ted was free for the evening.

Tonight, she told herself, beating a brisk tattoo on the knocker of the next door, belongs to us.

Chapter Twenty-One

The next day both the Inspector and Sergeant were on an early shift. They hadn't got within speaking distance of each other but they had exchanged waves from opposite ends of a corridor, she, vigorously, with her left hand.

The night had indeed belonged to them, lit by candlelight and toasted with a bottle of something special – or as special as that particular establishment was clearly able to provide, as the Inspector had remarked, ordering it with a resigned air after scrutinising the wine list and finding, as he'd put it, mostly a collection of bin-ends from the wrong part of Le Havre. And then, remembering something else from his night school course on wine appreciation, had gone on to give her a talk on north and south facing slopes, while the Sergeant listened as if fascinated, and stole glances at her ring.

And now she was on her way to the front office, to show it to a couple of women there who hadn't seen it the first time around.

Not long after that, the Inspector, gazing out of the window in his first-floor office overlooking the station car park, brooding on the escape of the armed robbers and his career prospects, had glanced down to see his fiancée again, crossing the yard from the building.

He and the Sergeant spent a great deal of their leisure time together doing various athletic things in shorts and plimsolls, and didn't believe in slacking on their respective journeys to and from work either. They usually left their cars behind and walked, briskly, turning the trip into another exercise session.

But it wasn't the fact that she was there, in the car park, which had made him move to one side of the window so he couldn't be seen. It was her body language.

If he hadn't got to the chapter on that subject in his text book on psychology and modern day policing, he might well have missed it. As it was, her back, for those able to read such things, spoke to him.

It told him clearly that the rest of her had something to hide.

He took another peep and pulled back just in time as she glanced up at his window. And when he had looked again she was getting into one of the new patrol cars.

Her use of it on official business was of course perfectly above board. But he was convinced that whatever else her business might be, it was not official.

The Inspector put two and two together and came up with Phineas Cook.

He grabbed his hat on the way out.

The Sergeant felt an absolute *rotter* driving away from the station, from under her fiancé's trusting nose, and with the sparkle of his ring newly back on her finger.

Which didn't stop her from indulging again the guilty pleasure of being engaged to two men at the same time, the unique feeling for her of being utterly desired and desirable. She felt like the femme fatale in the Mills & Boon she remembered, the one the men had gone mad about but who had been left out in the cold at the end when the ring went to another.

Except that in her case, at the moment, she was enjoying the perfectly delicious taste of having her cake and eating it.

Even her mother, a sophisticated figure, frequently seen in the society pages of *Country Life* and *Harpers,* who had long despaired of her gauche, unfashionable daughter, now so unbecomingly clothed in blue serge, had been impressed when the Sergeant couldn't resist ringing her up to tell her.

And now, taking the Batch Magna turn-off, she had to sternly remind herself of what she was on her way to do, leaving one unsuspecting heart behind and about to break that of another.

But the Inspector's heart wasn't in the least unsuspecting and he wouldn't be all that far behind either. He'd been delayed somewhat by the novel appearance, on a Sunday, of his boss, the Superintendent. When major crimes remain unsolved on their manor the brass lose their Sunday morning lie in.

No, Inspector Worth was afraid he hadn't anything new to report. But, he went on, tapping the side of his nose with a finger, and explaining what any minute now would be his absence from the building, he was just on his way out to have a few words in a certain quarter.

Which was precisely what he intended to have when he caught up with her. For one thing, that ring she was wearing had cost him over a month's salary, not to mention the meal with all the trimmings last night.

The Sergeant turned left at the village pub, the Steamer Inn, down a slope to the lane called Upper Ham running alongside the river.

There were three houseboats moored on that stretch. The *Cluny Belle* was the third boat along. Phineas's canary-yellow Sprite, she saw, was parked up on the verge in front of it. But then it had been parked there on the other occasions she'd called, so it didn't necessarily mean she was about to at last shed a fiancé. And looking at the state of it she wouldn't be surprised if it had broken down.

She went through what served as a front gate, a pallet top secured with orange baler twine. There was no sign of the dog which, as there had been before when she'd opened the gate, she thought might be promising.

She stood at the bottom of the gangway, opened her mouth to call Phineas's name, and squeaked.

The animal was suddenly there, standing in sinister silence, peering down at her from the top of the gangway, his upper lip lifted to display a set of hooked fangs.

And then he seemed convulsed by a sudden rage, growling and snarling and tossing his head about, as if he'd already sunk those dreadful teeth into something and was breaking its neck, jowls and spittle flying. While his other end, the part she couldn't see, was saying something else entirely, his stub of a tail working furiously. Bill Sikes was enjoying himself, and was inviting her to do the same, inviting her to play.

The Sergeant backed away slowly, and then turned and made a run for it.

Sikes realised then that she was leaving, and started barking after her, throwing himself into it, each volley rocking him back like the recoil of cannon.

The din could be heard up on the High Street, and certainly on the moorings of the next boat downriver, the *Cluny Queen*, where Jasmine was pushing her four-year-old son on a swing, giving him an aerial view of the world, taking him on a journey, while he held on tight with an avid expression and his eyes closed.

"… and now we're over Africa – and *Ohhh,* look, Cadoc! Elephants, a herd of them, trunk to tail. And rhinos, bellowing away like mad, and hippopotamuses having a mud bath. And lions, look, *roaring* and eating things, and tigers up trees, and there's giraffes, so we mustn't fly too low. And then we're in Spain," she said, unsure of the geography, but Cadoc liked bull fights. "And *what* do you know! There's a bull fight going on, with a matador and… Hold on, Cadoc, love, hold on while I see what that daft animal next door's on about," she said then, catching her son mid-swing.

When she came out into Upper Ham she found one of those new police cars from Kingham and a sergeant standing indecisively by it.

Jasmine hurried up to her. "What is it?" she asked, a dramatic hand up to her breast, her voice spectral. Whatever the worst was, in Jasmine's imagination it had already happened.

"Phineas Cook," the Sergeant said, looking thoroughly fed up. "I'm looking for Phineas Cook. I *never* seem to find him in. I mean, his car's here again, but…"

Jasmine looked disappointed. "Well, then, he's probably up at the Hall," she said, seeing that the pub wasn't open yet and the shop was closed, Mr Pugh, who was chapel, refusing to have anything to do with commerce on a Sabbath.

The Sergeant looked hopeful. "The Hall…?"

"The Hall. Batch Hall. He's been writing things up there. Look, go to the end of the lane there, follow it round and turn left. You can't miss it, a big black and white, it is, up on the left there." Jasmine hurriedly got that out of the way and then said, "But *what's* he done, darling?"

"I'm sorry, I'm not at liberty to tell you. But thank you for the directions," the Sergeant said, and left Jasmine gaping after her.

"Not at liberty to tell you," she repeated to herself. To her it had the same official ring as, 'helping the police with their enquires'.

She rushed in to telephone the Hall.

Chapter Twenty-Two

Humphrey, with George his helper trailing behind, popped up to the first-floor breakfast room to ask his guests, as he believed a good host should, if everything was all right.

The commercial traveller said glumly that he supposed so. But Brrm-Brrm and Clothesline were more forthcoming. The breakfast was lovely, they said, sitting back after it with a pot of tea, especially the sausages – they were *delicious*, Clothesline added, patting his stomach.

Humphrey, beaming his approval, sat down at the table and told them what was in them, where to get them, and how to get there, while George hovered by the door waiting to see if he wanted him for anything.

The two men told Humphrey's mother how much they'd enjoyed their stay, after coming back down with the holdall, and shopping bags with sticks of Aberystwyth rock in them and the various presents they'd bought. They would, they said, be back again.

"Anytime, boys!" Shelly said. "But best to book a couple of days before as we're usually standing room only."

Brrm-Brrm, to explain their presence in the area, had used the story the Major had told them he'd used at the Church Myddle left luggage office, and now said that they were off to study more old ruins, and all that.

They looked, Shelly thought, an unlikely couple to be studying anything. But if there was one thing she had learned since coming here it was that the English were an eccentric lot.

And the Welsh aren't far behind, she thought, going into the kitchen where Annie was frying the morning's onions

And by doing so missed the two departing guests returning far sooner than they said they would.

They had been about to trip down the small fan of steps to their car, when they froze, watching as an orange and white patrol car swept into the forecourt in a manner which suggested business a little more urgent than Conies and coffee.

Shelly was upstairs when the phone went and Annie had answered it.

"Phineas," she'd said, coming back into the kitchen, "that was Jasmine. She said a lady police sergeant called at the *Belle* and that she's now on her way…"

She hadn't got much past the words 'lady police' before Phineas, scooping his papers up from the kitchen table, was on his feet and heading for the door.

"What have you been up to then?"

"It's a long story, Annie, I'll explain later – but you haven't seen me, all right? I wasn't here!" he flung back on his way out, and almost collided with the two men darting back in to the hall.

Brrm-Brrm took the initiative. "Oh – er – oh, yes, we must have a look at the lovely gardens before we go, Mr Smith. I do believe one can get to them this way," he said in the sort of accent he imagined people who looked at lovely gardens would have.

"Down there, on the left," Phineas said without stopping, pointing to the drawing room on his way to the library.

"Oh, thank you so much," Brrm-Brrm said, and headed with the same sort of haste for the drawing room.

The two men went through the French windows at the other end of it, and out on to the terrace.

They were halfway across the lawn below the terrace steps when Clotheslines came to a halt with his mouth open.

"Cor! Look, Brrm-Brrm," he said, pointing to a peacock that had just appeared from behind a box hedge, dragging his tail behind him, the eye-studded, blue, gold and green feathers swimming with sunlight.

"What is it…?"

"I don't know," Brrm-Brrm said, glancing back at the house. "A chicken or turkey or something – come on!"

"It's *lovely*…" Clothesline said wonderingly.

Brrm-Brrm led the way across the lawns, and down a brick path through an archway into a walled kitchen garden, and out through another archway on the other side of it, and found himself in a cobbled yard of outhouses.

"Where we going, Brrm-Brrm?" Clothesline asked.

"I don't know, do I! We've got to find somewhere to dump the holdall," he said, glancing around. The yard looked deserted.

"Come on," he said, and hurried across to a building opposite with a half-door.

He peered in. "Horses," he said, referring to Clem's pair she kept there.

"Ahhh, horses," Clothesline said, taking a look. "I like horses."

There were no horses in the next stable, which didn't mean it was going to stay that way. And the building next to it was a room with horsey things in it. The door after that opened on a feed store.

He hesitated, before deciding that that wouldn't do either.

"What are we doing, Brrm-Brrm?" Clothesline wanted to know.

"We're – never mind, Clothesline. Just… Just, come on."

Brrm-Brrm was starting to sweat. Someone could show up at any minute – the police could show up at any minute.

He found what he was looking for on the other side of the yard, opening the door on an outhouse piled with junk, dust motes moving in sunlight pouring through a hole in the roof.

"This'll do," he said. "We'll bung it in here. Keep watch."

"And what if somebody comes?" Clothesline said in a complaining sort of way, looking as if the coach home hadn't turned up, wearing the novelty Western hat he'd kept and carrying the cheerfully-coloured bags of sticks of rock and the presents with A Gift from Aberystwyth marked on them.

"Tell 'em… Tell 'em we're looking for a cat."

"We're looking for a cat," Clothesline said, trying it out.

Brrm-Brrm started industriously burrowing into the junk to get at a row of tea chests he'd spotted stacked against the back wall, pulling away a bedstead, a galvanised iron boiler with a gaping hole in it, an old steamer trunk plastered with long-ago destinations, a mouldering carpet, perished harness, a copper dinner gong with a missing chain, a vacuum cleaner, a lawnmower with only one wheel, half a stepladder, a bicycle frame, a broken wooden wheelbarrow, a mattress with the springs poking out, a Marmet pram, minus its wheels and axle, a couple of rolls of rotting tennis netting, and a fridge with its door missing.

He took a breather and wiped sweat from his brow.

"Still clear, Clothesline?" he called.

Outside, Clothesline looked elaborately first one way and then the other.

"Yes," he reported.

Brrm-Brrm clambered over a rusting iron clothes mangle, and the remains of a Hepplewhite sofa, to get at the tea chests, and pulled the top three down from one of the stacks. He removed the balls of yellowing newspaper once used as packing from the bottom chest, and stood the big holdall in it on its end, because it wouldn't go in any other way.

He frowned at it sticking up by about a foot. And then had an idea. He emptied another tea chest of its packing, upended

143

it, and fitted that over the holdall. He then put the other two chests on top, and got to work again putting the junk back.

"That'll do," he said, back out in the yard, wiping at the cobwebs and dirt on his hands and dusting himself down.

Clothesline watched him close the door with a heavy frown.

"We just gonna *leave* it there?"

"No, of course we're not just gonna *leave* it there. We're coming back for it. Tonight, when it's dark." He looked down the yard at what appeared to be the entrance, an arch under a half-timbered gable, with a clock on its mossy red-tiled roof topped with a cockerel weathervane.

"Come on, looks like we should be able to get out that end. Let's get the hell out of here."

He made a mental note as they walked of the number of doors from the outhouse they'd used to the entrance.

He just hoped that today wasn't the day they decided to have a clear-out in the yard.

Chapter Twenty-Three

The Inspector hadn't minded the delay. He didn't need to tail her. He knew where she was going. And it would give them time to settle in, as it were, and for him to catch them in the act.

Batch Magna looked deserted, but in the High Street he stopped by a milk float and asked if by any chance the milkman knew which of the houseboats a certain Phineas Cook lived on. The milkman certainly knew which of the houseboats a certain Phineas Cook lived on, he'd left a certain Phineas Cook enough notes over the years, reminding him yet again that the bill was overdue.

Following his directions, the Inspector turned left past the pub, down into Upper Ham. The third houseboat down, he'd been told. But all that was parked up there was a yellow sports car.

He pulled up behind it and peered over what was meant to be a gate. It was the right boat, all right, its name painted crudely in white on the lid of a dustbin. And he could see what she'd meant when she described it as an old tub. He really would have appreciated a better class of rival.

There was no room in there to hide a patrol car, or any sort of car, which didn't stop him looking for it, peering suspiciously about, eyes narrowed. And anyway, it occurred to him she could of course have parked it elsewhere, out of sight.

He snorted a laugh at the subterfuge. You'll have to get up a good deal earlier than that, my girl, to get one over on me, he thought, pushing the gate to one side.

He was walking stealthily towards the boat, when he looked up at the deck and found Bill Sikes looking down at him, a growl gathering in his throat, his top lip up and rigid.

The Inspector hastily retreated, followed by another outbreak of frustrated barking. And on the moorings of the *Cluny Queen* Jasmine, bringing her son down to earth again, hurried out to catch the next instalment, and was rewarded by the sight of another police officer outside the *Belle*. And a higher up, important-looking one this time.

She watched agog as he drove off, wondering what on *earth* Phineas had been up to, and who she should tell about it first.

The Inspector followed Upper Ham round and up to the cross-roads and was about to turn right, back into the High Street, to take a drive round the village, just in case, when checking for traffic, he spotted the orange and white rear of a car turning off some way down on the left.

He didn't go tearing off in pursuit as another man might have, but waited.

Softly, softly, catchee monkey, he thought. Or rather, he added with a chuckle, *two* monkeys. Up their monkey tricks.

The patrol car had turned into the drive of what, when he passed it, a rather lurid bed and breakfast sign told him was Batch Hall. He was about to follow when another car swept down the drive at speed, a Wolseley, carrying a couple of civilians.

The driver came to an abrupt halt when he saw him, and turned in his seat as if about to reverse.

The Inspector sounded his horn and then flashed his lights when he had the man's attention, giving him right of way. The Inspector prided himself on remembering that his duties as a servant of the public went beyond that of nicking certain members of it.

He waited patiently as the Wolseley continued more cautiously towards the road, both men, he noted with a small knowing smile, looking thoroughly nervous. Other, less knowledgeable officers, usually, it has to be said, old sweats stuck in the past, like, for example, DI Berry, would have read their expressions as a sign of guilt and stopped them, thus adding to the public's case for police harassment.

We knew better now. Our weapons are no longer what the old plods are pleased to call a copper's nose, and an enthusiastic use of the truncheon. Modern policing has gone into the classroom and come out with a degree in psychology.

Those were the Inspector's thoughts as he beckoned the Wolseley out, letting the driver know the road was clear. What he was looking at was not guilt – the body language was all wrong for that – but simply the sort of reaction that many law-abiding citizens will sometimes have to the sudden appearance of a police officer, especially, it must be said, one at the wheel of a rather snazzy new patrol car.

The Inspector smiled a PR smile and lifted his hand in a salute. Mind how you go.

The driver, a young chap, returned a sickly sort of grin and carried on at a much slower pace towards the village.

It was also rewarding, the Inspector reflected, to witness the salutary effect a police car can have on those inclined to speed.

Chapter Twenty-Four

The Sergeant had rung the bell one side of the Hall's open doors, pulling a couple of times at the enamel handle, and waited politely. Unaware that the last time it had been heard in that house it had roused the butler Mr Peel from his pantry, a relic with the General of a shared past and a present they largely ignored, donning his black frockcoat before answering, and travelling to do so at a pace which befitted his position, no matter what sort of hurry the rest of the world might be in.

And she was still standing there when Shelly, carrying a tray with used breakfast things on it, came down the stairs.

"Hi!" Shelly greeted her. "You here for a Coney? Well, come on in, come on in, don't be shy. This is Liberty Hall."

"Actually," the Sergeant said, standing in the hall, "I was looking for a Phineas Cook. I tried his houseboat and a lady there suggested that he might be here…"

Shelly opened her mouth to say, sure Phineas was there, when Annie hastily appeared out of the kitchen and said he wasn't.

"No. No, he's not here. Not Phineas Cook, no," she said with a sort of careful honesty, as if to suggest that they did have a Phineas somewhere on the premises, but not a Phineas *Cook*. "No, haven't seen him for some time now, have we, Shelly, Phineas Cook?"

"No. No, I guess you're right, Annie, come to think of it," Shelly immediately agreed. After nearly three years living in Batch Magna she was used to sudden complications.

Annie gave a little laugh. "I thought you'd come for one of Shelly's Conies. What, never heard of Shelly's Conies!" she went on, when the Sergeant looked blank. "You must be one of the few who hasn't. Famous they are, in Kingham and Church Myddle. We get officers from there all the time, on their meal breaks, like. Coney and a coffee, very popular it is. Try one yourself while you're here, why don't you?"

"First one's always on the house," Shelly added.

The Sergeant's shoulders slumped and she sighed.

"So he's not here then?"

She could see no end to it, really she couldn't. She could see herself starting married life with a both a husband *and* a fiancé.

"Come on, darling, come and have a nice cup of something, anyway. You look like you need it," Annie said, hoping to learn what she wanted with Phineas, and leading the glum and unresisting Sergeant by the arm.

While across the hall, standing behind the library door, Phineas listened through the gap he'd left when closing it, and despised himself. If he had phoned her yesterday as he had told himself to, he wouldn't be here today, eavesdropping behind doors.

However did I get *into* this frightful situation, he thought vaguely, while wondering if that aunt of his in Kent had a room free for a couple of weeks.

He watched Annie leading the Sergeant into the kitchen. Good old Annie. Pure Welsh gold. He'd get her a box of chocolates or something before packing.

He made a break for it then, turning his back on the kitchen as he scuttled past its open door, and tripping down the steps just as the Wolseley took off as if to a fire.

That was the trouble with people today, always in a *hurry*, he reflected, following on down the drive, and thinking about his aunt in Kent.

He had parents, of course he had, like anyone else. And a suspicious pair they were, too. And he had friends. Jeremy Bryant, a fellow crime writer, living in best-seller splendour in Hampstead for one. He'd have given him a bed, he had enough rooms to spare there. But then he'd have to put up with listening to his latest sales figures.

No, he'd give the old aunt a ring. She was a bit stiff for his liking, and worse she was a teetotaller. And one moreover who expected those who stayed under her roof to abstain with her. But any port in a storm, as the Commander would no doubt advise, and the home waters of the Cluny were definitely not the place to be with this one brewing.

He could always send Sally a postcard – urgently called away on family business, will explain later, he thought, hurrying down the drive, anxious to put distance between himself and the car outside the Hall, and almost walked straight into the path of another one of them, appearing suddenly from around the screen of rhododendrons.

He nipped to one side with a pained, picked on expression, as the Inspector gave an admonitory toot on the horn and carried on up the drive.

And while the Sergeant's two fiancés passed each other unknowingly and went their ways, one intent on dodging her, the other on finding her, the Sergeant was sitting in the kitchen of the Hall with thoughts for once of neither of them, enjoying herself.

She was with two other officers from Kingham who had just dropped in, and Clem and Annie, listening to Shelly telling them about another police officer, a date of hers back in the Bronx, who had wanted to bring his handcuffs into the bedroom.

It was rather risqué, but after all, she was nearly a married woman now – nearly married twice in fact, to two men at the same time, she reminded herself, and laughing even louder wondered if she was about to have hysterics.

The patrol car from Kingham that the Inspector had followed in wasn't the Sergeant's, but one manned by two officers on their way back from investigating a minor traffic accident, and ready for a Coney break. And it wasn't their car, which as usual was parked round the back, he came across, but the Sergeant's, parked in front.

He didn't yet know what she was up to, but it hadn't escaped his notice that the hippy-type sign on the roadside had mentioned bed, as well as breakfast.

The Inspector pulled at the peak of his uniform hat, and swagger stick in hand, went to investigate.

He paused alertly on the steps, his eyes narrowed at the sound of laughter coming from within.

His eyes narrowed again then, when he crept into the hall, at the sight of four one-armed bandits against a wall. He'd be interested in seeing a gaming licence for those – after, that is, he'd dealt with the business in hand.

The laughter was coming from a room on his right.

He presented himself, suddenly, in the doorway of the kitchen, and took in what he was looking at – or rather not looking at.

The business in hand was there all right, along, mysteriously, with another two of his officers. But there was no one present who might answer to Phineas Cook.

The Inspector frowned and waited for an explanation.

While the Sergeant gaped at him and wondered if the game was up, the two other officers stood.

"So you've discovered Shelly's Conies as well, sir," the younger of the two said brightly.

The Inspector's frown deepened.

"We are on a meal break, sir. We have logged it in, and we'll be logging it out, as per the book," the other said, and sat down again, a man who knew his rights.

"Yes, well," the Inspector said, frowning on, "there's no rule about where you take your breaks, providing of course you don't exceed the allotted time. But what I don't understand is, there's only one car outside. Where—?"

The Sergeant found her voice, and told him another lie.

"That's my car, Te – Inspector. They're parked round the back here, by the kitchen door. And in case you're wondering what *I'm* doing here," she said with a little laugh, "I'd heard about Shelly's Conies, as they're known at the station, how absolutely delicious they are, and decided, as it was also my meal break, that I simply *had* to try one," she said, smiling with toothy sweetness at him and confessing her indulgence with a little feminine lift of her shoulders, while Shelly and Annie exchanged glances.

The Inspector, all eyes now on him, cleared his throat and said, "Yes, well, I happened to be in the village on other business, and seeing one of our units turning in here, I – er—"

"Ah, that would be us, sir," the younger officer piped up. "We were on our way back from a RTA on the A-four-five-eight," he rattled off.

"I see," the Inspector said, and sucked on a tooth.

And then he looked at the Sergeant again. And the Sergeant, who hadn't believed a word of his story about just *happening* to be in the village, saw that something was needed to divert him from mentioning the name Phineas Cook, and was inspired.

Ted, she knew was a snob. And in her more vulnerable moments, when she didn't feel in the least desired or desirable, just fed up, really fed up with herself, and when the latest Mills & Boon, with its promise of perfect love meeting in the last pages, was hurled across the room, she told herself scornfully that Ted wasn't thinking of *her* when he said he loved her, but of her family, her socially prominent mother and her father, a senior circuit judge sitting in Wales and the borders.

"But let me introduce you to the ladies, Inspector," she said. "This is – er—"

"Annie," Annie supplied, stirring the pan of hotdogs at the stove.

"And I'm Shelly," Shelly said. "Hi!"

"And this is Lady Strange," the Sergeant got in quickly, "the chatelaine of Batch Hall." Lady Strange was how Annie had politely introduced her to Clem, and Clem had immediately invited her to call her Clem, as she did now, to the Inspector.

He had merely nodded to the other two, but his hat came off for Clem, and he gave her his full, smiling attention.

"Delighted to make your acquaintance, Lady Strange."

"Well, thank you," Clem said with a small embarrassed laugh. "But, please, it's Clem."

Shelly slapped him on the back. "Siddown, Inspector, take the weight off your feet," she said with an accent straight out of *Annie Get Your Gun*. In a red gingham shirt, blue jeans with deep turn-ups, and sneakers, and her hair cut short and with another strawberry-blond dye job, she was going through a Doris Day phase.

"Have a Coney and a cup of coffee, set yourself up for the day."

"The onions are ready," Annie told him. "We're just heating up the hotdogs. Jumbos, they are," she added, familiar with the male appetite.

"And seeing as it's your first time here, Inspector, it's on the house," Shelly added.

Clem laughed. "She knows that after one bite you'll be back."

"Ohhh, they're delicious, sir, they are. *Very* tasty," the older of the two officers assured him.

"It's the relish what does it," Annie said. "Made from an old family recipe that Shelly brought over with her, from America, like," Annie said in her gossipy way. "Shelly of course is Clem's mum-in-law, the mother of her husband, Sir Humphrey, who's out at the moment, picking up a new sign from Nether Myddle for Open Day. We open once a week in the summer to the public, see. We do cream teas then."

"Rather romantically," the Sergeant put in, "the recipe for the relish is a family secret, an heirloom handed down from generation to generation."

"Alchemy from the New World, as the Commander, a friend of ours, describes it," Clem said. "Although he did add that it no doubt got there on the *Mayflower.*"

The Inspector hesitated, but the combined social weight of Sir Humphrey and Lady Strange, and a Commander of something somewhere in the background, proved too much for him.

"Well, when in Rome," he said with a chuckle, joining his officers at the table, and ignoring another two slot machines, standing either side of one of the kitchen windows.

The Sergeant looked across at him, lifted her shoulders again, and giggled.

She felt quite heady with success. Tina was absolutely right. When it came to men a little white lie, or two, did indeed simplify things.

While out in the stable yard, Humphrey's helper, George, was standing in the outbuilding Brrm-Brrm had not long left, staring wide eyed at the bundles of money in the holdall he'd just found.

He was looking, he told himself wonderingly, at riches beyond the dreams of whatever it was his teacher had once said. He'd never seen so much money.

He had no idea how much might be there, or what he was going to do with it – but made an immediate start with the sweets counter in Woolworth's, and then his eyes got bigger with thoughts of the train set laid out in all its busy glory on the floor of the toy department in Pennington's, and the wrapped and shiny newness of the bikes waiting in a line outside Webb's.

Chapter Twenty-Five

Sitting complacently at his desk with the phone in front of him, the pawnbroker dug into a pocket of his waistcoat and released the cover of a solid gold full-Hunter watch, engraved with a note from someone else's life and left, unredeemed, on the shelf.

The waistcoat went with his almost new tailored pin-striped suit, something else hocked and never redeemed. He'd polished his black Oxford business shoes again, and once more his yellow leather driving gloves sat next to his Homburg hat, ready for the start of his journey to a new life.

It was almost time. In another thirty minutes he'd ring for a taxi to drop him near the bingo hall. He was almost there.

And then the phone went.

He hesitated before picking it up.

"Hello…?" he said then warily.

And somehow wasn't altogether surprised to find Brrm-Brrm on the other end. Brrm-Brrm with another story to tell.

He listened to it with a grin he was unaware of.

"So, what do I do now, Mr Sneed?" Brrm-Brrm wanted to know.

"Eh…?" Sneed said.

"What do I—"

"Tell me what happened again, son, please."

Brrm-Brrm told him. "I don't think nobody will find it there. It's buried under a load of tat, in a building no one seems to go in."

First bed and breakfast and now this. This wasn't anybody's Plan. He knew what this was. This was life. His life.

"And where are you now?"

"I'm in a phone box in a lane somewhere. I just wanted to get clear away from there, know what I mean...?"

"Mr Sneed...?" Brrm-Brrm said into his ear.

"How far are you from this Hall gaff?" Sneed asked.

"Not far. I just wanted—"

"What, just up the road sort of thing?"

"Yeah, five minutes, or so."

"Well, nip back and get it then," Sneed said with a little laugh.

"Yeah, but what about—"

"Go back and get it, Brrm-Brrm!" he screamed, rage ballooning in him, lifting him to his feet.

Brrm-Brrm listened to him breathing raggedly on the other end, and then said cautiously, "Mr Sneed...?"

The pawnbroker sat down carefully, looking aged by it.

"Yeah..." he said.

"Mr Sneed...?" Brrm-Brrm said again, not sure what Sneed had said, or even if he'd said anything.

"Yeah. Yeah, I'm still here."

"Well, what I was going to say—"

"Sorry I shouted at you."

"That's all right, Mr Sneed."

"I didn't mean to do that."

"Yeah, well..."

"You're like a son to me, Brrm-Brrm. You know that."

"Yeah, I know that, Mr Sneed."

"Like the family I never had. Well, I did have one," he added with a sour laugh. "But not for bleeding long..."

Brrm-Brrm shared a brief familiar silence with him, and then went on quickly, "But the thing is——"

"I wasn't always like this, you know, Brrm-Brrm, stuck here."

"I know that Mr Sneed. But——"

"I had my dreams." And look where they'd got me, that's what his tone said. Look where they had ended up.

A character in the TV soap *Crossroads* had said that line about dreams once, and he'd heard his own life in it. His life and the life that might have been his, had things been different. And as his life over the years had turned into a game of Monopoly, one in which he felt he was being played with rather than playing, the number of times the dice promised riches before landing on another Go to Jail card, that other life had taken root in his imagination and had prospered there. A life rich with success, lit with smiling images like TV ads of an adoring family, and with the respect of friends and neighbours and business peers.

And over those years vague resentment had slowly grown into something else, and it became no longer the life he might have had but the life he should have had. A life he had come to believe he'd been cheated out of.

"Yeah, I know that, Mr Sneed, but what I was going to say was——"

"Yeah, go on, son."

"Well, it's just——"

"Don't mind me…"

"Well, it's just that I'm running out of change for the phone, like. But I was gonna say, what about the fuzz? They're all over the place here – there was another patrol car coming as we were leaving – or if one of the women there clocks us, seeing as we're supposed to have checked out. Know what I mean, Mr Sneed? Mr Sneed… ?"

"Yeah, I'm still here."

"Well, what shall I do then?"

"Yeah. Yeah, you're right, son. It's too much of a risk. Too much at stake. Just have to be patient."

"And it's well hidden there. So—"

"Patience and cunning, Brrm-Brrm. That's what you need in this life. Patience and cunning."

"Right, Mr Sneed. Well, shall I just carry on to the Major's, like you said? Then we could pick it up tonight, when it's dark…"

"*No* – no. No, don't do that. Look – er – look, give me your number there first, in case the pips go."

He jotted it down and stood staring at it, his mind, with everything so neatly in place there only a couple of minutes ago, now bare.

"Mr Sneed…?" Brrm-Brrm said.

"Yeah. Look, give me – give me an hour. All right? Be there in an hour. And I'll ring you then. When I've had a think. OK?"

He put down the phone carefully.

Apart from anything else, what the hell was all that police business about? Cops all over the shop, patrol cars buzzing in and out. Had Brrm-Brrm and Clothesline just had bed and breakfast in the local police headquarters?

Well, whatever was going on there, it was going on with the money sitting under their noses. It didn't bear thinking about.

But that's precisely what he had to do.

He could tell Brrm-Brrm, he decided, after sitting at his desk staring at nothing, building Plan D from the ashes of Plan C, to drive back as arranged to the bingo hall, where he'd meet them. He could then say that, as the shop was still under surveillance, he was going to hide the Wolseley for now. He could tell them to take the rest of the day off, have a break. They deserved it. Oh, and if Brrm-Brrm would tell him where the money was hidden he – no, more reassuring if he said *they*, Tony and the Major as well, *they'd* pick it up when it was dark.

And then he and Clothesline could meet them for the share-out at the Major's.

He considered it. It wasn't perfect, but he had time to dress it up a bit, make it a little more convincing for Brrm-Brrm, before the Wolseley got back.

He picked up the phone, and was about to ring the number Brrm-Brrm had given him, when he remembered that he probably wouldn't be there.

He rang it anyway, and listened to it ringing on.

He wouldn't be there for another hour. And in less than that, he realised, Brrm-Brrm and Clothesline, in the story he'd given Tony and the Major yesterday, were due at the Major's. And if they didn't turn up there when expected then Tony, paranoid Tony, would be on the blower – or worse, turn up at the shop. He had to stall them.

Sneed had so little experience of telling the truth, that it took him a while, trying out various untruths, for him to realise that all he had to do, basically, was to tell the truth.

He got the Major first, called to the phone in the hall of his lodgings, and then Tony, grabbing it from him. He told them exactly what had happened and how he had told Brrm-Brrm he'd ring back in an hour when he'd had a think about it.

And then added a small invention of his own, and said he'd now had a think about it and decided that Brrm-Brrm should drive straight to the Major's as arranged, and then when it was dark they could all drive to this Batch Magna place and pick up the money.

He thought afterwards that considering how little experience he had at telling the truth, he'd obviously done it rather well. He'd expected suspicion and argument from Tony, and had got neither. He must, he told himself in a sudden mood of flippancy, do it again some time.

He made himself tea, and sat working on the story for Brrm-Brrm. He didn't have to worry about Clothesline. He could tell him anything, and did. But Brrm-Brrm's brains hadn't been pounded to porridge in the ring.

He was on his second cup when he heard a car pull up.

He leapt to his feet and standing one side of the window sneaked a look through the bars.

It was Tony and the Major, paying off a cab.

He pulled his head back, snarling, his mind jumping to the loaded Enfield in his desk.

You're not thinking straight, Harold, he told himself then fretfully, fearful of what he had in mind. What about the bodies, what would you do with the bodies? You've no car. And what about the noise? And the blood? You wouldn't be able to get the evidence out of the carpet, nagging at himself as if listening to someone else nagging at him, his back flattened against the wall, at bay, the voice going on and on in his head and the doorbell ringing.

And then someone started banging on the door.

That'll be Tony, so you'd better let them in, hadn't you, before old Payne takes it on himself to report a disturbance. You know what he's like, you know what old Payne's like.

The pawnbroker was trying to control his breathing, taking slow, deep breaths, in, shakily, through his nose while counting up to eight, and then out slowly through his mouth as he'd been taught, eyes closed on an image of an indoor garden in Lewis's department store.

He had come in out of the cold, an urchin in charity boots and clothes smelling of the streets, and had found summer in a country garden on the third floor. He had been transfixed, gazing enchanted at the shining flowers, the sound of water falling over rocks and birds twittering unseen under lights warming him like the sun.

It was like – it was like, he'd thought wonderingly, trying to tell himself a special story about it. But couldn't think of anything. He had nothing to compare it with. There were no special stories in his world, only rumours of them when Christmas was in the shops, or the Salvation Army sang about the Kingdom of Heaven on a street corner. There were no stories of any sort in his world, only his own, the bare, hard places of his life.

And when he was discovered there, warming himself among the flowers, and marched back down to the street, he had taken the scene away with him as if it were something he had stolen.

Years after that he had read about a calming technique using some remembered beautiful, peaceful scene. And although he had seen much of the world since, some of it under five-star foreign skies on the few occasions he hadn't drawn a Go to Jail card, and although he had long been aware that probably the only thing real in Lewis's indoor garden had been the water, his mind had gone straight back there.

He opened his eyes now, head jerking as if he'd nodded off, and felt the brief exhaustion he usually felt afterwards, like something left behind after the tide had gone out taking a turbulence with it, exhausted but safe, for now.

He walked carefully through into the shop, carrying his new-found calm like something fragile, his step as measured and as dignified as a butler's, a reproof to the vulgar clamouring on the doorstep.

Tony had his face up to the glazed top of the door, hand over his eyes, peering in, and banging on the wooden side.

The pawnbroker opened up and glanced at the window across the street. "Talk about drawing attention to yourself," he remarked mildly.

"Have you phoned him yet?" Tony barged in, followed by the Major, nodding a smile at Sneed, and carefully coming in sideways, back turned on the undertaker's.

The pawnbroker took his time locking the door again.

"Have you *phoned* him yet?" Tony demanded.

"They're still up there, you know," was all Sneed said. "I saw one of them earlier. The other one. The tail you collected as it happens. Keen to make up for losing you, no doubt."

"So what?" Tony growled, and turning showed himself through the glass top of the door. "There's no money here to *find!*" he shouted across at the undertaker's window, arms up, offering his hands as if to show them empty, or as if for handcuffs.

"Come on, Tony," the pawnbroker said soothingly, understandingly, sharing his calm. "Come on, son, let's talk about it in the back."

He led them through the shop, piled with household and personal goods, the last-ditch defences pawned to keep life at bay for a few more days, trays of jewellery, clothes, musical instruments, toys, radios, presents in their boxes, clocks, record players, ornaments, power tools, cameras, radiograms, and television sets showing the test card.

"I have to say, Sneed, that Tony has a point," the Major grumbled, following on behind. "After all, we did the job on Friday and now it's Sunday. If the labourer is worthy of his hire, and all that, you know. And I'd assured my landlady that I would have the rent for her without fail on Friday evening. In cash. Seems there was rather an embarrassing error concerning one of my cheques. I've complained to the bank, of course. Took it the highest level."

"Would you like a cup of tea?" the pawnbroker enquired politely, seeing them into the office and playing for time.

"No, we wouldn't like a cup of *tea,*" Tony snarled. "What we'd like is—"

"Fortunately for me," the Major went on stiffly, "she's prepared to take the word of an officer and gentleman. Nevertheless—"

Tony put a hand in front of the Major's face, shutting him up.

"Well, really!" the Major protested.

"Have you phoned him yet, Harold?" he said again, quietly, like a threat.

"I take it, Tony, that you are referring to Brrm-Brrm?" The pawnbroker hadn't yet decided whether he had or hadn't phoned him yet.

"Yes, I'm referring to Brrm-Brrm. Who else d'you think I'm referring to?"

"Well, what *I* want to know, Tony, is what you're doing here. You could ruin everything."

"Yes, I must say," the Major huffed, "I did rather—"

"An hour, you said." Tony stabbed a finger at his wristwatch. "You were gonna phone him in an hour. And it's gone that now. Unless you've done it already, of course, and don't want us to know for some reason…" His eyes were busy with suspicion.

Sneed ignored the remark. He calmly removed his own watch from his fob pocket, opened it and considered the dial. And then looked up at the electric wall clock.

"Fine timepiece, Sneed," the Major remarked. "Full-Hunter."

"It was somebody's anniversary present, it says on the case," the pawnbroker said slowly, his mind elsewhere. "Um – it's – er – it's antique. Twenty-two carat. Um… Beautiful movement, lovely precision. Fifteen rubies. Gold – er – gold plated wheels. But it's running a bit *slow*," he added sharply, and snapped it shut like a rebuke.

If there was an advantage to be had in telling them he'd already phoned Brrm-Brrm then he couldn't think of it.

"To answer your question, Tony," he said in a tone befitting a man with a full-Hunter, "no, as it so happens I have not rung him yet."

"Better get on and do it then, hadn't you, Harold," Tony said. "You know Brrm-Brrm, he don't like to hang about. Maybe you'd like me to ring him."

"No – no, I'd better do it. Might make him suspicious. There's a lot of it about," he added, picking up the desk phone, and hoping that Brrm-Brrm didn't know, or if he did had forgotten, the Major's old address.

Brrm-Brrm answered on the second ring.

"Ah, you're there then, son. Good. Right, well, what you do is drive straight to the Major's. As I arranged with you," he added for Tony's benefit. "And we'll take it from there — 'Ere, hold on a sec," he said then quickly. "I did give you the right address, didn't I? Didn't give you the Major's old one, by any chance? What did I give you...?" he asked, and then startled the Major by suddenly staring at him and grinning fixedly.

Sneed was hoping for inspiration. His mind seemed to have gone off station like a radio, and he was desperately trying to tune it back in, to remember, among the babble of thoughts, there suddenly like voices in his head, what was real and what was imagined, which of the Major's addresses actually existed and which was the one he'd made up.

And then just as suddenly the din cleared.

"Say that again would you, son, there was a bit of static on the line... Ah, right, well, it's a good job I checked, because I gave you his old address. Comes of having to think of everything," he said, and meant it. "Hang on, and I'll get you the right one."

Thankful he hadn't chucked the Major's new address back in the bin, and left with no alternative now but to give it to Brrm-Brrm, he read it off. And then said, yeah, that's right, son, agreeing with him that he didn't have to bother about parking problems, not at the new address, doing so absently, his thoughts already searching for a way out.

But by the time the minicab they'd arranged to take them to the Major's had arrived, he was reduced to a Plan E that even Clothesline could have come up with.

Chapter Twenty-Six

Phineas had also packed his bags, or at any rate one bag, telling Bill Sikes all about it while he was doing it, how they were off on a trip, taking a short break in Kent, and how he'd like it there, sniffing and cocking a leg round the dog runs in the local park.

But then, when he rang his aunt, a neighbour of hers answered. She was there, the neighbour said, to water his aunt's indoor plants while his aunt was away, on her first day of a fortnight's bird watching holiday in the Outer Hebrides.

Phineas put down the phone and told Sikes that he could forget about the dog runs in Kent.

Well, if he had to stay there then it would be just as well if he knew who was where and who could tell Sally what.

He rang the Hall.

Humphrey, who had just returned, answered.

Phineas, although he'd spoken to him earlier, asked him how he was. Splendid, splendid, he said, when Humphrey said he was fine, Phin, thanks. And then Phineas said it again then, when Humphrey told him the new sign was fine as well, and went on to agree that, yeah, it was great weather for Open Day.

There was a hole in the conversation after that, and Phineas, with an air of finding something to fill it, asked was there by any chance a lady police sergeant in the kitchen?

"A lady police sergeant," Humphrey repeated, as if reminding himself who he was to look for, and told him to hold on.

Humphrey came back and said, nope, there was no lady police sergeant in the kitchen, and waited, as if Phineas might want him to look elsewhere. Phineas apologised for running him around, and said in that case, how about Annie. Was Annie there by any chance?

Humphrey said he didn't see her there but he'd check. Then came back and said no, there was no Annie either, just his mom and Clem. Annie had apparently nipped back home before they started to get busy.

And then Phineas said again that he was frightfully sorry, and all that, but wondered, as she was there, if he might speak to Shelly?

"Shelly," Humphrey repeated, and went off to get her.

"Hello, Shelly," Phineas said, when she picked up the phone.

"Hi, Phin," Shelly said, and waited.

She did not, he noted, offer her congratulations. All may not yet be lost.

Unless of course Annie had got the Sergeant to open up when Shelly was out of the room. Annie was good at that, getting things out of people. She should be in uniform herself.

"Shelly, how *are* you?" he said then, heartily, making up for forgetting that she was on the other end.

There was a pause, and then Shelly said, "I'm swell, Phin, thanks. How are you?"

"Can't grumble, Shelly, thank you. Well, I suppose I could, but there's not much point, is there, as no one listens," he said with a little laugh. "Anyway, I was just – er – I was just saying to Humph, that – er – that the weather's excellent for Opening Day, isn't it. Couldn't be better, in fact. Cream teas under the horse chestnuts, and all that. Splendid."

"Yeah, we've been lucky," Shelly agreed, and waited again.

"Right, well, in that case, Shelly, I'll let you get on with it."

"OK, Phin, thanks."

Shelly didn't waste much time wondering what that had been about. She didn't know Phineas as well as Clem or Annie knew him, but after two years she knew him well enough.

Phineas next decided on a visit to the *Felicity H,* to sound Annie out.

He made his way down the Owens' moorings, watched by Megan, the long-eared milking goat with that look of hers which suggested that whatever the secret was, she was in on it.

Owain, in a battered straw hat, vest, belt and braces, a red-and-white kerchief round his neck and short stubby pipe clamped in his mouth, was doing a bit of re-caulking, scraping away at the bottom of his upturned fishing punt with a painter's filling knife. He was working in the tilting shade of a couple of alders, the punt, along with a pram dinghy and a rowing skiff, beached on a low bank to the fore of the paddler, a man completely at home there, at peace in his world.

Phineas could only envy him.

"Lovely day, Owain," he said glumly.

"Oh, hello, Phin. Ah, it's a hot 'un, all right," he agreed.

When Phineas then wondered, as if idly, if Annie was about, Owain, pausing to re-light his pipe, blew out smoke and told him she was up top with Ffion – having a women's talk, he confided, lowering his voice. Owain could only guess what that might mean, but the words were enough to keep him well away from any room the females engaged in it were.

A few seconds later came the sound of a splash from the river.

An unhappy conclusion by the sound of it, Phineas thought, gloomily making light of things, and reminded himself that he could always take that way out himself.

"That's our Ffion, gone back to her swim. So everything's all right now," Owain said with relief.

"Hello, Phineas!" Annie called.

Phineas shaded his eyes with a hand. She was leaning over the bow rail, a Welsh-dark figurehead gilded with the sun, face avid for gossip.

"Lo, Annie."

"Fancy a cuppa?" she said, motioning enticingly towards the stern and the kitchen.

"You having one, Owain?" Phineas asked, hoping he wasn't. Annie may not open up fully with Owain there.

"No, I'm all right," Owain said, perfectly content where he was. "You go on up."

As Phineas reached the deck of the paddler, Ffion Owen was climbing back up the steel ladder fixed to one side of the vented, fan-shaped paddlebox. Both of the boat's paddleboxes carried her name in fairground flourishes around their tops, and were painted still, as was the rest of the vessel, in the Cluny Steamboat Company's livery of Trafalgar blue and dark gold, the funnel of the *Felicity H*, which, as they did on the other boats, nowadays sent up smoke from a winter stove, ringed in the same colours.

Ffion came through the open gate in the rail, sleek with water, and it seemed to Phineas that she had shot up a few sizes almost overnight, the extra, generous inches tanned a dewy caramel and packaged in a gorse-yellow silk bikini.

She brushed the river from her dark hair and grinned at him.

"Fee," he said, shaking his head, "you must have the lads *queuing* up."

"Ah, and that's the trouble," her mother said.

"I had a postcard from Dan yesterday," Ffion said cheerfully. "With Donald Duck on it."

Daniel, his son from the first of his three marriages, was doing a post-graduate degree in America in higher mathematics, and Phineas could only wonder where he got the brains from.

Yesterday, or last week at the latest, so it seemed to him, he and Ffion had been the love of each other's young lives, sworn to undying devotion. And now he was just the name of another lad, and she just another of his friends to send a jokey postcard to.

Ffion clambered back up onto the paddlebox, and jumped from it again instead of diving out of sheer exuberance, the only *possible* response to being young on a day such as this and with the river waiting, whatever problem she had shared with her mother something else that was now in the past.

"Come on, Phineas, bach, and we'll have a nice cup of tea together, eh? Indoors, where it's cooler," Annie said persuasively, linking her arm through his.

"Do you want to tell me something, then, love?" she asked in a low voice, couldn't wait to ask, immediately they were in the kitchen. "Sit down. I'll put the kettle on in a minute," she went on, settling herself across the table from him, not taking her eyes from his, drawing him into her gaze.

"Tell you something about what?" he asked, leaning casually back in the chair.

"The *Sergeant*, Phineas," she said solemnly, leaving the Inspector out of it for now, until she knew how much he knew.

He started playing with the pepper pot on the table. "Why, what did she tell you?"

"Nothing. She didn't tell us nothing. Said she was sorry but she wasn't at liberty to," Annie said, and bit her lip, hearing, as Jasmine had, his imminent arrest in the words. "I mean, me and Shelly, we just thought it was another ticket for speeding or something." Her expression suggested just how wrong they had been.

Phineas gave a laugh with relief in it.

"Well, that's what it *is* about, Annie. A ticket for speeding. Which I haven't got round to paying yet. That's all. I'll sort it out first thing tomorrow. My word – talk about a waste of police resources. No, I – er – I just dropped in for a chat, you know, to pass a friendly word with a neighbour. That's all," he added, looking at her, his eyes as blue and open as the sky.

Annie could have wept for him.

She, along with Shelly, *had* thought that that was what it was about, a minor traffic offence, although, having more experience of these things than Shelly, she'd considered it odd that a sergeant, and one from Kingham, in a high-speed car, should be after him for it, when that sort of thing was usually dealt with by a constable from Church Myddle in a Panda, when he wasn't on a bike.

But then, not long before Phineas's arrival, Jasmine had dropped round to tell her not only about the Sergeant calling at the *Belle*, which of course she knew about, but, soon afterwards, a much higher-up officer calling there, and looking very serious about things, which she hadn't known about, her jaw dropping at the news.

That would be the Inspector! The one who turned up at the Hall afterwards, she'd told Jasmine.

"But he didn't mention that he was looking for Phineas – funny that, seeing as she did, the Sergeant…"

And it was only after Jasmine had gone that it occurred to Annie that it wasn't that the Inspector *hadn't* mentioned it, but that the Sergeant *had*, mentioned it when she wasn't supposed to.

That's why she'd looked guilty when the Inspector came in. She had blown her cover, as Miss Wyndham would say.

It made sense, Annie told herself.

And then her dark eyes grew wide as she went on to make sense of something else: Phineas's jumpiness lately when it came to the police.

She told herself not to be daft, and then almost immediately returned to it, appalled and fascinated. Before telling herself again not to be so daft, and then going back to it, until she didn't know what to think.

Or rather told herself she didn't know what to think, because she was already thinking it:

Phineas had been involved in the Shrewsbury job.

She could hardly believe it!

She had no idea of course who the rest of the gang might be, friends of his maybe from London. They do that sort of thing all the time down there, you only had to look at a newspaper to know that. And Phineas was easily led.

Annie smiled across at him now, a mixture of motherly concern and exasperation.

It would have been a game to him, of course. Be like in one of those crime books he writes, or another of his larks, and if he had a gun it would be a toy one, she added in his defence. Wouldn't be like real life at all, not the sort where people get hurt or go to prison, like.

Not that is until real people, in real police uniforms and driving real police cars started turning up. Then he'd do what he was doing now, looking all innocent, with the – it wasn't me, I didn't do it, and anyway, I don't know what you're talking about look she knew so well.

"What?" Phineas said suspiciously, suspecting by the way she was looking at him that she knew more than she was letting on.

Annie leaned towards him.

"Phineas… Phineas, bach," she said starting again, gently. "Are you *sure* now, love, there's nothing you want to tell your Aunty Annie?"

He gave another little laugh. "There's nothing *to* tell. I've already *told* you – it's about a speeding fine I forgot to pay, that's all. Honestly, what a ruddy fuss over nothing! Got any of those Shropshire Dunks, by any chance?" he asked then nonchalantly, peering over at where she kept the biscuit barrel.

Annie smiled her motherly smile at him.

"Yes. Yes, of course I have, darling," she said indulgently, and wondered where he'd stashed his share of the loot.

She knew what she'd do with that sort of money, she thought, putting the kettle on. Get a new car for a start, the floor's going on the old Land Rover. And one of them coloured cookers with a hood they've got in that shop in Kingham. And they could go on holidays, *abroad.*

"And I've got some home-made chocolate cake with marzipan, you like marzipan," she told him as she busied herself with the tea things, while Phineas sat with his hands behind his head whistling carelessly under his breath.

She couldn't decide if she should tell him what she knew, so that he could make a run for it, or whether they should hide him, move him about from boat to boat maybe, until the heat dies down.

She thought of nipping round to see Priny after she'd phoned Jasmine and told her, see what Priny thought.

But then it occurred to her that there was somebody who should be told before anybody, before she heard it from somebody else when the gossip started flying. It was only right.

And she was due home on Monday. So she'd wait until then, Annie decided, wait and tell Sally tomorrow.

Chapter Twenty-Seven

At that moment a toy gun also featured in young George's thoughts, a favourite of his, a pop-gun with a blue metal barrel and varnished wooden stock, about the right shape, if not the weight, of a sawn-off shotgun.

He didn't so much mind losing his Roy Rogers six-shooter, because one of the plates on the butt was broken. It had happened during a Red Indian attack when, out of bullets and determined to go down fighting, he'd accidentally bashed the iron leg of his bed with it.

George hadn't been interested earlier in accompanying Humphrey to pick up the new Open Day sign, choosing instead to play in the den he'd made in the hayloft of a disused stable until Humphrey got back. He'd been about to leave the building, to see if he'd returned, when he spotted, further down on the other side of the yard, the big tough-looking man he'd seen earlier in the breakfast room, standing by the open door of one of the outhouses.

He'd ducked back inside and watched as the big man's companion came out, brushing himself down, and furtively looking about. Then he closed the outhouse door and the two of them walked off towards the entrance.

George had waited a short while in case it was a trap.

If he hadn't seen what he'd seen he'd have known anyway that someone had been in there. He knew the Hall inside and out, and it was one of the places he'd plundered to furnish his den, taking among other things one of the tea chests to use as a table.

It had taken him longer to arrive at the back wall than it had Brrm-Brrm. He had to sort through the junk carefully, not knowing what he was looking for nor where it might be, but convinced that something had been hidden there.

But once he had arrived at the tea chests he didn't need his magnifying glass from his Junior Detective set to spot the first clue of the scrunched-up balls of yellowing newspaper scattered about in front of one of the stacks, and then that one of the chests, at the bottom half of the stack, had been put back upside down.

He toppled the top two tea chests so that he could get at those at the bottom. And when he lifted the upside-down chest off the other, carefully, in case they were booby trapped, found himself looking at the holdall.

It was up in his den now, its contents transferred to a large hessian potato sack from the feed store, which sat in a corner of the loft while he hesitated, pop-gun in hand.

But not for long. He'd have given far more than a favourite gat, as Humph would call it, to keep Humph from being sent downriver to the pen, and what that would mean for him and his family.

Because after clambering back up the stairs to his den, and finding the shotgun and Luger in with the money, all thoughts of Woolworth's sweets counter and even the train set and a new bike had fled.

He was looking, he knew, at the loot from the Shrewsbury robbery.

And it hadn't taken him long after that to come up with the rest of the picture.

Humph had not only been involved in it, he'd planned it.

He didn't know who the other two were, a couple of soldiers maybe, as Humph had called them when talking about New York gangsters. But whoever they were, Humph knew them all right, the way he'd been talking to them at breakfast. And he hadn't been telling them how to get to some tourist place, as he'd thought at the time, but where to stash the money and guns.

Humph had talked about being short of cabbage, as he'd called it, and now he had done what he used to do back in New York, when he was a gangland boss. He'd never actually *said* he'd been a gangland boss, or indeed any sort of criminal back in New York, but a nod had been a good as a wink to George. He knew what he knew.

George had removed the money and guns to stop his friend getting himself into trouble. He'd replaced them with his own guns and was now stuffing the holdall with wads of banknote-sized paper laboriously cut from piles of old newspapers he remembered having seen in the butler's pantry, the tip of his tongue out in concentration as if doing his homework, his face set, obstinate with loyalty.

He was going to put the holdall, with its new contents, back where he'd found it.

He had no real idea why he was doing so, except that he remembered Dick Drake, sleuth hound, doing something similar in one of his *Intrepid* comics, to help round up a gang of crooks. George didn't want to help round up a gang of crooks, or at any rate not all of them, and he had no idea what would happen then, or what his next move might be. He couldn't think beyond that, beyond what had happened in a comic, in a world that was his size.

Because George, despite his Junior Detective set, wasn't Dick Drake, sleuth hound. But a rather confused ten-year-old schoolboy who, under his capable, determined air, was somewhat lost and not unafraid.

The Major told his landlady, who popped her head out of her room as the pawnbroker and Tony followed him through the front door, that they were forming an amateur dramatic society and that another couple of members were due shortly.

And when Brrm-Brrm and Clothesline did turn up, and so obviously hadn't made their own arrangements with the money, he'd airily assured her that he would have the rent by tomorrow, dear lady, and the rest of the month's as well, if she so wished, before leading them up the stairs.

They sat aimlessly about in the Major's bedsit for a while, and then Tony suggested a game of poker, using Tony's cards and with Tony doing most of the winning, raking in their IOUs, to be redeemed when they returned with the money.

Sneed didn't mind, even though he was sure the cards were marked. At the end of the day, if all went well with Plan E, it would be he, Sneed, who would scoop the pot.

After a lunchtime sandwich and drinks in a local pub, it was decided to kill a few more hours by having a drive out to the Lickey Hills beauty spot, the Major when there complaining about the heat and the hills, Tony sullen and Sneed silent and plotting. Only Brrm-Brrm and Clothesline enjoyed themselves, as they did in the cinema that evening, sitting quite happily twice through the main feature, a western, until it was time to pick up the Wolseley.

Brrm-Brrm directed Sneed as far as the Batch Valley turn-off, and then they had more time killed for them, over an hour of it, caught in the lanes in the dark, until, like Brrm-Brrm had, they found themselves on the road leading to the bridge over the Cluny.

They thought there had been a power cut when they reached the High Street, only a couple of lights showing in the windows there, the one burning in the telephone box outside the shop a solitary street light.

The Hall too was in darkness when they pulled up outside the gates.

There was a good deal of whispering, with Tony stubbornly insisting that he was the one who should accompany Brrm-Brrm.

The two men quietly left the car and flitted from shadow to shadow up the drive to the stable yard, as the owls called across the village.

Tony kept watch while Brrm-Brrm was inside the building, stealthily moving the junk he'd been relieved to find was still there to one side, his torch moving now and then in the window, a smear of light behind the years of cobwebs and grime.

Tony had the collar of his suit coat up, his shoulders hunched as if against the cold. The country night unnerved him, its darkness and quiet and the alien smells and sounds, and the feeling of eyes watching from the shadows.

One of the horses in the stables further down blew through its nostrils, and a hoof was stamped, and he jumped again at a sudden owl hoot, sounding much nearer now, and as if trying to spook him.

"C'mon – c'mon," he muttered.

"What's he *doing* in there?" he said again, awhile later, eye jumping.

"Got it?" he whispered then, as Brrm-Brrm emerged, puffing a bit and carrying the holdall.

"Is it all there?" he couldn't resist adding, suspicion a reflex with him.

Brrm-Brrm came indignantly to a halt.

Not only had he done all the work, he had also not disappeared with the lot when he could have. When he'd thought of doing so again, on his way back to the A458, and wished now that he had. It would have been easy. Ask Clothesline to get out and check that his brake-lights were working properly, and then just drive off. Pick up his old mum and buy a bungalow on the Isle of Wight. She'd have liked that.

"What d'you mean, Tony!" he demanded. "I was the one who hid it there, remember? I could have just had it away, nicked the lot. All we bleeding well—"

"Shhh!" Tony hissed.

"*All* we bleeding well took," Brrm-Brrm insisted, "was expenses. Out of our share."

"OK, OK," Tony said, his hands up and glancing nervously about.

Brrm-Brrm dropped the holdall on the cobbles, George's guns clanking, and unzipped it.

"Count it if you like," he said, switching on the torch and handing it to the other man. "Go on – count it."

"Put the light out, you fool!" Tony snarled.

"Well, go on!" Brrm-Brrm said again, and turned the beam full on the holdall. "*Count* it."

"Why don't you shout while you're at it, eh? Why don't you do that? Maybe they ain't heard you yet. Put it out, you idiot!"

"Well then," Brrm-Brrm muttered, zipping the bag up.

"And come on!"

"Well, don't accuse people of taking things when they bleeding well ain't," Brrm-Brrm went on sulkily, trailing after him.

Sneed wound down the window when they appeared. "We thought you'd scarpered with it," he said with a little laugh.

Brrm-Brrm came to another halt. "It was hidden, Mr Sneed," he said pointedly. "I had to hide it. Behind a load of junk. And I had to clear all that junk away first to get it again. Because, you know what? Funnily enough, it don't shift itself."

"Come on, come on," Tony said, "let's get out of here."

"Never mind, son, we've got it now. Close the door quietly."

"It's all there then, is it?" the pawnbroker said then, about to switch on, glancing in the rear-view mirror at Brrm-Brrm, sitting, holdall on lap, in the back with the Major and Tony.

"What d'you mean, Mr—?" Brrm-Brrm started up.

"Yes – yes, it's all there!" Tony snarled. "Now can we get out of here! This place gives me the creeps…"

Compared to his other plans Plan E was a blunt instrument. Sneed, that criminal Mr Big, that master craftsman in Swiss-precision clockwork plots, was going back to the street for this one.

He was simply going to point a gun and take the money.

He was going to wait until the others were eagerly crowded around the holdall in the Major's bedsit, and then step back and produce the loaded Enfield.

Backing out with it and down the stairs would be the tricky bit. Clothesline would still be trying to work it out, frowning in that way of his, but the other three, seeing their wages disappearing out of the door, might perhaps be driven to desperate measures. But if he had to shoot one of them in the leg to show he meant business, he'd do it. He did not, when it came to plans, intend going any further up the alphabet.

And then straight for the M1 and his future.

And now, back in the Major's room, the holdall on the table, he had got as far as the stepping back part of it, his hand closing on the butt of the gun in the coat pocket of his going-away suit, when Tony, after unzipping the bag, eagerly dug into its contents and brought out a handful of cut-up newspaper.

Chapter Twenty-Eight

George's Sunday had been a rather strained one.

He'd hidden the sack first in one of the abandoned glasshouses, and had then decided that it wasn't safe enough there. He tried several places after that, before telling himself that they weren't safe enough either, trudging about the yard and grounds with it, while some of the Open Day visitors added him to the things to be looked at, even photographed, a scowling stable lad or gardener's boy, humping a rural-looking sack of something on his back.

He'd thought of hiding it in one of the boats in the boathouse, but then remembered Humph saying that he was taking his family out on the river that afternoon for a picnic. George had been invited, as he always was, whatever the treat, along with his mother. George's father, like Humphrey's, had died when George was much younger, which, when Humphrey had learned about it, was enough for him to tuck George immediately under his large wing.

But his mother, George knew, was visiting a friend that afternoon in Horton Cross, and he now had other things to think about.

And that's what he'd been doing, up in his den again, thinking about it, the sack back in the corner.

What he needed was somewhere to leave it until that afternoon, when his mother and Humph and his family would all be out, and he could come back and take it home, and hide it in his room.

And it occurred to him that, as it was first hidden outside the Hall, it might be safer until then inside. And he knew just the place.

And as a group of visitors were leaving the Hall through the French windows at the back, he went in the other way, through the front.

Clem and Annie were busy with cream teas on the lawn, while Shelly was sitting just inside the doorway, involved in the goings-on in the Sunday scandal sheet, the *News of the World*, a biscuit tin on a card table next to her filling up with the visitors' entrance money.

"Hiya, George," she said cheerfully. "Whadda you got there – rabbits?"

Sion Owen, the estate's game keeper, often took George rabbiting, something from which the Hall, George's mother, and Sion's pot all benefited.

"No, Mrs Strange. It's for upstairs. Work stuff for the room that had the rain come in," he said, on his way towards the end of the hall, for the door tucked in under the curve of the big staircase one side of a fireplace which in winter scented the house with wood smoke.

He went through into a worn flagged passageway, with service rooms off it, and up the back stairs at the end of it, which at the top brought him out into a narrow corridor with a slanting ceiling.

He was heading for what had once been one of the maids' bedrooms. The other rooms were now single guest bedrooms, but the roof above this one had sprung a leak, that section of the ceiling under it damaged, waiting for Humphrey to get round to it.

The carpet had been rolled up to one end of the room, the iron bedstead on its side in front of it.

He put the sack behind the carpet, pulling it up until it was hidden.

Free of his burden for now, he went back down using the main staircase, just as Humphrey was on his way up with a group of visitors. Bemused-looking visitors, some of them, as the 9th baronet, in a shirt with palm trees on it, filled them in, as he put it, on his ancestors lining the wall of the staircase, a small gallery in the manner of Gainsborough of past squires and their families, in silk waistcoats and dresses, with lapdogs and fowling pieces, posed in the drawing room or grouped with their hounds on the lawns under the horse chestnuts.

"Hiya, Georgie!" Humphrey broke off, as George made his way through the visitors.

"Hi, Humph," George said

George didn't hold it against him. He reckoned it was not having had a dad that did it. He didn't have a dad, either, and if he'd been brought up in what he now knew of New York, he probably would have gone the same way.

And he was in enough trouble as it was, when he went home for his lunch to the rented cottage in the village.

"Why didn't you go to Sunday school?" his mother demanded immediately he walked in.

"Don't lie!" she warned him, when George opened his mouth. Having not long returned from church, she *knew* he hadn't. Mrs Evans, church organist and Sunday school teacher, had made sure she did.

But George hadn't opened his mouth to speak but to cough. A cough he'd been practising on the way there, his excuse for missing Sunday school, throwing himself into it as if taken by a sudden, explosive fit of it.

"What are you doing?" she asked, frowning suspiciously.

"I'm coughing," he stopped to explain hoarsely. "I've got a cough. An awful cough," he intoned. "That's why," he went on, the words seeming to cost him effort, "that's why I couldn't go to Sunday school, Mum. I didn't want to disinfect people," he said, and started coughing violently again.

"Infect," his mother corrected absently, frowning on at him, unsure. She'd have understood immediately had it being a school day.

She fed him a spoonful of cough medicine, and felt his brow, and told him that if he was still doing it tomorrow she'd take him to the doctor's in Church Myddle. She suspected that for some reason he was putting it on, while at the same time being concerned that he might not be.

George said that he wouldn't be surprised if it was gone by tomorrow.

He stopped coughing long enough to clear his plate of a roast chicken lunch, and his mother said that as the cough seemed to have cleared up, he might like to come with her to Horton Cross.

George shook his head. He'd like to, but he could still feel it here, he said, tapping his chest, and started coughing again to prove it. "People don't want me coughing all over them," he got out, and gave her the sort of look he thought someone with a bad cough might give.

"Well, in that case you stay in," she said sharply, still unsure and stung by concern. "And that means no going out on the river this afternoon, not if you've got a bad chest."

George gave a hollow laugh, as if he found the idea sadly amusing. "I'm not going out on the river, Mum, or anywhere else, don't you worry," he said, causing his mother to do just that. It was only last night that he'd been burbling happily about the boat trip today.

She thought it best, she told him, if she called off her visit.

"No, don't do that, Mum," he said immediately. "It's not a proper cough, as such. No, it's – er – it's just hay dust lung," he

184

said, remembering a local farmer complaining about it in the shop, and thinking about his den. "I've had it before. It goes away after a bit, after a bit of rest. I found a lot more old hay in my den earlier and cleared it all out. It's hay dust, that's what does it," he said on a cough. "Don't worry about me, Mum, I'll be all right, honest."

"Now you're *sure* you'll be all right," his mother said a while later, when ready to go, George slumped on the sofa.

"Yes, course I will, Mum. I'll just sit here having a rest. I'll have a read or something, or see what's on the TV. I wouldn't be surprised if it's gone by the time you get back."

"Well, if you're sure... I won't be long."

And before leaving she said, "And don't worry about your room, darling, not if you're not feeling well. We'll do it together later, hmm?"

He stared at the door she'd just closed after her. He'd forgotten about his room. After saying all week that he'd tidy it, his mother had insisted earlier that it must be done by tonight.

After he heard his mother's car pull away he got wearily to his feet, coughing, before remembering that he didn't actually have a cough.

He was beginning to wish he hadn't started this. He felt as if he'd done a day's work already. And now he had to go all the way back to the Hall, get the sack from upstairs, lug it back, and tidy up his room before hiding it. A room even he had been forced to admit needed a bit of tidying, and do it well enough to satisfy his mother, to stop her going in and doing it again. And all before she returned.

That night Humph came looking for him in his dreams, came for the sack. The familiar, cheerful Humph he knew, or thought he knew, turning then with an evil chuckle, as if whipping off a mask, into somebody called Big H, a cigar stuck out of a corner of his mouth and a Tommy-gun under one arm, bursting out of a page of the *Intrepid* and shooting up the dresser in the Hall's kitchen, while he tried to run and found he couldn't because he was hiding in a tea chest, listening to Big H chuckling evilly as he climbed the stairs to his den, after he'd given himself away by having an awful attack of hay dust lung.

George woke just before Humph got to him, sat up rigid, heart pounding, in a room his mother had said she'd hardly recognised when she got back, a room *he* hardly recognised when he switched on the light.

There was nobody coming up the stairs, and the sack was still there, under his bed. Still waiting for him to do something about it.

He sat on the edge of his bed miserably thinking about it. He couldn't take it to the police, because it might lead them to Humph, the other Humph, the one he knew, and he couldn't tell his mother about it, because that's where he'd end up, being taken straight to the police.

He needed an adult, a grown-up person, to help him. He went over all the adults he knew in the village, and saw as it were, as if in a rescuing beam of light, the figure of Phineas Cook, tapping away at his typewriter on the deck of the *Belle*.

Of course! Phineas Cook. The same Phineas Cook who had once told him that his alter go, or whatever he'd called it, was a certain Detective Inspector MacNail of Scotland Yard.

He couldn't think why he hadn't thought of him before!

George laughed briefly and triumphantly. A sort of, he'd show them laugh – or rather *they'd* show them, he and Phineas Cook and Inspector MacNail of Scotland Yard.

They'd show them all right! he told himself gleefully, getting back into bed, much comforted, even if he did leave the light on.

Chapter Twenty-Nine

Nobody else moved or said a word in the Major's room when Tony brought out the first handful of what turned out to be cut-up newspaper, and then snatched up more of it with the same result.

Apart from Clothesline, who was still waiting stolidly for the money to appear, the difference between what they'd so avidly expected to see and what they were looking at was too great to do anything but wordlessly gape, watching as Tony dug deeper, feverishly burrowing into the holdall, scattering more newspaper over the table and on the floor, until he was satisfied that that was all that was in there, that and two toy guns.

Brrm-Brrm's mouth dropped open even further then, when Tony picked up the Roy Rogers six-shooter and pointed it at him.

"Good joke, Brrm-Brrm" he said, and eye working overtime, pulled the trigger.

"Well, if it is, it's in damn poor taste," the Major barked "What...?" he added on a less certain note, and looked at Brrm-Brrm with a faint, hopeful smile, as if waiting to be told that that was all it was.

Sneed and Tony were also looking at Brrm-Brrm.

Tony's hand slid into his inside coat pocket. But it was Sneed who claimed Brrm-Brrm's attention.

Out of nowhere it seemed, another gun had appeared, a real one this time, and the pawnbroker was holding it.

"What did you do with the money, Brrm-Brrm?" he asked, as if finding the joke highly amusing, his eyes stretched bright with merriment.

A joke that was now over, that's what his expression then said, switched suddenly, and fear took Brrm-Brrm to another place and the memory of a clown. A clown he'd seen once making an upside down smile, that's what the pawnbroker reminded him of now, and laughter bubbled and then turned to something else in his throat when Sneed cocked the gun and aimed it stiff-armed at his thigh.

"Where is it? Where's the money, Brrm-Brrm? What did you do with it? Come on, son, tell me, tell your dad." The pawnbroker spoke quietly, as if for Brrm-Brrm's ears only, as if drawing on something between them the others wouldn't understand, and looking sorrowful, with his clown's sad face, for what in a moment he might have to do.

Brrm-Brrm opened and closed his mouth a couple of times on words, and then said, "Eh – *eh*, now wait a minute – wait a minute, Mr Sneed, we didn't do this, this is nothing to do with us, is it, Clothesline. Clothesline…!" he said, trying to get the big man's attention while keeping an eye on the pawnbroker.

But Clothesline was involved with whatever was going on in his head.

Still in his black cowboy hat from Aberystwyth with the marshal's silver star on the front, he was holding George's pop-gun and looking from that to the newspaper pieces that should have been money and back again to the toy gun that should have been a sawn-off shotgun.

The Major cleared his throat sharply and glanced at the door of the bedsit. "Better tell him, Brrm-Brrm. There are people asleep in the building," he said, nodding with a pained smile at the gun.

Brrm-Brrm was holding his palm up as if to stop a bullet. "We didn't take it, Mr Sneed, on my mother's life. I mean if we was gonna nick it, we've have just nicked it, wouldn't we. We had the car, we could have gone anywhere with it. So why stay and do all this stupid stuff? I mean, it don't make sense, do it. And Tony, I said to you outside that building, I said you can count it if you like. I unzipped it and offered you the torch, didn't I. Well, I wouldn't have done that, would I, if I knew what was in it. I'm not that bleeding thick. I mean, come on..."

Brrm-Brrm ended on a note like a sob, and stood sniffing and breathing as if he'd been running.

"'Ere..." Clothesline said then, having put it together, "what happened to the money?"

"Good question, Clothesline," Tony said.

"It's gone, Clothesline," Brrm-Brrm told him, his eyes still on the pawnbroker. "They think we took it."

"And the guns. They were all in the bag here," Clothesline told himself.

And then the last bit got through. "He – y, we didn't bloody take it! We didn't take the money," he said, ponderously indignant.

"That's what they think, Clothesline. They think it's us. They think we nicked it," Brrm-Brrm said, edging nearer to his bulk, something to get behind if Sneed started shooting.

The Major cleared his throat again. "I have to say, Sneed, that it doesn't make a great deal of sense," he said reluctantly, saying goodbye to a last hope of getting it back, which, if they had taken it, wouldn't have been too difficult, not with Sneed in one of his moods and with a cocked revolver in his hand asking the questions.

Sneed came back among them.

"I'd forgotten I had this in the shop," he said conversationally, looking at the Enfield with interest, as if he'd just found it. "I brought it along in case we ran into trouble."

189

He released the hammer. "All right, son, OK," he went on, putting the gun away and getting down to business. "Well, if it wasn't you and brains here, then who did lift it?"

Brrm-Brrm spread his hands. "I tell you, I don't know, Mr Sneed. Honest. I know we didn't."

"We didn't," Clothesline echoed heavily.

"Well, somebody did. Somebody nicked it," Tony said, his eyes moving between the two men, but with his hand no longer in his inside pocket.

"When did you last have it, when did you last see the holdall?" Sneed asked.

"In my bedroom, at this Hall drum. I took out some expenses for us and then locked it in there. And then the next day – well, you know what happened then."

"Well, if the switch was made then," Sneed said, "it means somebody in the house did it. Was the door still locked when you got back?"

"Yes, it was, but they'd have the key, wouldn't they. I mean, if it was them, the owners, or somebody."

"Or perhaps someone saw them, witnessed them hiding it," the Major put in.

"Then why not just take it, if that was the case?" Sneed wondered. "Why go to the trouble of doing all this?" he said, waving a hand at the table. "That's what I don't understand. It doesn't make sense."

"Maybe it was kids," Tony suggested, nodding at the guns. "Looks like kids to me. The sort of thing kids would do. Any kids there?"

"They've got a nipper, but she's a girl, a little girl," Brrm-Brrm said. "There was a young kid, a boy I saw about the place a couple of times. I don't know if he belongs to them or what."

Sneed looked doubtful. "Would he have a key?"

"I dunno. He might have."

"Well, we know one thing. It's unlikely whoever took it told the cops, or we wouldn't have all this nonsense."

"Maybe it's the law that found it," Tony said. "You thought of that? Some of them rozzers he said was all over the place. Maybe they've got it. Maybe they were there after drugs, or something, and found it when they were turning the place over."

"Then stuffed the holdall with all that and stuck a couple of kid's guns in with it."

"Yeah," Tony said, nodding.

"What would they do that for, Tony?"

"Well, to cop us bang to rights of course, when we…" Tony trailed off.

"When we picked it up, you mean?" Sneed finished for him with a small smile.

"Yeah, all right, all right," Tony muttered, and moved his mouth as if chewing.

Brrm-Brrm had been thinking. "I reckon it's him, the big bloke, what runs the place. I reckon he took it. He's a Sir Somebody—"

"A Sir Somebody," Tony sneered.

The Major looked scandalised. "Really!"

"Yeah, but he don't sound it, or look it. He's a Yank for a start, and I think it might be a cover. I think he might be an American gangster, hiding out over here. And the guns, the kid's guns, what they might be is a message to us," Brrm-Brrm went on, warming to a memory of something like that in a film he saw once. "A warning, like, telling us that we're out of our league – stick to the playground, youse punks!" he snarled in a passable imitation of Humphrey's Bronx accent.

"I've told you, son, you watch too much telly," Sneed said. "Well, whether it was the Mafia, the FBI, or Comic-bleeding-Cuts, somebody's got our money. And I want it back."

"Then let's go and get it, if that's where it is," Tony said. "Let's go down tomorrow and put the frighteners on them."

"Yeah," Clothesline said, making a contribution.

"Tony, Tony," Sneed said, shaking his head. "That's blunt instrument stuff, son. I don't know, I thought you might have learned a few things, working with me. For a start, the law seems to regard the place as a second home. And I'd give a lot to know what that's about."

"What do we do then, Harold? Eh?" Tony said, smarting. "What do we do — knock on the door and ask *Sir* Somebody, please can we have our money back?"

Sneed pulled out the full-Hunter from his waistcoat pocket and consulted it.

"Well for one thing, Tony," he was able to tell him, "it's tomorrow already."

He snapped the case shut. "And for another, it would be too soon. They'd expect that, if we were going to do something about it, expect us to go steaming in. No, we'll wait. Put a bit of distance between us and it. I suggest we leave it till the end of the week."

"What, and give them time to hide it somewhere?" Tony said.

"Where? Where would they hide it, apart from there, at the house? Big place like that. And they can't very well bank it, can they, can't just turn up with a hundred grand in notes and a paying-in slip. I've told you, son, leave the thinking to me. No, we'll wait till the end of the week, then pay them a visit. And meanwhile, get some sort of plan together."

A plan this time, he told himself, that he would just have to make up as he went.

"Then all may not be lost," the Major said, and beamed optimism at them.

For the Major there was always that, always a bright side of life waiting somewhere, some sunlit uplands above the tiresome realities. A place where for him things really do work out in the end.

Chapter Thirty

Before Phineas left the *Belle* that morning, he made a phone call – he *had* to make a phone call. He had to do *something*.

Because it was now Monday, and Monday, today, this morning, was when Sally returned from Jersey. That's where he was on his way to now, to Shrewsbury, to meet her off the coach from Birmingham airport.

While the fiancée he'd managed to acquire while she was away was not a million miles from there in Kingham, doing whatever it was she did in the police station. The same Kingham, he reminded himself again, in which Sally lived, not a million miles from the police station.

The possibilities didn't bear thinking about.

At least he hoped that's where the Sergeant would be, in the police station. Because if she wasn't, if you can't speak to her, can't throw her off the scent, you're in it up to your neck, he promised himself – and it will all be *your* fault, he'd added, putting the blame for once squarely where it belonged.

But when he made the call he'd spent the past week putting off making, not expecting her to be there, now that he wanted her to be, because life doesn't usually work like that, she was there.

He was told, quite casually, as if it were just any enquiry, that yes, Sergeant Cholmondeley-Jones was on duty, and would he please hold the line.

He waited, preparing himself to say what he'd been practising to say, another bit of fiction he'd come up with, inspired both by the need to get off the hook, and by guilt. It would, he considered, be a face-saver for her and, as a man who had retained a sneaking suspicion that even our smallest doings are recorded somewhere, a deserved penance for him – he would forever be expecting the hand of the law, as it were, to fall on his shoulder, to bump into an off-duty sergeant while shopping in Kingham, or pull up at the traffic lights and find her sitting in the car next to his.

It's me, he said, owning up immediately when she answered. Phineas. Cook, he added, as if confessing to the rest of it. And the Sergeant slumped in her chair with relief, seeing the end of this ghastly business finally in sight, seeing herself able to look Ted in the eye again.

Thank goodness! she said. I've been trying and *trying* to contact you.

And she was about to break it to him gently, to say the things *she'd* been practising to say, a different sort of fiction, about two lonely hearts wandering, lost, and meeting under the ill-favoured stars, and love on the rebound, when he got in first.

Open lines have ears, he said tightly, so please don't talk. Just listen. He told her he had to go away. Abroad. Far away, he emphasised. On a mission. A secret mission, he remembered to add. He wasn't allowed to say where, because, well, because it was secret, he went on, while she tried to get a word in. But if it should be that she doesn't hear from him again she should fear the worse. And if that is to be his fate, then remember, as he would till the last, what they once had, however briefly, and be glad.

The Sergeant got a word in then, just before he put down the phone, the romantic in him as much involved in the story as he imagined the Sergeant to have been, calling his name when he said a regretful goodbye in what he took to be a wail of anguish.

He felt an absolute rotter! As bad as her first fiancé – no, worse, much worse, he decided, not sparing himself.

See it, he advised her, picturing her weeping in the Ladies', as she'd told him she had over her first fiancé, as making room for a new chap waiting in the wings, someone who this time will *really* appreciate you.

Third time lucky, and all that, you know, he added, encouragingly as he saw it, stilling his guilty heart as the Sergeant would have put it.

But he *had* to do it. To be cruel only to be kind, he told her, and himself, on his way out, after giving Bill Sikes an extra helping of dried pigs' ears before leaving him behind, just in case.

He only hoped the rest of that particular quotation didn't apply. Something, if he remembered correctly, about bad, or maybe even worse, beginning.

After his mother had left for Church Myddle and work, now that his hay dust cough had completely cleared up, George, after nipping over to the Hall to see if the holdall had gone, took up the sack once more and set out in better heart for Phin's place.

Other adults in the village, largely introduced to him by his mother, or either Humphrey or Clem, were given their proper title, Mr that or Mrs the other. But when Humphrey had introduced Phineas to him, he hadn't hesitated in introducing him not just as Phineas but Phin. And George hadn't had to think twice about addressing him as such. It was, both he and Humphrey seemed to feel, something that was in the natural, unquestioning order of things.

Instead of going the shortest way to the river, straight down the High Street, George, sack on back, took the long way round, just in case, up the lane running alongside the churchyard, and over a stile, skirting the village and taking to the fields until he reached the lane down to Taddlebrook Leasow, a long stretch of pasture running down to the Cluny.

He left Taddlebrook and walked back towards the village along the riverbank until it turned into Upper Ham, where he came to a surprised halt.

Ahead of him, parked up on the verge, should have been Phin's car. But the Frogeye wasn't there.

Perhaps he's hidden it somewhere, he thought, for no particular reason.

He hadn't gone beyond this, Phineas and the *Belle,* and he went through the gate anyway, and called his name from the bottom of the gangway.

But Phineas obviously wasn't there.

Phineas wasn't there but Bill Sikes was, narrowing his eyes at him from the deck, a growl rumbling.

George ignored him.

He hadn't realised just how much he'd expected Phin to be there. He felt he'd been led to believe he would be, as if that's what was *meant* to happen next. He had arrived as it were at next week's instalment to find there was no next week's instalment. Just him, left holding the sack.

Well he'd had enough. He'd done all the work so far. He'd made the switch under the noses of the crooks, and had done all the lugging about the grounds with the money and guns, hiding them in the Hall and then having to go out with his cough to get them again, and then tidy his blasted room so his mum wouldn't find them, and then cart them across fields and over stiles and through hedges and up and down lanes, and he'd had enough.

Whether Phin liked it or not he was going to leave the sack there.

Let somebody else do the work for a change, he grumbled to himself as he humped it up the gangway to where Sikes waited, his scut of a tail ecstatically busy, a chewed-looking tennis ball dropped invitingly at his feet.

George gave the boxer's great head a couple of pats on his way past, and followed hopefully by him with the ball, carried on towards the stern and through the first door he saw open, and left the sack there, in the kitchen, dropped his burden, and went off to play with Bill Sikes.

Instead of driving straight to her flat after he'd picked up Sally, she suggested that they stop off first at Batch Magna with the holiday presents she'd bought for a few people.

And then, she said, lightly resting a hand on his leg, we could go back to my place if you like, for a spot of lunch.

Phineas laughed. "That's what they call it in Jersey, is it?" he said, looking at Sally and Sally looking at him, and nearly drove off the road.

They dropped off the presents on their way to the *Belle*, stopping at Miss Wyndham's, Tom Parr's, the Hall and the rest of the paddlers with a mixture of duty-free drink and tobacco and perfume.

She even had a present for Bill Sikes, a brightly-coloured squeaky ball, which, after abandoning his old tennis ball, he immediately started to play with, squeaking and growling his way round the deck with it.

Phineas suggested a cup of something, and he had filled the kettle and put it on before he noticed the potato sack propped up against the fridge.

He frowned, opened the top to look in, and almost immediately closed it again.

"What's that, then?" Sally, sitting at the kitchen table, asked with mild interest.

"Hmm?"

"The sack. What is it?"

"What, that? It's – er – it's a sack," he said, and gave a little laugh.

"Yes, I can see that. I meant what's in it?"

"It's – er – it's a potato sack, Sally," he said with another little laugh. "With potatoes in it."

"Awful lot of spuds."

"Well, yes, I suppose so. I – er – I buy them in bulk. Yes, it's – er – it's much cheaper that way. Much cheaper. Buying them in bulk."

Sally was immediately interested. "Oh. Where's that? Penycwn?" she asked, referring to a discount shop across the border.

"No. No, not that shop. Another shop. I don't think you know this shop. It's a potato shop – well, I say a potato shop, it's a greengrocer's shop, I suppose you'd call it."

"Oh, where's that?"

He stared at her, seeing what he'd done, and wondering, with his wide experience of women, why he'd done it, why he'd mentioned 'shop' and 'cheaper' in the same sentence. She'll never leave it alone now.

"Church Myddle," he decided. "Yes, in Church Myddle. But not a part you'd know, I don't think. It's just a little shop in one of those little side streets near the station, you know? It doesn't even look like a shop. Looks like somebody's front room turned into a shop. That sort of shop. You could walk past it without realising it was there. Actually, when I say I buy them in bulk, it was a one-off really. I was driving past one day and saw the notice. Cheap potatoes, I think it said, something like that. It's closed down now, I think. Turned back into a front room. It was probably a closing down sale – now, Sally, why don't you park yourself outside while I organise things here. Relax, look at the river. You're still officially on your hols. No – do as you're told for once, Nurse. Off you go," he said, steering her to the door. "I'll bring the tea things out."

As soon as she'd gone he took another look

God knows how much was there, but it was real all right. It wasn't pretend money or have the word Sample stamped on it, and it was endorsed by the Bank of England and with Her Majesty's head where it should be, and holding a couple of them up to the light he could see the silver threads embedded in them. There didn't seem to be a note with it.

He stood looking at the sack with an expression which suggested he was trying to remember what it was doing there.

All right, he'd had a few drinks in the pub last night. And who wouldn't, what with one thing and another lately. But *surely* he'd have remembered if a sackful of banknotes had entered into things at some stage?

And come to think of it, he couldn't remember it being there when he made coffee earlier, and had to go to the fridge for milk. And he'd have remembered had it been there then, surely?

It was bizarre.

Bizarre and utterly inexplicable, he told himself again, out on deck afterwards with Sally, smoking a duty-free Gauloise after tea, under the Martini sunshade from the Patio Living pages of one of Bryony Owen's catalogues. It was, beyond the least doubt, simply the most bizarre and inexplicable thing that had ever happened to him.

There must of course *be* an explanation, but he couldn't for the life of him think what that might be.

Maybe it was a mistake, left at the wrong address, the wrong paddler. But then who...?

No. No, not even his imagination, which was able to accommodate all sorts of implausibilities in his books, could tie anyone on the river in with a sack stuffed with banknotes.

It didn't make sense. It did not make *any* sort of sense...

"Are you listening, Phineas?" Sally wanted to know.

"Hmm...?"

"I said are you listening. You seem to be—"

"Yes, yes, of course I'm listening. No, I was just picturing your plate of – what was it again?"

"French seafood. Plateau de fruits de mer. Absolutely delicious. Of course the island is part French."

"Oh, quite."

"Some of the perfumes there! *Heavenly…*"

"Yes, I imagine," he murmured.

And Sikes, it occurred to him. What about Bill Sikes? The curious incident of the dog that didn't bark – or snarl, or do anything else. Or if he did, whoever delivered the sack either knew him or was prepared to call his bluff. Even more bizarre and inexplicable.

"And all duty free, of course."

"Of course."

"I treated myself to a bottle of L'Heure Bleu."

"So I should think."

"I'll wear it for you today, if you like. When we get to my place," she added, the swell of promise in her low voice luring him from thoughts of money, from pondering just how much might be sitting there in his kitchen.

Would it, he wondered, when following her down the gangway, be enough to buy a pier?

Chapter Thirty-One

Annie went through the door which led to what had once been the booking office and waiting room of the Cluny Steamboat Company, and out on to the old hay wharf that had once been the CSC's landing stage and was all now part of the moorings of the Cunninghams' paddler, the *Batch Castle*.

Both the building and landing stage looked much as they did in those days. There was a wooden triangular pediment still under the eaves, like that of an old branch line station, hanging baskets of geraniums, a couple of them dressing a Victorian lamp post that had once flared in the river mists, and begonias blooming in fire buckets, and yellow ramblers and crimson roses under the office windows a velvet sweetness on the air.

She thought how pretty it looked, and how nice and tidy it all was compared to the *Felicity H's* junkyard. Proper little home it is, she thought with a rush of sentiment.

A proper little home she was about to suggest that they leave.

And not only that, she shouldn't, she reminded herself again, even be in the *position* to suggest what she was there to suggest. Because what she was there to suggest was a result of something Priny, in a moment of weakness, had told her last week, and had then told her not to tell anyone else.

But she *had* told someone else — two someone elses, in fact. Clem and Humphrey. Because she'd then had an idea.

And while Clem and Humphrey had listened of course with great sympathy when she told them what Priny had told her not to tell anyone, they lost no time at all in agreeing to Annie's idea – especially Humphrey, who had not only agreed, but in his excitement reminded Annie of a child, a rather large one, it's true, who'd just learned what he'd been given for Christmas.

He'd wanted to rush off there and then and tell them. But Clem had suggested it would be better coming from Annie, who had known the Cunninghams far longer than either of them. The same Annie to whom the confidence which had started this had been solemnly entrusted.

The same Annie who was now walking up the gangway, half hoping that they, and in particular Priny, weren't in, while suspecting they probably were, because their car was there, parked up on the verge.

The Commander certainly was in, smoke from his pipe drifting through the open door of what he called the wardroom, and their Welsh collie, Stringbag, named after the Fleet Air Arm's nickname for the Swordfish aircraft, was also in, sprawled below the wardroom's short flight of steps.

The dog lifted his head to get a look at the visitor, moved his tail dutifully a few times when he saw who it was, and then went back to the warmth of the deck and the sun.

Annie found Priny in the sitting room, busy with a carpet sweeper, in large orange hair rollers under a Hermes silk scarf, and wearing one of her husband's old county check shirts over a pair of red toreador pants.

She'd cleaned the sitting room several times over the past week, and the bedroom, and kitchen and bathroom, which wasn't at all like Priny, something which the Commander had noted and had spent the past week wondering if he ought to comment on it.

"Oh, you're busy – I'll come back later," Annie said quickly, turning to leave again.

But Priny, peeling off a pair of daffodil-yellow kitchen gloves, said she was glad of an excuse to stop, and that anyway she'd been thinking of making tea.

And while she was making it Annie sat in a sitting room smelling of furniture polish, and rehearsed again what she was going to say.

As soon as Priny had taken the Commander out a cup, and they were sitting at the table with the tea things between them, she took a breath and said, "Priny – Priny, you know what you told me last week about your arthritis getting worse and how you weren't looking forward to another winter on the river, and all that, and told me not to tell anybody...?"

"Yes," Priny said simply, pouring tea.

"Well, I did. I did tell somebody. I told Clem and Humph," Annie confessed, and bit her lip.

"I see," was all Priny said, looking unsurprised. "Try one of those chocolate biscuits, darling. They're rather tasty. Got bits of hazelnuts in them."

Annie ignored the biscuits, her eyes on her friend.

"You're not mad at me, then?"

Priny shook her head. "No, I'm not mad at you."

"Because I did it – well, the reason I told them, Priny, is that I had an idea."

"I see," Priny said again.

Annie got the rest of it off her chest.

"My idea – and I hope you don't mind me suggesting it to them – my idea was – and Clem and Humph liked it, especially him, mad keen, he was on it – my idea was that the estate has the *Castle* and you and James have the vacant Masters' Cottage – the one with a hole in the roof, but Humph says he can fix that and the rain damage inside easily before the winter," she said in a rush.

"That was my idea..." she added lamely.

Which was something else Priny didn't look surprised to hear.

"Don't let your tea get cold, darling," she said.

Annie took a sip, her eyes on her friend.

"So what do you think then?"

Priny put her teacup down.

"Well, it's all very sudden," she said, not looking as if she found it anything of the sort.

"Well, as you said yourself, Priny, a decision has to be made."

"Yes," Priny agreed, "a decision has to be made. And thank you for thinking of us."

"Well then…?"

"Well, I suppose it would meet the business of paying rent. Some of the sums people are asking these days, even for a one-bedroom flat in Kingham – what with that and the price of gin."

Encouraged, Annie went on, "And it means you wouldn't have to think about leaving the village, to go to Kingham or anywhere else. And you'd be as near to the old river as you can get without sitting on it. That's the main thing, Priny. You wouldn't be on the water come the winter."

"But all other considerations aside, Annie, the cottage, with or without a hole in its roof, must be worth far more than the *Castle*. One must be practical about these things," she added vaguely.

Annie had an answer to that. Humphrey had suggested a straight swap, the boat for the deeds to the cottage. But Annie knew the Cunninghams, knew what they would and would not consider.

"Ah, well, what it is, see, is that you'd have the cottage until you – er – well, you know…"

"Until we go to sleep with the fishes," Priny said with a laugh. "Until we die, you mean, darling."

Annie wasn't having anything quite so final. "Until you don't need it no more," she said firmly. "Then it goes back to the estate, like."

"I see," Priny said, seeming to be perfectly satisfied with that.

"You'd have it, like us estate pensioners, rent free. And they're nice little cottages – two bedrooms, gardens front and back. Well, you know that yourself. Lovely little homes, they are. And you'd be just across the road from the river. You can *see* it from the windows. Well, from the front, anyway."

Annie waited.

Priny looked around the room as if already saying goodbye to it.

"And what does he have in mind to do with her?" she wanted to know, before saying anything else.

Annie shifted an eager bottom on the chair. "Ah – ah, that's the other bit I have to tell you. You'll never guess. Humph was talking about getting the old *Castle* out on the river again. Working her, like. Next summer." She laughed. "He was getting all excited about it, he was. Talking about getting the engine going again and doing trips up and down to Shrewsbury, like she used to. Like they all used to. What about that then?"

"My word," was all Priny said.

"And that's not all. He wants the Commander to be master. And Tom doing his old job as engineer, but with Sion as fireman, now that Tom's getting on a bit. Got the shoulders for it, our Si has. I know it sounds daft, and all that, Priny. But if you think about it, she's sound enough, your boat. I mean, you don't have to keep the pump on for most of the time, like we do, do you. And they've already done all that work on the old engine," Annie said, meaning the Commander and Tom Parr, an ex-CSC engineer.

What was left of the *Castle's* engine had been slowly added to with the working parts salvaged from the PS *Sabrina,* the fifth vessel of the CSC that had blown a boiler in a river race and lay upstream, a diving board for generations of village children and with moorhens nesting in her broken wheels. And Priny hadn't minded them playing with what she called their Meccano set, hadn't minded their dreams, as long as they washed their hands before they sat down to eat.

"Well, what do you think then, Priny?" Annie asked, and then nodded and grinned at the sheer on-the-river fun of it, when it became perfectly clear what Priny thought.

"I'll get James," she said.

The wardroom, which had once been the wheelhouse of the *Batch Castle*, now served as a small study and bar. A room stuffed with books and bottles, and copies of ancient charts, like storybook charts, marked with brimming treasure chests and spouting whales, and warnings of monsters, and cherubs with winds on their breath.

Here, the Commander pursued his studies into the nature of such things as earth time, the fourth dimension, the Bermuda Triangle, the location of lost Atlantis, and the unconquered oceanic worlds he was convinced existed in chasms deeper than Everest is high.

He left the heavens to their maker. He never bothered with outer space, except to wonder at the stars. Whatever waited beyond those he addressed in church each Sunday.

It was his contention that God had given us enough to think about on this world without wandering off, like bored inattentive minds in a classroom, with thoughts of what may or may not be happening on other worlds. The Commander, as far as he was concerned, hadn't finished yet with this one.

And now, in an old pair of ducks with a Royal Yacht Squadron tie for a belt, and wearing an ancient rowing cap, he was busy with his present preoccupation concerning the nature of time as we know it – or rather don't know it.

This new study of the time phenomenon was prompted by a remark he came across of St Augustine's, that if no one asks him what time is, he knows what it is. But if he is asked what it is, he no longer knows. And that, periodically during his current exploration into the subject, was Priny's job, to ask the Commander what is time.

So far, he had been unable to give her a satisfactory answer.

But due to a quite unexpected revelation the other morning he felt he had moved a step nearer, had at least, as he put it in his notes, established a direction of flow.

The Commander, who didn't bother with the tedious business of trying to understand a thing before deciding whether to believe it or not, had ploughed with mounting impatience through theories on linear time, vertical and horizontal time, absolute and relational time, and time, as it were, happening at the same time, in simultaneous futures, presents and pasts, before deciding that they were all looking at it the wrong way up, or rather round.

He had travelled beyond Newton's clocks, Einstein and Relativity, Bergson and Duration, Gödel's loops, and quantum theory, and had arrived the other morning in the kitchen, with a force of revelation similar to a witnessed apple falling or Archimedes in his bath, at the evidence of his wife's egg-timer.

An hourglass, that ancient ship's aid to navigation, linked to the stars and the magnetic compass.

It revealed to him in that instant that the past emptied into the present and became the future. That time was unchanging yet constantly changing, whether horizontal or vertical, latitude or longitude, or any variations on them (although he couldn't yet see its place in the jigsaw, it hadn't escaped his notice that to precisely locate points on the earth's surface, degrees longitude and latitude have been divided into minutes and seconds). The past becoming the present, and then the future, and then the past again.

In short, time, he had discovered, went round in circles.

Which was precisely what the Commander was doing at that moment, under the heading on his notes of 'The Circular and Repetitive Phenomenon of Time', finding himself frustratingly back once more where he'd started from, when he had to suffer another interruption by the First Lieutenant, calling, "Ahoy the bridge", or some such nonsense, and bearing, he had no doubt, another cup of tea, when he hadn't started yet on the first one.

He regarded her sternly with his good eye. In the other, Ringwood, a foxhound by Stubbs, had its tail up.

"James – we have a visitor," she said.

Something in her tone alerted him, and he suspected that it might be a representative of the bank, there to press their damn impertinences in person.

Well, he was more than ready. It would save him having to spell out what he thought of the cut of their jib in another letter to them.

Leaning on his badger head stick, his leg stiff after sitting for a couple of hours, he came awkwardly back down the wardroom steps and determinedly followed his wife along the deck, listing a little but under full sail and ready to engage.

And found Annie Owen sitting at the table, nibbling on a biscuit.

"Annie, my dear," he said, removing his cap, and peering round the room in case they'd parked the banking person somewhere.

"I thought you might have been the bank manager – or account executive, or whatever absurd, puffed-up, self-important title these people award themselves these days. We had another of their blasted letters the other day, an impertinent, semi-illiterate drone obviously dictated by an I-speak-your-weight machine. I was—"

"Sit down, James, please," his wife told him. "Annie has something to tell you."

Chapter Thirty-Two

As soon as he was decently able to do so, Phineas told Sally that he had to be back in Batch Magna to see Clem about some more advertising she had in mind. Sally said she also had things she wanted to do and suggested she come over later and do dinner.

"Some sort of salad I think, in this weather."

"And I'll sort out a bottle of something decent to officially welcome you back aboard," Phineas said with a quick goodbye peck.

Back on the *Belle*, having lost no time in getting there, he absently patted Bill Sikes, waiting for him on the top of the gangway, and headed for the kitchen.

It was still there. He hadn't dreamt it, or imagined it. It was still there. A sackful of money sitting in front of his fridge.

Leaving Sikes on deck to guard his back, he shut the kitchen door and putting the sack on a chair started unloading it on to the table to count it.

And then he froze as the door opened and George, followed by Bill Sikes with his tail busy, strolled in and told him casually that he'd find a couple of gats in there as well.

"*Real* guns. Take a dekko," he invited him cheerfully, and parked himself down at the table. "I dumped it in here, Phin, 'cause you were out. I thought you'd know what to do about it."

Phineas had his mouth open, gaping at him.

"Go on," George said, smiling and nodding encouragement at him. "They won't bite you."

Phineas did as he was told, feeling curiously detached from it as he did so, as if dreaming it, as if watching himself bringing out more money and then the guns.

He stared at them, laid them gingerly on the table, and then looked at George as if awaiting further instructions.

George, an old hand at this by now, laughed.

"They're not loaded, Phin. The shotgun was but I took the shells out, home-made jobs by the look of 'um. I put a couple of my own gats in their place. Got any lemonade?"

Phineas opened his mouth to say something, and found he couldn't think of anything.

Moving as if in a trance, he got George lemonade and a glass and the straw he liked to use, and automatically added a plate of chocolate biscuits.

And then sat down, slowly.

"Got the picture yet, Phin?" George asked, sharing a biscuit with Sikes.

Phineas didn't look as if he had.

"The big un, in Shrewsbury The wages job. On Friday," George elaborated. "There's a hundred thousand smackers there all together," he added casually, nodding at the banknotes and the sack sitting on the chair.

George shook his head. "You gotta hand it to the guy," he said, sounding like Humphrey, or rather sounding like Humphrey sounded when he was trying to sound like a gangster.

Phineas found his voice.

"What guy?" he asked faintly.

"Humph, of course."

"Humph…?"

"Yeah. He was the brains behind it."

"Humph was the…?" Phineas's sense of unreality grew.

"The brains. The mastermind. Mr Big. That's why it's here, Phin. That's why I brought it to you, so he don't get caught."

George then went on to tell him the rest of the story, the things Humph had told him about his days in New York, and how he'd come to make the switch after remembering him talking to the crooks at breakfast and putting two and two together.

While Phineas sat staring at him, digesting it.

"These two men, George," it occurred to him then with a start. "Are they still there, at the Hall?"

George looked at him. "Course they're not. They're keeping low somewhere, till the heat's off. And then Humph'll deliver their share of the loot to them. The old briefcase switch in a busy airport or railway station, I wouldn't be surprised. Or in a park, on a bench. Or when feeding the ducks," he said, looking less sure of that one.

"Course here, he'll prob'ly just drive out into the country somewhere to make the drop. That's what he'll prob'ly do," he decided, and went back to his lemonade.

"Well, why then, George," he said carefully, "if you're right, why go to all that trouble? Why not simply take their cut and go? Why stay overnight? And why then hide it? Hmm…?"

George's shoulders slumped in an exasperated sigh. "'Cause he *told* them to."

"Yes, but *why*—?" Phineas started.

"He's got his plans," George said darkly. He shook his head. "He's his own worst enemy," he added, having heard his mother say that about someone.

Phineas was trying to think what to say or do next. It occurred to him, not for the first time, that real life was often a good deal less tidy than fiction.

And do Clem and Shelly know about it? he caught himself wondering. No, no, of course they don't! he told himself irritably. Nor does Humph.

"Now look, George," he started firmly. "Look, George," he said again, appealing to him. "Look – well, let me put it this way. I don't know what that was about, the conversation in the breakfast room. But… But well, whatever it *was* about, I don't think Humph would… And well, Humph as a mastermind of anything. It just doesn't… well, it just doesn't, that's all…"

And then something else occurred to him. "Have you checked yet to see if the big bag is still there?"

George stopped sucking long to tell him that yes, he'd checked, and no, it wasn't.

Phineas could only wonder what that might mean, when whoever got the thing back to wherever, and opened it.

"I've got their number, you know," George said then.

"What number?"

"Their number. Their car number."

"You've got their car number…?"

George nodded over his straw, and then said, "I saw the other crook, not the big tough one, the other one, going in with the bag when I was coming round the side, from the kitchen. I had my car number book on me so I took theirs down," he said, and went back to his drink.

"Well, George, don't you see?" Phineas said. "All we have to do is to hand it to the police, let them sort it out. And you'll get a reward, you know. Ten percent I think, that's the usual amount. Ten thousand pounds. Ten thousand *pounds*, Georgie! What would your mother think of that!" he said enticingly.

But George wasn't to be bought. He was staring down at the table top, shaking his head slowly and implacably.

"No!" he said firmly. "No, we *can't* do that. It would in – it would incrin…"

"Incriminate?"

"Yes. Yes, incriminate. It would incriminate Humph. We can't do that," he said again, simply, the end, as far as he was concerned, of the matter.

"George – Georgie," Phineas said, trying to think of the best way to put it. "George, I don't think Hump was involved, I really don't." He put up a hand. "Now, I understand why you thought so, but I—"

George was shaking his head again. "We are not going to the cops, Phin."

Phineas tried again. "Look... look, George, old chap, I applaud what you did, I do really. It took initiative and considerable courage, and was the act of a true friend. But these tales of Humph's about New York gangsters, and all that. They're just – well, they're just that, tales, stories," he went on, not without sympathy, always ready to believe a good story himself.

"I mean, if he had actually *been* a gangster, he wouldn't have talked about it, would he?" he asked reasonably.

George gazed steadily at him. "Wouldn't he, Phin?"

"Well, no. No, he wouldn't. I mean—"

"What, never heard of a double bluff?" George said. Because Dick Drake, sleuth hound, had.

Phineas stared at him for a few moments, and then at the money and the guns, his expression showing the difficulty he was having in making it add up to Humphrey.

For one thing, it occurred to him, putting aside for the moment the thought of Humphrey masterminding anything, how did he *know* there was a wages robbery waiting to be masterminded?

He opened his mouth to voice that, and then closed it.

Now he came to think of it, he remembered a few weeks back Humphrey telling him about driving round the outskirts of Shrewsbury, trying to get up into the town centre and getting hopelessly lost. He could have seen the money being delivered then. That was a Friday. He remembered it because it was Owain's birthday, that's what Humph was doing there, looking for a present.

No! No, it was absurd – *absurd,* he decided firmly.

And then he remembered the reports describing one of the robbers as a big man.

"You've got me at it now," he said fretfully.

George looked at him over his straw with an expression suggesting that it was not before time.

"Wait a minute," Phineas said then. "You said one of the two crooks was a big chap, yes?"

George nodded.

"And all the reports of the robbery mentioned a big man. Not *two* big men, George. *One* big man. The same big man presumably you saw keeping watch in the yard. So... Wait a minute," he said again then, slowly. "*Wait* a minute! Even better. The robbery was on Friday morning, wasn't it. I was up at the Hall then, and you were working with Humph on the lodge. He was with you all morning. Wasn't he?"

George nodded again.

"Didn't nip off at any time to get his stocking mask, did he?"

George shook his head.

Phineas laughed, not unkindly. "Well, then..." He spread his hands, resting his case.

George sighed impatiently.

"Well, you don't expect him to ac'ually be on the robbery do you? He's a Mr *Big*, Phin. And a Mr Big with an alibi. Clever, isn't he. Fiendishly," he added, remembering a remark of Dick Drake's.

"All right, then, George. All right," Phineas countered, after thinking about it. "Well, what about the rest of the gang? What about them, then?"

"What about them?" George said round his straw.

"Well, where would he have got them from? I mean," Phineas said with another laugh, "he could hardly advertise in Situations Vacant for that sort of thing."

George smiled almost pityingly.

"What — never heard of the International Organisation of Crooks, Phin?"

It was obvious Phineas hadn't.

But George had. And so had Dick Drake. There was a serial involving that secret organisation currently running in the *Intrepid*.

"It means, Phin," George took time off from his drink to explain, "that a Mr Big can operate anywhere in the world. A Mr Big can go to a foreign country to plan a job, and after he's planned it, all he has to do is to ring a certain number and he'll have a gang of ruthless crooks ready to carry it out. 'Smatter of fact, I doubt there's a major robbery anywhere in the world that doesn't have the dabs of the IOC on it," he said casually.

Phineas smiled to himself at it, the amused, detached smile of the adult. But then couldn't think of anything adult to say to go with it.

"Look — look, George," he said instead. "Look, old chap, leave it with me and I'll — er — I'll have a think about it. OK?"

"OK, Phin," George said, knowing that it wouldn't just be Phineas who'd be thinking about it, but also Detective Inspector MacNail of Scotland Yard.

"I'll hide it somewhere for now, and then I'll — er — I'll have a think about it. Decide what's the best thing to do, and all. OK?"

"OK, Phin," George said.

"We'll sort it out, don't worry, Georgie. One way or the other, we'll sort it out."

"OK, Phin," George said.

"And George... Well, just keep your eyes open when up at the Hall. And *be* careful. Just be *careful*. I don't know about Humph and share-outs, and all that," Phineas went on worriedly, as much to himself. "But I do know that the money is now missing and that whoever *is* involved will no doubt very much like it back, having gone to the trouble of stealing it."

Not adding that the toy guns might also, to whoever, point directly to George's involvement in the disappearance of that money.

"And the den," he added. "Stay away from the den for now, George. You understand? Just in case," he said, when George wanted to know why.

"If, or rather when, they come back, they might well have a poke about in the yard, and... Well, as I say, just in case."

George nodded. "Got ya, Phin."

"And, George... Well, I don't know," Phineas said then reluctantly. "Just – just keep an eye on Humph as well. See if he – see if he appears any different from usual, that sort of thing... OK?"

"OK, Phin," George said.

Chapter Thirty-Three

Phineas had a bottle chilling and the glasses out when Sally's Morris Minor pulled up outside the *Belle* later that day.

"You look," he said when she appeared on deck, "*Marvellous.*" The sky-blue of her dress bringing out the blue of her eyes, like flowers, he told her, that and a holiday tan he felt he could feel, as if she'd brought the sun back on her skin.

"*Mmm,*" he murmured into her neck, breathing in L' Heure Bleu for the second time that day.

"Nibbles later," she said prosaically, thrusting a plastic shopping bag at him instead. "There's the making of a chicken salad in there."

"Nurses!" he said.

He put the shopping in the fridge and then popped the cork on a bottle of Chablis that had been nestling on the deck table in a silver-plated wine cooler from another of Bryony's catalogues – 'Guaranteed to impress at dinner parties'.

They were on their second glass when Sally, out of nowhere, asked, "Is there any mayonnaise in the fridge?" And when she learned that there was, said that in that case that's what she'd do, she'd make a potato salad to go with it.

"We both like potato salad."

"Indeed," he agreed.

And then, "Aargh! We can't. I've just remembered. I'm completely out of spuds. Had the last on the weekend. And the shop's closed."

Sally looked at him. "But you had a sack of them in the kitchen earlier."

Phineas, about to add that he could always nip off to Church Myddle for a bag, was left with his mouth open for the second time that day.

"Ye-s," he admitted then. "Yes – yes, indeed I have – or rather *had* – a sack of spuds in the kitchen earlier today. That is perfectly true. They were on the floor there. Sitting in front of the fridge," he said with a show of candour.

"Yes," she said with a little laugh. "Well, where are they now?"

He stared at her.

"I gave them away," he said, clutching at the first thing that came into his head. "To the poor," he added.

"What poor?" she said with another little laugh.

"What poor she asks."

He shook his head as if at the fact that she *had* to ask, while giving himself time to think.

"The poor, Sally, the poor. Those who are always with us. That poor."

He pointed an indignant finger in the direction of the Masters' Cottages. "People like Tom Parr and the Tranters, and old Mrs Parks, that's who. Eeking out a state pension while the rest of us uncaringly chuck the stuff about. Living on scraps from society's table," he said, warming to it. "Foraging for what little they can find to keep body and soul together, the end of their days a bare field in winter. That's who, Sally. There's your poor. Not a million miles from where we sit sipping Chablis and discussing the menu."

She was unmoved. "Well, I don't know about Mrs Parks and the Tranters, but Tom Parr grows his own vegetables. And besides, they live rent free."

Phineas made a scornful sound. "They may live rent free, but they still have to do a jolly lot of eeking out, I can tell you. And anyway," he went on irritably, "I didn't mean that I actually shared the spuds out over there. I was simply using them as an illustration. There are unfortunately plenty of poor elsewhere you know, Sally. Of all ages. Ask a few vicars, they'll tell you."

"Vicars?"

"Yes, Sally, vicars. And one vicar in particular. In a certain town on the Welsh side of things. Faith, hope and charity, Sally, and the greatest of these is charity."

She laughed again. "What, are you saying you—?"

"I'll rather not go into details, if you don't mind."

"Well, if that is the case, why on earth didn't you tell me…?"

"If you would do good, Sally," he said with gently reproof, "then do it by stealth."

"Well, I must now view you in a new light," she said, and while he looked down with a sort of modest piety at the table top, wondered what it was really about.

According to Annie he had not so much been helping the poor as helping himself. She hadn't of course for one moment believed Annie's nonsense about Phineas and the wages snatch in Shrewsbury. Ten days away had given her a fresh perspective on the place, and she'd put it down to a bit of Batch Magna pottiness.

But that still left her with Phineas's unlikely story, as Annie told it, of two senior police officers chasing after the non-payment of a speeding fine, and now that of the spuds, another story she frankly found unlikely.

She decided to at least have a go at the speeding fine story.

"Oh, by the way, Annie phoned after you'd left, to thank me again for the holiday prezzies."

"That was nice of her," he said warily.

"Yes. And she told me some story about two police officers, two *senior* police officers, from Kingham, turning up separately at the *Belle*. On a Sunday. All for a non-payment of a speeding fine." She looked both quizzical and amused.

Phineas relaxed. "Yes, I know. I wasn't there at the time, but Jasmine told me about it. And I got immediately on to the station to complain about it, I can tell you. In no uncertain terms. I asked was that, did they think, a justifiable use of police resources? Is that, I demanded to know as a rate payer, where our money goes?" he said, tapping sharply on the table. "Haven't you anything better to do!" he went on, getting worked up about it. "Is there not—"

"Like investigating an armed robbery in Shrewsbury," she put in.

"Ah. Ah, you know about that, do you," he said, and gave what Sally thought was a sort of shifty laugh.

"Annie told me."

"Did she. Yes, well, as you say… Anyway," he said, moving quickly on, "I was told that it's all down to a new head of traffic there, a new broom and all that. Nice chap, the officer I spoke to. Said he had every sympathy with me, being a motorist himself. Reckoned this new bloke turned up unexpected, and cleared the canteen, everybody scrambling to find something to do – twice, in my case. But it's all sorted out now. And I've sent a cheque off, so we won't be hearing again from *that* quarter. More wine?"

Sally lifted her refilled glass and looked at him over it.

Phineas tensed. He'd seen that look before, or something very much like it, only yesterday, in Annie's kitchen.

"Phineas – darling," she said on a softer note, putting the glass down, "is there anything you want to tell me…?"

"Who? Me?" he said, pointing to himself and looking surprised, astonished even. "Have I got anything to tell you…?" He made an elaborate show of considering it, and then shook his head. "No. No, I don't think so. Why?" he asked, and laughed carelessly.

Sally laughed with him. She had to, at the thought of Phineas with a stocking over his head waving a gun about. It was ridiculous. *Quite* ridiculous. Whatever it *was* about, it certainly wasn't about that.

"Nothing, darling," she said, deciding to leave it for now. "Nothing at all."

Which didn't fool him for one moment.

She surely couldn't know about the spuds not being spuds, and she *certainly* didn't know about the Sergeant, that was obvious. So what had Annie told her?

Annie didn't know about the Sergeant either, that also had been obvious. But women didn't actually have to *know* something to know it. Just as they didn't actually have to *say* a thing to talk about it. They can talk about one thing while telling each other something else entirely. It was a code which, to the male ear, was simply unbreakable.

Or maybe it was just that she hadn't entirely bought the spuds business. The spuds which weren't really spuds but banknotes, he had to remind himself, introducing a note of reality. One hundred thousand pounds' worth of banknotes from an armed robbery, parked with the guns that were brandished at that robbery, only yards from where they were sitting, in the dinghy tied up at the stern.

He'd thought a few times about simply taking off with it, all that money waiting in a sack like Christmas morning. Idly daydreaming of the sun shining on the sort of seaside pier he remembered when he was a boy, with flags and bunting, and a ghost train, and rides, and an amusement arcade, with a What the Butler Saw machine, and all that, and a summer show For all the Family at the end of it, before getting back to what he was really going to do with the ruddy stuff.

He needed help from another adult, a *sensible* adult – which, he thought, ruled out the rest of the river. Although he did give Priny some consideration but decided that, although unflappable, and practical, he supposed, in the way of nurses, he wasn't altogether sure she merited the description 'sensible'.

And then it came to him – of course, Miss Wyndham. The very person. He wasn't altogether sure she merited that description either, but she somehow *felt* right for this sort of caper.

As soon as he was able he'd take the problem over to Petts Lane. He felt less burdened already.

Chapter Thirty-Four

And the day after George's conversation with Phineas, Humphrey, working now on the Masters' Cottage in Upper Ham, the Cunninghams' future home, asked George, out of the blue and quite casually, to let him know if he saw anybody nosing about the Hall, and that kinda thing.

"Anywhere 'ticularly in the Hall, Humph?" George had asked innocently.

Everywhere. Inside and out, Humphrey told him. Just keep an eye open for people nosing around, Georgie.

When George asked with the same air of innocence what sort of people might be nosing about, Humphrey hesitated, if about to say more, and then said vaguely, just people, George. Just keep an eye open for people nosing about, and things.

"What things?" Phineas wanted to know, when, instead of going straight to the Hall for lunch with Humphrey, George had said he wanted to go to the shop first, and that he'd walk up. And had then sneaked across to the *Belle* and reported the conversation.

"Dunno. He just said keep an eye open for people nosing about, and things. I reckon that proves it, Phin. I reckon he was talking about undercover tecs," he said, and waited to see what Phineas thought, his expression a mixture of concern and fascination.

"Well, there's something going on, but I don't think it's that," Phineas said. "If the Old Bill thought the money was there, George, they'd simply steam in with a warrant and a couple of dozen bobbies, and turn the house and grounds over, believe me."

George did, both Phineas and Detective Inspector MacNail.

"And if they were going in undercover then they'd probably do so as guests, a couple of tecs maybe posing as a married couple. They did that in *Death by Room Service*," he said, referring to one of his books. "So what did he mean?"

"Dunno, Phin. He just said people nosing about, and things."

"It's that '"things"' I don't understand. What things?"

Phineas looked at George and George looked at Phineas, and then Phineas said simply, "Why don't I ask him? He's up at the Hall now. I'll give him a ring, and ask him. There's probably a perfectly innocent explanation, Georgie. You'll see."

"You won't say I told you, Phin, will you?" George asked anxiously, following him down the deck to the sitting room.

"No, no, of course not. Leave it me."

When Humphrey came to the phone, Phineas came straight out with it and asked him if by any chance they'd had any trouble with people snooping about, and things," he added, emphasising the last two words.

There was a pause on the other end and Phineas glanced at George.

And then Humphrey asked, what things? You know, Phineas said, things, snooping about, and things. And Humphrey said no, they hadn't had any of that, far as he knew, and then, casually, wanted to know why he'd asked.

Nothing really, Phineas said. It was just something he'd overheard in the pub, someone mentioning something about people snooping about, and things, in Kingham, he thought it was, in hotels or guest houses, that sort of thing. He thought that they might have meant sneak thieves and was just passing it on, that's all.

Humphrey thanked him and Phineas put down the phone thoughtfully and looked at George.

"He said they didn't have any trouble with anything like that, but I noticed that when he came on and I said, '"and things"', he didn't reply immediately, as if considering his answer. It doesn't of course necessarily mean anything. He might have been eating something. But then he sounded somewhat cautious after that. There's no doubt that something is going on up there…"

He looked at George with concern. "So – so, just be *careful*, George. Remember that whatever it's about, it involves dangerous men. And whatever it *is* about, I can't escape the feeling that any day now it's going to go off with some sort of frightful bang."

While up at the Hall Humphrey returned to the kitchen and the three women sitting over a lunch of cold cuts, slices of Stretch's pork and game pies, and a salad bowl.

"He wanted to know if we had any guests snooping about, and things."

"What things?" Annie asked.

"I'm not sure…"

"Guests snooping about?" Clem said, eyes narrowed.

"Yeah," Humphrey said, nodding. "Yeah, that's what I was thinking. Said he'd heard somebody in the pub talking about some people snooping about in hotels, or guest houses, in Kingham. He thought they might have meant sneak thieves and was warning us."

"Hey, is this about—?" Shelly started.

"It might be, Shelly," Clem said. "It just might be. Well, there is one thing if it is," she went on, looking at them. "Forewarned is forearmed."

When George wasn't watching out for people snooping about, he was keeping an eye on Humphrey. And when he wasn't keeping an eye on him at the Hall, he was doing so at the Masters' Cottage, which, after putting aside for now work on the Hall's lodge, they were busy working on in order to have it ready for the Cunninghams and winter.

And when they weren't there, they were aboard the *Batch Castle*, as they were now, where the talk had summer in mind, next summer, when, with a good tail wind, as the Commander had it, the Cluny Steamboat Company's booking office would once again open for business.

There, with the Commander, Tom Parr and new recruit Nigel, Tom's nephew, who had married a girl from the other side of the border and now had a garage in Cwmdach, they were gathered round a rough blueprint Tom had made of the engine, spread out on the flat roof of the engine room, while George sprawled on the other side of it, face cupped in his hands.

And that old CSC hand Tom conjured out of the familiar talk of blower valves and drain cocks, coupling and connecting rods, a memory as fresh as if it were yesterday. One in which he could almost hear the throb of the pistons pushing power into the drive shaft, and feel the deck come alive under him as the paddle wheels turned again.

"We'll get all that, Nigel, the copper piping and the gland fittings, and that, and give you the right length and angles needed, if you'll do the rest. OK?"

"No problem, Tom," Nigel said.

Nigel was giving his services for free, for family reasons, he'd told his wife after Tom had phoned him, and with an expression that suggested it was all a bit of a nuisance. And had then shot off for Batch Magna at the first opportunity.

"And we'll need a steam whistle," Humphrey put in enthusiastically.

The Commander grinned at him, the light of something like mischief in his eye turning him into a boy again. "We've got one, Humph. It's still there, in the wardroom – which of course was the wheelhouse. And will be so again. As with all her upperworks, when we've turned the rest of the living quarters back to what they were. The old duck," he added, gazing at her.

"Cor – a steam whistle," George said.

"We'll let you have first go, Georgie," Humphrey promised him.

"And we've got a wheel now, to go with it," the Commander said. "Tom and I salvaged it from the old *Sabrina*. Our wheel," he told Nigel, "ended up on the back wall of the pub here. And we know the rudder's still there and moving, because young Ffion Owen, off the *Felicity H*, she was good enough to go down and have a look for us. And her rudder shaft's all right. So that's her steering under way."

"What about the rest of her?" Nigel asked.

"There's nothing wrong with her other bits and parts," Tom said firmly. "The fire-box is sound, and we know the boiler don't leak. And the flu in her funnel's all right, we know that as well, 'cause they've got their stove plumbed into it. What we don't know about, Nigel, is the state of the wheels. Their steel's much thinner of course than the hull. But we won't know what's what there till we get the sponsons, the paddleboxes, off. And the nuts'll be a bugger, I can tell you. They're well rusted in after all this time."

Nigel shook his head. "Not a problem."

If Nigel had a problem with any of this then he hadn't come across it yet. "But how we going to do that then, Tom, with the half that's in the water?"

"With our hands," Tom said, demonstrating. "Push 'un round. They'll go, if they ain't caught up in a load of debris. 'Sides, there's not half in the water but only about a quarter. Then we can get a good look at 'um from the deck, the wheels themselves and the floats and feathering rods, and that."

He chuckled at Nigel's incomprehension.

Tom had been chuckling a lot since first hearing the news. The thing which over the years he had never entirely stopped hoping for, had miraculously turned up one day like rescuing smoke on the horizon. This time-locked Lord Jim had at last been picked up by the past and taken back to the days when he still mattered. A past he was used to half-talking to himself about and which now it seemed everyone wanted to hear.

"The floats," he explained, "are the blades, the paddles, the things that make these vessels move. And the feathering rods keep each float near vertical when they're in the water. Increases speed and stability, see."

"I see. Well, unless the wheels are completely shot," Nigel said, "we can patch up almost anything with a bit of welding, especially steel. But what I'm wondering, Tom, is why these boats didn't just have one wheel on the back, like you see on films, and that. Be less of them to get up and down the river then."

"Ah, well, in the first place, the old General's dad had to buy what he could get at the time. And as it turned out he was lucky that they *were* doubles. 'Tis true the two paddle-boxes put more beam on 'um, but it's these side-wheelers that are best for rivers, especially here, with all the twists and turns going up to Shrewsbury. They give extra, what's called manoeuvrability, see. Better control, like, 'cause the floats are set to move at different rates, and in different directions, forward and reverse, for tighter and quicker turning. Put a stern-wheeler round some the bends in these waters, and by the time she's come round you'll likely end up with her wheel bashing the bank."

He looked at the Commander. "The zigzags are easy enough to tack in and out of. You just have to get the timing right. The hardest part is keeping her on a straight course in the midstream current. But you'll soon get the hang of it."

"Under your tutelage, Tom," the Commander said, "I haven't the least doubt."

"Right – so what do we start on first, then?" Humphrey asked, rubbing his hands as if to get down to it there and then.

"Well, the heart of the boat, Humph," Tom said. "The engine. Get that properly re-fitted and see how it runs."

"See how it runs..." the Commander echoed, turning the words into poetry, his good eye tender with the thought.

Tom tried to stay aloof from such amateurish enthusiasm, but grinned, slowly.

"Ah..." he said.

"What about her bodywork?" it occurred to Nigel then.

"What, her hull, you mean?"

"That's sound enough," the Commander said. "It's galvanised steel on the outside. Her innards have had a couple of plates welded on them over the years because of rust. But she's tight enough there. I don't think the surveyor's report will say any different."

"Then you'll need – what? To get the go ahead, like?"

"What won't we need," Tom said with a laugh. "You could get a fire going in her box with the paperwork. River worthiness certificate. Passenger insurance certificate. Safety certificate. Navigation certificate. Then there's a passenger license. And a Master's license. And you'll pass that all right, Commander," he assured him. "One eye an' all, once I've done with you. Once we've paddled her up and downriver a few times. You'll be all right."

"Is *she* gonna be all right, Tom?" Humphrey wanted anxiously to know, frowning at all the official stuff that had now unexpectedly entered into it. "Is she gonna pass this river worthiness thing, and the safety thing, and all the other stuff?"

"Oh, her'll pass all right, Humph, don't worry. Her'll be all right, you'll see."

Tom looked about him, gazing fondly on all her works.

"Her won't know herself by the time we've finished with her."

Chapter Thirty-Five

Miss Wyndham was in similar sort of state already, not knowing herself – or rather not knowing, and wasn't at all sure she wanted to, that rather silly creature who, with a fortune sitting in her coal shed, found herself at times idly daydreaming her way through it, before, scandalised, having to remind herself that it was not hers to spend.

She had still been in her dressing gown early on Tuesday morning, feeding her cats, when she'd been startled by a couple of sharp, imperative raps on the kitchen door, and opened it to find Phineas Cook on the doorstep.

Morning, Hattie, he'd muttered tersely, and glancing furtively about hurried inside. He hadn't, he told her, putting up a hand as if to stop the conversation there, much time. Sally, being a nurse, was a light sleeper, and was suspicious enough for some reason as it was, he confided, shaking his head over it.

Anyway, what it amounted to was this, he said, and told her about a potato salad Sally had wanted to make last night, and how a sack of spuds that had been in his kitchen earlier was found to be missing. Except it wasn't actually *missing,* but sitting in the dinghy, where he'd hidden it.

"So I had to tell her I'd given it away. To the poor. Yes? OK?" he said, peering at her, willing her to keep up.

"I see," she said vaguely.

"Good. Right, now, for spuds, Hattie, read banknotes. Rather a lot of banknotes, in fact. One hundred thousand pounds' worth of banknotes to be precise, if reports are correct. I haven't had a chance to actually count them. Ring any bells, yet...?" he said, and waited with a small expectant smile.

"The proceeds," he elaborated when it didn't appear that it did, "of the robbery. The Shrewsbury job. The wages snatch. From Wrekin Engineering. On *Friday*," he added with a touch of impatience.

He lowered his voice. "Well, that money, Hat, is outside in the car. Sitting on the passenger seat. But not the guns used," he assured her. "I chucked those in the river. So what it boils down to is this – if you would, Hat, I'd like you to hide it for a couple of days, just till we get things sorted out. OK? Now, there's no need to worry about the gang, they're not likely to know about this place. And you can forget about the police," he scoffed, "they're too busy chasing law-abiding citizens such as yours truly over an speeding fine. On a Sunday. Two of them, in separate cars. That's where your taxes go."

He glanced at his watch. "Anyway, must dash," he said, edging towards the door. "It's frightfully good of you, Hattie. I really am most grateful. And as I say, it should only be for a couple of days."

He nodded a smile at her. "OK, Hat? All right?"

Miss Wyndham, still holding the spoon and empty cat food can, had her head on one side, ear cocked and jowls agitated with the effort of trying to make sense of what she'd been listening to, like a receiving mechanism overwhelmed by incoming signals.

And then she frowned and carefully put the spoon and can down on the table.

"Am I to – do you mean to say – are you telling me, Phineas, that you were somehow involved in the Shrewsbury robbery...?"

He tutted. "No. No, of *course* I'm not telling you that. It's nothing to *do* with me. It's George."

"George…?"

"George Hadley," he said impatiently, shooting another look at his watch. "The lad who helps Humph at the Hall. OK? Now—"

"Young George? Young George Hadley was involved?"

Miss Wyndham's jowls shook with fresh bewilderment.

"Well, no, not exactly involved. Not directly, at any rate."

He looked at her, anxiously vibrating, and sighed, resigning himself to having to stay and give her the full story.

"That's George's contention, anyway," he said, after rattling the rest of it off. "That Humph is the mastermind behind it. The very reason we can't simply take the money to the police. Now I really must *go*, Hat. As I say, it will only be for a—"

"I don't believe it," Miss Wyndham got out then.

He sighed again, heavily. "What don't you believe?"

"This business about Humph being the mastermind behind it. I simply don't believe it."

"Yes, well, I have to admit the idea does take a bit of getting used to rather. It's not suggested, incidentally, that he was actually *there*, on the job itself. George can give him an alibi for that morning. He was working with him on the Hall's lodge. And the reports of one of the robbers being a big man must refer to one of the men George saw hiding the money, not Humph. Frankly, Hattie, I don't believe any of it either. But there's something going on there all right," he said, and added the bit about Humphrey telling George to keep an eye open for anyone nosing about the place, and things.

"Anyway, I really must go. As I say, it will only be for a couple of days, till we know what's what, and all that. I'll just nip out and get the swag. Won't be a tic," he said, and returning with it like a cheery deliveryman deposited it on the table.

"It's absurd," she told her two cats, indifferently cleaning themselves after their breakfast, while Phineas roared off back down Petts Lane.

"Quite *absurd*... But what if there's some truth in it? What if Humph *has* been up to some foolishness – what would happen then to Clem. To Clem and the little one?" she asked tremulously of the cats. "And to Shelly, his mother?"

She drew a sharp breath as something else occurred to her. "Unless – unless of course Shelly herself was involved. Unless *she* was the mastermind behind it. His mother," she said, remembering the Tommy-gun toting Ma Barker and her boys in one of her *True Crime* magazines. The same Ma Barker said by the FBI to have masterminded the robberies carried out by her sons.

"No, no, no!" she told herself, and the cats, firmly. "It's all perfectly ridiculous. Ri*diculous*."

She regarded the sack disapprovingly for a few moments, and then glancing around, as if to check she was unobserved, gingerly approached it and peered in, her eyes widening at what she saw there.

And Miss Wyndham, a vicar's daughter, who knew well where the path of covetousness and avarice led, and for whom honesty was not only the best policy but the *only* one, forgot herself long enough to stretch out an eager hand, as avid and unthinking as a child finding a sudden wealth of sweets, fingers spread to grab as much as possible.

Really, Harriet! she admonished herself sharply, and touched at her cheeks as if blushing.

And then she dithered, head quivering in a sudden spin, wondering where on *earth* she was going to hide it.

She rejected the idea of the loft almost immediately because she couldn't get up there, the back of the piano because there wasn't room, under her bed or in the wardrobe because she would then never get any sleep, discarded the idea of the two spare bedrooms for the same reason, immediately pooh-poohed thoughts of the washing machine and the oven, considered burying it in the garden, and then thought again because the gardener was due tomorrow, before finally settling on the coal shed, to where she carried it and heaped coals on it.

And there it now sat, out of sight but not of mind.

The thought of it following her throughout the day and to bed, where she clutched the bedclothes to her and waited for the sharp squeak the coal shed door makes when someone opens it.

While Tom Parr, in his shipshape cottage in Upper Ham dreamt of the PS *Batch Castle*. An iron ghost waking, shrugging off rust and her mooring cables, turning his head from the heat of her fire, as smoke was made and her wheels stirred from their long years on the river bed, and turned again on their journeying.

The drizzle of spray and soot falling, and the scream of her steam whistle as she thrashed her way upriver, making him smile with a sort of wonder in his sleep.

Chapter Thirty-Six

After a sleepless night spent waiting for the robbery gang to turn up, Miss Wyndham could take no more.

Before making herself a cup of tea, or even feeding the cats, she unearthed the sack from the coal shed, and balancing it on the wicker basket of her bicycle, wheeled it through the village like a delivery of Christmas post.

She was heading for the river. She didn't intend returning it to Phineas because she felt guilty about not keeping it for the couple of days she was sure she'd promised. She was taking it to Priny. Priny would know what to do.

The Cunninghams' car wasn't there, parked as it usually was up on the verge. But someone was aboard because she could hear banging coming from the deck.

It was Tom Parr, loosing up an old piping joint on the *Castle's* engine with a hammer, surrounded on the deck by various lengths and angles of shiny new copper waiting to be fitted. Tom, who'd been up much earlier, *had* had tea before leaving, and a fry-up, as he used to in the old days on the paddlers. Tom, once again, had work to do.

Priny and the Commander had left for Penycwn to stock up in the discount shop. Got a special offer on gin, they have, this week, he told her, and Miss Wyndham nodded and smiled vaguely, her mind elsewhere.

She knew of course about the swap Humphrey had done with the Cunninghams because of Priny's arthritis, and what Humphrey intended for the *Batch Castle*. But had refused to believe it, because she wanted so much to.

The Cluny Steamboat Company was Miss Wyndham's past as well as Tom's.

She wore her engagement ring still and her fiancé's signet ring, given to her by his parents after his death. She had met him on the river, while day-tripping on the *Cluny Belle* in the glory days of the CSC. A young solicitor, free for the day in a boater, who had teased her about her hair escaping from under her hat, and who, at the end of that summer, went to a war he wasn't to return from.

She had never married. There had been a brief upheaval in the Fifties, when a local vet had admired her, and made her for a while think of what she might be missing, and of the years waiting ahead. But in the end she had turned him down, as she had known she would. Miss Wyndham had already given her heart.

"Is it true then, Tom?" she asked, and quivered expectantly.

"Ah," Tom assured her. "It is, Hattie."

"After all this time…" she said wonderingly.

"Yes, well, her's sound enough, you know. Her don't leak. We'll have this turning any day now, see how it runs," he said, nodding at the engine, "and blow a bit of steam through her. And we'll have the plates off soon, as well, tek a look at her wheels. There'll be parts of 'em that'll need replacing, no doubt. But my nephew, Nigel, the one in Cwmdach, he's took an interest now. And there's not much he can't sort out, what with the welding equipment and all the other gear he's got in that garage of his."

Tom went on to tell her about the engine, what he was doing and what needed to be done, while Miss Wyndham listened with uncomprehending delight.

She may not have known what he was talking about but she knew what, next summer, it might all add up to, and her heart was full of it.

So much so that she forgot about the money until, with a start of surprise, she saw it again, still sitting there, where she'd left it, propped up against the front wheel of her bicycle.

An albatross, she thought, around one's neck.

What *was* she to do? Jasmine's car wasn't there either. And after considering involving Tom, and almost immediately deciding against it, because it wouldn't somehow be right, she had resigned herself to pushing her bike back up to the High Street and down again to the *Felicity H* to see if Annie was there, when Jasmine's car swept down into Upper Ham and pulled up outside the *Cluny Queen.*

Chapter Thirty-Seven

Jasmine put the kettle on and once more the proceeds of the Shrewsbury job sat in a Batch Magna kitchen, the two women sitting at the table while Miss Wyndham told her how it had got there.

"So I wanted to ask you, Jasmine," Miss Wyndham went on, "if you wouldn't mind looking after it for a couple of days."

"No, darling, course I wouldn't," Jasmine said, eyeing it up.

"Just until things are sorted out," Miss Wyndham added vaguely.

Jasmine turned her attention back to what she'd just been told.

"So it *was* Phineas then!" she said with shocked relish. "Annie said it was. And I had a sort of feeling about it beforehand, of course, professionally speaking," she got in. "And then we had that sergeant and then an inspector turning up after him. Well…!"

Miss Wyndham, opening her mouth to say that no, of course it wasn't Phineas, frowned.

"A sergeant and inspector?"

Jasmine moved her bum on the chair. "From Kingham. In them new high-speed cars they've got now. First one, then the other. *Roaring* about everywhere after him they were, at the boat, up at the Hall. An unpaid speeding fine, *he* said. Well, I ask you…"

"Yes, yes," Miss Wyndham said impatiently, "he said something about that. I take it this sergeant and inspector were in uniform?"

"Yes. Yes, they were," Jasmine confirmed eagerly, as if feeling that that would clinch it.

Miss Wyndham smiled at her naivety.

"It would be a CID job, Jasmine," she explained. "The criminal investigation department. Not, for an offence of that nature, the uniform branch. The CID officers might, indeed probably would, be accompanied by uniform colleagues were an arrest imminent. But not the uniform branch alone."

"Oh, I see," Jasmine said, reluctantly bowing to what she knew to be Miss Wyndham's superior knowledge in such matters.

"But while I think of it, please don't tell Phineas that I gave it to you to hold. I promised *I'd* look after it for a couple of days, but… but, well…" Miss Wyndham went into a mild flutter.

"I know, darling, I know. Now don't you worry. You just leave it to me," Jasmine said, feeling expansive with a fortune sitting in her kitchen.

"No, you have it completely wrong about Phineas. It's nothing to do with him," Miss Wyndham went on. "Well, not entirely. It was George, young George—"

"George Hadley…?"

"Yes. He—"

"June's son?"

"Yes, June's boy, George. He—"

Jasmine gasped. "Ohhh, and she's a *lovely* lady," she said on a note of anguish, her heart going out to another mother.

"No, no, no," Miss Wyndham said testily. Jasmine *would* gallop away with a story. "You misunderstand. Young George, as with Phineas, wasn't of course involved in the robbery. He simply saw two of the men that obviously were, hiding the money from it."

"Go on, Hattie," Jasmine urged some minutes later, having had to make the tea in the middle of Miss Wyndham telling her what Phineas had told her, throwing in New York gangsters, double bluffs, and something called International Crooks Limited.

"At least I think that is what it's called," she said vaguely. "It's a sort of international labour exchange for criminals, as I understand it. The principle behind it being that if you, in a foreign country, and not knowing any crooks there, case a job and need men for it, you just ring a certain number."

"Well, I never!" Jasmine said, putting the tea things down.

And then she frowned. "But do you mean then, Hattie, that *Humph* had something to do with the robbery?"

"George thinks so. No sugar for me please, dear. In fact, he believes Humph to be the mastermind behind it."

Miss Wyndham then told her about George seeing Humphrey giving what appeared to be directions to somewhere to two men in the breakfast room, but which afterwards, George thought, must have been Humph pointing out the outhouses in the yard as a good place to stash the loot. Because a little while later George saw them doing just that, and how he'd then made the switch, and taken the money home with him in a potato sack.

"He hid it from his mother in his room. And the next day took it to Phineas who hid it in his dinghy. And then the day after that, Phineas gave it to me to hide because Sally apparently was suspicious about something. I cannot now remember what."

"That'll be because Annie phoned her and told that she thought Phineas was one of the gang," Jasmine said, absently nibbling on a chocolate biscuit, still occupied with the news about Humphrey.

Miss Wyndham's jowls shook in a brief flurry of disapproval at such loose talk, and then she said, "Well, anyway, I – er... Where was I...? Oh, yes, George. George hid it from his mother in his room, and then took it to Phineas, who hid it in his dinghy before taking it to me. And I hid it in the coal shed, before bringing it here," she said, mentally ticking off the sequence. "That's why, I'm afraid, it's not as clean as it might be."

She smiled over at the sack, a slight, vague smile with something of sympathy and apology in it. It had, it seemed to her, begun to acquire a sort of unwanted air.

Jasmine shook her head. "I don't know," she said, more to herself, "I would have said Humph's aura was all wrong for that sort of thing. But then you can't always tell, I suppose. It's the little one, I'm thinking of. Hawis. It's always the little ones who pay in the end."

"Precisely why we cannot take the money to the police."

"No, of course we can't," Jasmine agreed immediately, glancing in a proprietary way at it.

"And anyway, we can't be entirely sure that Humph *was* involved." Miss Wyndham paused, and then went on with a sort of fretful honesty, "But then only the other day he apparently asked young George to keep his eyes peeled for anyone snooping about the place."

She looked at Jasmine as waiting her verdict on it.

"Well! There you are then. That proves it. Hey...! Hey, come to think of it, they said one of the robbers was a big man!"

"No," Miss Wyndham said firmly, "No, we can't place him on the actual job, Jasmine. George is able to alibi him for the morning in question. And as regards the reports of a big man, one of the two crooks George saw fitted that description. And that man wasn't Sir Humph."

"Oh, I see," Jasmine said.

But Miss Wyndham hadn't finished.

"But then one would hardly expect the mastermind behind a robbery to be involved in the actual execution of it."

Jasmine thought about it and then shook her head.

"That's the bit I can't see, Hat. Humph as a *mastermind*. I mean..."

She looked at Miss Wyndham, her expression inviting her to find it as unlikely as she did.

"Precisely what I thought," Miss Wyndham agreed. "As indeed did Phineas."

And then she lowered her head and peered at Jasmine.

"But perhaps that all along, my dear, is what we were *meant* to think."

"Whatever do you mean, Hat?"

"I mean, Jasmine, that we may be dealing with a very clever criminal indeed. A master of concealment and disguise."

Jasmine stared at her. "What, you mean Humph isn't Humph but somebody else?"

"In a manner of speaking," Miss Wyndham said. "I mean Humph not being Humph but simply pretending to be... well, Humph. I mean that he is who he says he is, and is in his rightful place, but is not the genial, rather... Well, not the Humph he presents himself to be."

"I see..." Jasmine said slowly.

"There was never a doubt in my mind that immediately after the job the loot and guns were handed on to what is called a sleeper – a member of the gang installed beforehand in some hotel or guest house in the area. And then moved again, to Batch Hall, either following a pre-arranged plan or because circumstances at the time dictated it."

"Well! Who'd have thought it?" Jasmine said, thinking, not without a certain pride, of the Humph she knew.

"On the other hand," Miss Wyndham went on, speaking now for the defence, "we should also consider the possibility that he was perhaps coerced into it, the real Humph, that is.

Or, foolishly, talked into it. That it was put to him that no one would get hurt and that it was simply a matter of supplying a suitable hiding place for a couple of days until the heat was off."

"And here's a few thousand for your trouble," Jasmine said, and smiled generously at the thought of someone else's luck. "Well, I mean, anybody would be tempted, wouldn't they."

"And they, like most of us, are rather in need of money," Miss Wyndham concluded.

"You can say that again," Jasmine agreed with a laugh.

"So is it all there then, in that old sack?" she said, looking coyly at it sitting up against her washing machine. "All that money they took?"

"So I believe." Miss Wyndham lifted a finger. "But not the guns used. They, I am informed, are now at the bottom of the river."

"One hundred thousand pounds," Jasmine breathed, gazing at it. It was better than winning the pools.

She looked at Miss Wyndham and grinned. "Hey, Hattie, we could just disappear with it. I've got the car outside. We could go to Acapulco."

"I wish it would just disappear. I'm beginning to feel – where on earth is Acapulco?"

"Dunno. Heard somebody say it on the radio once, and thought, ooh! I'd like to go there. Acapulco... Or Africa," it occurred to her. "We could go to Africa, me and the kids, like. And then Spain, and – er..."

"I'd go on a cruise," Miss Wyndham put in when Jasmine got stuck after Spain. "A luxury world cruise, visiting the Greek Islands, the Caribbean, Egypt and the pyramids. The trade winds on one's face, and red sails in the sunset..."

The two women shared a silence, each basking for a few moments in thoughts of the sort of suns that half a sack of banknotes each could buy.

"Anyway, Jasmine," Miss Wyndham said, returning first, "the thing to do, is to do precisely nothing with it for now. Until we know what's what – or rather who's who. In other words, until we know who Humphrey really is," she said, leaving for now his name as they had first known it, until she could be sure that he once more deserved the affectionate diminutive.

"And what if he's the other Humph, the master of disguise, and all that? What do we do then?"

"We take the matter straight to the police," Miss Wyndham said firmly.

"Oh," Jasmine said, hand to her breast, "that poor family."

"Indeed."

Miss Wyndham carefully put down her cup.

"Unless of course they were involved with him. That's to say, one family member specifically. His mother. Shelly," she revealed, leaving Jasmine with her mouth open.

"It happened in America," Miss Wyndham began, emphasising the connection, and told her the tale of the Tommy-gun wielding Ma Barker and her boys in the blood-soaked landscape of the 1930s Midwest, and her death with two of her sons in a last shoot-out, while Jasmine listened agog and let her tea grow cold.

She saw Batch Hall under the same sort of siege, and Shelly with a Tommy-gun snarling defiance at one of the windows, and Big Humph dead, and Clem, tragically and innocently caught by a stray bullet, seeing with a mother's dying look of relief her little daughter being rescued at the last moment, and had to be nudged a couple of times by one of her young sons to get her attention.

"Mam, Mam, can I have something to eat, Mam, can I? I'm starving," he was saying, taking a break from the activities outside, the sound of the rest of Jasmine's brood and their friends like that of a school playground.

Jasmine gazed at him with a smile of such tenderness that he took a step back.

"Of course you can, Thorin. Course you can, cariad. Help yourself, darling."

Thorin cut himself a doorstep of bread spread lavishly with butter and damson jam, and was on his way out when he spotted the sack and immediately veered off to investigate.

"What's that, Mam? Spuds, is it?"

"No. Leave it alone, Thorin. It's not spuds, it's – er – it's…" Jasmine floundered

"It's newspaper, Thorin – cut-up pieces of old newspapers," Miss Wyndham said, prompted by a dim memory of someone recently mentioning such a thing. And then quickly came up with a further invention. "For your mother's stove," she said, referring to the wood-burning stove in the paddler's sitting room. "Ready for the winter."

"Now, don't you worry, Hattie," Jasmine said a few minutes later, when Miss Wyndham said that she really must go, that she hadn't fed the cats yet. "I'll look after it. Be as safe as houses with me, it will."

"Thank you, dear. And do remember, that until we can be sure who's who, mum's the word."

"Oh, yes," Jasmine agreed. "Tat-tar, Hattie."

"The fewer that know about the money, Jasmine, the better."

"Yes, yes, of course."

Miss Wyndham popped her head back in.

"Because do bear in mind, won't you, my dear, that whoever was or wasn't involved, there's still a gang of ruthless crooks out there who no doubt would very much like it back."

"Oh, yes, of course."

Miss Wyndham's head reappeared round the door.

"Even if it wasn't theirs to begin with."

Jasmine closed the door after her – couldn't wait to close the door after her.

She had peered briefly in at the bundles of banknotes when they had first turned up, and was now eager to get better acquainted.

After checking that her brood were still busy out on the moorings, she hurried with the sack along the deck to the sitting room and through into her bedroom. She wedged the door shut with a chair, shook the money out on to the bed, and gazed on it.

It lay there in all its different denominations and colours, spread before her like a map of some exotic country. A country she could before only dream about. A country where you no longer had to count the coppers, where there was no scrimping and making do, no borrowing till the giro was due, no patching and mending, and shoving unpaid bills at the back of a kitchen drawer, and then having the phone or electricity cut off because of it. A country of ease and plenty.

And now it was hers. Now it was her turn.

All she had to do now was to find somewhere to hide it until she'd decided how she was going to spend it.

And after that she'd ring Annie, and leaving out the bit about spending it, tell her about it. Wouldn't be fair to Phineas, for one thing, to let her go on thinking he was involved.

And besides, Humph as a criminal mastermind trumped Annie's revelation about Phineas any day. Not to mention Shelly.

Chapter Thirty-Eight

Phineas's undoing that evening, as he'd lost no time in pointing out to himself the next morning, head in hands as if holding the pieces together after waking on the sofa, had been to open the bottle of Annie Owen's patent blackberry whisky.

He should have left it as it was, minding its own business, harmlessly gathering the years and dust in the wine rack. But that of course, as he told himself with unsparing sarcasm, would have required what he believed was something called common sense.

Because after the cork was popped, its bottled breath released like a genie, and the first sip tentatively taken, and then, with a look of startled pleasure, another, he was lost, as stronger wills than his have been, to Annie's way with a late summer hedgerow. Lost to the sunburst of flavours on the tongue and the embracing warmth of an old and dear friend, one who understands and instantly forgives all.

He decided that the overtone was that of a good vintage port, even one of the swankier vintages. But couldn't quite put a finger on any of the undertones, despite a judicious savouring of several more glasses. And found by then, that not only did he no longer care, he could no longer remember what it was he was supposed to be looking for.

He gazed with enraptured admiration at another fresh glass of the liquid, the swill of magenta light winking enticingly back at him, and could only wonder at the alchemy, the sheer *alchemy*, Annie could conjure from the humble bramble.

"I have," he told Bill Sikes, curled up next to him on the sofa, "walked past hedges of blackberry many times. Many, many times – *masses* of times. And never guessed. Simply *never* guessed. Never, ever guessed… Who would have guessed? Hmm? Not I. Not me, Sikes, old boy. Count me out. I would never have guessed. Never…

"Never would have guessed," he said, returning to it a while later, and leaning back with another empty glass smiled beatifically at nothing, finding it somewhere up on the wall opposite, just above a window burnished with reflected light from a dying sun and the river.

"It's all the same to me," he murmured, thinking of nothing in particular, just drifting with the current and the feeling of the sun on his face like the kindest of blessings.

"… In boats or out of 'em, it's all the same to me… All – the – same – to me… As Ratty knew… as good old Ratty knew…" he said dreamily, and nodded.

And then sat bolt upright, eyes wide, seeing it all as clear as if he were reading the headlines the next day.

He not only now knew what was what, he knew who was who.

And it wasn't Humph.

Of course it wasn't. Of *course* it wasn't! Not Humph, not old Humph.

Dear old Humph, he thought on a rush of affection, welcoming him almost tearfully back into the bosom of the family.

He looked at Bill Sikes.

"Humph's no crook," he told him, as if appealing to his reason: you know Humph! Big chap, buys you pork scratchings in the pub and has a habit of scooping you up as if you were a puppy and running round the deck with you.

"Humph's not a *crook*," he said, shaking his head and chuckling as if the misunderstanding, and an absurd one at that, had been the dog's.

"He was forced into it, Bill, by a threat to Hawis, do you see," he explained patiently. "Do what we tell you or the kid gets it, that sort of thing. And he'd do anything for little Hawis, Humph would. You know that. Do *anything* for the dear little thing, he would. The damn swine! Well, now – *now* Sikes, m'boy, now it's their turn – and let's see how *they* like it!" he said, and laughed cruelly, a pirate with the upper hand.

He leaned confidingly towards the dog.

"What we'll do – what we're going to do, Bill, is to lure them back to the Hall, see. We'll lure them to the Hall and we'll tell 'em – we'll say, the money's been found, all you have to do is to come and get it. And then, my boy, then we'll lie in wait for 'em. In the butler's pantry off the hall," he said cunningly, and lifted a cunning finger. "Remembering of course not to step on the squeaky floorboard in there.

"And then, Bill, then, when they arrive, we'll leap out and – *bang!* We'll hit 'em with all we've got! We'll give 'em what for – we'll *give* 'em what for, all right. We'll learn 'em!" he cried, lurching to his feet.

"We'll rush 'em with pistols and swords and sticks, and we'll whack 'em, and whack 'em, and whack 'em!"

He paused abruptly, gripped by another thought. "And blow me," he said wonderingly, "if Badger doesn't know of a secret passage from the riverbank to the Hall. Which comes out, if I remember rightly, in the very place," he went on excitedly. "The very place! The butler's pantry. Of course! That's why the floorboard squeaks. Otter found out what was what and where, when round at the back door of the Hall with his brushes, disguised as a sweep," he said, getting things mixed up a bit but he knew what he meant, he knew well how the story went. And it was one that was on their side.

Good old Badger. Sion and Humph, back to back in Cutterbach Wood, slaying the baiters with the jawbone of an ass and a baseball bat.

He laughed again briefly.

"We'll give what for all right. We'll learn 'em. Good old Badger!" he cried, almost tearfully, and sat down again, abruptly, his face screwed up in an expression of great perplexity as he tried to remember Sion Owen's telephone number.

After a garbled phone call from him about otters and badgers and a secret passage, Sion drove over to the *Belle* from the Keeper's Cottage to make sure Phineas hadn't gone in over the side, and found him asleep on the sofa, his head resting on Bill Sike's.

He recognised the bottle sitting on the coffee table immediately. It was one of Annie's, from her store of hedgerow mischief, all innocently labelled, like jam.

He saw how little was left and winced in sympathy at the thought of the hangover waiting in the morning. Sion had also been on the receiving end of his stepmother's home-made spirits.

He took off his friend's deck pumps, plumped up a couple of cushions one end of the sofa, and settled him there. And then covered him with Phineas's old duffel coat before leaving, closing the door of the sitting room quietly behind him.

Phineas the next morning felt obscurely that it was imperative to ring Humphrey, and did so even before putting the kettle on.

He had, he said when Humphrey came to the phone, something important to tell him, *very* important.

The only trouble was, he felt obliged to add, that at the moment he couldn't altogether remember what. But whatever it was he, Humph, wasn't to worry, that was the gist of his call.

Because whatever it was, it was well in hand. He, Phineas, could assure him of that.

"OK, Phin," Humphrey said patiently, and then asked if there was anything else as he wanted his breakfast.

Phineas said there wasn't, not at the moment. But as soon as he remembered he'd get straight back to him. Meanwhile, don't worry. That's the message from this end, Humph old chap. Do not worry.

"OK, Phin," Humphrey said.

Chapter Thirty-Nine

Jasmine was dreaming over the ironing, in a room with ornamental plates and the children's artwork on the walls. Their school photographs, and brass and copper knick-knacks, and a small china world of bonnets and crinoline on every available surface, and martingale straps of polished leather and painted brass decorating the upright support timbers.

She had decided against Acapulco and was off to Africa, in a camper van, with the kids and the sack of money. Well, it's not every day, is it, she told herself.

They'd have a look at the animals first, in their natural habitat, as they say on the telly, and then off to Spain for a bullfight for Cadoc, and then – well, whatever comes after Spain. They could go anywhere, they could, free as gipsies. And it wouldn't be like *stealing*, like robbing people, because somebody's already done that. No, it was sort of – well, sort of *lost* money now it was. And finders keepers, everybody knows that.

And why not? She was between boyfriends at the moment, so that was all right. And she wouldn't miss Batch Magna, not really… Well, she'd miss Annie and Owain, she supposed, and Priny and the Commander, and Phineas, and the others, like. And the old river, of course. Well, bound to, after all this time, she told herself, and sniffed, welling up at the thought of it.

And then she gasped. But what about the little ones? *What* about their education? You'd forgotten about them, hadn't you, she accused herself. You can't just uproot them like that, from their schools and friends, and all, wouldn't be right.

So there you are then, you can't go, she decided firmly, and with relief.

She'd only been pretending to keep the money, or told herself she was only pretending, and then meaning it again, and then telling herself that she hadn't meant it, not really, until she didn't know where she was.

All the money had done for her so far was to give her a headache. And now she couldn't disappear with it, whether she wanted to or not. So that was that.

Not with little Cadoc joining the twins, Rhiamon and Gayner, at primary school in the autumn, you can't, she told herself, lifting Sulta the cat from the pile of clothes waiting on an armchair, and contentedly starting on one of the girl's dresses. And Morwen and the two boys at the juniors, and doing well there, their teachers said, well, behaving themselves at any rate, most of the time, like, and Romney, Thorin and Meredith at the senior school in Kingham, and getting good marks, they were, at the old exams, and that.

She was going through them again, making sure she hadn't left anyone out, when her head went alertly up, listening.

Listening for what she couldn't hear and should be hearing: the background din of her family.

She switched off the iron.

She tried the Uptops, as they were known, first, the two large bedrooms built by a boyfriend on top of the upperworks and reached by companionways, the children stacked there at night in tiers of wooden bunks. Where, when high winds struck the shallow-draught vessel, they squealed and screamed in the swaying and rocking dark as if getting their money's worth on the big dipper.

The rooms were in their usual state of disarray but empty of children. Nor could she see them on the river.

And there was no sign of them on the moorings either when she went down to look. Then she heard voices coming from the bell tent she'd put up for them, her work tent, used for outdoor events.

They were all there, her brood and some of their friends from the village, sitting round in a circle like Red Indians, busily stuffing themselves on a variety of sweets, adding to a debris of wrappers, silver paper, and cellophane. Trevina, her two-year-old daughter, was sitting between Meredith's legs, with no knickers on and a clown's mouth of chocolate.

"Lo, Mam," Thorin said indistinctly.

Jasmine stood in the entrance, taking it in. "Where d'you get all that? All them sweets?"

"Dunno," Thorin said.

"From the shop, Mam," Cadoc told her happily.

"And where did you get the money?"

"We found it" – "A lady gave it us," Morwen and her brother Arian said as one voice, remembering at the same time two of the stories suggested in case of discovery.

Jasmine looked at her eldest daughter, the sensible one, with a career in social work in mind, and who was now trying to hide what was left of a box of Black Magic chocolates behind Trevina's back.

"Meredith," she demanded, "where did you get the money? Come on, my girl!"

"In the sofa," Rhiamon, one of the twins, said, helping her sister out when Meredith appeared to have trouble remembering.

Jasmine gasped.

"*What* were you doing in there!"

That was where the money was hidden. The sofa had storage space under its seats and she'd removed some of the linen normally kept there and buried the sack under the rest.

"Only having a look, like," Arian said, sounding aggrieved.

"Where d'you get it, Mam?" Romney, her eldest son, wanted to know.

"Never you mind. It's—"

"Have we won the pools, Mam?" Meredith broke in avidly.

"No, we haven't won the pools. It's not our money."

"Where d'you get it then?" Romney asked implacably.

"Never you mind where I got it or didn't get it. It's not ours to spend, that's all you need to know, Romney. It's stealing, it is. *Stealing*. Lewis Hoskins," Jasmine went on, singling out one of the village boys, "would your mam and da like you stealing?"

Lewis Hoskins looked down abjectly and shook his head.

"No, Mrs Roberts," he muttered.

"Of course they wouldn't. They'd hate it – *hate* it, they would, because it's a sin, stealing is. And lying," she added, coming up with another one. "They're abominations in the eyes of the Lord, they are," she told them, an echo of old terrors thundered from the chapel pulpit, words she was convinced were addressed directly at her, and the sins she'd started enthusiastically to discover behind the junior school bike shed.

"Ashamed of you, I am. A*shamed*!" she flung at them, bosom heaving.

"Sorry, Mam," Meredith said then, leading a ragged, mumbled chorus of apologies.

"I've a good mind to warm your breeches for you. Well, you lot needn't think you're going to Africa now, 'cause you're not," she told her puzzled family. "You'll be lucky after this if you get to Borth Zoo this year. Right, so how much did you take? Come on, how much?"

"Didn't take much. Just enough for a few sweets, like, that's all," Thorin said sulkily.

"A few sweets, is it? Looks like it, I don't think. There's another lie, Thorin. And don't think the good Lord didn't hear it. He hears everything, He does. Right, well, come on, I'll take whatever's left, after your *few* sweets!"

She picked up an empty Roses chocolates box and went round the circle grim faced, holding it out like a charity tin, filling it with notes and coins.

Gayner said she hadn't any of it left, said it with an innocence which caused her mother to stand over her with pursed lips and the box held out, waiting.

Gayner made a face, and modestly lifting her skirt dug out her change, a few coins wrapped in a ten pound note and secreted in her knickers.

"You can keep what's left of the sweets – with any luck they'll make you sick. And serve you right!" she said on a parting note.

And she, she decided, after stuffing the banknotes back into the sack, and wondering if she should put an IOU with them, would keep the coins. Only right, after all the trouble it had caused her.

After sleeping fitfully, in between checking on the sack again under the bed, and then getting up to hide it in the wardrobe, and getting up again to put it back under the bed, she slept past the alarm going off, waking at the time she was supposed to arrive in Water Lacy, upriver, for a reading.

She rang the client to tell her she'd be late, and without stopping for even a cup of tea, told a chastened-looking Meredith to get breakfast for the rest of them.

"Where you going then, Mam?" Meredith wanted to know.

"Where d'you think I'm going, my girl, dressed like this? Somebody's got to turn a penny or we'll *starve*," Jasmine flung back at her, disappearing down the gangway with the potato sack of money.

She intended dropping it off at the *Felicity H* on her way, because with Annie she wouldn't have to spend time explaining things.

"Just for a couple of days, Annie, till things get sorted out, like," she rehearsed on the way there.

But it was Annie and Owain's turn to be out when the bearer of the sack came calling. Which, discounting Phineas as, to oblige Miss Wyndham, she must, left Priny and the Commander.

And she knew they were there because she'd seen their car parked outside on the way round.

She roared off back up Lower Ham, into the High Street, round the pub, and down again into Upper Ham, and pulled up with a screech of brakes behind it.

Chapter Forty

They were on deck, with Sion Owen, who, as future fireman of the *Batch Castle*, had dropped by to check the progress on her engine.

Tom Parr had gone to Kingham, so the Commander showed him over the latest bit of restoration, the new growth sprouting from the old. Where once was ruin, rust and dereliction, now shone polished brass fittings and copper piping, bright as newly-minted coin, the engine smelling healthily of lubricating grease and oil. They were, the Commander was able to tell him, his good eye full of it, almost there.

And now they were having tea on deck at a round glass-topped table, in the shade of a floral parasol, both table, chairs and parasol familiar to browsers in Bryony Owen's catalogues.

"A splendid day," the Commander said with satisfaction, leaning back with his pipe and looking out over the river to where summer sat in a haze on the hills.

"Too good for work," Sion, who was on his way to some, said, and then watched with interest as Jasmine appeared from the gangway in one of her working dresses, a sea-green silk adorned with golden sun faces and zodiac circles, hugging to her generous bosom what looked like a sack of potatoes.

She blew hair from her face and wiped at her brow with the back of a hand.

"I'm late, I am," she announced.

"I see, darling," Priny said. "No time for a cuppa, then?"

She shook her head above the sack.

"I'm due for a reading and I overslept." She looked at Sion. "I wanted to see Annie, but they were both out."

"Ah," Sion said. He batted away a caddisfly. "What you got there then, Jas? Spuds?"

Jasmine shook her head again and carefully leaned the sack against one of the gangway's stanchions.

"No. No, it's not spuds. It's – well – well, what it is…"

She started again. "What it is," she said with a small hesitant smile, "is money, see. A tidy bit of money, like."

The Commander laughed briefly and vaguely, out of politeness, and shared it with the other two, who merely looked blank.

"It's – well – it's from the Shrewsbury robbery," she said apologetically. "The wages snatch, like. At that factory. But not the guns, though. Phineas dumped them in the river," she added, and offered another small smile.

When nobody said anything, simply stared at her, she said, "Look, I haven't got a lot of time, but what it is, is this…"

She came confidingly near, and starting with George finding the money after seeing Humph talking to the men who hid it, then gave a quick account of the sack's journey from the outhouse at the Hall to George's den, and then to his bedroom, and from there to the *Cluny Belle*, and from the *Belle* to Miss Wyndham's coal shed, and from there back to the river, to her place.

And now there, on the *Castle.*

"So that's what Phineas was on about the other night…" it dawned on Sion. "Bugger me!"

"How ex*trao*rdinary," the Commander said.

"I was going to hold on to it," Jasmine went on, "like I promised Hattie. But then the blooming kids found it, the little devils! *Diawl bachs!*" she repeated in Welsh for extra emphasis. "Started helping themselves to it. I could have lamped them, I could. Anyway, so here I am," she said, looking anxiously at them.

"I see," Priny said.

"Well, what I was hoping," Jasmine went on, fiddling with one of her abraxas rings, "was that you'd look after it. Hide it for a few days. Just till things get sorted out, like, that's all."

"Till what things get sorted out, darling?" Priny asked.

"Well, you know, who did what, like, and that…"

"So, who *did* do it?" the Commander, who'd been grappling with it, asked, frowning up at Jasmine.

"That's what has to be sorted out, James," Priny said reasonably.

"Well, according to Annie, it was Phineas that was involved," Jasmine was able to tell them. "But according to Hattie, because of what Phineas had told her George had told him, it was Humph, as a master of disguise, and all that. Or Shelly, Hattie said Shelly could be the mastermind behind it, like Ma Bacon, or somebody, in America."

Priny ignored it. "So, meanwhile, in there," she said, indicating the sack with her cigarette holder, "is all the cash from the Shrewsbury robbery? Is that right?"

"Yes."

"One hundred thousand pounds…?"

"Yes. Well, almost."

"My word," Priny said, and fluttered her eyelashes at it. "May I take a little peek, Jasmine? I've never seen a hundred thousand pounds before."

Jasmine said yes, of course she could, and was it all right if she went now?

"Yes, of *course,* darling," Priny said breezily.

"Just a minute – hold on, Jas," Sion broke in. "Why didn't any of you just call the police?"

Jasmine looked scandalised.

"We can't do that, Sion! What if Humph is the mastermind, and all that? We can't call the police on him. Wouldn't be right."

"My word," Priny said, peering into the sack. "All that money… There's *oodles* of it," she said with a delicious little shiver.

"Who would have thought it," the Commander pondered.

"Who would have thought what, darling?" Priny said, sitting down again, and leaning on the table beaming, chin in hand, at her husband.

"Well, Humph. A master criminal, and all that, you know?"

She laughed, sounding light-headed. "This gets weirder. A sackful of swag from a wages snatch sitting on one's deck is fantastic enough – but Humph as a master criminal…!" she said, and tinkled another laugh.

"You never can tell, Number One," her husband told her. "There are more things in heaven and earth, Horatio, than are dreamt of—"

"Well, somebody did it," Sion broke in prosaically. "And that somebody's not just going to leave it like that, are they. Not going to go, oh well, can't be helped. They're armed robbers, professional criminals, for God's sake. They'll be back."

"Unless of course," the Commander said, his pipe indicating Jasmine, moving impatiently from one foot to the other, "it was as Jasmine said. That Humph, as unlikely as you might find the proposition, was not only *involved* in the robbery but was, indeed, the brains behind it."

"You've been leaving your hat off in the sun again, James," Priny told him. "And it wasn't Jasmine who said that, but Hattie."

"Well, anyway, I must go now. I—" Jasmine started.

"And Hattie, allow me to point out, Number One," the Commander said, regarding his wife with his good eye, "knows about these things."

"Well, why don't we just ask him?"

The Commander transferred his gaze to Sion. "Who?"

"Well, Humph of course."

"My dear fellow," the Commander protested, "we can't just go around accusing people willy-nilly like that."

Jasmine offered another little smile, "Well, is it all right, then?" she said, starting to edge towards the gangway. "Only I—"

"Who else knows about it, Jasmine?" Sion asked.

"Knows about what?"

Sion sighed. "The money, love. You know? The one hundred grand's worth from an armed robbery, sitting over there in a potato sack? That money. Who else knows about it?"

"I dunno. Not many. There's us of course. And George. And Phineas. And Hattie. And the kids – well, they don't know where it's from, like. But anyway, I must—"

"What about Annie? Does she know about it, or think she just knows who robbed it?"

Jasmine hesitated.

Sion narrowed his eyes at her. "You told her, didn't you... Didn't you. Come *on*!"

"Well... Well, I might have mentioned it to her in passing, like, yes."

He made a sound like a laugh. "Oh, well, that's it then. You might as well just put an ad in the paper. It'll be a toss-up who gets to hear of it first, the fuzz or the robbers. If I were you," he said to the other two, "I'd get on the blower now to Kingham and get them to come and pick it up."

"And Humph along with it, I suppose!" the Commander said, regarding Sion sternly. "Dragged out in front of his family, with little Hawis screaming and clinging to her daddy. I rather think we owe the family more than that."

Jasmine tried again. "Blimey, look at the time. Look, I must—"

"Yes, yes, of course you must, darling," Priny said. "Off you go."

The Commander, re-filling his briar from an aged leather pouch after Jasmine had bobbed off back down the gangway, shook his head. "Just goes to show..."

"What," his wife wanted to know, "goes to show what, James?"

"Well, I mean to say, Humph, of course."

He shook his head again. "It just goes to show."

"What nonsense," Priny said.

"And all that, you know," the Commander added vaguely, and struck a match to his pipe.

"Bloody *hell*," Sion said then, unable to resist taking his look at the sack's contents.

"Quite," Priny said happily.

"What are you going to *do* with it?" Sion asked.

"I know what I'd *like* to do with it," Priny said, as if she had all kinds of glamorous things in mind, and then realised with a sort of mild dismay that she couldn't offhand think of anything.

It must, she thought, be age.

"Well, speaking for myself," Sion said, "if it was mine, like, I know what I'd do with it. I'd get a Harley. A Harley Davison, that's what I'd do," he said, sitting down again.

"Yes, that's it," the Commander said. "We should have a share-out. That, I believe, is the usual form. Each take a cut — that's to say all those who know about the money."

"That means half the village," Sion put in, "seeing that Annie knows about it. And tomorrow the other half."

The Commander considered the arithmetic. "Even generously, for argument's sake, putting the number involved at fifteen, it would come to – er... Well, whatever it comes to, it's not to be sniffed at." He thought again. "Although of course, Humph, having masterminded it, would understandably expect the larger cut. But even so, even so..."

Priny was looking at her husband and shaking her head.

"What this place does to people's brains," she said wonderingly.

"Yes, well, that's one suggestion, Commander," Sion said. "Now all we need is a sensible one."

"Well, that's not hard to find," Priny said briskly. "We simply do as Jasmine asked us to do. Put it somewhere safe for a few days until, as she says, things, or rather people, get sorted out."

The Commander smiled at him. "There, you are, Sion. Is that sensible enough for you?"

Sion shook his head. "I give up."

"Comes from having been a nurse, you know," the Commander said, beaming proudly at his wife. "They never make a fuss, never run, and like nanny, always know best. Well never make a fuss, that is, until they find you cluttering up their ward. Couldn't wait to get me into bed she couldn't, when first we met."

An old joke, which he never tired of making and she never tired of hearing, going back to the last war and a Southampton hospital, where she was a staff nurse and he a patient.

And maddeningly sexy she was too, he thought, remembering again her starched bustle up and down the ward, in black stockings and cuffs and frilly hat, and with that nursery upside-down watch on her breast.

The Commander leaned back, pipe in mouth, as if savouring the memory.

And then he came forward in the chair and smacked the table, rattling the tea things.

"Got it! The very place. To hide it," he explained. "We'll—"

Priny shot up a hand. "Don't tell me, James, please. I don't trust myself. We haven't paid the phone bill yet."

264

Chapter Forty-One

Sergeant Cholmondeley-Jones sighed from the heart on her way back to Kingham after her lunchtime Coney break at the Hall on Saturday, back up through a valley bright with summer and followed by the pealing of church bells.

It was, she thought glumly, a perfect day for a wedding.

She'd mentioned to the Inspector earlier in the week that they were hosting a wedding reception at the Hall on Saturday, and had suggested that they might do the same, hold their reception there – *when*, that is, she'd added in a coy, pointed sort of way, they'd fixed a date.

And he'd frowned and looked serious, a man who had more things than a wedding to think about. It was, he'd said, a difficult time, what with the current staff shortages, and he wasn't at all sure at present if he could juggle the rosters in such a way as to synchronise their annual leaves, if she knew what he meant. For their honeymoon, he'd added with a smile, offering the word like a sop.

But the Sergeant had heard it all before.

And quite frankly she was glad now that she'd lied to him about sending the letter.

And that wasn't all. When she got to speak to Phineas Cook again, and if when she did so she could get a word in edgeways, she intended lying to him as well, intended telling *him* that she'd sent the letter. A letter which he would never get, because she hadn't sent it. And she hadn't sent it because she still hadn't got round to writing it.

The Sergeant at present wasn't anybody's Petal.

She didn't even feel inclined to respond, as she normally would have, to the Inspector flashing his lights and honking his horn at her when, back in Kingham and approaching the police station, he was coming away from it, travelling towards her.

Normally she'd get a small thrill from the exchange, especially the making of unnecessary noise contrary to the Road Traffic Act, Section 75. Subsection 4 (noise, smoke, bells and horns). It wasn't quite risking all for love, as the heroine of her current Mills & Boon was doing, but it would have earned them both a reprimand of some sort.

A reprimand she once would have gladly, proudly, accepted.

But now all she could bring herself to do was to lift her hand in a brief ambiguous wave as they passed each other, a wave which could have being saying hello, or goodbye.

And the Inspector, taking advantage of a traffic jam to regard himself in the rear-view mirror, wondered idly, *now* what's the matter with her?

He was on his way to where the Sergeant had just left, for *his* Coney break. Inspector Worth had joined the club.

After his first, dutiful bite to show social willing, the Inspector, a healthy-eating zealot, a man with a colour coded nutritional chart taking up half a wall of his kitchen, had fallen, brought down not by an apple, but a hotdog and the alchemy of Shelly's special pickle relish.

In the short space of not quite a week he was a regular there. With the added enticement of a kitchen presided over by Lady Clementine Strange, Clem, the now familiar use of her shortened first name a source of pleasure and satisfaction.

But when he turned in through the gates of the Hall he found he could get only a short way up the drive, the rest of it was clogged with cars. He'd forgotten about the wedding reception.

He could have left the car and walked up, but although his visit was perfectly above board, the thought of doing so made him feel vaguely exposed. A man who had trod his career path with as much caution as ambition, the Inspector had a very sensitive back.

He reluctantly reversed down the drive and found himself blocked in by another car turning in through the gates.

He waited for it to let him out.

Chapter Forty-Two

"What's he doing – what's he doing?" Tony, in the back of the other car, muttered, and gnawed on a fingernail.

"He's leaving, Tony. That's what he's doing," the pawnbroker said with elaborate calm, bobbing his head and acknowledging the Inspector's salute with a brief wave after the police car had backed out, and headed off towards the village.

"What I'd like to know," Sneed added, "is what he was doing there in the first place."

The Major, who had pulled the brim of his brown trilby down over his eyes and appeared to be searching for something in the glove compartment, looked up as they turned into the drive, and saw the jumble of cars lining it.

"My word," he said.

"It's a wedding reception, Major," Sneed said. "They told me to expect difficulties with parking when I made our reservations. We'll have to walk up."

They collected their luggage from the back seat, piled next to Tony because Sneed had said he hadn't had time to get the boot lock fixed, and trudged, straggling, up the drive.

"Delightful house," the Major said. "Elizabethan, of course. The half-timbers, the tall, red-brick chimneys. Its whole standing four square still, speaking for old England. There are those who talk of the influence of the Italian Renaissance in the Elizabethan style. I," he pronounced, "am not among them. I see in its solidness and courtly elegance the—"

"What if he comes back?" Tony, who'd been thinking about it, cut in abruptly, barging roughly past him with his suitcase to talk to Sneed. "Eh? What do we do then?"

"Perhaps a stay in such surroundings might benefit your manners, Tony," the Major huffed.

"What if who comes back, Tony?" the pawnbroker enquired.

"And I do think that that white tie and black shirt are ill-advised," the Major added primly. Bristling with tweed, an ashplant tucked under an arm, the Major had dressed for the country.

Tony, about to snarl a reply, changed his mind and returned his attention to Sneed.

"The rozzer, of course, in the motor. Who'd you think I'm on about!"

"We don't do anything, Tony. Why should we? We know from Brrm-Brrm that they're always in and out of here for some reason. If you're going to start coming apart every time you see a uniform—"

"I'm not coming apart. I just—"

"The thing to bear in mind, Tony, is that we are businessmen, respectable, law-abiding citizens. With no more to fear from them than any other law-abiding citizen. Long as you remember not to use your real name when you check in," he added, leading the way up the Hall steps.

The pawnbroker gave the brass hand bell on the hall table a couple of business-like shakes, and lifted his Homburg when Annie appeared from the kitchen.

"Good day to you, dear lady. I am Mr Havington-Wilkes," he said in an accent to go with the double-barrelled name. "And these gentlemen are my business associates, Major Blashford and Mr Coma."

"Como," Tony corrected him, and winked at Annie. "Like Perry."

"Perhaps you are the lady I spoke to on the telephone when booking the rooms?" Sneed enquired.

"Was she English, American, or Welsh?" Annie asked, opening the register on the hall table.

"I got the impression she was English."

"That was Clem then. Lady Clem."

"Ah," Sneed said.

Annie asked if they wanted just bed and breakfast or the full board option. Full board, Sneed told her. Even if they left no richer than when they arrived, there was always one of the Major's cheques to fall back on.

"If you'd sign the register, please, I'll get the keys and show you up," Annie said, heading for the kitchen. "Won't be a tic."

The pawnbroker removed his yellow driving gloves and placed them, one on top of the other, on the table and then in the same deliberate way took a fountain pen from the inside pocket of his going-away suit.

He then stood aside for the other two to sign and showed his teeth in a smile as Annie reappeared.

"We noticed—" he started, when a group of wedding quests, carrying a couple of champagne bottles and glasses, tripped, chattering and laughing, into the hall and headed for the drawing room and the way out to the terrace.

Sneed's smile came and went indulgently a couple of times at the merriment.

"We've got a wedding on," Annie said. "The caterers put a marquee up on the lawns. The bride was born in the village and went to London. But came back here to be married, in the village church. Looked lovely, she did."

"Ahhh, how very romantic," Sneed said. "As I was saying, we happened to notice a police car leaving when we arrived. Nothing amiss, I hope?"

"Oh, no. They're always here. They come for the – ah, here's Lady Clem now," Annie said, as Clem bounded in from outside. "The booked guests, Clem."

"Hello, you chaps," Clem said. "Welcome to Batch Hall. We hope you enjoy your stay."

"They've signed the book. They want full board."

"Splendid," Clem said, giving them an extra smile.

"Will you show them up, Clem?" Annie said, handing her the keys. "I'm on my own for now in the kitchen."

"OK, Annie. If you'll follow me, gentlemen. Your rooms are all ready."

"A fine staircase, if I may say so," the Major remarked, following her up it. "The house of course is Elizabethan."

"Yes, yes it is. But the staircase is believed to be a bit later. Early Jacobean."

"Ah. Of course. I should have known. The exuberance of its ornamentation. The arabesque scroll work on the balustrading, and the newels surmounted by—"

Sneed headed him off. "Major Blashford has got an interest in old buildings. In fact we all have, haven't we Mr Como."

"That's right. We all have," Tony agreed.

"We're not as knowledgeable as the Major perhaps, but we do appreciate these old places, part of our national heritage, and all that. One of the reasons, actually, we decided on Batch Hall and its amenities, having picked up one of your brochures on a previous business visit to the area. So I hope you won't mind if we wander about the old place while here, having a general look at things, and that. Drink in the atmosphere, so to speak."

"No, of course not. Make yourself at home," Clem said cheerfully, and couldn't *wait* after showing them their rooms to get back downstairs.

"*Annie!*" she hissed, poking her head round the kitchen door and motioning her out into the hall.

Clem had the register open when Annie came out of the kitchen.

"They've just asked for permission to have a look around the place while they're here. Which is just the sort of thing I'd expect them to do."

"Who?" Annie said, drying her hands on a cloth.

"Mr Havington-Wilkes, Mr Como," Clem quoted from the register.

"Like Perry," Annie said.

"And Major Blashford. Sounds like aliases to me. Sounds very much to me like people who are here incognito."

"Incog...?"

"In disguise."

"Oh."

Annie's eyes grew bigger. "*Ohh*! Oh, you don't mean they're—?"

"They could be, Annie. They certainly could be."

"Well, what did they say when they booked?"

"Just said they were coming to the area looking for business opportunities, and weren't sure how long they'd be staying. Which is also the sort of thing I'd expect."

"What do we do, then?"

"Nothing. Just carry on as normal."

Clem thought about it. "Well, perhaps keep an eye on them. But nothing too obvious."

"Nothing too obvious, I see."

"And if you see Humph or Shelly before I do, tell them."

"Yes, yes, I will. And I'll put a mop over the kitchen floor, and wipe the tops down, and that."

"And I'll give Dilly a ring, see if they've been there yet. They don't declare themselves of course. They just check in, stay for a while, and make their report," Clem said, referring to the hotel and guest house inspectors the pub had warned them about some time before, passing on a rumour that they were in the area.

"And the Italian one looks like he might be something to do with catering. Oh, and Annie," she added, stopping her on her way back to the kitchen. "Not a word to anyone outside of this house."

"Wouldn't dream of it, me," Annie said, looking offended.

"Yes, you would. But you mustn't. This is serious, Annie. A lot may depend on it. If it is them, and they get to hear we knew it beforehand, then… Well, I don't know what would happen, how it might rebound on us. It might end up with the tourist authorities simply ignoring our existence – which would be disastrous for us. A lot of visitors from this country and elsewhere go on their recommendations. So I want you to promise, Annie, that you won't say a word. Not even to Owain."

Annie's expression was solemn. "I know I'm a bit of an old gossip, Clem, but I know what this place means to you. And to me."

She shook her head firmly. "I won't *utter* a word. To anybody."

Clem, never having heard Annie confess to being any sort of gossip before, was reassured.

She smiled at her. "Good chap," she said, and Annie swelled.

It was an accolade that Clem, who, by tradition and temperament, was not given to effusion, usually reserved for persons, of either sex, who had shown mettle in the hunting field.

Annie, she knew, was in good company.

Upstairs the three men had gathered in Sneed's bedroom.

They had left Clothesline and Brrm-Brrm, two faces known at the Hall, behind, and they were determined that, this time, the money would be leaving with them. And it was Sneed's idea that when it did, it would do so in one of the two suitcases he'd brought with him, filled now with the cut-up newspapers from the holdall, ready to leave behind in place of the money.

Sneed was a man who liked to have the last word.

"I'd still like to know what the rozzers are doing here," Tony said fretfully, and nibbled on a nail.

"Well, it's obviously not a secret, is it," Sneed said "She was about to tell us, wasn't she, that Welsh woman. She's a gabber if ever I met one, so we won't be in the dark for long.

But meanwhile, don't forget, we have the advantage here. In my opinion whoever took the money must have seen them hiding it there – seen *them,* Brrm-Brrm and Clothesline. But there's nothing to link us, three respectable businessmen from Nottingham, with a couple of half-baked villains from Brum, is there."

The Major turned from the window overlooking the festivities on the lawns below.

"And an advantage in the field, as Wellington observed, is worth an extra battalion of men. And this time, gentlemen," he said, beaming optimism at them, "I have the inescapable conviction that we shall retire from this engagement victorious."

While at the front of the Hall, young George, busy with his car numbers notebook, was working his way through the windfall of them on the drive.

He was halfway through the number of the last car, when he paused and then flipped back through the pages of the notebook.

And gasped.

He was right! It was the same car, the same number he'd taken down a week ago.

The two crooks were back.

Chapter Forty-Three

The following Monday Inspector Worth and his CID colleague were again summoned to Superintendent Jenkins's office.

Their boss held up a copy of a local newspaper. It was over a week now since the robbery and the front page of the *Kingham News* was asking how the money could have vanished without a trace, and further wanted to know what the police were doing about it.

The Superintendent indicated that he rather wanted to know that as well, and tossing the newspaper down on his desk, sat back and waited.

The CID Inspector shifted in the visitor's chair. "Well, I wouldn't say completely without a trace, sir. I mean, we know—"

"Yes, yes, Mr Berry," the Superintendent broke in testily, "we know that the getaway car and lorry were both stolen in Birmingham. And that, as they yielded neither fingerprints nor any other sort of clue, is all we do know. Quite frankly gentlemen, our side of the scoreboard at present does not bear looking at. And I would appreciate, when next the Chief Constable rings this office, having some movement on it to offer him."

"With respect, sir," the DI pressed on doggedly, "I was about to say that the fact that they *were* stolen in Birmingham gives us at least one lead. I'm working closely with Birmingham CID, and I think I can say with some confidence that—"

"And with equal respect, Roger," Inspector Worth cut in with a small thoughtful frown, "I do think we should be careful here of tunnel vision."

It was the Superintendent's turn to frown. "I don't think I follow you, Inspector."

Inspector Worth nodded understandingly. He was used to that, to people having difficulty keeping up.

"Well, sir, both vehicles were taken from the same area, on two successive weekday nights. And their recorded mileage indicates a journey from Birmingham to Shrewsbury only. All of which points to a local gang. But is that what we were *meant* to think? It's easy enough to rig mileometers, as we know. So, could it be that whoever stole the vehicles came from elsewhere?" he said, as if he knew the answer to that and was teasing them with it. "I was struck, for example," he went on, giving them a clue, "by the fact that they were both taken at around the same time. I was also struck by the proximity of New Street Station to the two sites, the fruit and vegetable market, from where the lorry was lifted, *and* the theatre car park the Triumph disappeared from—"

"The registered owner of the car's a dentist, sir," the CID Inspector said, making a contribution.

"Is that relevant?" the Superintendent asked, while suspecting that it wasn't.

"Well, no, sir, it isn't, actually," the DI had to admit.

Superintendent Jenkins nodded, looking tired. "Go on, Inspector."

Inspector Worth, who'd transferred his attention to the carpet when interrupted, frowning, lips pursed, at it, looked up. "I was about to say," he went on, as if not at all sure they deserved to hear it, "that as a consequence of this, I checked the arrival times of all trains at that station on both those evenings. And I found that London Euston, and London Euston alone, has a regular weekday service which gets into Birmingham New Street one hour before the two vehicles were taken."

"Mmm," the Superintendent murmured, chewing on it.

"Of course," Inspector Worth added with a modest shrug, "it may be just coincidence. But on the other hand, gentlemen, it could be that we've been handed a couple of red herrings for us to obligingly run after," he said, and sucked on a corner of his mouth.

There was a thoughtful silence, and then DI Berry said, "Well, of course Birmingham was the obvious place to start. And it would be remiss of us not to thoroughly investigate that end of things. But as I've said, I have never ruled out other possibilities. And one of those very much in the frame has always been a London mob."

Inspector Worth regarded the carpet again, and smiled faintly.

"Well, wherever they came from," Superintendent Jenkins said, "and however they got there, I, and the CC, would very much like them caught. So, to that end, perhaps you wouldn't mind bringing me, and him, up to date."

DI Berry went first, brisk with confidence. "Local area intelligence. That's where our lead will come from, sir. Plain-clothes coppering with its ear to the ground. That's where the real work's done on this sort of caper," he said with a sideways glance at his uniformed colleague. "I'm in close liaison with forces both sides of the border, including," he emphasised, "the Yard. And I'm confident that it's only a question of time – some known chummy throwing money about, loose talk picked up in some dive here, a name in somebody's ear there."

"Yes, there's always that, isn't there," the Superintendent agreed gloomily. "Mr Worth?"

"Well, sir, whether a train comes into the scheme of things or not," he said carelessly, a man who could afford to lose the odd detail, "this is obviously a highly professional gang. That we have no reliable witness descriptions of the getaway car's occupants further attest to that – the speed it was driven, the way it was handled on a wet road. Someone, some Mr Big perhaps somewhere, fielded a top team for this one. And *that* is the point. Because the fact that they left no clues is, of course, itself a clue."

The Inspector narrowed his eyes in thought, and sucked on a smile.

The Superintendent waited expectantly. There had been times when he was of the opinion that Inspector Worth was mad. And other times that he carried in his knapsack a chief constable's baton.

"As I indicated," the Inspector said then, sharing it with them, "this is a top-drawer team. Not at all the sort likely to risk a stop. But very *much* the sort to plant a sleeper."

He let that sink in and then went on, "And with that in mind, I have as we speak, well-briefed officers steadily working their way through all guest houses, hotels and pubs in the area, looking at people who checked in within a week before the robbery and who left within a week after it.

"Or who checked in within a week pre the robbery and who are still there, in the area. Our sleeper. Sitting on the money until he, or she – we must include the ladies in everything these days – is convinced the dust has completely settled. In other words, gentlemen, I am very much of the opinion that not only is the game still afoot, it remains a home one."

He smiled at his boss, the bearer of good news. "I am also of the opinion, sir," he revealed, "that when we come to drawing stumps on this particular game, the scoreboard will look *very* much different."

The CID Inspector shook his head. "Not likely, Ted. Trust me, they're all long gone and spending by now," he said, and looked at the Superintendent.

"Yes, I have to say, Mr Worth, that I am not – er – not entirely convinced that – er…" the Superintendent trailed off, and smiled vaguely at him.

The Inspector sighed inwardly, a man with pygmies pulling at him, slowing him down. "Which is precisely what they'd *like* us to think, Roger!" he snapped, taking it out on the DI. "These are not some petty local tealeaves we're dealing with here, flogging stuff off in the pub," he said, neatly and brutally delineating his colleague's usual area of operations. "As I have indicated, these are top-league villains. First Division players," he added, looking at the middle-aged figure sitting next to him, making it clear which division he considered him to be in. "Which is why, incidentally, by the same token, your scenarios of loose talk and chucking money about in this case simply will not run," he said dismissively.

DI Berry wheezed a laugh. "What, so they left one member of the gang to make his little piggy way home with a hundred grand? You must have been round some very trusting villains, Ted."

Inspector Worth leaned towards the DI. "Someone needs a course on cognitive systems," he said playfully.

"Cognitive systems, Mr Worth?" Superintendent Jenkins was frowning again.

"Yes, sir," the Inspector said, sitting up straight and smiling brightly at him, as if offering himself as some sort of proof. "It's a new way of thinking, sir. A new way of looking at things. Vertical, horizontal, circular and lateral," he said, making the hand movements to go with it as if to a song. "The thinking police officer's tool kit in the search for new idea pathways, sir," he ended snappily.

"I see," the Superintendent said, as if humouring him.

"I'll lend you the text book I've just finished reading if you like, Roger," the Inspector offered. *"Big Picture Thinking in the Detection and Apprehension of Criminals.* Psychology, Roger. Psychology," he said, tapping sharply at his forehead. "It's the future of policing."

"Load of old toffee, you mean," the DI growled.

Inspector Worth, a much younger man with psychology and the future on his side, could afford to smile.

"Well, wherever they came from and wherever they are now," the Superintendent said, getting back to the present, "and whatever you use to get them, speaking for myself *and* the Chief Constable, I want them got."

He regarded his two senior officers, his expression suggesting he was trying to find confidence in them, and not altogether succeeding.

"So... So – so put a bit of topspin on the ball!" he cried with vague, sudden passion. "Get out there and take the field back. I want this brought home. I want some collars felt!"

Chapter Forty-Four

One of the collars the Superintendent wanted felt was at that moment no more than a few miles away in the Hall's kitchen.

He was investigating a broom cupboard and so had missed the sound of a car pulling up at the back door. He had just discovered that a promisingly large cardboard box with 'cleaning materials' scrawled on it contained cleaning materials.

He gave it a frustrated kick, and was closing the cupboard door when Sergeant Cholmondeley-Jones walked in.

"Hello!" she said breezily.

"Oh, goody – the hotdogs are on," she went on, looking over at the stove, a light on under the big preserve pan and the smell of frying onions in the air.

Presented with the sudden sight of a police uniform, Tony's eye went into spasm, his hand on its way to his inside breast pocket before he remembered the Welsh woman explaining that the local law used the place for their meal breaks.

"I was just looking. That's all, lady," he said, spreading his hands. "I used to be in the restaurant business, see."

"I see," she said.

"I was just taking what you might call a professional interest in the kitchen. Just taking a look, like. Know what I mean?" he said, winking at her and starting to edge towards the door into the hall.

"You're a guest here, then?" the Sergeant asked politely.

"That's right, lady, I'm a guest here. From Nottingham. I'm from Nottingham," he emphasised. "Here with two associates. Two business associates. On – er – on business."

"I see," she said.

Tony established the rest of his cover story. "Name's Como. Like Perry," he added with a wink, and disappeared.

"How very peculiar," the Sergeant said.

"You've got rather a peculiar guest staying at present, Clem," she said, when Clem came in a few moments later. "I found him nosing about in that cupboard there. An Italian-looking chap. In a black shirt and white tie. Like somebody in a gangster film."

"Mr Como," Clem said, suddenly alert.

"Yes, that's right. Como, like Perry. That's the chap. Said he used to be in the restaurant business and was taking a professional interest. But I have to say that I didn't altogether like the look of him. Thought him rather a shady sort."

But Clem wasn't listening. "I knew it! I *knew* it."

"Knew what, Clem?" the Sergeant asked. "What did you know?"

"He's – no, I'd better not tell you. It's all supposed to be... Well, it's all rather... hush-hush," she said with a little embarrassed laugh.

"Look, Petunia, have a seat. The Conies are nearly ready, and I'll do coffee. But I must find Annie first."

"How very peculiar," the Sergeant said to herself, as Clem disappeared back into the hall.

George also thought Tony looked like a gangster – which, unlike the Sergeant, he didn't find in the least peculiar, because he knew now that that was what he was.

When he'd established that there were no guests staying at the Hall who resembled the two men he'd seen hiding the money, he told Phineas that he thought he must have made a mistake when jotting down the number the previous Saturday.

"Easily done," Phineas said with some relief, as he was still dithering over what to do about it.

But then, on that Monday, when wandering past what used to be an orangery, George saw, through the broken panes of one of its tall windows, a man he knew to be a guest moving among the large wooden tubs which had once held hibernating citrus trees in long ago Batch Valley winters.

He appeared to be looking for something, and George hadn't needed to have his Junior Detective's hat on to recognise, when the man spotted he'd been seen, shifty behaviour when he saw it.

That man, he was later to learn, was the one who called himself Mr Havington-Wilkes.

And the following day, to clinch matters as far as he was concerned, he was able to link him and two others to the Wolseley when he saw them leaving it after returning from a trip out, one of the journeys they were forced to make now and then to back up their cover story, driving aimlessly around for a while or sitting in the library or a café in Kingham.

He was convinced then that he hadn't made a mistake with the car number, and putting it together came up with three members of the same gang, there to search for the missing money.

On his way to report to Phineas, he decided first to get as much information as he could about them. He found Annie Owen in the kitchen.

They were from Nottingham, she told him, leaning on the mop she was using. In the area on business, like. And George smiled to himself then in a superior sort of way when she told him their names: a Major Blashford, a Mr Havington-Wilkes, and Mr Como, like Perry, the singer.

But then she couldn't, he allowed, be expected to know about aliases.

"Why Georgie?" it occurred to her to ask then, considering what she and Clem now knew about them.

"Oh, nothing," George said, elaborately casual.

She studied him, wondering what he knew – wondering *if* he knew.

He could do, she decided. He always seemed to be popping up all over the place. He could have overheard Clem telling her of her suspicions about the three on Saturday, or even done so yesterday, when she'd told her about the Sergeant finding Mr Como inspecting the kitchen.

Annie, who'd been cleaning it again today on the strength of it, surprised George by poking her head out to check no one was in the hall, and then coming back to him.

"Look, Georgie, bach, look, if you know what I think you know, don't tell nobody, all right? Keep it to yourself, there's a good boy," she said, lowering her voice and leaving George with his mouth open.

"Not a word now, mind. For their sake," she added, glancing in the direction of the rest of the Hall. "The family's, like."

And then she smiled in a motherly way at him. "OK, Georgie?"

George, staring at her, nodded dumbly.

He didn't know what to say, or think.

He was once again no longer Dick Drake, sleuth hound, but a ten-year-old schoolboy in a world that was suddenly far more difficult to read than an *Intrepid* comic.

He left, hurrying out on his way with it to Phineas.

Chapter Forty-Five

Phineas, working at the table on deck in his Gent's Superior Panama, had his eyes narrowed with thoughts of another sort of robbery.

He had DI MacNail and his men staking out a bank, waiting after a tip-off for the arrival of the gang that planned to rob it, the tension ticking away like the watch MacNail kept checking.

He had guns and radio communication of the, 'Roger, over and out' sort, and was about to have a shoot-out, with bullets flying and passers-by screaming and running for cover. He was looking forward to it.

And then real life in the form of George came up the gangway.

George also had a story to tell.

"Crikey!" Phineas said, when George got to the part where Annie told him not to tell anyone about the three crooks for the family's sake.

"What *is* going on up there?" he said, more to himself.

"Beats me, Phin," George said, shaking his head, and absently patting Bill Sikes who'd wandered across to join in.

"I mean, if Annie knows about whatever it is, and she obviously does," Phineas went on, "then I'd expect you and me by now to be the only two people in the village who *don't* know. Which we obviously are *not*, or whatever it is would be the talk of the post office. Well, whatever it is, I don't at all like the sound of it. And why haven't they gone to the police, whatever it is? I don't understand it. I simply do *not* understand it."

George looked at him. He obviously didn't spend his Saturday mornings in the Kingham Odeon.

"They couldn't go to the cops, Phin," he said patiently, making allowances for him. "Not with Humph up to his neck in it. They have to keep it buttoned, see."

Phineas struggled with it for a moment, opened his mouth to say something, and abruptly stood up instead.

"Right. OK. Well, I'll ask her. That's what I'll do. I'll give her a ring. She'll tell me. I'll get it out of her. She can't keep anything under her hat for longer than five minutes."

He was back in just under that.

He sat down and shook his head.

"Said she didn't know what I was on about and that she couldn't talk now, anyway, she was busy, and put the phone down. She knows something, all right. I can tell when Annie's lying. Well, there is one thing. If they are here to search for the money it suggests, does it not, that Humph *isn't* involved."

"So what about him talking to the two crooks?" George wanted to know. "And what about asking me to keep on eye open for people nosing about – like the crook I saw in the orangery?" he said pointedly. "What about that then, Phin?"

"I don't know, frankly, George," Phineas admitted after doing a bit more struggling. "I'm not sure I know anything anymore. About anything."

He pushed a hand through his hair in frustration. "Look, what have we got? We've got you finding the money the first two gang members hid. And now it seems we've got three *other* gang members looking for it – presumably because they assumed the first two gang members are now known, having perhaps been spotted hiding it."

He paused. "But if Humph, as you say, knew the first lot, why then doesn't he know this lot? I mean, presumably he doesn't. Or does he? Is that what Annie meant?" he asked himself.

"Well, Humph wouldn't know *all* the gang the IOC sent, Phin," George said, with a little laugh at his ignorance. "He's a Mr *Big*. And the Mr Bigs don't."

"Maybe he double crossed them. Maybe – No! It's *ridiculous.*

"George – George," he said firmly, "I still cannot accept that Humph was involved in the robbery." He put up a hand to forestall him. "He's in there somewhere, in some way, I grant you. Or somebody at the Hall is. There's now no question of that. God knows what it's about, but whatever it is about, it seems to me we have two choices. We either hand the money over to the crooks or to the police."

"But what if we go to the police and Humph *is* involved?" George said, fretfully pulling at one of Sike's ears.

"But what if he isn't?" Phineas countered.

"But what if he *is*?"

Phineas opened his mouth to continue the argument, before seeing that it would only come back to him.

"Well, in that case I think we ought to take their ball away. And then, with nothing to play with, they'll go home. And we'll have Humph back. If, that is, he has managed somehow to get himself tangled up in it. So in other words, I think we ought to give it to the police, give them the money."

He shot up a hand again as George opened his mouth to protest.

"Anonymously."

"What's that?" George asked suspiciously.

"Secretly. Without divulging our identity."

George looked impressed.

"And what we need now," Phineas mused, "is a method of doing so."

He frowned out over the river, while George, leaving it to him, or MacNail, started playing with Sikes.

"I've *got* it!" Phineas announced a few minutes later, sounding surprised.

George took his seat again expectantly.

Phineas leaned forward. "Some years ago, George, in Buckinghamshire, a gang robbed a mail train of over two million quid. The Great Train Robbery, it's known as. The biggest heist on these shores until the Baker Street job a couple of years back. And then after it, someone, for whatever reason, left a mail sack stuffed full of banknotes, part of the loot, in a phone box in London, rang Scotland Yard and told them to come and get it."

Phineas slapped the table. "And that, Georgie, my boy, is precisely what I suggest we do."

"What, leave it in a phone box in London?"

"No, here somewhere. In the area. In Kingham, say. And then ring the police anonymously. That way, the crooks don't prosper, as the unrighteous shouldn't, and Humphrey, if he is up to his daft neck in it, won't get into trouble. We can then tell him we know all about it and that, whatever he's done, he's not to do it again."

Phineas beamed at him. "How's that?"

George thought about it, and then nodded.

"So he wouldn't have to go downriver then?"

"Downriver?"

George sighed. "To the pen. The joint, Phin."

"Ah, I get you. No. No, he wouldn't have to go downriver."

George shook his head. "I knew you'd come up with something, Phin. You and Inspector MacNail. So when do we do it then?"

"*We* don't. *I'll* do it. You've done enough. I'll just chuck it in the old Frogeye and… No, no, wait a minute, I can't, can I. I haven't got the money, have I. I gave it to Hattie, Miss

Wyndham, to look after – *crikey!*" it struck him then, "that was last Tuesday. I said it would only be for a couple of days. She'll be having kittens by now. Look, Georgie, you – you just leave it with me. All right?"

"All right, Phin."

"I'll give Miss Wyndham a ring now. And if she's there I'll nip across and pick it up. End of story. You'll see. You just leave it to your Uncle Phineas, Georgie. This time tomorrow you'll be wondering what all the fuss was about."

"OK, Phin," George said.

After George had disappeared back down the gangway, Phineas headed for the sitting room and the phone, wondering what he was going to say to Miss Wyndham.

But then, when he got through, he wasn't able to say much of anything.

Was it, she squeaked as soon as she knew who was calling, about the loot? He said that it was rather, Hattie, yes. And then before he could tell her that he was sorry for the delay, and how, what with one thing and another, it had completely slipped his mind, she told him how sorry *she* was, and went on in an agitated rush about her nerves, and how she hadn't been able to sleep for longer than five minutes that night, waiting for the gang to turn up.

"Phineas, I'm so sorry," she wailed. "But I simply *had* to get rid of it!"

Phineas, seeing her on the other end with her handkerchief out, told her she was not to worry, that he quite understood, and wondered if she remembered just what she had done with it? It wasn't terribly important if she couldn't, he hastened to assure her, not wishing to set her off again, and thinking that wherever it was it was probably just as good as a phone box.

Miss Wyndham, somewhat reassured, and with some of her dignity restored, said tartly that that was very kind of him, but she *could* remember, thank you all the same. She was, she admitted, prone to drop, as it were, the odd stitch now and then, but wasn't yet entirely gaga.

She had, she said precisely, as if demonstrating it, taken the sack from the coal shed where she had hidden it, placed it on the basket of her bicycle, and wheeled it down the High Street to Upper Ham and the *Castle*.

"Ah," Phineas said. "To Priny and the Commander. Right, thank you, Hattie—"

"But they were out. So I next thought of Annie and Owain—"

"Annie and Owain," Phineas said. "OK, I'll—"

"But then, as I was about to continue on round to the *Felicity H*, Jasmine appeared in her motorcar. So I asked her would she kindly look after it."

Phineas waited in case it had then gone on from there, before saying, "Jasmine. Right. Thank you, Hattie."

And after telling her again that she wasn't to worry, that he now had everything in hand, he rang Jasmine.

There was no answer.

There was no answer later that day either, and when he went round to the *Cluny Queen* the car wasn't there, and neither was Jasmine, nor was there any sign about the place of her family.

Chapter Forty-Six

While up at the Hall it was Inspector Worth's turn to walk in on a member of the gang searching for the money.

Needing, as he'd delicately put it to Clem, to wash his hands, he excused himself from the kitchen and went up to the bathroom on the first floor.

The small brass and white enamel plate above the door knob said it was engaged. But then it always said that. The lock was faulty. It was, Clem had told him vaguely, on Humph's list of things to do. And the handmade cardboard sign with 'Engaged' written in blue Biro on one side of it and 'Vacant' on the other, and which was usually hanging by a piece of string from the doorknob, now appeared to be missing. Batch Hall, as he'd had reason to observe before, was not the sort of establishment one could truthfully say ran like clockwork.

He knocked, a couple of times, waited for a reply, and getting none, walked in.

The Major, waiting for whoever to go away, and wondering if whoever could damn well read, was kneeling on the floor in front of the bath. Using his Swiss Army knife to remove the screws, he had just taken off the side panel.

The two men stared at each other.

The Inspector recovered first.

"Ah. Sorry. I did knock."

The Major, confronted with the sudden appearance of a senior police officer, was on his knees, shaken, but not yet out.

He came up with a cat.

He smiled feebly and then made a show of peering into the spaces around and under the bath.

He sat up and cleared his throat. "I can only suppose that it must have been the plumbing, the pipes, you know, in an old house like this. Silly of me. A cat," he explained, getting to his feet and dusting off his trousers.

"I could have sworn I heard a cat crying. Still, mustn't hold up a chap in need. I'll put the panel back after you've finished. And meanwhile, keep cave for you, seeing as the lock appears not to work."

"Thank you very much. That really is very good of you," the Inspector said effusively, making up for having at first mistaken him for a plumber, much taken with his accent, expensive-looking tweed suit and regimental tie.

"Shan't be long. Just a quick – er – you know…"

When the door closed the Major's first instinct was to bolt for it.

But he steadied the ranks, and waited, using the time to work on the rest of the story.

He chuckled in a self-deprecating way when the door opened again, the sound of the lavatory flushing thudding and banging through the pipes.

"I must confess that it's not the first time I've imagined such a thing. It all goes rather painfully back to the death of a pet cat in a flat I had then in London. Before, that is, I re-located for business purposes to Nottingham," he added, getting his cover story in.

"I see," the Inspector said politely.

The Major wiped dolefully his moustache.

"Foolish of me, I know. But I – I cannot entirely shake off the thought of her last hours under the floorboards, where the silly creature had somehow contrived to get herself stuck. I was away on business at the time, d'you see."

"Ah." The Inspector's face was composed sympathetically.

"Yes, I had – er – I had arranged for one of the porters to leave food for her in the kitchen. No business of his of course that it remained untouched. So no blame can be attributed there. She was found under the – er – under the drawing room floor."

"Ah, I see."

"Yes, the – er – the electrician chappies discovered her. When I later had the place re-wired."

"Oh, dear."

"I have to confess that I cannot go anywhere near Eaton Square these days without imagining her cries going unheeded. And sometimes… Well, as I say, this isn't the first time it's happened. And when it does I – well, I just have to make *sure*, d'you see."

"Yes. Yes, of course."

"All rather foolish of me, I'm afraid."

"Not at all, not at all. Does you credit."

"Well, good of you to say so. Yes, she was a dear creature. She was – em – she was an Egyptian cat, you know."

"Ah, an Egyptian cat."

"Yes. Called a Mau. An early example of onomatopoeia."

"My word."

"You are perhaps familiar with the breed?"

"No. No, I can't say I am."

"Spotted cats. In fact, they're the only naturally occurring spotted domestic cat in existence."

"Is that so?"

"Yes. They were duck hunters, you know, in ancient Egypt."

"Were they indeed! What, they actually used to hunt ducks?"

The Major hesitated. "They – er- they acted as retrievers," he decided. "The Egyptians would shoot the ducks, or quack-quacks, as they might have called them, with bow and arrow, and they would fetch."

"What, ducks on water, do you mean, or—?"

"Oh, yes, on water. Paddling about on the Nile."

"Good lord! So they're obviously good swimmers then."

"Oh, indeed."

The Major chuckled nostalgically. "And how fondly I remember that ancient instinct at play, the innocent summer hours spent together in Kensington Gardens, me chucking rubber thingies in the pond for her to retrieve. They wag their tails like dogs when happy, you know."

"Really!" the Inspector said, chuckling with him.

"Oh, yes. Quite beguiling creatures. And – er – and as I say, an ancient breed. Going back to Pharaonic times. Beginning with the eighteenth dynasty and ending with the twentieth," the Major said crisply, on surer ground now. "They were revered as deities, cherished as pets, and, as we have heard, employed in the pursuit of ducks. They often featured in the iconography of the sarcophagi, and on their demise were mummified and entombed in the pyramids, shut away from the vulgar gaze with the Pharaohs. While Fadia – that was her name, you know, Fadia. Princess Fadia, a name she wore as if a tiara – died like a common house mouse under the London floorboards. Her stiff, matted corpse mute, singing no more, no more."

The Major wiped again at his moustache.

"What a sad story," the Inspector said.

The Major's head came up as he remembered more from that volume in the prison reference library.

"They're known for that, you know, their musicality. Filling with song the days of those under whose roofs they choose to honour with their presence, chirping and chortling, and other, distinctly unusual vocalisations when stimulated."

"Just been chatting to a guest of yours upstairs," the Inspector said, back in the kitchen. "At least I assume he's a guest. Military-looking gentleman, in tweeds."

"Major Blashford," Clem said immediately.

"Major, eh. I thought as much. Ex-officer, and all that. Decent type. Had the panel off the bath there because he thought he heard a cat crying."

Inspecting the plumbing, Clem thought. They *are* thorough.

"Told me a rather sad story about a pet cat who died under the floorboards of a flat he had in London. Eaton Square, actually," he added, suggesting a familiarity with the address. "And how he can't now get the cries he imagined her making out of his head."

"Ohh, there's sad," Annie said over the onions. "He's here—"

"He's here on business," Clem cut in, in case Annie had been about to blunder on. "With two colleagues from Nottingham."

"Yes, he mentioned Nottingham."

"Looking for business opportunities in the area."

"Are they? *Are* they indeed! I find that *very* interesting. They're just the sort of people we need, businessmen of that calibre, seeking to invest in the area. As I was saying to the mayor only the other week, regeneration, that's today's watchword. Regeneration, not stagnation. I wonder if he plays golf...?"

After the Inspector had gone, and with Shelly upstairs with the vacuum cleaner and Hawis, who liked to chase after it, Annie, alone with Clem over the washing-up at the twin soapstone sinks in the kitchen, took the opportunity to ask her if there was anything she'd like to tell her.

"I mean, you know you can tell me, don't you, Clem. It won't go any further, if you say not to. You know that, don't you."

Clem frowned. "Tell you about what?"

"Well, Humph, like..."

"Humph? Tell you what about Humph?"

Annie smiled encouragingly at her. "You know..."

"No, I don't know look – would mind being a little less Welsh about it and get to the point?"

Annie's smile faltered. Perhaps she really didn't know. Perhaps it wasn't Humph after all. Perhaps Miss Wyndham had got it right. Perhaps it was—

"Is this about my marriage, Annie?" Clem demanded bluntly, breaking into her thoughts. "Do you think Humph's playing around. Is that what you mean?"

"No!" Annie said, aghast at the thought. She had no trouble seeing him as a robber, even, if pushed hard enough, as a criminal mastermind. But never *that*.

"No, no, of *course* I don't."

"Well, what—"

"Well, what about Shelly then?" Annie said, plunging on. "Is there something you want to tell me about her?"

"Annie – what *is* this about?"

"Well… Well, nothing really. I just wanted to be sure that – er – everybody was all right, like, you know. That's all…"

"Well, why *wouldn't* we be?" Clem said impatiently.

"I dunno," Annie said, busying herself again with the scourer and saucepan. "I just thought… you know… was everything all right. That's all I meant," she added, sounding offended.

Clem had no idea what it was really about, and had known Annie long enough to know that there was no point in pursuing it.

She confined herself to reassuring her that everything was fine, thanked her for asking, and then changed the subject.

"When we've finished this," she said, getting back to the washing-up, "we'll put the kettle on and get the Dunks out. Put our feet up while we've got the chance. We've got a few quiet days from now till the historical re-enactment bash on Saturday, fighting the battle of Batch Magna over again.

"Be a good way to end the week," she added on a laugh. "With a bang."

Chapter Forty-Seven

The following morning there was still no answer when Phineas rang Jasmine, so he rang Annie. Ffion answered and told him that her mum was up at the Hall and wouldn't be back till lunchtime. And that, no, her dad wasn't at home either. And no, she had no idea where Jasmine was.

He thought about ringing the Hall, but decided not to risk Annie not answering and the Sergeant being in the kitchen when whoever did answer told her, Annie, that he, Phineas, the same Phineas who was supposed to be incognito, on a secret mission abroad somewhere, was on the other end of the telephone.

He went round to the *Queen*. Jasmine's car still wasn't there, and neither was Jasmine. Nor were any of her brood around, the place strangely quiet without them, like a school closed for the holidays.

He wondered if, finding suddenly herself the richer by a windfall of a hundred thousand pounds, she simply hadn't taken off with it. Not that he would necessarily blame her, it was just that it would further complicate things somewhat.

Keeping his eyes peeled for patrol cars from Kingham, he headed for the post office, where Mrs Pugh, in her guise of post mistress, presided over a spy ring with tentacles reaching to Capel-y-Coch one side of the border and Little Batch the other, passing on the information with the stamps and postal orders. If Alwen Pugh didn't know where Jasmine was, then no one in the village did.

The bell above the shop door rang him in, and he was startled by Mr Pugh, who usually greeted his appearance with a sniff, a man who regarded the houseboats and the things that went on there as a latter day Sodom and Gomorrah, waiting only for God, or the council, to get round to them, grinning at him, the few yellowing strands of hair plastered across his bony skull lifting with a bob of his head.

Phineas carried on through to the post office, bought a book of stamps and then casually asked Mrs Pugh if by any chance she had seen Jasmine lately.

The post mistress leaned eagerly forward on her high chair behind the counter, the top buttons of her floral print dress straining under the impact of her plump body like a parcel coming undone.

"Haven't you heard, dear? She had to go to Betws Fesniog, to her sister's there. Called away, she was. Her husband's a builder and he had an accident at work. Fell off some scaffolding, he did. Touch and go it was for a while, by all accounts. She's there helping out with things, looking after the kids and that. Took some of her own lot with her, the youngest, like, and left the rest with her mother. Well, couldn't get them all in the car, could she," Mrs Pugh couldn't resist adding, her expression making it clear what she thought of Jasmine and her offspring, a frequent subject of scandalised discussion on the pavement outside the chapel on a Sunday, all born in sin, and not only that, a sin, considering the number of times she'd committed it, obviously enjoyed.

And then she lowered her voice. "But you've got your own problems, I hear, haven't you, dear?" she said, making a sympathetic face, hoping for something to add to the rumours about him.

For the second time since setting foot in the shop Phineas was startled.

Annie, he thought immediately. Bloody Annie. She'd either wheedled it out of the Sergeant or simply gone ahead and publicly aired her suspicions, the suspicions he had guessed she'd had in her kitchen the other day, presenting them as fact.

Either way, it was only a matter of time before Sally got to hear of it.

He regarded the postmistress sternly. "I will neither confirm nor deny common gossip," he said haughtily.

"And furthermore, let me remind you, Mrs Pugh, that there is such a thing as the law of slander," he added, and had to put up with Mr Pugh on his way out nodding and grinning at him again in what he now took to be a knowing sort of way.

Really – this place! he thought, closing the door sharply behind him.

But what the shopkeeper had demonstrated was not knowingness but ingratiation. He was treating Phineas as he would a favoured customer, which, if the rumours about him were true, he hoped he soon would be. A favoured and newly rich customer. Mr Pugh was hedging his bets.

Whether it was Phineas or Sir Humph, or, as some talk had it, even Sir Humph's mum, who had a hand in the robbery, if not the masterminding of it, then, even after splitting the proceeds with their gang, that would still leave a good deal of spending money when it came to buying the groceries.

Back on the *Belle* Phineas sat on deck thinking about it.

He'd spoken to Sally on the phone last night and all was calm then, so, unless Annie had rung her before leaving for the Hall, it hadn't yet reached Sally's ears.

So what he had to do now was to keep Annie from Sally.

He decided to ring Annie at lunchtime on some pretext and let it slip that Sally had gone away again, on a course, up north somewhere, say. And then ring Sally and tell her that he had to visit an ill aunt in Kent. That for now should keep Annie from Sally and Sally from him. Which would only leave the Sergeant who, acting on information received, would now no doubt be back staking out the *Belle*.

He decided that this time he'd reinforce his defences by hiding the Frogeye, and settled on John Beecher and his coal yard. John would do it for him, no questions asked.

He went back over it, checking he hadn't left anything out. Life had got tiresomely complicated again, and he was telling himself that it would be far easier to simply leg it, when George came up the gangway.

He glanced round as if to check he hadn't been followed, and lowering his voice asked how the drop had gone last night.

Phineas hadn't been serious about legging it, which didn't stop him sighing because he couldn't now anyway. He'd forgotten about the money.

He told George that the drop hadn't gone, and explained why.

"So she's either taken it with her or hidden it somewhere. Either way, when she gets back, which local gossip in the shape of Mrs Gasbag Pugh tells me shouldn't be too long, I'll make the drop then. OK, George?"

"OK, Phin."

"Oh, and George, if anybody asks do you know where I am, say you don't. OK?"

"What, anybody, Phin?"

"Anybody. Anybody at the Hall, anybody – anybody anywhere. Just say you don't know. You haven't seen me for a while. I'll explain it all later," he said, and winked.

George nodded knowingly. "Got ya, Phin."

"And meanwhile, keep an eye open up at the Hall – but, George, listen to me – no more than that, OK? Do please remember that these are dangerous men, so keep well away from them. All right?"

"All right, Phin."

"Well, just make sure you do, because I can't be there. I have to stay away for now, for reasons, would you believe, to do with the police – or rather a certain lady police sergeant, who, extraordinarily enough, has somehow managed to get it into her head that I asked her to marry me!"

He laughed briefly and spread his hands in a gesture of amazed incredulity.

George shook his head. "Dames, eh, Phin."

"Dames indeed, George. So I'm afraid in view of that, you'll have to be my eyes and ears there. What's called a watching brief."

George looked impressed. "OK, Phin."

Chapter Forty-Eight

But then not long after that George, coming across Tony, decided to do more than just watch.

Whether Humphrey was involved or not, he took the view that it would do no harm to let the crooks know just who they were dealing with.

Tony was standing on the Hall front steps, wondering where to search next, when George sidled up to him.

"He's not who he says he is, you know," he said out of the corner of his mouth.

Tony jumped.

"Who're you – who're you?"

"Never mind who I am," George said, remembering a line from Saturday morning at the Odeon. "It's who Sir Humphrey, as he calls himself, really is. He's known as Big H in New York. And Chicago," he added for good measure.

"Push off, kid," Tony said.

"'Smatter of fact," George went on, "he sleeps with a Chicago piano under his bed."

"A *what*?" Tony couldn't resist asking.

Tony, despite his black shirt and white tie, went immediately down in George's estimation.

"What – you don't know what a Chicago piano is? It's a Tommy-gun," he said, and mimed its action. "Fires off five hundred rounds a second," he improvised. "He took Jimmy Legs out with it, in a barber's chair. Blood all over the place, there was."

"What the hell are you on about?"

"And Fat Tony. Left him with his face in a plate of spaghetti. Ask the FBI."

Tony flexed his shoulders. "The FBI," he sneered.

"He used to be a hit man for the Mafia. You wanna watch it."

"You wanna watch it, kid, you wanna watch it."

Tony glanced around and then pulled out his flick-knife.

"See this?" he said, and sprung the blade.

George, his world suddenly bigger again, took a step back.

"I dunno who you are, kid – but scram, OK?"

"Just a friendly warning, that's all. From a friend," George got out, remembering another line from the same film, and trying to keep his voice steady.

Tony returned the knife to his breast pocket and brushed a couple of times at nothing on a lapel.

"*Beeeat* it," he growled.

Tony met Humphrey then, on his way back in, having decided that Sneed should be told about his encounter with George.

Humphrey, chomping on a cigar and in a birds of paradise shirt, was playing on a one-armed bandit in the hall, playing the slots, as he called it, bringing a touch of Vegas to Batch Magna. And although Tony hadn't of course believed any of the kid's nonsense, it struck him that Humph, as he'd insisted they call him, certainly looked and sounded the part. Tony was also in thrall to the screen version of American gangsters. It's where he got his dress sense from.

"Hi, Mr Como. How ya doin'?" Humphrey greeted him. "Hey, I've been meaning to say. There's not a lot to do round here when you want to relax after business, and that kinda thing, right?" he said, following on from a conversation he and

Clem had had about scoring extra points with the three men they now had no doubt were tourism inspectors.

Tony mumbled something, and Humphrey went on, "Now my wife, she was saying that it'd be no trouble to put a picnic together, if you wanna take one of the boats out. We've got a boathouse down on the river. It's something we offer all our guests. Hey – when you're under our roof, you're family. Right? Know what I mean?"

"No, thanks," Tony said. "We're – er—"

"Or riding. We've got stables out back. Swell country for riding round here."

"No, thanks," Tony said again. "We – er – we don't do that."

"Same here. You'll never get me up on one of them things. I leave all that kinda stuff to the wife. How about a spot of fishing then? You could go out with our ghillie," Humphrey suggested swankily, meaning Owain Owen. "We have a ghillie for our guests, as well."

Tony, edging his way towards the stairs, said no thanks, they didn't do that either.

Humphrey had another idea.

"Hey – how about shooting? You guys shoot?"

Tony was about to say that that was something else they didn't do, when Humphrey lowered his voice, looked around, and said, "Game's outa season now, but we can always find something to shoot at."

He clamped the cigar back in his mouth and winked. "Know what I mean?"

And Tony winked back, several times, rapidly, and hurried on upstairs.

The pawnbroker was lying on his bed, staring at the ceiling. He shot up when Tony burst in, and glared wildly at him, before seeming to recognise him.

"Harold—" Tony began.

"You should learn to knock before coming into somebody's room, Tony. It's only manners. Didn't nobody ever teach you that, eh?" he said mildly. A mildness under which turbulence was gathering.

They'd been there four days now without a sign of the money, and he'd been feeding on the frustrations, seeing his dream of London and a new life blocked at every move, making a mockery of the plans he'd laid so carefully, turning his life once more into a joke.

"Harold, there was this kid downstairs—"

"A kid, Tony? A kid? What kid?" Sneed said with exaggerated, puzzled amusement.

Tony, irritated, shrugged. "I dunno, do I. Just some kid," he said, and then told him what George had told him, and what Humphrey had then said, all of which seemed to afford Sneed further amusement, sitting on the edge of the bed, shaking his head over it and smiling to himself, a man still on top of things even if somebody else was clearly coming loose at the seams.

"I don't know, Tony. Kids and Mafia hit men. Whatever next?" he asked with a chuckle. "I think you'd better have a little lie down, like I was trying to have."

"Yeah, yeah, but what I've been thinking is—"

"There you go again, Tony, thinking. I've told you, son, you ought to leave that kind of thing to me."

"What I've been thinking, Harold," Tony insisted, "is that I said back in the Major's place that a kid was involved, looking at the toy guns. Well, what if it's him? I mean, he was going on about guns – well, what if it's him? What if he's the one what made the switch. What if he's the one that—"

"Yeah, I get the picture, Tony, thank you," Sneed said briefly. And then, "Who is he then, this kid?"

"I told you, I dunno. But maybe he's the one Brrm-Brrm said hangs about the place."

Sneed thought about it.

"And he'd have probably known where to put his hand on a load of old newspapers…" he mused.

"Yeah, that's right. That's right. That's what I was thinking. Maybe we should pick him up. Take him somewhere and put the frighteners on him."

"Well, it's worth looking into, mate. But before adding kidnapping to armed robbery, let's find out what we can about him first. Leave that to me. I'll – ah, Major. Please, do come in," Sneed said as the door opened again, Mr Havington-Wilkes graciously welcoming a guest.

"The Major," he went in the same accent, "volunteered to do a recce of their bedroom while our hosts are downstairs."

"He didn't knock," Tony pointed out. "You didn't say anything about *him* not knocking, did you. Didn't talk about *his* manners."

The Major inclined his head. "Quite right, Tony. An oversight on my part. For which of course I apologise."

"Never mind all that," Sneed said, Sneed again, getting back to business. "No luck, I take it?"

The Major, watched sullenly by Tony, said he was afraid not.

"Well, we've done the rest of their living quarters, theirs and his mum's. I can't see there's much left indoors."

After a desultory search of a few outhouses, they had decided to concentrate on the Hall, in their guise of enthusiasts of historical domestic architecture. And sharing out the rooms, and in addition to sneaking into the family's living quarters when opportunity allowed, had quickly ticked off the unoccupied guest bedrooms, including the single rooms on the top floor, once the maids' bedrooms, the two bathrooms, the breakfast room, dining room, billiards room, drawing room library, kitchen, the servants' hall, now used, among other things, as the guests' TV room, the butler's pantry and other service rooms off the back passageway, the basement, once a dormitory for male staff, a respectable distance away from the female staff under the eaves, and the cellars.

"The lofts," the Major said, directing a finger upwards. "We've forgotten the lofts."

"And how are we supposed to get up there?" Sneed wanted to know.

"I'll stand on Tony's shoulder," the Major volunteered.

"How about me standing on yours?" Tony said.

"Yeah, well, before you start doing your Laurel and Hardy act, let's finish the outside first. 'Ere, Major, you did search it properly did you, their bedroom? Only you were a bit quick about it. And if they have got it, and it's here, indoors, that's where I'd expect it to be, as we couldn't find it in their lounge."

"One did not want to hang about longer than was absolutely necessary, Sneed," the Major said stiffly. "I did not have time to remove the panels on the en suite bath, nor to take up the floorboards there and in the bedroom, if that's what you mean. And that apart, there wasn't much to search. A laundry basket in the bathroom, a double wardrobe and two dressing tables in the bedroom, and a late Victorian secretaire desk, the business heart of their enterprise, judging by the paperwork. And their child's bed, with no room in it, I assure you, for anything but a child. I checked its mattress, and that of their double bed, and of course, as with the child's, under it – a quite splendid four-poster, incidentally. George the Third, I should think. Corinthian capitals, yellow silk—"

"Was there anything there, anything under the bed?" Tony broke in.

"Like a piano," Sneed said, and shook with suppressed laughter.

The Major looked at him. He was lately of the opinion that the pawnbroker was slowly becoming unglued.

"A piano under the bed, Sneed? Oh, very droll," he said, chuckling, hoping that that was what it was, an attempt at humour, and not the prelude to the pawnbroker coming apart completely.

"A Chicago piano," Tony growled. "A Tommy-gun. He knew what I meant. You knew what I meant, Harold," he said quietly, his face speaking the loudest, and it was his face that got Sneed's attention.

The pawnbroker put up a hand, as if holding him off while he collected himself. "Take no notice of me, Tony. Just my little joke. I didn't mean anything. You know that, son, don't you," he said, smiling fondly at him. And then looked sharply at the Major.

"No, what I was on about, was while you were buggering around admiring the bleeding furniture, our Tony here was actually doing something useful. Like picking up something what might turn out to be a lead. Go on, tell him, son," he said encouragingly.

Tony, mollified somewhat, nodded. "Yeah, all right. Well, there was this kid, see," he said, and went through his story again.

The Major was frowning. "Well, I have to say that the lad sounds interesting, in light of the toy guns. But—"

"And the cut-up newspapers," Sneed said. "Don't forget that, Major. He could have took them from home, or from here somewhere. We know at least some of them were local."

"So could the so-called *Sir* Humphrey," Tony said.

"I do think, Tony," the Major said, "that you're reading rather too much into his remarks. It's the sort of sport after all that he would offer his guests, as a gentleman – even one who – er – who came rather late to the role," he said, delicately seeking a way to be polite about someone he liked. "Rod and gun, and the pick of his stables. I might take him up on the horse myself. It's been a long time…" he said wistfully, and lifted his head, as if hearing something, or listening for it, on some faint distance.

"Bumpity! Bumpity! Bumpity! Bump! If I was riding my charger! Bumpity! Bumpity! Bumpity! Bump! As proud as an Indian Ra-

jah!" Sneed threw himself into it, vigorously miming the action and singing out wildly, startling them. "*All the girls declare, I am a gay old stager! Hey! Hey! clear the way, here comes the galloping Maaaajor!*"

The Major looked a little uncertain, but briefly joined in, moving his head gaily in time with it, before turning back to Tony.

"And do remember, Tony, that our host is a baronet," he said primly, as if that settled it.

Tony, still staring at Sneed, dragged his attention away.

"A baronet!" he sneered. "He *says* he is. And anyway, he's a Yank. How can a Yank be a baronet? You tell me that."

The Major was glad to. "Because, Tony, interestingly enough, he's a modern beneficiary of the ancient law of entailment. The estate and title inherited by primogeniture down to the nearest male line descendant. As I say, it's an ancient law, feudal in origin, designed to—"

The pawnbroker, who looked as if he'd sunk into depression after the burst of hilarity, said in a flat voice, "Spare us the history lesson, Major. What we've got to—"

"It still don't mean he's not what the kid said he was," Tony said stubbornly. "He could still have been a hit man. He could have—"

"Yeah, well never mind him for now."

"He sounds like it. And looks it. And he talked about family, like they do on the films," Tony got in.

"Yes, well for *now*, if you don't mind, *Tony*," Sneed snarled, "let's concentrate on the bleeding kid. Because that's who my money's on. And aside from your Mafia hit man and his Tommy-gun, he's all we've got at the minute."

"I quite agree, Sneed. The rest, frankly, is all rather far-fetched," the Major said sniffily

"So what we've got to do," Sneed went on, before Tony could come back, "is to try and find out where he plays, and hides, like kids do. It's bound to be outside somewhere, so it might pay us to concentrate on the outhouses – a proper job this time, starting from scratch. And I'll talk to the gabby Welsh woman, see what I can find out about him. And then, if that fails, and there's nobody else in the frame, we'll do as Tony suggested," he added, looking at him.

Tony's shoulders moved in the jacket of his silk suit.

"Take him for a ride," he said.

Chapter Forty-Nine

Later that day, the Major, shirt sleeves rolled up, was sneaking back in for a wash and brush up.

He'd made an industrious start on some of the outhouses, and assuming that other people were as devious as he was, had begun with a thorough search of the one Brrm-Brrm had told them he'd stashed the holdall in.

He was tiptoeing past the kitchen on his way to the stairs, when Clem tripped down them and into the hall.

"Ah, Major," she said.

"Ah, lady Clem," he returned, and laughed briefly.

"Yes, I've – er – I've just been involved in what might be described as a dig," he said, and offered the palms of his hands as if in proof. "A sort of archaeological investigation of Batch Hall's history. Yes, I – er – I often find the past in places such as these speaks as eloquently in its outside ruins and abandonments as it does in the house itself. I'm on my way up now to wash and change."

He inclined his head. "Do excuse me."

"I was about to say, Major, that I took a phone call for you, as you weren't in your room. From Mr Worth."

"Mr Worth?"

"The police inspector. From Kingham," she elaborated.

The Major found his voice.

"A police inspector…?"

"Yes, the chap you spoke to yesterday. You told him a rather unfortunate story about a cat you once had in London. The one who died. Under the floorboards…?" she reminded him.

"Ah. Ah, *that* police inspector. Yes, I – er—"

"Well, he left a message."

"Oh, really," the Major said weakly.

"Asking if you might be free tomorrow afternoon for a round of golf."

"A round of golf…?"

"Yes," Clem said on a laugh at his expression. "You do play golf?"

"Well, yes, I – er—"

"Well, there you are. And he said not to worry about transport, he'll pick you up."

"Did he?" the Major said, looking cornered.

"I've got his office number here, if you'd like to confirm it."

Clem ripped the top page off the message pad by the telephone and handed it to him.

"Major…?" she prompted, as he stared at it.

"Emm? Oh, yes, sorry, sorry. Thank you. I'll – er…"

Clem smiled at him. "Not at all. It's all part of the service. Some establishments, I have to say, believe in doing the minimum for their guests. We believe in doing the exact opposite. Well, must get on. Have a good game if I don't see you before then," she said, and disappeared into the kitchen, leaving the Major standing in the hall staring at the Inspector's telephone number.

When Sneed heard about the invitation he sat thinking about it on the edge of his bed, while Tony worried at a fingernail and said again that he didn't like it.

"And not only that," the Major added plaintively. "He wants to pick me up. Give me a lift there."

"I don't like it," Tony said.

"Tell me again how you met this Inspector Worth," Sneed said.

And when the Major had done so, said, "Well, I think you should go. Why not?"

"Why not?" the Major said with a laugh, a man who could think of all sorts of reasons why not.

"What if it's a trap?" Tony said. "He'll be walking straight into it. What if it's a trap?"

"Precisely what I was thinking, Tony," the Major fervently agreed.

"What sort of a trap?"

Tony thought about it and shrugged. "I dunno – just some sort of trap."

Sneed smiled at it. "No, I don't think so, Tony. No, he's just taken a shine to him, that's all. Likes the cut of his jib, and all that. Or maybe he's a cat lover. Yes, I think you should go, Major."

The Major shook his head. "I have to confess, Sneed, that I'm not at all comfortable with the idea."

"Course you're not. Wouldn't be natural if you were. But no, I think you should go. Never know what you might pick up over a snifter, a G and T, and all that in the old club house."

"Yes, that's all very well, but—"

"'Ere, and there's another thing," it occurred to Sneed. "There's a lot of business done at golf clubs, right? The old pals act, and all that. The old school tie and the right accent, and that sort of thing. Well, maybe that's why he asked you. Seeing as we're supposed to be down here looking for business opportunities. So it might look a bit suspicious, mightn't it, if he thinks you're not interested. Might make him take another look at you – and us. You know what coppers are like."

The Major thought about it and then sighed.

"There's something in what you say, I suppose."

"So you'd better get a nice story ready for him. Anything will do to keep him happy till we finish our real bit of business here. One way or the other."

"Hey – hey, what about golfing clubs?" Tony, who still didn't like it, said. "He'll need golfing clubs. He can't go. He's got no golfing clubs."

"They'll have a spare set there, Tony," the Major said resignedly.

"Well, there you are then, That's settled," the pawnbroker said.

"I was thinking of taking up the game myself once," he went on, largely to himself, his eyes souring at the thought of membership of an exclusive Surrey golf club disappearing with everything else he'd planned for his new life.

The next morning, Tony, after searching a row of abandoned glasshouses on the north side of the gardens, and taking what he thought should be a short cut back to the front of the house, had briefly got lost and had blundered into a small pink, peach and apricot jungle of rhododendron bushes.

He had his fedora neatly removed twice by their branches, and swiped again at something trying to crawl inside his shirt collar, while cursing a countryside with things growing everywhere in it, before emerging between a stand of beeches near the bottom of the drive, in time to see an orange and white patrol car turning into it.

Instinct took over and he darted behind one of the trees.

But not before the Sergeant, at the wheel of the car, had spotted him.

"It's that gangster-looking type again," she told herself. "How *very* peculiar."

She stopped the car then, on her way round to the kitchen, and after thinking about it, reversed and parked on the forecourt. The Sergeant had had an idea.

She strolled in, humming innocently, and stood for a few moments listening to the sound of voices in the kitchen, before tiptoeing elaborately past its open door to the hall table and the register.

She found Mr Como's name and those of his associates and furtively scribbled them down in her notebook.

Inspector Worth was practising with a golf ball and a waste-paper basket on its side at the other end of his office when the Sergeant knocked and entered at his bidding, closing the door behind her quietly, like a conspirator, her face eager with what she was bringing him.

"You see before you, Petal," he said, before she could speak, "a man deep in thought. Sherlock Holmes had his fiddle, I have my putter. It's how I do my thinking," he explained, while she waited impatiently. "Give the hands something to do, and let the brain get on with it," he said, and tapped sharply a couple of times at his forehead.

"Well, I've been rather *clever*," she told him, and gave a little surprised laugh.

"Really," he murmured, narrowing his eyes at the waste-paper basket.

"I've unearthed something I think you'll find very interesting."

"Go on, I'm listening," he said, his tone suggesting that he was doing so even if he appeared not to be, that he could do that, listen and digest one thing while thinking about another, and at the same time concentrate on the game in hand.

"Well, there are three men staying at Batch Hall. From Nottingham. Or so—"

"Yes, I know about them," he said casually.

The Sergeant could only stare at him.

"Gosh, Tedders," she said, shaking her head admiringly, "you make it *awfully* hard sometimes for people to keep up with you."

The Inspector, retrieving the ball after cleanly potting another hole in one, merely smiled.

"So you know of course about directory enquiries. Of course you do," she added goofily, a woman who didn't mind in the least not being able to keep up.

The Inspector paused mid-swing.

"Directory enquiries…?"

"Well, yes. I mean—"

"What are you talkingabout?" he said.

She could hardly believe it. She was, it appeared, one step ahead of him for once.

Playing nonchalantly with the pile of papers in his Pending tray, her eyes cast modestly down, she told him in an off-hand sort of way that she just happened to note the suspicious behaviour of one of the guests staying at the Hall, a certain Mr Como, first in the kitchen and then on the drive, and how she had then contacted directory enquiries with his name and those of his two so-called associates and had been informed that none of them was listed as having a phone in Nottingham, or anywhere else in the country.

"I sneaked a look at the Hall's register, that's how I got their names," she finished, and paused, as if waiting for his congratulations.

And then she looked up at the Inspector and her smile died.

"Well, all I can say, Sergeant, is that I very much hope you were discreet about it," he said tightly, tapping his displeasure out with the putter on the heel of his shoe. "I very much hope you did *not* mention these ridiculous suspicions of yours when gossiping in the Hall's kitchen."

"But Ted—"

"*Because*," he went on, stopping her there, "I, and certain other people, would *not* like it to get to their ears. It would be embarrassing, to say the least."

"But—"

"These are three respectable businessmen, Petunia. Businessmen, furthermore, who seek to invest in the area."

"But Ted—" she tried again.

"I am in fact playing a round of golf with one of them this very afternoon. And it might interest you to know, that I have arranged for the mayor to join us in the bar afterwards. And that our own Superintendent," he went on, pointing upwards, "is taking time off from other pressing official matters to be there. That should indicate the level of importance we attach to their visit."

He looked at her, waiting to see what she had to say about that.

"But – but they're not even on the *phone*," she wailed. "I mean, surely if—"

The Inspector sighed heavily. "My dear girl, have you never heard of ex-directory numbers? These are no doubt prominent businessmen in their community. They don't want any Tom, Dick or Harry ringing them up whenever they feel like it." He shook his head. "Really, Petunia. You surprise me."

"Well, the one calling himself Mr Como doesn't look like a prominent businessman," she said, sulkily stubborn. "Looks more like a gangster."

The Inspector chucked briefly and without warmth. "I appreciate your knowledge of gangsters is somewhat limited. But believe me, it's only in films, my dear, that gangsters actually *look* like gangsters."

"Well I think it should be reported. In case, Ted," she dared to add, "you are wrong."

The Inspector looked startled for a moment, and then said silkily. "That is not a course of action, Sergeant, I'd recommend."

When it was obvious that she was about to say something else he went on sharply, "Sergeant – as I have already indicated, these people are considering putting money, much needed investment, into the area. And there we are – or at least a certain member of the force is – sneaking about behind their backs investigating them. That will not, I can assure you, go down well in certain quarters. So be advised by me, my girl, and drop the matter. Understood?" he added curtly, and addressed himself to the ball again, dismissing her.

The Sergeant stood glaring at him for a few moments, and then, blushing defiance, left, closing the door this time less quietly behind her.

Chapter Fifty

It was the misspelt sign in black paint on a stable door in the Hall's yard which alerted the Major.

'DANJER!
THIS BUILDIN IS NOT SAFF!!!

He checked the loose-boxes first, the dragoon in him noting the bad state of the brick flooring, the rest of the stable, like many of the other outbuildings he'd seen, badly in need of repair.

The lad's den would of course be above, in the hay loft.

He called out, and when no one answered cautiously climbed the stairs. The loft smelt of damp and mice, and the faint, lingering sweetness of hay.

"It was a *frightfully* long time ago!" he said into the empty room, briskly jovial, remembering his own den, in the grounds of another estate, in another place, another time, and chuckled at the skull and crossbones nailed to two upright wall timbers, crudely painted in black on a sheet the lad's mother, he wouldn't be at all surprised, would have missed.

A white-painted cane chair, the paint flaking, sat at an upturned tea chest for a table with a red brocade winged chair that had once perhaps graced the Hall's drawing room, its legs now gone but with the ormolu intact on the arms and back.

There was a dinner plate and table knife on the chest, with a glass mug and a quarter-full lemonade bottle, and a small collection of comics.

He smiled, leafing through them. The *Hotspur, Wizard, Intrepid.*

He wondered if they still published the *Gem* and *Magnet.* Harry Wharton, Tom Merry and Frank Nugent at Greyfriars, and the character he'd felt a sneaking empathy for, the Fat Owl of the Remove, Billy Bunter, and the postal order that was always in the post.

The Major sniffed, and wiped at his moustache, wallowing in a memory of that time. Part of him wondering again where it had all gone wrong, while another part owned up, guilty as charged, his expression hangdog with a show of contrition and regret, and as if with one eye on a judge, or a much higher power of appeal, hoping for leniency, for one more chance.

It was not that when he thought of his own boyhood he yearned for a fresh start, a new beginning – unless it meant that it wouldn't always end *quite* so badly. It was that he resented having had to leave there in the first place.

I was happy there, he thought plaintively.

And then he straightened his back, his mouth set, and without fully understanding why, out of vague obstinacy, and a memory perhaps of a time when he truly could have pleaded innocence, he resolved there and then, as if taking an oath, that he would not give the lad up, that he would not tell the other two that he had found his den.

Which didn't stop him doing a thorough search of it before leaving.

He was downstairs again, about to leave, when he paused, and then went back up into the loft.

He took the things off the top of the tea chest, upended it and put the bits and pieces inside. Using his Swiss army knife, he eased out the two nails securing the sheet with the skull and cross bones on it and folding it like a flag, added that to the chest.

The two chairs he moved to a corner of the loft, as if they'd simply been dumped there.

He poked his head out of the stable door to check no one was around, and then hugging the tea chest to him hurried with it down the yard to a building he'd searched earlier.

It had been the Hall's forge and still had its whetstone wheel and an anvil, the remains of long-cold anthracite ashes in the furnace hearth under a metal canopy, and a rusty hill of discarded horseshoes piled up against a corner.

The Major turned the tea chest into a table again with its contents on top, in front of a battered oak work bench low enough to be used as a seat. He then secured the sheet with its skull and crossbones to two of a row of iron pegs on a wall once used to hold tools.

If Tony or Sneed hadn't searched there yet, it was ready for them to find now. A little misdirection, another lesson learned at Sandhurst.

Chapter Fifty-One

The Major won the toss and teed off first with a 2-iron from his bag of borrowed clubs. The ball travelled low, just above the ground, and stopped a good distance from the hole.

"A damn worm-burner," he said.

"Unfamiliar club, Major," the Inspector was good enough to suggest. Dressed for the green in a multi-coloured Pringle sweater and tartan trousers, he did little better with his stroke, the ball high but falling wide.

"Hard *luck*, sir," the Major cried sportingly.

After that each man, for his own reasons, tried to let the other have the game. But it was the Inspector who, at the end of the round, and despite his best efforts, found himself the winner. When it came to deviousness, the Major had by far the best handicap.

When they entered the clubhouse bar the Major was finishing off an anecdote about another major, the secretary of St Mellons Golf and Country club who wrote the rules for games played during the last war.

"Rule Seven," the Major was saying, "states that a player whose stroke is affected by the simultaneous explosion of a bomb or shell, or by machine-gun fire, may play another ball from the same place."

The Major paused. "Penalty, one stroke."

The Inspector, feeling socially elevated by this major sharing a story with him from that exclusive golf and country club, chuckled his way to the bar.

"The drinks of course are on me," the Major said expansively, before taking his wallet out and finding it bare.

"Blast. Completely forgot. Meant to get to the bank. Too late now," he said, snapping off a glance at his watch, and then wondered, as if an afterthought, if by any chance he might cash a cheque.

When the bar steward saw the amount on the company cheque the Major had dashed off carelessly, he glanced enquiringly at the Inspector. The Major, with not just a club member but a police inspector as guarantor, had not stinted.

The Inspector, as if finding the steward's query impertinent, nodded abruptly.

"I shall be rather tied up at the Hall tomorrow with paperwork – preparing various growth projections, you know, all that sort of thing, " the Major explained. "Tedious but necessary, I'm afraid. And then of course we're into the weekend. And my bank, in the modern way of doing things, sees fit to shut its doors to its customers on a Saturday. So I'm obliged, my dear fellow."

The Inspector, heady with the Major's talk between holes of a consortium of Nottingham banks and businesses with more investment money than they knew what to do with, airily told him not to mention it.

The Inspector was where he wanted to be, not only in the right sort of company, but also part of the bigger picture. Where, as an executive officer in a modern police force, he considered he *ought* to be, taking a wider view of the needs of the community, other than that of merely policing it.

And doing so a short while later in the company of two fellow club members, Superintendent Jenkins and the mayor of Kingham.

The Inspector had wanted those two personages there not only as witnesses to his grasp of the bigger picture but also because he knew that it was more likely to reach the ears of the Chief Constable.

The Major for his part was glad of the support of his large whisky, beginning as he was to feel outnumbered when he learned who the mayor's companion was.

While the Superintendent, shaking the Major's hand, wondered where he'd heard the name before.

The Major had been relieved to find that the car which carried him away from the Hall to the golf course and which now brought him back didn't have 'Police' written on it.

It was the Inspector's own car, and when the young constable from Church Myddle, arriving a few moments later with his sergeant on a Coney break, passed it parking in the forecourt he recognised not only the driver but the passenger alighting from it.

I was right! he told himself. He is a local toff. A friend of the Chief Constable or a judge or something, being chauffeured about by one of the brass from Kingham.

The constable was out of the Panda almost before it had pulled up at the back door.

Telling his sergeant that he wouldn't be a sec, he shot through the kitchen, startling Annie and Shelly, and caught the Major on his way in.

The Major jumped as he popped out of the kitchen, and bringing his heels together snapped off a salute with a forefinger.

"Afternoon, sir! I never forget a face, sir. It's something I've trained myself to do, along with my reading on criminal type recognition," he said, hoping that it would get back to the Inspector, or even higher.

He chuckled at what he took to be the Major's struggle to do the same, to place his face. "Church Myddle railway station, sir. Last Friday," he reminded him crisply. "You were using the morning Birmingham service."

The constable straightened. "PC 08, Cooper, sir! Based in Church Myddle. Well, duty calls," he added with another salute, and disappeared back into the kitchen.

The Major recovered and walked slowly and cautiously to the stairs, as if wondering what was coming next and from what direction.

He was a man whose life seemed suddenly to be stiff with police officers, and he was touched with the uneasy feeling that, like a hand sizing up his collar, some sort of trap was being set in place.

While the constable was satisfied with his visit to the Hall and meeting again with the Major, he wasn't half as satisfied as his sergeant was.

While the constable was tucking into his Coney, his sergeant had taken his courage in both hands and did what he'd been failing to do for the past month or so.

When Shelly left the kitchen to go upstairs, he jumped up, followed her out, and just said it, blurted it out, there and then in the hall.

Would she, he'd said, like to go to the pictures tonight?

And while he was busy adding quickly that it didn't matter if she couldn't, he'd understand, being busy, and all that, it was just a thought, like, perhaps next week, maybe, Shelly, who'd been wondering for the past month or so if he was ever going to get round to it, said yeah, she'd love to.

"It's a lovely day, Constable," the sergeant told him in the Panda afterwards.

"A *lovely* day," he emphasised a few minutes later, and hummed his way happily back to the station, his head full of roses and Shelly.

Chapter Fifty-Two

Later that day, Superintendent Jenkins remembered where he had come across Major Blashford's name before. He dug out Sergeant Cholmondeley-Jones's report and phoned down to the Inspector.

The Inspector sighed. "Frankly, sir, there are times when I think wistfully back to the days when our female colleagues dealt only with women, children and stray dogs. Sergeant Cholmondeley-Jones came to me first with this. I told her there was nothing in it and that she should drop it. She obviously decided she knew best. Perhaps it's her sex, I don't know. But she seems *incapable* of grasping the simple fact that these people are prominent businessmen, and as such are of course likely to be ex-directory. We must be thankful, I suppose, sir, that it didn't reach their ears. At least the force has been spared that embarrassment."

"Oh, quite, quite. This – er – this Mr Como she mentions. Not the singer, I take it," the Superintendent said, and chuckled.

The Inspector chuckled with him. "Oh, very good, sir. No, he's a restaurateur, the Major tells me. A noted and extremely successful one, apparently. They're doing a bit of market research in that direction in Kingham, incidentally, with a really top notch, *haute cuisine* establishment in mind, imported French chef and sommelier, and all that. With guaranteed tables, I might add," he said coyly, "at any time for senior officers of a certain town's police force."

"Really? Oh, I say. Well, that certainly explains his interest in the Hall's kitchen. But what on earth is this business about him hiding behind a tree when he saw her car? Extraordinary behaviour."

"That, sir, is her interpretation of the incident, coloured I have no doubt by the fact that she thinks he looks like a gangster. As the name suggests, he's an Italian type, " he explained.

"Ah," the Superintendent said.

The Inspector sighed again. "Her action was also I suspect influenced by a total misunderstanding of an initiative of mine following the Shrewsbury robbery. You may remember, sir, that I instructed officers to do a check of hotels and guest houses, etcetera, in the area. But that was with people in mind who might have arrived within a week before the robbery and who left within a week after it. Or who arrived in the area within a week pre it and who were still there. Major Blashford and colleagues arrived at the Hall a week *after* the robbery…"

The Inspector paused, waiting for the Superintendent to catch up.

"Yes. Yes," the Superintendent said. "I see what you mean. Well, in that case I think we'll let this one go through to the wicket keeper, Mr Worth, hmm?"

"It's a complete no-ball, sir, I assure you. Oh, and there is one further point," it occurred to the Inspector.

"The Shrewsbury gang came to the area to take money from it. While the Major,' – the Inspector couldn't for a moment continue for chortling – "while the Major and his associates intend putting money *into* it!"

Chapter Fifty-Three

The next afternoon, Sneed, searching for Annie, wandered round a box hedge half-buried in a pale pink rambler rose, and came on her weeding the bed below the terrace.

"Somebody's busy," he greeted her with a smile, trying for a bit of charm.

Annie, glad of an excuse to rest on her fork, and the chance of a natter, wiped her brow and said, "Well, you've got to try to keep on top of it, see. When you've got the odd bit of spare time, like. Old Tom Parr from the village usually comes in a few times a week, to work on the main beds and the kitchen garden, but he's busy these days working on the engine of the *Batch Castle*, one of the paddlers on the river. He knows about that sort of thing, Tom does. Used to be an engineer on them when they were working boats. Years ago, that was. But they're hoping the old *Castle* will be doing it again. Next summer, with any luck. Hot one again today, isn't it."

Sneed, who'd been nodding away, waiting to get a word in, agreed that it was, and then went on quickly, "Actually, I was looking for a young kid. I don't know his name, but he always seems to be about the place."

Except, he thought, when you want to lay hands on him.

"Oh, you must mean our George. Young George Hadley."

"Ah, that's his name is it, George. I didn't know. Does he live here, then, at the Hall?"

Annie shook her head. "No. No, he lives with his mam. June. She's renting the Old Post Office in the High Street, just past the church. It's what used to be the village post office years ago, till the shop took it over, like, then it got turned into a cottage."

"Ah, I see. So where—"

"Well, I say years ago, but I remember it when I was a kid. The Prossers had it then. Mr Prosser died, cancer, I think, that was. Then not long after that Mrs Prosser retired and went to live with her married daughter in Leeds… Or was it Manchester? Anyway, then the shop took it over. They haven't been here long, George and his mam. She's a widow. Husband died young, of a heart attack while playing tennis. Nice woman, she is. Works in a chemist's in Church Myddle. So George gets looked after in the summer holidays, when she's at work, like, and helps out, here and up at the yards."

"Right. So where—"

"The hunt's yards, that is, at the other end of the village. The Batch Valley Chase. Lady Clem's joint master of it, she is. John Beecher, who's got a coal yard in the village, he's the other master. Course, they don't do any hunting yet. Not till the autumn. But the hounds still have to be fed and the horses looked after, and all that."

Annie drew a breath and Sneed jumped in. "So where might I find him then, this kid? Because he's been very helpful to us, showing me and my colleagues the old buildings in the grounds, and all that, knowing we were interested in that sort of thing. And I wanted to give him a small gratuity, in appreciation, like. A little something to buy sweeties with," he explained with an avuncular twinkle, when Annie looked blank.

"Well, I haven't seen him about lately, come to think of it But he could be anywhere. Out here somewhere," she said, indicating the rest of the grounds with a hand. "Or over at the yards. Or he might be helping Sir Humph down at the lodge. They're rebuilding it, see. Or the Master's Cottage. He could be there, at the Masters' Cottage. In fact, come to think of it, that's probably where he is. I should try there if I was you. It's been got ready for the Cunninghams, for the winter, see. The Commander and Priny, his wife, live on the *Castle* at the moment, the boat I mentioned. But what's going to happen is—"

"*Where is it!*" It came out suddenly and on a much higher note than he had intended, almost shrieking it, some of the growing desperation and frustration he'd been sitting on escaping.

Annie looked startled and then affronted, the light in her eyes a storm warning for those who knew her.

And then she did something which put her loyalty to the estate beyond all doubt: she held her tongue. She reminded herself who he was and said nothing, except to give him directions in as few words as possible – which for Annie was another way, if one not nearly as satisfying, of saying what she thought of his manners.

Tony, meanwhile, had found George's den – or what he assumed was George's den.

And like the Major, if for more clear-cut reasons, he, too, decided, that he would not tell the other two of its existence.

After hopefully searching the place, he left and found a vantage point in what had once been the coach house, further down on the other side of the yard but with a view of the forge.

Leaving one of the big doors ajar, he stood leaning against the other, watching and waiting, and allowing himself to daydream once more of Monte.

Chapter Fifty-Four

The Strange family had two cars, a red Mini and Henrietta, an old, large wooden-framed Bentley shooting brake, a wedding present from Clem's parents.

Sneed couldn't see how Humphrey could even get in the Mini, but he'd seen him coming and going a few times in the brake, and saw now that it wasn't there, parked in front of any of the Masters' Cottages.

The last cottage but one, the Welsh woman had said.

He drove slowly past it and saw as he did so, through the open front door, a young lad crossing the hall from one room to another.

And it seemed to him that the way had been made clear for him, like something meant to be. And with that, suspicion was turned into certainty. He *knew* then that it was the kid, he had taken the money. He hadn't believed, and still didn't believe, Tony's nonsense about the Yank, but he'd been right about the kid. It had been him all along.

Calm yourself, Harold, calm yourself, he told himself, driving on past, and starting to get the story clear in his head.

He'd tell him that he was a recovery agent for an insurance company. He'd say he knew all about him and the money, so there was no point in lying. He wasn't there to judge, he understood, he'd been a kid himself once. All he simply wanted to do was to recover the money. And if he, George, would help him do that then he, George, would be entitled to an official fee of five per cent, he'd say, coming up with the lower figure out of habit, and then upping it to ten, seeing as he wouldn't be paying anything.

Ten thousand pounds, George, and no more said about it. Ten thousand pounds. Think what you and your mum could do with that.

The pawnbroker was rehearsing this while turning the Wolseley round at the end of Upper Ham, coming back, parking in front of the cottage, and walking up the front path and through the open door.

He found George in what would be the Cunninghams' front room, sitting on a bag of plaster, reading a comic.

George recognised him immediately and shot to his feet. On pain of Phineas telling his mother what he'd been up to, he'd been told to stay away from the Hall after the business with Tony and the knife. If he wasn't with Humphrey, then he had been made to keep his head down on the *Belle*, where Phineas, who had reasons for keeping his own head down, could watch out for him.

And now the Hall, as it were, had come to him.

"Hello, George," Sneed greeted him matily.

"Doing a bit of renovation, eh?" he went on, looking at a section of exposed roof timbers, the walls under it stripped of rain-damaged plaster.

George just stood there, looking at him.

"My name's Mr Havington-Wilkes, George. Yes, I know your name. And your surname. It's Hadley, isn't it," Sneed said, smiling in what was meant to be a friendly, reassuring sort of way, while George started to edge slowly towards the door.

Sneed held up a hand. "Now there's no need to worry, George. I know all about it," he said, and was about to tell him what it was he knew all about, when he jumped.

"Hiya, Mr Havington-Wilkes!" Humphrey boomed, coming up behind him. "How ya doin'?"

Sneed took a few seconds to turn round, and then, as if surprised to see him there, said, "Hello, Sir Humphrey."

"Humph, please," Humphrey reminded him.

"Humph. No, I was – er – I was just passing, like, Humph, you know, having a bit of a drive round, and that, and I saw this little place was being done up. And I wondered if it was going on the market. It's a charming spot Batch Magna, and I'd been thinking about buying a little weekend cottage in the country. You know, somewhere to get away from it all, from the stresses of the city and business, and all that."

"Yeah, you said it, Mr Havington-Wilkes, it's a great little place. But gee, I'm sorry, it's not for sale. We're doing it up for somebody. And I don't know any place in the village that is."

"Oh, that is a pity. It would have just suited me. On the river, and all that. Know what I mean?"

"Yeah. Yeah, I do," Humphrey said earnestly, and George wondered if they were talking in code.

"Gee, I'm sorry," Humphrey said again, and meant it. He had almost been lost to the place himself once, had almost sold it cheap, in pursuit of money, before realising, just in time, its true worth.

Humphrey smiled in sympathy at him – laughing at him, Sneed would later come to believe.

Chapter Fifty-Five

Sneed tried again later that afternoon, after locating the Old Post Office on the other side of the village.

It was one of a terrace of cottages a few doors down from the church on the same side. He'd parked the Wolseley in front of the lychgate, suggesting someone was visiting the church, and was now slumped low in the seat, waiting for George to come home.

He had been there, to be on the safe side, since five o'clock. He'd rung the chemist's in Church Myddle before that and had been told they closed at five-thirty. He had no idea if George's mother had a car or used the bus. Either way, he thought it reasonable to assume she'd be home sometime around six and George also.

He needed both speed and luck for what he had in mind. He had to throw up dust, create worry and confusion, giving him no time to think.

He planned to get out when he arrived and tell him with rushed urgency that Lady Clem had asked him to pick him up. She was at the hospital because his mum had been taken ill at work. Now he wasn't to worry, the doctors say it's going to be all right, but his mum had been asking for him – so get in, George, get in, and I'll explain more on the way.

And then he'd take off with him, drive up into the hills. There'd be no more coming at it sidewards there. He'd instil a bit of terror first, and if that didn't work then he'd use the tyre iron he had ready under his seat.

Either way, he'd talk. He wasn't going to leave him alone until he did.

And then he'd be gone, along with the money, well before the kid could walk back and raise the alarm – if, that is, he could walk at all.

Well, needs must when the devil drives, and you can't make an omelette without breaking legs, he told himself, chuckling over the play on words, a man who might, at last, have something to laugh about.

And then he jumped for a second time that day when someone rapped on the window, and he swung his head round and met Humphrey's meaty face grinning in at him.

Humphrey was on his way to the builders' merchants in Kingham for the plasterboard and roof timbers he hadn't had room for on his last trip. He was in a hurry to get there before it closed, but thinking Mr Havington-Wilkes might need help, grabbed at a chance to impress one of the tourist inspectors.

Mr Havington-Wilkes didn't at that moment look in the least appreciative. Then he produced a smile, and wound down the window.

"Hiya again, Mr Havington-Wilkes. I thought you might have broken down, or something, wondered if there was anything I could do."

"No. no, nothing like that. Thanks, anyway"

"All part of the service," Humphrey said.

"No, I was – er – I was just admiring the church, like, and about to have a look at it."

"Saint Swithin's. Yeah, great, isn't it. It's *old*," he added on a confiding note, making a face at just how old it was, in awe still of it.

Sneed, regarding it as a statement of the blindingly obvious, put it down to Humphrey being an American.

But what Humphrey had really meant was that his family was old there, in that place, home to the alabaster repose of the first baronet, Sir Richard Strange, with his wife Lady Hawis and his sword by his side, and the plaques on its walls to the family's sacrifices in war and a service to empire. And the box-pew below the altar in which squires of Batch Magna had bent the knee since Jacobean times, the faded colours of the Strange family's escutcheon painted on the wall above it. A pew in which this squire, in his Brooks Brothers executive suit from another time, another world, diffidently, almost apologetically in the presence of all that past, now took his place with his family each Sunday.

Sneed had told Humphrey he was there to look at the church, and that's what he did, even after he'd seen Humphrey drive off, he looked at the church. He went in and he looked at the carved roof timbers and the pews, at the stained glass and the altar, at the font and rood screen, at the brasses and the history of Humphrey's family on the walls, and the tomb of Sir Richard, looked with a distracted, jumpy air, waiting for the American to pop up again.

While Humphrey, whistling carelessly, was well on his way to the builders' merchant with George.

Afterwards, he would drop him off at the cottage on their way back, by which time his mum would be home.

That evening, the pawnbroker was lying on his bed, staring again at the ceiling, when the Major knocked briskly and came in.

"Forgive the intrusion, Sneed, but I happened to spot in the entertainment columns of the local newspaper that a string quartet is sitting this evening in the Assembly Rooms in Kingham."

"Eh?" Sneed said.

"A string quarter," the Major said, and gaily mimed the vigorous dance of a bow. "A composition for four players of string instruments. Two violins, a cello and viola. Quartets composed in the classical period, typically consist of four movements with a structure similar in ambition to that of the symphony. The outer movements are allegro, sometimes even prestissimo, the inner consisting of larghetto, or, if slower, largo, and a dance movement of some kind – minuet, scherzo, furient, that sort of thing. Although," he cautioned, "not necessarily in that order."

Sneed, looking suddenly and deeply tired, had a hand up, as if to ward him off.

"A feast of classical music, Sneed, not to be missed. A whole four *hours* of it. Just think!" the Major enthused, as if to rally him. "Haydn, Debussy, Beethoven, Mozart, Schubert, Tchaikovsky's *Andante cantabile* and Mendelssohn's fugues, and Strauss of course," he added, and animatedly hummed a few bars of the *Pizzicato Polka,* his head wobbling in time.

He smiled invitingly at the pawnbroker.

"Thought you might like to accompany me. Tony declined, said he was having an early night."

"No. No, not for me, thank you, Major. Not tonight."

The Major looked disappointed. "Oh. Just me, then."

"Yes, 'fraid so. Got a bit of a headache, you know."

"And an upset tummy?" the Major enquired solicitously.

"No, I haven't got that. Just a headache."

"Ah, well, it's not something going round, then. I didn't have a headache earlier, just the tummy. Which is still a bit dicky, I have to say," he said, patting it.

"Still, no doubt you're doing the right thing, resting. Well, I'll be off. Mustn't miss any of it. Oh," he said then, on his way to the door. "Almost forgot. There is one thing. I can't seem to get hold of a taxi. They're all booked solid. Friday night, I suppose. That is why, I must confess," the Major added, dipping his head sheepishly, "I was rather more than usually keen on your company. But as you are *hors de combat,* I wonder, Sneed, if I might borrow the Wolseley? I'd *hate* to miss it. And it's for one night only."

The pawnbroker sucked dourly on nothing, considering it.

"Yeah, all right," he said then reluctantly. "But don't – don't crash it, or anything, will you. And don't leave it unlocked."

"Certainly not," the Major said shortly.

"Yeah, well, the keys are over there, on the chest of drawers."

"Thank you, Sneed. Most kind of you. I shall of course take the greatest care of it."

"Yeah, yeah," Sneed said. "Well, just make sure you do, that's all."

"As if it were my own," the Major assured him. "And I do hope your headache's better in the morning."

"Me too," Sneed said gloomily, sinking back on the bed.

The Major stopped on his way down the drive, the Wolseley shielded from view round a bend in it.

Nipping smartly out, he dived into a clump of rhododendron bushes and retrieved the suitcase he'd sneaked out while the others were at dinner, pleading then an upset stomach to excuse his absence.

He tossed the case on to the back seat and set off again.

Chapter Fifty-Six

After a morning wrestling, in pursuit of his circular definition of time, with theories of three and fourth dimensional space, poring over books from the reference library in Shrewsbury, the Commander was perfectly happy to be informed by the First Lieutenant that they had a visitor and that she'd put the gin and tonic on.

He left the wardroom, trailed by Stringbag, and beamed at his wife and friend and the waiting arrangement of bottles and glasses in the shade of the red-and-white striped sunshade.

"Your health," Phineas said, after Priny had done the honours.

"And yours, old chap, and yours," the Commander said.

"Indeed," Priny echoed.

The Commander leaned back with his glass and regarded them fondly. "What fun."

"Actually, James," Phineas said, "I called – did Priny say why I called?"

"No point in saying much about anything when he's in the wardroom, darling. He's mostly elsewhere."

The Commander leaned forward confidingly.

"Deep in the third and fourth dimension on this occasion, Phineas my boy. Absolutely *crucial*, my dear fellow, to any understanding of time. The third serving as space and the fourth as time itself. According to the Euclidean perceptions of space, d'you see, the universe—"

"Phineas has come about you know what," Priny broke in.

The Commander frowned.

"*Do* I?"

"The money, James. The loot."

"Ah, that."

"Yes. You see, I've just been speaking to Jasmine," Phineas said.

"Ah, she's back, is she," Priny put in. "And how's the brother-in-law?"

"Em? Oh, he's fine, I believe, yes."

"Out of hospital?"

"Yes – well, not quite apparently, but any day now. Anyway, Jas told me about the – er—"

"The loot," the Commander said, helping him out. "From the Shrewsbury job. Yes, yes, m'boy, go on."

"Yes, the – er – the loot…You see, I gave it to Hattie to hold, after George, young George Hadley—"

"Yes, we know all that, darling," Priny said. "And then it came down the line to us."

"Yes, that's it," the Commander said. "And we're sitting on it until…" He looked at his wife. "What *are* we sitting on it for, Number One?"

Priny, cigarette holder in hand, blew out smoke.

"Until we're sure who's who, darling."

"Until we're sure who's who," the Commander told Phineas, and then brightened. "Yes, that's it, of course. We know that Humph was the brains behind it, but—"

"But he wasn't," Phineas broke in.

The Commander looked surprised. "Wasn't he?"

"No, of *course* he wasn't," Priny said.

"He had nothing to do with it," Phineas said. "Not directly, at any rate."

"I do wish people would make up their minds. So who *was* behind it?" the Commander asked querulously.

Phineas glanced around before speaking.

"The answer to that one is, as we speak, up at the Hall."

Priny grinned at him. "Don't tell me, darling. It's Ma Bacon, with a Tommy-gun."

"Barker," Phineas said shortly. "I think you mean Ma Barker."

"Or Shelly, as we know her," Priny said.

"Shelly, is it?" the Commander said. "Well, well."

Phineas sighed. "It's nothing to do with Shelly, either. I was referring to three guests, three men, who checked in there last Saturday."

He told them about George spotting the Wolseley and then coming across one of them in the orangery, and how another one of them had produced a knife, and George telling him, Phineas, what Annie had told George.

Priny became serious. "I really do think it's time the police were brought into it."

"That was my idea – in a way," Phineas said, and outlined his suggestion of leaving the money in a phone box for them.

"I was thinking of something a little more direct," Priny said.

The Commander, who'd been poking at the bowl of his pipe with a hairpin, blew once, furiously, down it and glared at them.

"To the devil with all this pussy-footing! Waving knives about! *I* think it's time these people had something put across their blasted bows. We've enough shotguns sitting about the place. I suggest we rope in Sion and Owain, march up there and tell the blighters to hop it!"

The Commander's good eye was fierce with it, while in the other, Turner's sky went up in flames over Norham Castle.

"And what about the money?" Phineas asked.

"Tell the police to get their damn boots on, and come and get it. And we'll share the insurance reward. Ten per cent, I believe is the usual amount. Which means drinks all round and fish and chip suppers. I'll give Owain and Sion, a ring," he said, about to get up.

"Wait a moment, James, please," his wife said. "I'm not at all sure that it's as simple as all that." She looked at Phineas. "Have you tried asking Annie what she meant?"

"Waste of time. Said she didn't know what I was talking about. I phoned her, and I phoned Humph. Phoned them all, in fact. Nothing obvious, of course. Just asked if there was anything wrong, anything they wanted to talk about, that sort of thing."

Priny looked at him. "Awful lot of phoning, darling. Why didn't you simply pop up there and do it where all the talking's done, in the kitchen? More chance of getting things out of them that way."

Phineas laughed briefly. "Yes, well, I haven't really been able to – er – to walk all week. Not properly. I – er – I stupidly tripped, and sprained an ankle, or something. So I've been confined to quarters rather," he said, and laughed again. "Well, apart that is, from hobbling back and forth to the shop, for essential supplies, you know, that sort of thing. It's all right now," he added, waggling his foot at them.

"You should have given us a shout, my dear fellow," the Commander said, concerned. "That's what friends are for."

"I expect he has Sally dropping in when she could to minister to him, didn't you, darling," Priny said, watching him.

"Well, no, actually, Priny. Sally's – er – Sally's away. She's not here."

"Yes, that's what away usually means. Not on another holiday, is she?"

"No, no, of course she isn't. She's only just come back from one."

"Has she left you? Come to her senses at last?"

"No, she hasn't *left* me."

"Ah, good," the Commander said vaguely.

342

Priny regarded him, head on one side. "Haven't done her in, have you, darling? Haven't buried her up in the hills somewhere, or weighed her down and dumped her overboard?"

The Commander narrowed his good eye at Phineas and waited.

Phineas laughed. "No, no, of course I haven't! No, she's away."

"Yes, we've established that," Priny said.

"On a course."

"I see," Priny said.

"Yes, a course. She's on a course. Up north somewhere," he remembered then. "That's where she is. Up north. Leeds, or somewhere. Be back soon."

"I see," Priny said again, and wondered what it was really about.

"Anyway," Phineas said, moving quickly on, "as I was saying, in my opinion Annie was lying. And the others were quite frankly evasive."

"Annie keeping something to herself?" Priny said. "I don't at all like the sound of that. What *is* going on?"

"And what are we going to *do* about it, if not storm the place?" the Commander demanded.

"Well, whatever it is," Priny said briskly, "I really don't think, James, that that's the answer. We can drive them off but they'll surely be back. And who knows what might happen then. Happen to the family, that is. We really can't risk it. I propose that we give them what they came for – the money."

Phineas nodded. "Yes. Yes, that was something else I considered doing. And I rather think, Priny, that it's now the only way. If we were to involve the police the family might then find themselves later on the receiving end of a nasty bit of revenge. Yes, I second that."

"Well," the Commander said reluctantly, "I don't at all like the idea of showing the white flag to the scoundrels, I have to say. But yes, all right, I agree, I suppose. Yes, yes," he added more positively, "of course I do. The safety of the family must be paramount."

"Priny smiled. "Oh, well, easy come, easy go, I suppose. But it was nice rolling in it for a while."

"How do we do it, then?" the Commander wanted to know. "Simply hand it to the blighters, or what?"

"Well, I was going to leave it for the police anonymously," Phineas said. "And I suggest we do that. I'll do it, if you like. Leave it, say, in that phone box on the valley road, and then ring them using a disguised voice, and—"

"Why, do they know your voice, darling?" Priny asked.

"Well, no, actually, they don't."

The Commander waved an impatient hand at his wife. "That's how it's always done, Number One. Carry on, m'boy."

"And tell them – well, tell them that – er – that the family had nothing to do with its disappearance, and as I didn't want them to get in trouble over it I was returning it. And – er – and tell them to come and get it." He smiled brightly at them.

"And what if," Priny pointed out, "someone meanwhile uses the phone, or chances by and spots it?"

"Ah, yes… Yes, well in that case I'll park nearby with the bonnet up, pretending a breakdown, you know? And keep an eye on it from there."

"Yes, that's something else they always seem to do," the Commander approved. "Right, well, that's settled then. I'll go and fetch it."

Phineas put up a hand. "No, not yet, Commander. They've got these historical whatnot things on all day today, at the castle and then at the Hall in the afternoon."

"Yes, we're looking forward to that rather," the Commander said.

"Well, I'll leave it until that's all finished, and the place is clear of visitors."

"Well, do be careful, darling. Don't go and get yourself plugged," Priny said vaguely.

"Oh, don't worry, Priny, they'll be too busy with thoughts of the money to take any notice of me."

"You know, I have to say, that for someone, in whatever role, in the middle of all this, Humph's bearing up remarkable well," the Commander said a short while later, with another gin in front of him and his briar pulling.

"I saw him only yesterday, working on the cottage with young George. Whistling away as if he hadn't a care in the world."

Chapter Fifty-Seven

Both the pawnbroker and George were late showing that morning. Sneed because he'd slept badly and woke late and George because yesterday his mother had brought a present home for him, *The Bumper Adventure Book for Boys*.

And after she had left for work, he'd sat at the kitchen table with it, finishing the story he'd told himself again would be the last, before starting on another.

And after leaving the snowy wastes of Alaska and a tale about Sergeant Hawk of the Mounties, was soon lost to the steamy heat of an Amazon forest, where natives lurked behind trees with poisonous blowpipes and alligators waited to be mistaken for logs as the square-jawed hero navigated treacherous swamps, and hacked his way through undergrowth, home to deadly spiders the size of dinner plates and ants that could strip him to his bones in seconds, in pursuit of the villain.

George breathlessly followed his brushes with death until the last page, when the villain, a foul brute given to whisky and swearing, and who needed a shave, got the drop on him from behind, tied him up, and was about to finish him off with a machete, when a giant python, waking up hungry on the limb of a tree above him, slithered down with silent intent and wrapped him in his powerful coils.

The hero, turning his face away from the horrible sounds the villain made as the snake tenderised him, and knowing that he was next on the menu, struggled with his bonds, and freeing himself in the nick of time, snatched up the machete and decapitated the monster.

George blew a sigh of relief, and then saw the time.

He closed the book firmly and hurried guiltily out.

But the shooting brake wasn't parked outside the cottage when he got to Upper Ham, and Humphrey wasn't at work inside.

And neither, when he went across to the *Belle,* was Phineas at home.

He played for a while with Sikes and his new squeaky ball, and then tried the cottage again. Humphrey still wasn't there.

So, as Phineas wasn't around either, to tell him not to, he went up to the Hall to look for him.

Tony, meanwhile, was waiting patiently again in the coach house for George to turn up at the forge, and Sneed was standing on the bank of the Hall's stretch of the river, gazing at the water.

The pawnbroker hadn't washed or shaved this morning, or even combed his hair, his greying locks after a night spent tossing and turning, wild looking, his eyes lit with a brittle light. His going-away suit looked now less optimistic, less confident of his future, as if weathered by failure, by the frustrations and disappointments he'd suffered, the trousers he'd kept pressed under his mattress in Birmingham creased from lying on his bed, the coat he no longer bothered to hang up rumpled.

He'd missed breakfast. Not that he'd have stopped for it. He had, he'd told himself, springing out of bed with vague urgency, things to do.

And after wandering aimlessly about the grounds for a while had ended up on the river.

He was wondering – was driven to wondering by this time – if the money was down there somewhere, in a waterproof box or sealed drum with a few house bricks to weigh it down.

He had an image of himself groping about naked on the riverbed, and made a sound like a laugh.

"You can't even swim, Harold," he told himself dismissively.

He had another look at the boathouse the Major said he'd searched, just in case, and was on his way back up to the Hall, thinking about the lofts. He was pondering how he might sneak in a pair of steps or a ladder – wondering where he might *get* a pair of steps or a ladder, when someone came out through the French windows and on to the terrace.

Sneed scuttled for the cover of a nearby horse chestnut, all thoughts of ladders and lofts flown.

It was George. George on his own.

He was standing on the terrace peering around, as if looking for someone.

Or checking to see if the coast was clear, Sneed thought eagerly, and immediately he'd thought it, *knew* it, knew that he was right. He'd spooked him yesterday and he was on his way now to check that the money was still wherever he'd hidden it.

He peered round the tree, and watched intently as George came down the terrace steps and wandered across the lawns in the direction of the stable yard, stopping now and then and looking around again.

"Go on, son, go on, nobody's watching you. Only your Uncle Harold," he muttered gleefully.

Careful, Harold, careful, he warned himself then, making a dash for the cover of another horse chestnut.

He reached it just in time, as George stopped abruptly, turned, and walked back in his direction.

He *is* cautious, he thought, flattening himself against the trunk.

The pawnbroker went slowly round it, keeping it between them, and then darted back to the first tree after George had walked past it, and then, in case he glanced behind him, ran almost on tiptoe at a wide oblique angle across an exposed stretch of lawn to a yew hedge bordering overgrown flower beds. He followed him along it, stooping, and when running out of hedge, scurrying from bush to bush, and then on his knees in a small wilderness of weeds and tall summer grasses, stalking him with mounting, almost breathless excitement.

He was almost there. He was sure of it. He was at last, despite everything, about to come out on top. And the kid was going to do it all for him.

George was walking determinedly now – now he was sure no one was watching, Sneed thought, showing his teeth in a grin. Heading straight for the row of abandoned glasshouses, the ones Tony said he'd searched the other day. But maybe not thoroughly enough.

He was about to make a dash for the cover of a wall sheltering what had once been asparagus beds running in front of the glasshouses, when out of a gap between two of them strolled the American, whistling.

Sneed shot off to the left, darting behind a clump of azaleas, his face twisted in a snarl.

He made a space among the fat summer blooms and peered through it. He couldn't hear what was being said, could only seethe impotently and watch as they walked away together, the American with one large arm around the kid's shoulders.

"Yeah, Lady Clem's been talking about doing 'em up, something extra to offer the guests, you know?" Humphrey was telling George, after George had said he'd been looking for him, and had then remembered him mentioning the old tennis courts.

Humphrey grinned. "Me, I've got other plans. They'll make a swell couple of pig runs, with housing and that."

"Pigs?" George said.

"Yeah, pigs, Georgie. Big Tamworths. Like Ken Hollywell's got," he said, naming a local farmer. "The wire fencing's all right, and you don't need that much space with pigs. Easier to keep than cats, Ken says."

"I like pigs," George said.

"Me, too, George," Humphrey agreed enthusiastically. "All them pork cuts and bangers. Anyway, don't say anything for now to Lady Clem. I gotta soften her up first."

"OK, Humph," George said.

"We can get a couple of hours in at the cottage before lunch, if you like. It's Conies and Annie's chips today. Then after we eat we've got this historical acting thing. Where we kick the butts of the Roundheads again, you know?"

"Great!" George said.

Sneed stared after them as they disappeared down the side of the Hall together, towards the drive, his eyes rancorous, a man who had almost been handed the lot left again with nothing.

"Well, the game's not over yet!" he told himself, and them, on a sudden shrill note.

He marched across to the glasshouses. He had no doubt that the kid had been making a beeline for them, but checked what lay beyond first, and found two abandoned tennis courts. He went back to the glasshouses.

There were six of them and he searched them all, thoroughly. And then stood in the last one thinking about it.

And then it came to him, out of the blue. And he wondered why he hadn't thought of it before.

What if the money wasn't above ground at all? What if it was below? What if he'd buried it, and had been on his way to check that it hadn't been disturbed?

Well, they couldn't find it in the Hall and they couldn't find it in any of the outhouses. And that's the kind of thing a kid might do, thinking of buried treasure, and all that.

He looked at the earth floor of the glasshouse.

There were no signs of digging there but then all a clever kid like him had to do, with soft earth like this, was to flatten the spot afterwards with something and scatter dirt over it.

He checked the other glasshouses for evidence of digging, and despite finding none, became increasingly convinced that he was right. So much so that, by the time he'd finished, not finding it and finding it came in his mind to the same thing.

It just meant that, unless he got lucky, he'd have to work a good deal harder, that's all.

And he remembered then, as if he were meant to, the shed in the kitchen garden on the other side of the grounds, the shed he'd searched himself a few days back, and saw again the tools in there, which, he was sure, had included a spade.

He took off, striding eagerly back across the lawns, his eyes manic with cunning.

Chapter Fifty-Eight

Phineas was enjoying himself. He was sitting in the Steamer Inn with another pint of Sheepsnout cider in one hand and a comely wench, as he thought of her in the present company, almost in the other.

And if he hadn't quite got his arm around her then it certainly wouldn't be long now, or his name wasn't Phineas Cook – no E on the end and one of the Os doesn't work, as he'd told her when introducing himself, making her giggle.

The place was heaving inside and out with Cavaliers and Roundheads calling a lunchtime truce after the re-enactment show up at the castle. The Commander, Priny, Jasmine and Owain were sitting out on the terrace, but there was only elbow room there and in the public bar.

There was slightly less of a crush in the bigger bar, and pushing through with his pint he'd spotted a space on one of the settles, the comely wench, a blonde camp follower in jeans and a Led Zeppelin T-shirt, shoving up to give him room.

She was, he'd lost no time in establishing, on her own. Her name was Isadora, Izzy for short.

He told Izzy a joke someone had told him the other day. He completely messed up the punchline, but she giggled anyway, her pert breasts, bra-less, if he was any judge, quivering, and laughing so much she had to lean against him.

Phineas's arm slid with practised ease round her waist.

When he went to get more drinks he had to ask Dilly, happily making hay while the sun shone, to put them on his slate. To come to this, he thought, he who had known such wealth, even if it was somebody else's.

He was back on the settle, his arm around Izzy again, where it seemed to him it now belonged, when he looked up and found a Puritan gazing steadily down at him. A Puritan with cropped head and a pale, full round face, the austere Roundhead uniform, made for conflict and nothing else, a rebuke to the frills, lace and wigs of the Cavaliers in the bar.

He was standing in front of their table with a pint of bitter in one hand and the remains of a cheese ploughman's in the other, his expression suggesting to Phineas that either he was struggling with a confusion of pressing thoughts, or was constipated.

Either way Phineas found his presence irksome, and was about to enquire, as languid and mannered as a Cavalier, but with a suggestion in it of steel ready to be drawn, if he could help the fellow, when the Roundhead, transferring his gaze to Izzy, spoke.

"Lo, Izzy," he said, in a flat Midlands accent.

"Hi, Graham," she said.

"Lost me helmet," he said lugubriously. "And by the time I'd finished looking for it the coach had gone. Had to walk down."

"Did you find it?" she asked.

"No. I reckon somebody took it. Reckon somebody's got two helmets now," he said, while Phineas sighed loudly and waited for the fellow to go away.

"What do they want two helmets for?" she said.

Graham shook his head. "Dunno."

"Well, I shouldn't worry about it, old chap. These things have a habit of finding their own way home, you know," Phineas said encouragingly, and pointedly turned his attention to Izzy.

Graham ignored it. "Where's Bruce?" he asked.

Izzy shrugged offhandedly. "Had to work. Said he might be able to get off in time for the second gig. I came on my own."

He removed his gaze to Phineas. "Bruce is her boyfriend."

"He doesn't own me, Graham!" she said sharply. "He doesn't own me," she said to Phineas on a softer note, the words like a promise, prompting him to weigh up the risk of sneaking her aboard the *Belle* afterwards.

Graham chewed on the last of his lunch, his eyes moving from one to the other, and then swallowed and said, "He's our Sergeant-of-Pike, Bruce is. Used to be in the real army. He's an ex-Para. And a Hell's Angel."

"Is he really," Phineas said with bored indifference, a bored indifference born of several pints of Sheepsnout cider, and the feeling of a sword at his side, sprawled with his long legs out, a booted gallant, taking his ease with a tavern wench, being pestered by a damn Iron Head.

"He won't like it," Graham said flatly.

Phineas looked amused. "Won't he indeed," he drawled, and laughed carelessly, a man who in his time had left a trail of defeated Bruces in his wake.

"Well, my fine young friend, I'm afraid that if Master Bruce doesn't like it then Master Bruce must perforce do the other. With knobs on."

Izzy looked at him as if seeing him for the first time and nestled into him.

Phineas held her there. "All's fair in love and war, you know. Now how about toddling off and having a look for your helmet. There's a good chap. Never know when you might need it."

"I'm in no hurry," Graham said, and took a leisurely drink of beer to prove it.

Phineas, tiring of him, waved a foppish hand. "Begone, sirrah, begone."

"You wanna be gone. 'Fore Bruce gets here."

"Graham!" Izzy protested.

"You'll cop it then," Graham promised him. "And you will, Izzy."

"What!" Phineas sat up abruptly, seized with indignation and rush of Sheepsnout to the head. "You dare to threaten a lady in my presence! You scullion! Bootless fustilarian! I'll tickle your damn catastrophe for you!"

"Eh?" Graham said, frowning heavily, not liking it whatever it meant.

"You tell him, mate," the Cavalier sitting on Phineas's right, who'd been taking an open and lively interest in the exchange, put in.

Phineas intended to. "You are a rogue, sirrah, and a scoundrel. A meddling shorn-pated, young fry of treachery. An onion-eyed codpiece. A damn beetle head!"

"Eh! You wanna watch it," Graham said, and put his pint down.

"Just ignore him, Phineas. He's not worth it," Izzy said, clinging to him as if to hold him back.

Phineas, his wrath turned aside, smiled tenderly down at her. "Dearling, honeybucket, bachyboo," he murmured, and kissed her head.

"What are you looking at, Graham!" she demanded.

"I'm just wondering what you're up to, Izzy."

"Mind your own business!" she snapped.

"Tell him, girly," Phineas said. "Before the mewling comes to grief on my sword."

"You ain't got one," Graham was quick to point out.

The feather in the Cavalier's hat moved again in Phineas's direction. "I'll lend you mine if you like, mate," he offered

"You keep out of it, Kenny," Graham told him.

And then Phineas, about to say something else, looked at Graham's glass.

"Is that, perchance, my rampallian newt, Black Boy bitter you're quaffing?"

355

"Yeah, why, you gonna buy me one?" Graham said with sly humour, and his round face opened in a slow, wide grin like a new moon, watched with some fascination by Phineas.

"Are you Tweedledum or Tweedledee?" he wondered. "Well, whichever you are bear in mind what happened to them. They fell off a wall and came a cropper. So let that be a lesson to you. Doubtless they too had mislaid their helmets."

"You'll come a cropper," Graham said, "when Bruce gets here."

"Oh, grow up, Graham!" Izzy told him.

"Or do I mean Humpty Dumpty?" Phineas asked himself.

"Humpty Dumpty, mate," Kenny supplied. "He was the one who fell off a wall."

"Humpty Dumpty. Yes, of course. Thank you. Humpty Dumpty," Phineas said, passing it on to Graham. "Anyway, as I was saying—"

"Why don't you just... Just *shove* off, Graham!" Izzy, who'd been staring hard at him, burst out.

"Yeah, just shove off, Graham," Kenny said, and laughed.

"You wanna mind your own business, Kenny," Graham said.

"Anyway, as I was saying—" Phineas started again.

"Lost your pot, Graham?" Kenny said. "Gra's lost his pot," he told a mate sitting next to him.

The other Cavalier grinned. "Oh, dear. Hope he don't get a sword bounced off his bonce."

Phineas tried again. "Anyway—"

"It probably got picked up, Gra," a Roundhead on Izzy's left broke in. "And slung in the back of the lorry with the rest of the gear."

"Yeah, right. Thanks, Tel," Graham said. "Only I liked that helmet. It was a good fit. I've got me name and that inside it."

"Anyway—" Phineas said again.

"There you are, Graham. You can go and have a look for your little helmet now, can't you. Off you go," Izzy said, dismissing him with a flick of her hand.

"I'll go when I'm ready," Graham said.

"I'll go when I'm ready," Kenny mimicked.

"Shut your gob, Kenny," Graham said.

"As I was *saying*!" Phineas's voice rose, firm as a schoolmaster's above the discord. "If you are drinking Black Boy bitter, then, sirrah, you are drinking the royal health. Black Boy bitter," he pontificated, while Graham, head lowered, gazed stolidly at him, "was first brewed in this pub in sixteen sixty-two, when tankards were raised to a restored monarch. And on each anniversary in May of the young prince's return to London, when the bells rang out again and bonfires were lit across the land, the children of this valley pinned their clothes with oak leaves. Children. Little *children*," he emphasised in a sentimental appeal to the rest of the company.

And then put back his head and eyed Graham as if under the brim of a hat with a feather in it. "The Black Boy, the name of the bitter you're drinking, was an affectionate – and mark that word, sirrah – an affectionate sobriquet given by his people to their king, Charles Stuart."

"Good old Charlie!" Kenny cried.

"A merry sort – unlike some one could name," Phineas confided to Izzy. "When the Warty One had the reins it was all uphill. No wonder they threw a party when Charlie came riding home. And afterwards they dug old Iron Sides up and spiked a pole with his head – and serve him right, the damn regicide. *And* he banned Christmas."

"Well, that's the last I'll drink of that," Graham said, after seeing the rest of his pint off first.

"Here's to the General!" he cried, brandishing his empty glass and finding an echo among the other Roundheads.

"Well said, sir! I like a man who sticks to his colours," Phineas said, while Graham looked suspiciously at him. "And try this next time," he went on, lifting his own glass. "Good, honest yeoman's cider, from our own orchards – even if most of the apples are French. Sheepsnout. That's the stuff to go to war on."

"Ah, I will," Graham said, as if accepting a challenge.

Up at the bar, to where Phineas had followed with two empty glasses, he airily told Dilly, addressing her as ale wife, to add Graham's drink to his slate.

Dilly, long used to Phineas's nonsense, stooped to the wooden cider barrel mounted behind the bar, the name of the brew stencilled on it like a warning.

Phineas put a hand on Graham's shoulder. "Let us, my young friend, lay our weapons aside at least long enough to drink together – if not from the same glass."

"Ah. Right. Thanks mate," Graham said.

Phineas passed him his pint, and regarded him gravely.

"And remember, Graham, remember that in the end it comes to the same thing."

"What does?"

"This war. This sundering of our country. *Our* country, Graham. Not mine, not yours, not... Not anybody's," he finished vaguely, with a sweep of his hand. "But ours, Graham. *Our* country," he said again, while Graham, a bought man, frowned with interest.

"Because no matter what uniform we face each other in. No matter what flags we meet under in battle. No matter what tunes we march to. Our true colours, Graham," Phineas carried on – felt *obliged* to carry on, with a member of the younger generation all ears, "our true colours are those of our country. No matter what our beliefs and allegiances, we stand in the end on the same ground under the same pale English sky. In the *end*. Because you see, Graham, in the end – curiously," he put in, because he wasn't too sure of this bit himself. "*Curiously*," he emphasised, "we are both right and at the same time wrong.

"Do you see? Do you *see*, Graham?" he asked earnestly, feeling he was on to something, if not altogether sure what, gazing into

Graham's moon face which was nodding ponderously back at him.

Graham, after buying a drink for Phineas and Izzy, and finding himself happy to do so, and accepting another on Phineas's slate, and then doing the honours again, was back on station in front of the table as if on some sort of duty, but was now ignoring the couple, who, it seemed to them, had found each other, and were now sharing another lingering kiss to prove it.

After taking a tentative sip of his first pint of Sheepsnout, and then frowning and holding it up to the light, he had persevered, and had now nearly reached the bottom of his fourth. Whatever was happening wherever Graham was now, it was perfectly all right with him.

And then a short while after that the Cavalier called Kenny, back with another refill, broke off an animated conversation about football, and banging a fist on the table broke into song.

"*In sixteen hundred and forty-three those Roundheads they were after me. But we were on a winning spree. Fighting for good old Charlie!*" he roared, taking the other Cavaliers with him, the words heard again perhaps under the ancient timbers of a pub that had first been named the Black Boy.

And Phineas, to whom a song was a song, even if one he hadn't the remotest idea of the words to, couldn't resist joining in, making it up as he went, after first kissing Izzy, and then kissing her again, a last, snatched, regretful kiss, as if saying goodbye, a man off to follow the drum.

The Roundheads also had a song learned for their part in these events, and didn't wait for the other side to finish theirs first, a song about the Cavaliers being all around, but the gentry will come down and the poor shall wear a crown, with a chanting chorus of, "*Stand up now! Stand up now!*" the combined din drawing people in from the other bar and the terrace.

After that it was a free-for-all, with songs such as 'The Wild Rover' and 'Home Boys Home', and 'The Black Velvet Band'. And then somebody sang about a young soldier dying on foreign fields, his voice off-key and wobbling with emotion, the bar, at this stage in the drinking, according him a respectful hush.

And somebody else, on one of the settles, head back to dreamily take in the words, opened his eyes, and found himself looking at the pub's wall clock.

He stared at it, and then shooting to his feet shouted, "Bloody hell! Look at the time!"

"What's up with the fellow?" Phineas enquired.

Kenny put down the pint he'd just hurriedly finished and wiped at his mouth.

"We're late. Supposed to have mustered for the second show an hour ago. We're supposed to take one hour for lunch, not two."

Phineas waved a hand at mere details.

"One hour, two hours, what does it matter? They can't start the war without you."

"Where is the next gig? Anybody know?" somebody asked.

"It's called Batch Hall," somebody else said. "Anybody know where that is, Batch Hall?"

Phineas stood. "I know. I'll take you," he said solemnly. "If you must."

He regarded them, Roundhead and Cavalier, gazing mistily at them, their flushed, eager young faces. Divided by creed, united in folly.

"I'll take you," he said again, and held out a hand to Izzy. "Come, girly, let what must be done, be done."

The hired lorry and coach, which had gone ahead, were parked in front of the Hall, the colours and the long, sixteen-foot pikes, and cannon, muskets and drums unloaded and waiting on the lawns, when Phineas, with Izzy, his prize, at his side, led the way up the drive, past the parked visitors' cars lining it.

His band of brothers, as he thought of them, embracing both sides, the old guard and the New Model Army, straggling, happily, after two hours in the pub, behind them, singing their way to war.

Chapter Fifty-Nine

The pawnbroker had turned over all six floors of the glasshouses and had then done it again, going deeper down, the more he dug and found nothing, the more convinced he was that there was something to find.

He was resting now, fully clothed on his bed. Exhausted by his labours and wearied by the dream of that new life that had left him in the end on his knees in the last of the glasshouses, scrabbling about in the dug earth with his hands in a last, desperate search for it.

He turned his face to the pillow and slept briefly and fitfully, struggling on in his sleep. And when he came awake, when he opened his eyes, there it was, staring him in the face, grinning. It was the American.

It was the American. The kid and the toy guns of course had been just a smoke screen. It was the Yank, of course it was. He was the brains behind it, and he couldn't *think* why he hadn't seen it before.

Everybody else had, he thought vaguely, sitting up and looking amused by it, a man who had at last seen that the joke was on him, and who was taking it in good part.

He even managed a chuckle. Sometimes, Harold, he told himself, you can be too clever for your own good. There you were, chasing shadows, and he was there all the time, hiding behind that grinning, village idiot act of his. Even Brrm-Brrm had come nearer to it than he had.

It was what all the business with the kid had been about, of course it was. Every time he'd got near to him the American had suddenly been there, popping up, grinning and whistling away, playing with him.

He tried to chuckle again, but the sound was more like a sob.

They were all in on it, he saw that also now. The Yank's wife, his mother, the gabby Welsh woman. They'd known all along who he and the others were, what they were there for. Course they had. It's what all the extra attention had been about – 'Hope you're enjoying your stay. Hope the food's to your liking. Hope the beds are soft enough. If there's anything we can do to make your stay more comfortable, don't hesitate to ask. It would be our pleasure.'

They'd been rubbing their noses in it, laughing at them behind their backs.

The pawnbroker shook in a sudden gale of anger.

"Steady, Harold," he told himself with vague fretfulness, heart thumping. "Steady."

And then a few moments later, or minutes, or an hour even, he couldn't be sure which, Sneed, a man who never imagined things, wondered if he was imagining things, standing at the window of his room, looking down on the lawns. Or maybe he was asleep and dreaming it, as he couldn't remember getting off the bed.

Down there, under thickets of long pikes and the battle colours of both sides, Roundhead and Cavalier struggled again for the ground of Batch Magna. Cannon and volleys of musketry went off like firecrackers, their smoke drifting over the milling figures. And there were bloodthirsty screams and yells, and the steady beating of drums setting the marching pace, urging both sides forward, as they met, retreated, reformed and met again.

And down there somewhere was the Yank, and he had his money.

He knew now that he wasn't dreaming or imagining things. He knew the sort of tourist thing he was looking at, and it might have been something that took place under his window every afternoon, for all the curiosity and interest he showed.

The combatants had made full use of the lawns running down to the river, the spectators thronged both ends and either side of them. He peered intently down, face almost up against the glass, looking for the bulk of the American, in one of his shirts.

He searched again, carefully picking his way among the onlookers, and when he still couldn't see him felt he had somehow been wrong-footed again. As if the American were taunting him, as if he were behind him, grinning, or maybe over there, or there.

He felt dizzy with it for a moment, disorientated, and anger came out of nowhere and took him in a couple of strides back to the bed.

He sank to his knees as if in prayer, and reaching under it hauled out one of his suitcases. He opened it and found the Enfield service revolver, waiting among the clean shirts he'd never got round to wearing, felt the loaded weight of it in his hand, before shoving it in a side pocket of his coat.

"You have the advantage here, Harold. They don't know you know," he told himself, as if someone else were telling him, feeling distanced from it, and only half listening, wiping distractedly at the dried mud on his going-away suit, and frowning, as if wondering how it had got there.

He had to remind himself to take his Homburg, the hat he'd first coveted as a young man, the headgear of a man of substance, of someone who meant something.

He carefully positioned it, his uncombed hair sticking out from under it in greying wisps, and straightened his tie, and then digging into the fob pocket of his waistcoat consulted his full-Hunter, a man with affairs to attend to.

He thought vaguely about taking the suitcase with the cut-up newspapers in it, before remembering that it stayed there, to be found after he'd left, the last laugh on them. And he'd collect his other suitcase when he had finished here, when he had done what had to be done – done what it seemed to him now he was here to do.

He shivered briefly when closing the door of the bedroom behind him, as if coming down with something. A symptom of something much worse to come.

Chapter Sixty

Graham's body lay under the broad spread of one of the horse chestnuts on the lawns, a casualty of war and two hours in the Steamer Inn. Graham had done his bit and now slept.

He had not found his helmet and had not stopped to look for it. He had discovered that Sheepsnout was indeed the stuff to go to war on, and when he arrived there couldn't wait to get started. He'd been in the thick of it, sometimes indiscriminately, not caring particularly which side he lent his pike to.

And had then felt a sudden and overwhelming urge to lie down, and had staggered away from the conflict, clapped on by nearby spectators applauding the dramatic detail of a young Parliamentary soldier falling in the English shade of a horse chestnut.

While down on the river bank, Phineas and Izzy continued to get to know each other, dreamily isolated in their togetherness from the struggle above them.

Sergeant Cholmondeley-Jones was enjoying herself, standing with the other spectators, eating a Coney Special on a paper plate from the Owens' De Luxe Cook Centre.

It had been borrowed for the afternoon, along with a trestle table for the tea urn and soft drinks, and joined the line of stalls one side of the lawns. Stalls selling books on the Civil

War, and riding tack, and clothes and boots, and a stall for outdoor pursuits, where men in tweed tried the sweep of a shotgun or a rod for casting. And Jasmine's bell tent was there, the board outside advertising her world-famous powers, with a special rate for pets, and the ice-cream van from Penycwn, the chimes of 'Men of Harlech', played at full pitch over and over to remind people it was there, mixing stirringly with the clash and cry of battle.

Phineas's girlfriend Sally was also at the show. She'd seen the event advertised in a local newspaper, and had arranged to go with a friend, as Phineas was away in Kent, at the bedside of a stricken aunt. And there were times, she'd thought, after he'd phoned and told her about his errand of mercy, when she had to admit that she had misjudged him.

Bruce, Sergeant-of-Pike, ex-Paratrooper, Hell's Angel, and boyfriend of Izzy, was also present. He had got off work in time for the second show, and when he arrived at the Hall had started immediately to make up for missing the first, throwing himself into the nearest heaving scrum of combatants with a zest. Bruce liked a good scrap.

The pawnbroker left the Hall through the front doors, to approach the lawns from the rear.

And it was on the forecourt that he noticed that his car wasn't where he usually parked it. There was a coach and a lorry in front, and cars all over the place, there and either side of the drive, but he couldn't see the Wolseley.

It diverted him briefly, standing there frowning, wondering in that case where he *had* parked it, before remembering that he'd lent it to the Major last night. And hot on that realisation came the thought that he hadn't seen Tony about lately either.

So that was it. Rats leaving a sinking ship, taking his car and the stash of jewellery with them. Except that what they didn't know was that this particular ship wasn't even leaking, let alone sinking. This ship, his ship, the ship he'd spent a lifetime waiting for, was about at long last to come in.

He laughed, the sudden, high shrill sound startling a middle-aged couple wandering about with a National Trust handbook.

Sneed lifted the Homburg, and inclined his head as he passed, as if acknowledging their greetings. They didn't know him but Sneed knew them, or rather Mr Havington-Wilkes did. They were a class of person he expected to meet there, in that other world, the life that might have been his. A place that Sneed was on his way to now – once he had dealt with the obstacle standing in Mr Havington-Wilkes's way.

The pawnbroker lifted his hat again then, to that obstacle's mother, waiting for any latecomers at another trestle table borrowed from the Owens, sited at the entrance to the back of the Hall and its lawns, with what was left of the programs of the event and books of tickets on it, the takings in a bucket at her feet.

She looked up from the paperback she was reading.

"Hiya, Mr Havington-Wilkes!" she greeted him, taking in the state of his going-away suit, and his tie, pushed up under one side of his shirt collar as if someone had tried to throttle him.

"How much is the entrance fee, dear lady?" Mr Havington-Wilkes grandly enquired.

Shelly waved a hand. "Nothing to you, Mr Havington-Wilkes. It's on the house."

On the house for the Hall's paying guests, she meant, but Sneed heard what Mr Havington-Wilkes wanted to hear.

"Most kind of you," he said, accepting his due with modest dignity.

It was Shelly's opinion that Mr Havington-Wilkes had been hitting the sauce, as she watched him making his way with a deliberate sort of step round to the lawns and the din of battle, before going back to her book.

Chapter Sixty-One

And as battles went it was, as far as George was concerned, a letdown.

The cannon and muskets he'd seen waiting so promisingly on the lawns sounded like fireworks, and not very good ones at that, and it was obvious they were only pretending to run each other through with the swords and the spear-heads of the long pikes.

There was no blood, and the only dead soldiers he'd seen had got up again after a few moments, or turned out to be asleep, one stretched out behind the stalls, another snoring away under a horse chestnut tree, and he counted three more curled up in the rhododendron bushes.

So he was on his way now to the drive, to fill up his car numbers notebook and bag a coach and a lorry while he was at it.

And that's when Mr Havington-Wilkes, or rather Sneed, spotted him.

The pawnbroker darted in among a group of spectators, his back turned to him as George wandered up in that direction.

Absently dealing with the repeated attempts of a toddler, sitting on his father's shoulders, to remove with ice-cream fingers his Homburg, he waited until George had walked past.

And then he moved swiftly after him and grabbed his arm.

"Ow!" George cried, startled.

The pawnbroker put his mouth to George's ear. "Where is he? Where's the Yank?" he hissed.

"I dunno! I dunno! Honest!"

"Tell me!"

"*Leggo!*" George yelled.

"Tell me or I'll—"

"Help!" George shouted. "*Help!*"

And Sneed, aware that they were now attracting attention, turned into George's uncle, concerned and understandably annoyed.

"You little devil running off like that. Your mum and dad have been worried sick!"

"He's lying – he's lying!" George desperately told a small audience of visitors finding something new to look at.

"He's a crook. Him and his gang did the wages snatch in Shrewsbury. Call the police!"

"Honestly! You and your *stories*," Sneed said, an uncle amused by it despite himself, shaking his head and sharing it with a few of the onlookers who, with children of their own, smiled back understandingly "His mum and dad have been looking everywhere for him."

"Let me go!"

"Oh, no, you don't, me lad. You're coming home with me."

"He's lying! I don't have a dad. Only a mum. He's lying. He's a crook!"

"Come on now, George, there's a good lad," Sneed muttered through a clenched smile, George struggling to get free.

"He's here with his gang to search for the loot. Call the police!"

"Come on you little—" Sneed snarled, the mask slipping, and George yelped with pain as his fingers dug in.

"I don't know where he gets them from," Sneed said, trying for an avuncular chuckle.

But a few of the visitors no longer looked quite so convinced, taking into account now perhaps his appearance. And one of the women, middle aged, in a tweed skirt and sensible shoes, decided to take charge and walked firmly towards them, her face set with a few questions she obviously felt she was entitled to have answers to.

Sneed knew her sort. They sat on the Bench. Women a few of his other plans had ended up in front of in the past. And before that they were house mothers who slapped your bare legs raw for your own good, and made you sleep in the sheets you kept wetting.

And it was suddenly loud where Sneed was. The air was rowdy with the sounds of mock battle, but for the pawnbroker, as he watched the woman approaching, his eyes at bay, they became real, a turmoil building in his head, becoming so clamorous that he couldn't think straight.

Using George as cover he fumbled with his left hand towards his right hand pocket and the gun.

And then Annie appeared.

"I see you found him then, Mr Havington-Wilkes," she called, walking briskly towards them, carrying a large tray.

He stared at her, suspecting some sort of trick, a diversion while the American sneaked up on him. He glanced quickly around and behind him, and his hand touched the butt of the Enfield.

He gripped it, one hand on the gun, one foot on the edge of the abyss.

And then something shifted in him, and he pulled back, came back, and lifted his hat instead, Mr Havington-Wilkes graciously acknowledging a greeting.

"Mrs Owen! Mrs Owen!" George cried. "He's—"

"Can't stop now, Georgie," she said, hurrying on past, on her way to the kitchen. "We've run out of rolls. Selling like hot cakes they are, the Conies."

"Mrs Owen!" he called after her plaintively, and watched as she lifted a hand and waved without turning round, leaving him alone with Sneed, now that the small audience they'd collected had turned back, reassured, to catch up with the Battle of Batch Magna.

And desperation gave him strength. He threw himself into it, twisting round in the pawnbroker's grasp and kicking out at his shin.

Sneed grunted and relaxed his grip, and George jerked his arm free and made a bolt for it, sprinting off in the direction of the house.

Sneed knew he had no chance of catching him and considered shooting him.

He giggled at the thought of firing off all six rounds at his fleeing back, and missing, the kid zigzagging, dodging them like a cartoon character at the end of Loony Tunes – "That's all, folks!" he cried in a high, squeaky voice.

He felt light-headed, frivolous even, and had to compose himself then, when he saw that he had regained the attention of a few of the visitors.

Mr Havington-Wilkes soberly doffed his hat in their direction, and continued on his way, on his search for the American.

Chapter Sixty-Two

Phineas's comeuppance waited for him in what the program of the re-enactment described as a 'push of pike', the pikemen of both sides meeting, weapons at the vertical, in a heaving solid block, pushing against each other until one side was forced to give way.

This time it was the Roundheads who gave ground, steadily forced down to the river end, the spectators there hastily giving them room as they were driven backwards through their ranks and sent sprawling down the river bank in a tangled heap of pikes and men.

Bruce who, as Sergeant-of-Pike, had been in the forefront of things, scrambled to his feet, pike in hand, ready to join battle again. He glanced first down the steep bank at the river, where some of his side in the rear might have ended up, just as the couple sitting below finished kissing.

He looked away, and immediately looked again.

"*Izzy!*" he roared, and scattering some of his men climbing back up the bank, ran blindly down it.

"Oh my God!" Izzy leapt to her feet, followed immediately by Phineas, who had lost no time in putting two and two together and coming up with Bruce.

Izzy went one way, Phineas the other. Bruce, the momentum with him, and holding, out of habit rather than any intent, sixteen-foot of solid ash, tried too late to slow his charge or alter course sufficiently, and sailed, legs peddling, off the deep ledge of the bank into the river.

He came up gasping, and immediately started to strike out for the bank, before realising he could stand, the water there up to his knees. He still had his helmet but when he looked round for his pike saw it bobbling away downstream.

Further enraged by the thought of the five-pound fine levied on pikemen who lost their weapons, he bellowed something indistinct but leaving Phineas, struggling up the bank through an interested audience of Puritan pikemen, in no doubt as to its general meaning.

Bruce waded ashore and hauled himself dripping up the ledge back on to the bank. He didn't bother looking for Izzy, who was watching from a safe distance off, hand to mouth, but took off determinedly, squelching in his ankle boots, leaking water, after his rival.

Humphrey had just arrived back at the show, after wrestling with a window in one of the single rooms under the eaves.

The guest had complained to Clem that it was stuck, and Clem knew who was to blame. Her husband had got round to painting the room last winter and had, she knew, done what he'd done before when painting rooms up there in cold weather: he'd closed the bottom sash of the window before it was completely dry.

The top half of the window in that room didn't open because the cord was broken, and now the bottom half was paint stuck. And Clem had pointed out that, as she was busy on the Coney stall, *and* had to look after Hawis, and as he was the one who had caused it to be stuck, he should be the one to unstick it.

The window, Humphrey thought grumpily, when up in the room, staring accusingly at it, didn't even look out over the lawns and the fun he was missing, not to mention what he regarded as the best ice-cream either side of the border.

He shook it, pushed and pulled at it, hit it a couple of times with the side of a fist like a mallet, and then stood glaring at it, before stomping off to find a hammer and filling knife. And when the filling knife didn't do it, he stomped off again, and after a visit to the lodge came back with a bolster chisel, which, after banging away at it with the hammer, did.

Before he hurried off back downstairs, he conscientiously made a note, mentally adding it to his list of things to do, that the bottom half of the window now needed wood filler and repainting.

He'd treated himself to a triple-decker vanilla, strawberry and chocolate ice-cream after all that, and coming away from the van paused mid-lick to watch with interest, but no particular surprise, as Phineas went haring past, followed by a Roundhead who had obviously been in the river. The fact that it *was* Phineas explained things in a broad sense immediately. Those who knew him could more or less fill in the rest themselves.

Phineas didn't run far. He had taken to his heels out of instinct and now the effects of Sheepsnout, that brew to go to war on, caught up with him, and he turned, his blood stirred to drama by the sounds of battle and the rousing notes of *Men of Harlech* ringing out again.

He'd halted on the slightly higher ground at the top of the lawns, a Cavalier picking his spot, a Cavalier with a careless laugh on his lips, as his adversary grimly advanced on him.

He stuck up his dukes, as he believed the fists were called in this sort of situation, and wondered vaguely what the old one-two was he'd read about somewhere, which, he seemed to remember, had proved so effective.

Bruce also had a laugh on his lips, or at any rate a smile, a smile with relish in it as he put up his dukes, large tattooed ones, Phineas couldn't help noticing, and doing so in a manner which suggested that he *did* know what the old one-two was, and a bit more besides.

Phineas adopted what he imagined to be a boxing stance, did a little shuffle, and tried out a few jabs.

And then Izzy came to his rescue.

Despite telling herself to forget it, to forget him, and go home, she had chased after them, running past Humphrey, who had showed the same degree of interest and lack of any great surprise as he had when Phineas went by – he had already filled in the detail of a female being involved in whatever it was about.

And now Izzy was flushed not only with running but with temper.

She came to a halt and blew hair from her face. "Bruce…!" she growled.

He waved her away with an abrupt movement of his hand.

But Izzy hadn't finished. "Stop it, Bruce! Leave him alone."

"Leave *me* alone?" Phineas laughed scornfully, and went into a fighting crouch. "Come on, Brucie, let's see the colour of your blood."

"Be quiet, Phineas," she said, flapping a hand at him. "This is none of your business. It's none of yours, either," she told Bruce, who, taking Phineas at his word, was about to make a start. "Who I go with or don't go with. You don't own me."

Bruce looked indignantly at her. "But you're my girlfriend!"

"But you're my girlfriend," she mimicked.

"Hush, girly. Stand aside, this is men's work," Phineas said, practising a bit more jabbing, getting the hang of what he now thought must be the old one-two. "Women are for weeping."

"Oh, be *quiet*, Phineas!" she said, as if about to stamp her foot.

"Yes, I am your girlfriend," she went on to Bruce. "Or was. 'Cause you can forget it now. And when I was your girlfriend, how did you treat me, Bruce?" she demanded, and without waiting went on to tell him. "Like that bike of yours, that's how."

"Now come on, Izzy! You know that isn't—"

"Just another bit of your property. Something you took for granted."

"That's not true!"

"Isn't it? Isn't it, Bruce? All right then. When did you last tell me you loved me?"

Phineas sighed and lowered his hands. Bruce, he knew, had already lost the argument, although judging by his expression he was still struggling with it. When women introduce the subject of love into such exchanges, for most men the game's over.

"I *do* love you," Bruce said then, furtively, lowering his voice and glancing at Phineas.

"I don't think you know the meaning of the word. This is all your fault, you know," she went on, indicating Phineas as if he were some small disaster he'd lumbered them with.

"You're stupid, Bruce – really *stupid!*" she burst out, eyes welling with sudden tears.

Phineas sighed again and folded his arms.

"Look – Look, Izzy, I'm sorry, all right? I mean – well, I do, you know. I do love you," Bruce muttered.

Izzy touched at the corner of her eyes with a finger.

"You're all wet," she said, and sniffed.

"I went in the drink."

"I know," she said, sniffing again, and then smiling. "I saw you. You'd better get out of that lot before you get pneumonia."

"I've got nothing to change into. I came on the bike in this, helmet an' all. Lost me pike in the river," he said with a laugh, cheerfully saying goodbye to a fiver now she appeared to be coming round.

"I'll have to get home, I suppose, get changed. I wonder if – well, I wonder if you'd come with me, like… Then we could go out on the bike somewhere," he said, and watched her start to walk away.

"Izzy…?" he said plaintively.

She turned and motioned with her head. "Come on then," she said, as if reluctantly. "Well, come *on* then… Before you catch your death."

"Well!" Phineas said then, watching them walk away without another word to him, not even a backward glance, just walking off together, one hand finding another.

"Well!" he said again.

He walked aimlessly down the lawns after that, past the stalls, and the busy De Luxe Cook Centre, and Jasmine's tent, in which Jasmine was passing on to its owner the grievances of a normally waggy cocker spaniel, given of late to moods and surliness, and the ice-cream van, where Humphrey, after the rest of the details on Phineas's latest shenanigans, tried to bribe him with a triple-decker.

Phineas smiled wanly and said he wasn't in the mood for ice-cream, thanks very much. He felt deflated, let down by love, spurned, the effects of Sheepsnout which had fired his blood turned now to ashes and a dull headache.

He wandered on, drawn as if by homing instinct to the river, and his mind elsewhere, almost walked straight into the arms of the law in the shape of Sergeant Cholmondeley-Jones

The Sergeant had been helping to search for a missing child who'd been found wandering among the stalls, and was now on her way back to her car to return to Kingham.

She came to a surprised halt.

"Phineas…" she said to herself.

"Phineas!" she said in a louder voice, and one sharp with suspicion

"Ah," Phineas said, seeing the problem immediately.

He didn't consider himself to be a man given to self-pity, but it seemed to him that there were times, and this afternoon, if he was any judge, was one of them, when he could make a case for victimisation.

"Ah!" he said again. "Ah, Petal, I've – er – I've been looking for you. I thought you might be here. But hold on a sec, please," he said, putting up a hand as if stopping the traffic. "I'll be back in a minute. I've forgotten something and it's rather important," he threw back over his shoulder as he made a run for it, hoping that he was giving a convincing impression of someone who'd forgotten something rather important.

"Phineas!" she shouted, no longer Petal but Police Sergeant Cholmondeley-Jones, and hitching up her skirt determinedly gave chase.

Humphrey was talking to the Commander and Priny, who were about to treat themselves to ice-cream, and had started on the story of Phineas been chased by a water-logged Roundhead, and then a female, when Phineas went by again chased by a woman police sergeant.

"Stop! Phineas – *stop!*" she shouted, people browsing the stalls making way for a police emergency.

"So it *was* Phineas after all!" Annie said aghast to Clem, pausing over the hotdog onions as he went past, the Sergeant coming up fast behind.

And Sally and her friend, along with other spectators, had turned away from the battle to see what was going on, in time for Sally to see Phineas heading towards her.

"Phineas…" she said to herself, as surprised to see him there as the Sergeant had been. As surprised as Phineas was to see *her* there, before remembering that she wasn't actually on a course up north somewhere.

"I can explain!" he cried, veering away from another sudden complication, running on with the river in mind, his haven from the squalls and storms of life, while knowing that this time he wasn't going to make it.

And then the pawnbroker appeared.

Chapter Sixty-Three

Sneed didn't see Phineas run past him. He didn't even see the police uniform when the Sergeant went by. He wasn't looking for them.

He had made several circuits of the lawns, searching among the visitors, wound up like a clockwork toy. A clockwork toy that came to a halt when he saw who he *had* been looking for.

A clockwork toy that had stopped and now started again, gun in hand.

He advanced on Humphrey and pulled back the hammer.

"What the devil…!" the Commander said.

"*Where's my money! Give me back my money!*"

This was the pawnbroker screaming about more than money. This went much further back than plans laid in a Birmingham backstreet. This was Sneed talking about his beginnings. A seven-year-old in an overcrowded slum family with too many mouths to feed, pushed out as if from a nest on to the hard stone of the streets and the charity of the parish. A pinched and snivelling waif unloved and unlovable, who had spent the rest of his childhood running away from boys' homes and the things that happened there, and on the streets. And what had taken the place of tears after that had never left him.

This was Sneed talking. And this time someone had better listen.

"Give it to me. Give it back to me!"

Humphrey looked with furtive unease at one of the tourist inspectors pointing a gun and shouting wildly at him.

He had the feeling he was supposed to know about this. It must, he thought, be something to do with the historical acting thing, Mr Havington-Wilkes entering into the spirit of it for the tourists. Mr Havington-Wilkes, made up with mud on his suit and his tie like that, maybe acting as some guy back then who had shot the squire over money, or something.

He grinned and glanced, embarrassed, at the visitors the scene had attracted, wondering what the heck he was supposed to do, what his part as squire in it was.

It was that grin that did it. The grin that pushed Sneed over the edge. That grin again, laughing at him behind it, mocking what he was and all he wanted to be.

The pawnbroker had no more to say.

The Enfield was perfectly steady, rigid in his hand, as he lined it up on the large, bright target of Humphrey's chest and found the heart, his finger stiffening on the trigger, when Sergeant Cholmondeley-Jones, as she would later describe it in her report, attended the incident.

The Commander, badger head stick at the ready, had started to creep up out of sight of what he hoped was the gunman's range of vision, but the Sergeant beat him to it.

She had almost got her hands on Phineas Cook, the end of her problem within grasping distance, when it struck her that what she'd just run past was not in some way part of the show, that Mr Havington-Wilkes should not be wandering about looking like that with a gun in his hand.

She turned, and running back saw she was right. She didn't hesitate. She came up behind him and put all those leisure hours spent on the judo mat at Kingham Polytechnic, and her frustrations and humiliation at the hands of Phineas Cook, into it.

She dealt with the gun first. She punched his arm up with the heel of her palm under his elbow and the Enfield went off, fired above his head like a starting pistol. His legs were swept from under him, his arm wrenched up his back, and he found himself face down in the grass.

She was pinning him there, one knee on his back, when the sergeant and constable from Church Myddle appeared. They also were on a Coney break and had gone to assist.

But the pawnbroker came quietly enough, once he had been allowed to retrieve his Homburg, brushing at it fastidiously, and as if nothing untoward had gone before. Or if it had the details were beneath him, already on his way back to that other place, that other life, Mr Havington-Wilkes and a Homburg hat.

The Sergeant handed her prisoner and his gun over to the two Church Myddle officers to take to Kingham to be booked, while she finished up there.

Clem, who had rushed to her husband, was patting his chest vaguely, as if feeling for holes, and asking repeatedly if he was all right, the stiff upper lip quivering, while Humphrey, with a small thoughtful frown, a man who had still to fully catch up, murmured that he was fine, honey, fine. Clem then thanked the Sergeant, showing a gratitude she could only express by pumping her hand and telling her she was a good chap, a good chap.

"But why did he try to shoot him?" Clem wanted to know then, asking herself that as much as the Sergeant. "We're not *that* bad a guest house, surely? Couldn't he have just marked us down, or something?" she said, making light of it out of relief.

The Sergeant looked blankly at her.

"He's a tourist inspector," Clem explained.

"He's *supposed* to be a businessman," the Sergeant said.

"That was his cover – or rather their cover," Clem said. "There are three of them. All tourist inspectors."

The Sergeant looked confused.

"Look, Clem," she said, unbuttoning the notebook pocket of her tunic, "let me get the details of the eyewitnesses down first before they wander off."

"He knows no more than we do," Clem told her then, after the Sergeant returned to them, her notebook opened on a new page ready for Humphrey. "He simply pointed a gun and shouted something about money."

"What can I tell you? That's all I know," Humphrey added.

"What money?" the Sergeant asked. "What did he mean by that?"

Humphrey shrugged. "Beats me. I don't know anything about any money. I don't know what got into the guy."

Annie, who had followed Clem with Hawis in her arms, and who'd been looking on, chewing fretfully at her lower lip, said, "He wouldn't have meant it, Sergeant. Not really," she added with a smile, inviting the Sergeant's understanding.

The Sergeant frowned. "Who wouldn't?"

"Phineas," Annie said, as if that explained it.

"Phineas…?" Sally echoed, standing with her friend among the group of onlookers.

"Phineas Cook…?" the Sergeant said, hoping that it wouldn't be, but knowing that it would, feeling a vague foreboding, some official disaster waiting for her in those two words, and seeing the face of Ted frowning at her again.

"Yes. Phineas," Annie said with a little laugh, as if sharing her knowledge of Phineas with her, and then extending it to the others. "Be like a game to him, it would."

"What would?" the Sergeant wanted to know.

"The Shrewsbury robbery. Be a sort of lark to him, like. You know," Annie said, making an indulgent face.

The Commander cleared his throat and glanced at his wife.

"I think, darling," Priny said to the Sergeant, "that we can perhaps explain."

Chapter Sixty-Four

Upriver from the *Batch Castle*, in the sitting room of the *Cluny Belle*, Phineas Cook was also doing some explaining, to Sally.

Sally, after excusing herself to her friend, had headed straight there, knowing that's where Phineas would be, battened down, as he called it, a woman in search of answers and hotly determined to have them, starting with armed robbery and a sick aunt in Kent.

And he was now busy clearing his name of the armed robbery bit by telling her what, at that moment, Priny and the Commander were telling the Sergeant, starting, as they had, with George, while George, who had fled there after escaping the clutches of the pawnbroker, played carelessly on deck with Bill Sikes and his new squeaky ball.

It was Phineas's hard-won experience that a silent woman was a dangerous one. And Sally had then gone silent. She hadn't moved from where she'd stood after bursting in, standing, arms folded, by the open door of the sitting room, suggesting that she was ready any minute to leave through it.

She listened from a stony distance as he stumbled through the far more difficult part of explaining the need of a sick aunt in Kent, explaining the Sergeant, offering up from the sofa where he'd sunk in near collapse after his flight, the gestures and expressions of a man more sinned against than sinning, a man martyred by events and his own reasonableness in the face of them.

While the Sergeant, the person he was striving to imply was somehow responsible for this 'extraordinary misunderstanding', was pulling up with Priny and the Commander outside the *Castle*.

The Sergeant was having quite the opposite time of things, so much so that she hadn't even minded Stringbag getting in the back of the new patrol car with the Commander. First the breaking of the Shrewsbury robbery case had fallen, out of the blue, into her hands, and now this.

She had exhausted her notebook getting the story down. She could hardly believe what she'd been listening to, and wasn't altogether sure that she had the complete picture. But she'd been too full of what she did have to stop for details.

She now knew that Phineas was a cad and a lying rotter, and that there was a Sally, who was supposed to be in the north somewhere, and that she could at least console herself that she hadn't been, however briefly, engaged to an armed robber. She knew who the other two members of the gang were, and knew also that at least two others were still at large.

And now she knew where the money was. And that, as far as she was concerned, was quite enough to be going on with.

She followed the Commander and Priny through to the landing stage with mounting anticipation.

And there the Commander came to a halt.

He smelt it first, and then saw it, wisps of smoke in the air above the paddler, lifting idly from the funnel ringed with Trafalgar blue and dark gold. And then he heard it, a couple of backfires and then the hammering of piston rods, a series of hesitant blows first at the air, before it picked up the pace as if remembering, after all these years, how it went, the music of a twin cylinder compound diagonal steam engine in full flight heard again, a song from the Cluny's past.

"Tom…" he said faintly.

Priny was grinning, her face alight with it.

"He's done it. He's *done* it! He said he intended trying to, to finish the engine today. As a surprise for you. He filled the boiler up earlier, while you were at the library, and asked John Beecher to cart up coal and kindling after we'd disappeared to the show. It's why last week he got Nigel to disconnect the stove and patch the funnel up. He said…"

She saw her husband's expression and her voice trailed off.

"Darling!" she said then, her eyes widening. "*Darling* – is that where…?"

The Commander nodded. "I'm afraid so, Number One. The fire box. And I thought I was being *frightfully* clever. Camouflaging it under sheets of scrunched up newspaper, to suggest to any prying eyes the preparations for a fire. A fire waiting only for kindling and coal. And Tom."

"Oh, dear," Priny said. "Oh, *dear.*"

"Why, what's wrong?" the Sergeant asked.

The Commander smiled apologetically at her, and was seeking words to break it to her gently, when the river air was split with the scream of a steam whistle, something else that hadn't been heard on the Cluny for over thirty years.

"What on *earth* is that!" the Sergeant said.

"That, my dear Sergeant," he told her, sounding on the verge of laughter, or tears, torn between sheer pleasure at the din, and thoughts of the insurance money, the fish and chip suppers and drinks all round, "is the sound of one hundred thousand pounds' worth of banknotes going up in smoke."

Chapter Sixty-Five

The Sergeant had dutifully phoned her immediate superior, Inspector Worth, before leaving for the *Batch Castle* – couldn't *wait* to phone him.

She told him where she was calling from, and quite casually asked for assistance in rounding up two more members of what she coyly referred to as a certain little gang, and waited for his response.

"What gang?" he barked impatiently, and for a moment she considered not telling him.

"The Shrewsbury wages snatch gang, if you must know," she said sulkily. "I've already arrested a third member of it. The one who's *supposed* to be a prominent businessman," she couldn't resist getting in. "Mr Havington-Wilkes should be with you any minute now. In handcuffs."

There was a silence at the other end.

"Mr Havington-Wilkes?" the Inspector said then, wonderingly.

"That's the chap," she said flippantly.

"You've *arrested* Mr Havington-Wilkes?"

"Yes," she said, and chuckled. "Although whether of course that actually is—"

"On what evidence, may one ask?" he cut in, and she could almost feel him frowning at her from there.

"Oh, there's plenty of that," she assured him. "Half of Batch Magna seem to know about it. And there's lots of eye-witnesses to the attempted murder."

"Attempted murder…?"

"Yes," she said, and giggled. "Gosh, sorry, Ted, I'd forgotten about that. Mr Havington-Wilkes, or whatever his name is, tried to shoot Sir Humphrey Strange. It's how I came to arrest him. And then Commander Cunningham and his wife off one of the houseboats, told me everything," she went on chattily, and told him what Priny and the Commander had told her.

And now she added, quite casually, she just happened to be on way to collect the proceeds of that certain robbery.

There was another silence after that, a busy silence, in which the Inspector was doing his figures, adding it all up and trying to decide what it came to, what it would mean for him.

And then he rallied. She was not, he instructed her, to pick up the money or take any further action until he got there. And was that clear?

The Sergeant had just said thank you, pretending she hadn't heard the last bit, and hung up.

And now here she was, back at the Hall, without the money – which was something he *couldn't* blame her for.

Although when he did arrive he managed to suggest that if she had obeyed orders it wouldn't somehow have happened. And when he did arrive, she noticed, he did so without any CID accompanying him, but with what seemed like the entire complement of the new patrol cars parked in a line along the lane outside the Hall, because, as the show was still going on, there was no room on the drive.

The Sergeant may not have returned in triumph bearing the stolen money but she did, a short while later, bag herself a second member of the gang, while the Inspector was in the kitchen with the family, Annie, and Priny and the Commander, listening to his hopes of the Sergeant having got the wrong end of things as usual disappearing as they verified her story.

The Sergeant was outside at the time, on the forecourt, talking to two colleagues after the bedrooms of the suspects had been searched, when Tony, his dream of Monte turned to boredom and sore feet, after standing in the coach house most of the day waiting again for the kid to show up, decided he was hungry.

He was on his way into the Hall, pretending he hadn't seen the three uniforms, when the Sergeant came up behind him, took an arm and told him he was under arrest.

Unlike Sneed Tony didn't come quietly. But after a brief struggle he was subdued by the three officers, relieved of his flick-knife, and lead away by the Sergeant's two colleagues to join Sneed in custody at Kingham.

The Sergeant then tripped in that gawky way of hers up the steps into the hall and popped her head round the kitchen door.

"Apologies for interrupting." she said cheerily, someone who was having a *splendid* time, if no one else was. "But I thought you might like to know, Inspector, that I've just arrested a second member of the gang. The chap who calls himself Mr Como. Like Perry," she added, and giggled.

"Must rush," she excused herself with a toothy grin. "Got the paperwork waiting."

Humphrey shook his head after she'd gone. "I can't believe all this. I *cannot* believe it."

It was obvious that Clem could. She was prosaically pouring tea, upper lip once more properly stiff.

"So that leaves Major Blashford," she said. "Or whatever his real name is."

And me, the Inspector thought. That leaves me and the Major, and the Superintendent, and the mayor of Kingham, and the large cheque at the club which I endorsed, and which of course will bounce. And... He couldn't go on.

"Yes. That leaves Major Blashford. Or whatever his real name is," he agreed, staring gloomily into his future.

Chapter Sixty-Six

While elsewhere the Major was stepping optimistically out to meet his.

The Major's real name, as the Inspector would shortly learn, was Smythe. But he was no longer that, nor Blashford, but Buckingham, Colonel Buckingham. He had promoted himself in the Gents' at Euston railway station, after reluctantly saying goodbye to his moustache, shaving it off in one of the cubicles. Buckingham was the name of the firm which supplied the paper towels he'd used when drying his hands before leaving.

He had gone to Kingham last night, as he'd told Sneed, not to feast on music at the Assembly Rooms, but to the railway station. There he had left the Wolseley in the car park and boarded a train for Euston, changing at Birmingham, and leaving that city again with scarcely a backward glance.

He'd spent the night in a bed and breakfast and the morning busily emptying at various banks the company cheque book he'd brought with him from Birmingham, a small pension to tide him over for the next few months, before heading for Waterloo station and the train to Bournemouth and a new start.

He had a feeling that the photograph of him the authorities had on file, the one with a hangdog expression and a moustache, would shortly be taking its place alongside those of the other members of the Shrewsbury wages snatch gang, peering out of the daily prints and on news-time television screens.

The Major, as Sneed would have it, was one of the rats leaving a sinking ship. Or as the Major thought of it, adopting the same position on strategic withdrawal as Wellington, he was daring to retreat.

Sitting back in the first-class compartment, purchased by the last of the Major's cheques, the Colonel had pondered on what that future might hold for him.

He came to realise that his new name was fortuitous. Colonel Buckingham, it seemed to him, combined a suggestion of both dash and probity, as well as social standing. It would, he considered, prove alluring to females of a certain age, class, and romantic inclination, a yearning still unsatisfied, its fulfilment hoped for still. The sort of woman who would see any alliance he might be able to manoeuvre her into as a recklessness of heart, a feeling of being carried away by it, while keeping both her feet, as well as his, comfortably on the ground. He felt that he knew her already.

She would be a widow, a woman of property and financial soundness, perhaps even wealth, given to wondering what that really came to when added up in the lonely hours.

He hoped to meet her over a rubber of bridge, or while on a morning promenade, or among the blue rinses at the Conservative club, or perhaps a local church where she would do the flowers.

He'd indulged himself briefly, after ringing a number in the Rooms to Let columns of a local newspaper, aggrieved that his dreams of Bournemouth should end up there – end up back there, it seemed to him. In another bedsit in the sort of run-down street that over the years had become depressingly familiar, the stucco peeling on the porch pillars, and a stale, tired sort of smell in the hall and on the stairs, a smell which followed him into a room with a pattern of orange swirls trodden into the carpet, and grease on the Baby Belling.

The smell, he thought, wiping at a moustache that was no longer there, of failure, of other lives that had ended up there, and of his own, less than heroic, defeat.

He wondered when the window in the room had last been opened, and after struggling with it, told himself he might as well throw himself out of it, peering lugubriously down at a basement area with dustbins in it.

And then he found that if he lifted his eyes, he could see the sea. That if he stuck out his head far enough, and at an angle, he could glimpse a slice of the bay with the sun on it. It was enough.

It wasn't much, with the rest of the street and half a leisure centre in the way, but it was enough.

It seemed to him that in its glitter danced a promise of horizons far beyond the view from there, the pittance that that room, that street offered. He had always believed, in that part of him that even a cell door slamming on another attempt at the sunlit uplands couldn't daunt for long, that tomorrow truly was another day.

And as he breathed in his current ration of sea air he was struck by the inescapable conviction that, for him, it had at long last arrived.

Changed into blazer and flannels, and new Panama hat, Colonel Buckingham adjusted his regimental tie in the fan-shaped mirror above the tiled fireplace and gas fire, and picking up a silver-topped Malacca cane, bought before leaving London, along with the Panama hat, for sunnier times ahead, squared his shoulders and jauntily humming the *Pizzicato Polka,* went back down the stairs to meet it.

The End... Almost

Three Months Later…

Petunia Alicia Anne Cholmondeley-Jones, as her name appeared in the announcement of her engagement in *The Times,* sat going through the trial papers, the bulk of it consisting of witness statements ranging from that of an ten-year-old schoolboy to village spinster Miss Wyndham.

The trial of the Shrewsbury robbery gang was set for tomorrow. Sneed, or Mr Havington-Wilkes, depending on what day, and sometimes what hour, it was, would appear with his co-defendants in the Crown Court of that city, Tony having lost no time informing on the Major, Brrm-Brrm, and Clothesline in the hope of a more lenient sentence. Only the Major would be missing from their ranks when they trooped up the stairs from the underground cells to the dock where 'the big one' had ended up.

The Sergeant had been on the front pages of all the local newspapers, the *Shrewsbury Journal,* that had scooped the story, featuring a picture of her back on the lawns of the Hall, showing her teeth for the camera and with one foot on a prone reporter. She had even made a couple of the nationals, and had received an official commendation from the Chief Constable with tea and biscuits in his office afterwards.

And while this was going on, it had not been forgotten by the Superintendent that Sergeant Cholmondeley-Jones had aired her suspicions about the prominent businessmen who turned out to be nothing of the sort in a report to his office. A report that he, acting on the assurances of Inspector Worth, had then binned.

It gave him some satisfaction afterwards to reflect that while he, the Superintendent, hadn't stood at the wicket with the applause that might have been his falling about him, he, the Inspector, had been clean-bowled by his own declared no-ball.

For the Inspector, now in charge of a sub-station on the other side of the county, was once again a sergeant, and the Sergeant, in a reversal of roles that could hardly be neater, was now an inspector.

And that's not all.

Among the congratulations that had been hers that day, were those from a young man, one of the spectators at the re-enactment. He was a physical education teacher at the grammar school in Kingham, and it showed. He shone with health, and a fitness he seemed barely able to contain, as if about to start running on the spot, or even to do a handstand or back-flip. The Sergeant had instantly approved.

He was, he'd told her, new to the area, and complimenting her on her judo technique, said that he used to enjoy the sport himself, and had been meaning to take it up again. The Sergeant had recommended the sessions she attended at Kingham Polytechnic.

And there, on the hurly-burly of the judo mat, among the weekly sweat and grunts of grapples, chokes, foot sweeps, hip throws, heaves and falls, her heart submitted and she was won, as she thought of it, as if reading it on the last page.

The last page of the last story she would tell herself – would *need* to tell herself. The other stories, with Mills & Boon covers and Ted and Phineas Cook in them, the ones in which she, for once, was desired and desirable, and had made the most of it, had just been that, stories.

Something to read, as if were, while waiting for the real thing to turn up.

And now the Sergeant was an inspector and sat at a desk with flowers on it, and wore on her finger a new engagement ring.

It was for her, as Phineas had once promised it would be, third time lucky.

The End – *for now.* The story of Batch Magna sails on in *Clouds in a Summer Sky.*

Preview

Living in an old steam boat on a river deep in the Welsh Borders has numerous charms, but the Commander's wife Priny is suffering from arthritis, a condition not at all improved by their water-based lifestyle. They take up an offer from Humphrey, the squire of Batch Hall, of a straight swap: their boat, the *Batch Castle*, for one of the Masters' Cottages facing their beloved river.

The *Castle* is restored to river worthiness and starts plying successfully as the Cluny Steamboat Company to Shrewsbury and back. As a result it takes a good deal of profit away from a taxi firm in a local border town. The English owner of the firm, Sidney Acton, enlisting the aid of two corrupt Welsh councillors, plots against the new venture. Only time will tell if his sabotage attempts will bear fruit or blow up in his face…

The Batch Magna Chronicles, Volume Four

COMING SOON

About the Author

Peter Maughan's early ambition to be a landscape painter ran into a lack of talent – or enough of it to paint to his satisfaction what he saw. He worked on building sites, in wholesale markets, on fairground rides and in a circus. And travelled the West Country, roaming with the freedom of youth, picking fruit, and whatever other work he could get, sleeping wherever he could, before moving on to wherever the next road took him. A journeying out of which came his non-fiction work *Under the Apple Boughs*, when he came to see that he had met on his wanderings the last of a village England. After travelling to Jersey in the Channel Islands to pick potatoes, he found work afterwards in a film studio in its capital, walk-ons and bit parts in the pilot films that were made there, and as a contributing script writer. He studied at the Actor's Workshop in London, and worked as an actor in the UK and Ireland (in the heyday of Ardmore Studios). He founded and ran a fringe theatre in Barnes, London, and living on a converted Thames sailing barge among a small colony of houseboats on the River Medway, wrote pilot film scripts as a freelance deep in the green shades of rural Kent. An idyllic, heedless time in that other world of the river, which later, when he had collected enough rejection letters learning his craft as a novelist, he transported to a river valley in the Welsh Marches, and turned into the Batch Magna novels.

Peter is married and lives currently in Wales. Visit his website at www.batchmagna.com.

Note from the Publisher

If you enjoyed this book, we are delighted to share also *The Famous Cricket Match*, a short story play by Peter Maughan, featuring our hero Sir Humphrey of Batch Hall, defending the village with both cricket *and* baseball…

To get your **free copy of *The Famous Cricket Match*,** as well as receive updates on further releases in the Batch Magna Chronicles series, sign up at http://farragobooks.com/batch-magna-signup

Printed in Great Britain
by Amazon